V/
REBEL ANGELS VOLUME ONE

Vampires and angels are locked in a deadly war. But first, they want their daughter back.

Half vampire/half angel, Violet, was abandoned amongst the humans in London as a baby.

Suddenly discovering monstrous powers on her twenty-first birthday, she thinks she's the most dangerous creature to prowl the streets. She's wrong.

When a snarky angel falls into her lap and her adopted sister disappears, Violet is forced into a new role: Huntress. But the deeper she's dragged into this supernatural world, the more she struggles to survive.

On the run, Violet'll have to rely on a sexy vampire geek, while facing off the harem boy angel threatening her sister. And there's only one way she'll win: by letting out the monster...

FANTASY REBEL

FANTASY REBEL

VAMPIRE HUNTRESS: REBEL ANGELS VOLUME
ONE@copyright2018RosemaryAJohns

The moral right of the author has been asserted.

*All characters, places and events in this publication,
other than those clearly in the public domain, are
fictitious and any resemblance to real persons, living or
dead, is purely coincidental.*

ALL RIGHTS RESERVED:
No part of this publication may be reproduced, stored
in a retrieval system, or transmitted, in any form or by
any means, without prior permission in writing of the
author, nor be otherwise circulated in any form of
binding or cover other than that in which it is published
and without a similar condition including this condition
being imposed on a subsequent purchaser.

ISBN-13: 978-0995557949
ISBN-10: 0995557942

Book Cover Designer: Rebecca Frank
Fantasy Rebel Limited

rosemaryajohns.com

1

Vampires? Angels? All I know is they're both bastards.

And I hunt bastards.

In the beginning, I made games about them. None of it was real, only play. I was human, after all, in a world of humans. At least, I reckoned so. The gamer and developer, lost in make-believe.

Until everything changed, and the monsters fell from above.

Except, they tasted of sugar and blood.

It was a Friday. But not a regular Friday, where I worked with my best mate Gizem on creating the games you play when you stagger in from college or work.

Instead, it was the type of Friday where your new boss circles in for the kill.

I rubbed my palms down my jeans and snuffled against the stuffy office heating. The silver star lights sparked a migraine pulsing behind my eyes.

How could I concentrate on battling to protect

our dream project, when I was fighting off a fever?

Not your regular fever either.

It blazed higher, as I clutched my desk. Ever since my twenty-first birthday, I'd been shaken with an illness that I didn't understand. One that terrified me.

Slam.

A wave of intense sweetness hit me.

The *slam* of sugar tinged with copper — which I could even taste at the back of my throat — had been crashing over me since I'd turned twenty-one a month ago.

Try explaining *that* to your doctor.

I'd been knocking back tequila shots with Gizem in a dive of a bar where they played live rock gigs because if there's one night when you can get drunk and forget...everything...it's your birthday, when the fever had started.

The heat had begun somewhere between my shoulder blades, before burning inwards and throbbing into my gums.

Then I'd quaked with a rush of rage that had flared the dark bar to violet.

I'd crushed the shot glass; shards had pierced my palm.

Gizem had been hollering, yanking on my elbow. But I'd panted, sweat sticking my ash blonde hair to my burning forehead, unable to sense anything but a new power...waking inside me.

And it'd been monstrous.

A month later, the fever hadn't died. It burnt higher.

I typed on my Apple iMac in frantic *clicks* to distract myself, playing with the figures to impress my boss.

The secret voice in my head was in nagging nurse mode.

You've been burning up with these sugar tingles for over a month now, Violet-cakes.

I've had to listen to J, my resident voice, since birth.

And once the rages, sugar tingles, and fever had broken out like a freaky second puberty, I'd come to realise J had his own power.

J thought he was real. Who was I to say he wasn't?

Except, no one knows about J but me because who likes to be labelled *different*?

I was already different enough, growing up as the orphan kid, named after the dead woman whose grave I'd been abandoned on and the violet feather I'd clutched in my hand.

Do you reckon I posted on social media about the sassy bitch who lived in my mind?

I glanced anxiously around the rainbow office of Spirit and Fire Gaming Company, slouching down in my candy pink plastic seat.

You can't ignore the danger. Or the changes transforming you inside.

What the hell's wrong with me? It's more than the slam of sugar blood, J. It's the anger. I see a flood of violet, the world turns to nothing but that colour, and then I snap—

Bang — Mr. Stanbury smashed his fist down on my cherry computer desk; it shuddered. 'Are you with us, *Feathers*?'

Only my boss could say my nickname like a cross between an insult and a come-on.

I grabbed a pencil from my desk, twiddling it between my fingers. The over-bright office lights haloed Stanbury's Devil in a Suit effect. 'Sorry, zoned for a moment.'

Stanbury blinked. Then he smoothed his tan wool suit, before wagging his finger at me like I was twelve, rather than twenty-one. 'The problem is, sweetheart, the expensive project you're developing for us here...'

I glanced at Gizem, who was marching up and down between the regiment of buzzing computers in her orange dress, like a streak of primal fire. She smiled at me, but her cheek twitched just below the scar.

Crack — I stared down at the remains of the broken pencil in my hands. Dark stained my palms.

Two best friend orphans, one high-flying job, and a bastard of a boss.

Add in the not always friendly voice in my head, and then watch the feathers fly bloody.

Frantically, I scrubbed the pencil marks away on my denim jeans. When I looked up, Stanbury was glaring.

Mr Stanbury is going to kick your pretty little ass, unless...

'Shut up,' I muttered.

'Not a chance,' Stanbury's eyes narrowed. Then he flicked a button by the door, and a monitor on the canary yellow wall burst to life with our latest game in development.

And the reason behind Stanbury's important meeting — and tantrum — today.

On the screen, a female warrior angel, with gold wings and blazing sword, fought on the edge of an abyss.

...Slam...

A wave of copper flooded me, stronger than before.

I juddered, sucking in my breath.

Vampires crawled monstrous from the pit, but the warrior hacked through the fanged fiends.

...Slam, slam...

I lurched forward, gasping at the intense sensation of candy blood invading me, until I tingled head-to-toe.

Gizem stopped pacing to watch me instead.

The warrior glowed in her victory, flying upwards towards one more level of perfection.

The game was awe-inspiring. My addiction.

... Slam, slam, slam...

I gasped, pressing my hands down hard in my lap not to have a big 'O' moment right there in front of my boss.

And *that* was the stuff of my nightmares.

'See, it may turn *you* on,' Stanbury paused the computer game, perching on the edge of my plastic desk; when his gaze lingered over my body like grubby fingers, I dragged my khaki jacket closer around me. It only took one look from him to dampen the happy tingles between my legs. 'But *Angels vs Vampires...*? Let me tell you something, research highlights one simple fact: men desire guns, cars, and zombies. I guess that's hard for you to understand, being dickless.'

You show that asshole just what you can do without one of his precious dicks, girl...

Rage. It bunched in every stiff muscle. Flooded my eyes. Scented the air.

A fury so strong, I trembled, hell *wept*, from it.

Everything became clear and simple when the world flared to violet. Then it was as if I stood above a land of bones, on a mountain of feathers, and I controlled the world.

And all I had to do was *ask...*

'Say that again,' Gizem's voice was low and dangerous. Her hand curled around a monitor like it was Stanbury's throat.

Stanbury shrugged. 'People don't want to become the hero. They want to let out their monster. And this obsession with *perfection...*? But then I don't have to ask where that comes from, do I?'

He leaned forward, staring at my cat's eye mirror sunglasses. As if he knew what was behind them.

Yeah, he knew.

One violet eye, and one black one. I'd been born that way. At least, found that way in Hackney Cemetery, before I'd been taken to Jerusalem Children's Home. And Gizem had become like my big sister.

Why do I bother hiding? As if kids hadn't always called me *freak*?

For the same reason no one knows about J. We all have secrets to survive.

I swallowed convulsively. 'You're shutting down our project.' It wasn't a question.

'More like firing you.'

Gizem gave a strangled cry, before storming to the window out over London. Her curling hair jumped on each step.

I knew what it meant.

The same cold ball froze my guts: Christmas coming up, kid sister, and bills to pay.

We were screwed.

Stanbury stalked predator-like around me; I tensed, at the *tap, tap, tap* of his brown brogues on the mahogany floor. Musky cedarwood, as if he'd woven the aftershave into his suit, caught me by the throat. When he tucked a strand of my ash-blonde hair gently behind my ear, I startled.

Tell that shady dick to go find a fashion runway for Christian Grey wannabes to die on.

Despite myself, I sniggered.

Stanbury twisted my hair. 'Why not come out to dinner? We'll discuss this. I'm certain we can solve our little problem without such...drastic measures.'

I wrenched away from his teasing fingers. 'I have a boyfriend.'

'So, hands off, muppet.' I jumped at the sudden voice from above our heads — for once, *not from inside my head* — which sounded like an Irish, pissed off god.

We peered at the shining pearl dropped ceiling.

Somebody was hiding up there...

The gleam of the pendant lights shanked icicles of pain through my throbbing forehead. I twisted away, huddling behind my sunglasses.

Thump — flakes of ceiling, like dry snow, floated down.

Crash — the ceiling was falling in, or someone was falling from the ceiling.

I shrieked as I was showered in shattered PVC panel...and punk.

The plastic swivel chair cracked, and we both tumbled backwards in a tangle of limbs.

Of course, it's hard *not* to notice a bloke when you have a lapful of him: red leather bondage trousers and leather jacket studded into armour. His hair was a spiked mess of red flame. And his kohl smudged *violet eyes...?*

I hissed.

Don't get excited, Feathery-toes, just because the punk has violet eyes too.

Although he also has an ass that's just

begging to be ridden to the Grand National. That's right, grind against mama...

A strange punk Irishman's arse on my crotch.

What. The. Hell.

Why've I never seen anyone else with the same colour eyes as me?

Slam.

I doubled up, as sweetness, like thick treacle, choked me.

At least by the bulge in the gorgeous punk's scarlet trousers, and the tremors quivering through him, I wasn't the only one struggling.

Help me, or I'll have a Harry Met Sally moment right here with this stranger on my lap.

I thought you'd never ask.

And just like that? The fever died.

Whatever was affecting me, the voice in my head could control it.

Or control me.

I shoved off the punk. He tumbled harder than I'd expected to the side, banging his head under the desk.

I smirked, until he turned the puppy dog eyes on me.

How was the punk able to look innocent, with that spiked black collar around his long pale neck?

Tap, tap, tap. Brown leather brogues. Tan wool suit. And Stanbury's immaculate wave of brunet hair above a sour, prim face, as if he hadn't just been sexually harassing his staff. A.K.A – me. 'Boyfriend?'

I shot up, scrambling for my saddlebag. 'I've never seen him before. But I'd go with stalker.'

'Stalker?' Stanbury squealed, fumbling to pull out his mobile from his trouser pocket, forgetting his Mr Suave act.

'Hold on, now,' the punk straightened in a twirl of red and black leather, 'I made a balls of the entrance but—'

'You fell through the ceiling, wallad.'

'Hold on, no need to be calling me an idiot. Nobody's perfect. Not even an angel.'

'Right, that's it. Security?' Stanbury jabbered into his iPhone as he edged towards the door. 'Get your fat arses up here. We're trapped with a nutjob. For god's sake, he could have a gun!'

The punk's eyes widened. He peered around our office, which looked like a rainbow had vomited it up, as if he'd catch sight of the *nutjob*. Then he stepped towards me, his voice low and urgent, 'I'll save you.'

I slipped the pepper spray out of my saddlebag and blasted it into the bondage punk's face.

He screamed, before rolling about on the mahogany floor like he'd never been sprayed with pepper spray, bleach, or acid until now...

Bitch must never have lived in Hackney.

'I'm blinded!' The punk gasped, clutching at his streaming red eyes (points on the waterproof eyeliner), but then he grinned around his panted pain, 'Fair on you, princess.'

You go, girl, teach him to be a peeping tom. Next time though? Not the eyes. Those babies are for the gods.

The sun glinted through the long windows out over London. I winced, even with my sunglasses. The feathered line of skyscrapers and tower blocks winding around the Thames were greyed to ghosts.

When the punk dragged himself to his knees, I caught a blur of orange and...

Gizem drew back her Dr Martens and — *boot* — got in a hard kick.

The punk groaned.

'You come to my yard and bother my girl...?' Gizem shoved her hair back from her forehead, shrugging. 'Let's bounce.'

The punk was struggling to his knees again, wiping his sleeve across his weeping eyes.

I nodded, tiredly. 'We're fired. I don't need it shared on the company website to get the message.'

'You're not leaving me alone with *him*...?' Stanbury threw himself towards me like I was *his* guardian angel, digging his fingers into my shoulders.

I recoiled at the enshrouding musky cedarwood; bruises ached under my skin. My pulse pounded. My legs trembled. My cheeks flushed.

It's happening again... J?

Silence.

Don't go all Queen Bitch on me: I need you.

'I thought blokes like you craved guns, soldier?' I didn't recognise the hardness in my voice, or the crushing grip I used to prise Stanbury's fingers from my shoulder. He whimpered. 'Anyway, what can I do? I'm dickless, remember?'

Stanbury clutched his injured hand under his armpit. He scrutinized me like he could see through my sunglasses. 'I guess I got it wrong. You've already let out the monster.'

Light-headed, I bounced up to the balls of my feet. I cocked my fist, only for one cool arm to encircle my waist from behind and another to close gently around my fist.

I struggled.

Spikes and studs dug into my skin. A roaring rush ballooned louder and louder in my ears.

Slam.

Stronger than ever before, the sweet coppery tang exploded on my tongue. I'd never eat again because it'd be like the beat of a single drum after dancing to the heaviest tunes in banging unison.

I was lost in it: the rage, heat, and desire.

Then the world bled to black.

Violet.

Confused, I gaped at the toes of my violet knee-high boots.

My arse was numb; I shook. Then I turned my head to the side and hurled.

Someone nuke me from orbit.

And you call me the drama queen.

You're back, then? Way to help a girl.

I was never gone. And who says I've ever helped you?

J was like having both an angel and a devil trapped in my mind. I never knew which one would battle for control and sass me.

'So, I made a holy show of myself before,' the punk peered down at me. He lounged against the glass front of Spirit and Fire with infuriating ease, his hands in his pockets.

I mumbled something. I'm not sure it was English.

Then the fog cleared and...

My gaze cooled. The numbness of my arse was because someone — this *punk* — had carried, and then dropped, me, with my head between my knees, on the veined marble steps outside my own office.

Except I reckon it's not *your* office, if you're fired.

'Where's everyone else?'

'With that muppet of a boss. I trapped them in when you swooned, and then—'

'I don't *swoon*. Who are you?'

'My name's Rebel.' The punk took a wary step towards me.

'Rebel? What the hell sort of name is that?'

His eyes sparked with flames, and I gasped. 'The sort you earn.'

I scrabbled up, clasping my saddlebag to me like a shield. I couldn't taste anything now but my own watery sick. The dizzy exhaustion from my migraine was catching up on me.

Migraine induced hallucinations...? Today was messed up.

When Rebel stuck out his hand towards me, like he was following through on a learnt script, I shied back. 'You get me kicked out from the one job I've ever... You've no idea how hard it was for someone like me to even be allowed through the door of a company like that. And then you reckon I'll shake hands with you?'

He raised his pierced eyebrow. 'Cop on! You didn't need me to lose that job. You did that all on you own.'

Boom! The collared redhead has just read you some realness.

I shoved Rebel against the clouded glass skyscraper, pinning my arm across his throat. The safety pins in his ripped black t-shirt pricked my guts. His breath was fast and hot across my cheek, but he stilled. His thick eyelashes curved onto his cheeks as he looked down. 'Belt me one, if it'll make you feel any better, princess.'

It coiled — like it'd been coiling for months now — a darkness.

I could mess up his sweet face. Teach him what happened on the Utopia Estate when you *disrespected*. Take what was offered sacrificial from the stranger.

This *angel*.

But I didn't believe in angels. And definitely not ones that fell out of the ceiling into my lap.

I snorted. 'I don't gank crazies.'

I pulled away from Rebel, but couldn't help waiting for the moment his eyes opened, before I marched towards Hackney.

Gizem was locked with Stanbury. The worst that could happen to her was dying from boredom, until security freed them. But I had a sister who'd be home from college and I needed to get back and explain just why I'd lost my job...almost a month before Christmas.

I pulled my jacket tighter around myself against the bite of the wind as I trudged past the Caribbean supermarket — which was a red and green vegetable blaze in the grey day — and the boarded-up Vietnamese one next door. The line of empty properties squatted in tattered threads, amongst Turkish kebab shops and the hard glare of CCTV cameras. A greasy pall blasted from a burger bar.

I grimaced, wiping my face.

Don't look now, your Feathery-highness, but someone may be following our fabulousness.

The pretty boy in red leather will get himself beaten up looking like that on these streets.

My, one would almost reckon you cared.

Don't push it.

Or what...? You'll punch yourself in the head or not talk to yourself?

I grinned.

I'll stop playing, that's what I'll do. Hasn't this all been a game? Since I was born?

I'm hurt. You're mine. I raised you. I'm inside you. I don't play about that.

I shivered. The bass of a grime song blared from

a beat-up Ford cruising by, pounding my migraine harder.

I stopped, before calling over my shoulder, 'You're not stealthy, bro.'

Rebel's head popped out from a side alley. He bit his lip, before sauntering towards me, as if his pale skin wasn't blushing. He shrugged. 'Look, I'm not awful good with all the...blathering and...' His pink tongue licked out, swiping his lips. 'It's been a long time, what with...'

'Being locked up?'

'How'd you know?'

'Wild guess.' A gang of kids on bikes circled like eagles. They'd pulled up their hoodies and dragged scarves over their faces. Their gazes were sharp and assessing. 'Trust me, you'll be shanked wandering around all punk rocker without a clue.' One of the boys spat in front of a bin; another swiped his hand through the globules of spit. A drug deal gone down. Then they both patted their navy schoolbags like a salute. We all knew the warning; they were carrying a knife, ammonia, or meat cleaver. I snatched Rebel's hand, tugging him after me. 'What is it with me and strays?' I muttered. 'You don't even know my name.'

'I do: Violet. But your mates call you Feathers. It'd be a fine thing if I could call you...'

I crushed Rebel's wrist; he howled.

'Listen here, you're not my mate. And I don't need a fanboy. So, you're going to tell me how you know all this. And if it involves cameras and the internet...?'

I rolled his wrist from side-to-side; the bones rubbed against each other with a *crunch*.

'Jesus, will you stop that woman and wise up. I already told you,' Rebel's smile through his pain was suddenly dazzling, 'I'm an angel.'

'Yeah, and I'm a unicorn, not the Bitch of Utopia Estate.'

He laughed. The punk stood there quivering in my hold and *he laughed*.

I threw down his wrist like it'd burnt me. 'You've been watching me?'

Shame flooded Rebel's face. He dropped his gaze to the pavement, rubbing at his bruised wrist. 'Can't help it. I'm addicted. A month now.'

'*You...*?'

The *slam* of sugary copper couldn't be because of *Rebel...*?

I imagined the taste of his blood in my throat and its sweet kick, before shaking my head. *I* was a freak, but angels weren't real.

I staggered back from him. 'Whatever you are, don't come near me, you get me?'

'It's not safe...'

A flash of silver, tumble of black, and then Rebel was yanked into a side alley.

I froze.

A bald bastard clutching a knife — his face tattooed with wings, like birds had exploded free from his mind — pinned Rebel to the redbrick wall, before punching him in the guts.

A hook to the chin, and Rebel crashed into overflowing recycling bins.

Rebel struggled up, shoving back the attacker.

'Just give him your phone,' I growled because I'd seen enough muggings to know the drill.

Distracted, Rebel glanced over at me, and missed Bird Tattoo's knee to his balls.

I winced, creeping closer.

When I peered into the shadows, however, the sun glinted off the shank...

My knees buckled; I swayed.

The new powers burning through me since my

15

twenty-first meant nothing in the face of that blade.

And despite a flush of guilt, I abandoned Rebel and I ran.

2

Shanks, blades, or knives: call them what you like, I hate the bastards. The sleek primitive power that promises *respect*, but offers up some poor kid's grave.

Yet there's nothing like the *gasp* as your mates watch the tip slash, and knowing one more push to the left or right could save or end your enemy's life. Then as the quarry's wide eyes watch yours, waiting on your decision, even if you never intended to kill them before you were drawn into the dance...

In that moment, *you're the god.*

When you grow up as an orphan, alone on Utopia Estate in London, the centre of drugs, gangs, and prostitutes, you learn how to survive.

As a kid, I'd been nicknamed the *Bitch of Utopia.*

I hadn't just looked different, even if I'd tried to hide behind sunglasses, I'd learnt to pull off that edge of swagger, which is backed up by a shank.

Until the day the blade had been turned on me.

When I finally collapsed onto the faded purple swings in the playground on the Utopia Estate, holding myself against the biting cold of the chains, I knew why I'd deserted Rebel in the alleyway, leaving him to the mugger with the wing tattoos.

It was the memory of a knife cutting into my neck. And Gizem's scar.

I sighed, scuffing my foot in and out of a muddy track as I swung.

Drizzle ghosted from torn clouds; rain tears caught and shone down the slide. The broken monkey bars bared themselves like fangs. Somewhere high in Tower Block B, a baby bawled.

Hey, scaredy cat, you left our pretty boy to bleed.

The bloke — angel — wears a silver skull on his chain bondage trousers, J. If he can't handle himself, he deserves to be knifed.

My, we are in a lying to ourselves mood today. The first jackass you ever kissed, right here on these swings...

I scrambled to jump off mid-arc, hissing as I landed hard on my ankle. I caught my sunglasses before they could tumble from my nose.

...holds a knife to your throat, and then—

I don't need the replay.

You need reminding we control, we're not controlled. I didn't raise you that way.

You didn't raise me at all.

Gizem warned you not to sneak out of Jerusalem Children's Home to see tall and shanky, but you ignored her. And that's right, Little Miss Fabulous here warned you too.

Then Gizem, your best mate, gets a blade in the face for rescuing you and a scar as a

memento.

Now go back and rescue pretty in punk.

I shoved my hands into the pockets of my jeans. 'I can't hear you,' I slung my saddlebag onto my shoulder, 'too busy ignoring you.'

I glanced up, caught in the shadow of the two concrete and purple tower blocks that glowered from either side. I pressed my sleeve across my mouth; the air was thick with traffic fumes and the stench of cooking fats.

When I booted a beer can skittering, it crunched under the lopsided merry-go-round. Then I prowled towards the stairs, which wound up Tower Block A.

A gang of my boyfriend, Toben's, drug soldiers lounged on the concrete steps up into the block. They smoked joints with bored swagger as they waited for the deals to go down.

They nodded to me.

I slipped my iPod out of my jacket pocket, worming in the earbuds, whilst I plunged into the stairwell's shadows.

The heartbeat bass of EELS' "Mental", pulsed in time with my migraine. Then the aggressive, despairing vocals kicked in, along with the shock of the drums; I was caught in the disturbed howl, so raw it ripped at my soul.

This wasn't my iPod — it was Jade's.

I must've picked up my sister's by mistake this morning, whilst rushing to get ready for the big meeting with Stanbury.

My sister? I'd always been alone, but Jade was the brightest point in my world. I'd adopted her from the streets, or she'd adopted me when she'd agreed to stay. Either way, we called each other 'sisters'.

And she'd become the only family I had.

I lifted my hand to pull out the earbud, as if I'd peeked at something private, because someone's playlist is their life stripped bare.

Then I hesitated.

I'd heard this song playing through the thin walls between my room and Jade's for days now.

I swiped down the list.

It was the album my little sister had fallen asleep to: *Beautiful Freak.*

Jade had been quieter for weeks, although with the whole emo black hair with pink streaks and stripy socks look going on, it was hard to tell. It was simply a mask to hide the shy girl I'd rescued.

Like me, Jade had been through the system and thrown out at sixteen. Unlike me, she'd had no one watching her back to save her from the monsters.

Until she met me.

Yeah, I have a thing about rescuing strays.

Since the new term, Jade had been hanging around with a boy at college; she hadn't hidden the love bites. But quietness, love bites, and alternative rock music don't add up to an intervention.

An interrogation though...?

I wrenched out the earbuds, winding the iPod neatly, before dropping it back into my pocket.

Bang – I startled, as a door slammed, echoing somewhere higher up the block.

Only for thick fingers to wrap themselves around my neck, and dash me against the graffiti-sprayed stairwell.

My jaw cracked together, slicing my teeth through my tongue. When the tangy blood hit, I groaned, closing my eyes. The memory of a flame-haired Irishman consumed me...

Yet when the hold at my throat tightened, and I opened my eyes again, I found myself staring into the narrowed gaze of Bisi, the top boy of the Estate.

And for *top boy* read *boss*.
Thinking violet.
Nothing: not even an irritated itch.
I was as calm as a zen master.
Go violet...or...you wouldn't like to piss me off violet style.
Nothing again, except now I'd sniggered into the outraged face of Bisi.
The tiniest kid in class, Bisi had always been the first to get medieval with knives, acid, or guns. He'd taken over the gang when he was thirteen.
Reckon that's a joke?
There's bros who did too, until they found out first-hand that Bisi was more addicted to that moment when the knife goes in than I'd ever been.
And yeah, Bisi reckoned he was a god.
Why can't I find my inner mojo, J?
If I don't get to play with the punk, you don't get to play with your toys.
Remember what I said about J being both angel and devil? I reckon J was all pouting devil right now.
I clawed at Bisi's fingers; panic choked me.
'Baby girl, this is your man's time for selling food.' That's what all drugs (spice, weed, cocaine, or whatever met demand), were called – *food* – as if it was as innocent as baby milk in a bottle. 'So, what looks shady is why you be back from your...?' Bisi thumbed up and down like he was shooting Big Bads on his controller.
Wrong console, bitch.
I shuddered. 'The only reason I stay with Toben is because you're cuckooing my apartment.'
Here's a story London style.
One day a fat cuckoo shoves you out of your nest, moves in guns and *food*, and promises if you keep your mouth shut, then rainbows and

unicorns… sorry, wrong fairy tale…then holes won't be hacked through your heart.

Or your sister's.

Bisi grinned; his golden teeth gleamed. 'Then what you be doing here?'

For a moment, I gaped.

What kind of screwed sidewise day was it when *getting fired* had slipped my mind? 'I lost my job.'

Bisi's laugh was like a seal suffocating on its own smugness. 'The good girl geek ain't such an angel, after all.'

I shrugged but couldn't help the grin. 'Nobody's perfect.'

'Seems to run with you up in Number 333. First your man's short—'

My grin died. 'How much does he owe?'

Bisi shoved me back, before letting go of his chokehold. I could feel each finger still bruised deep. 'It doesn't matter. Short is short. Now I have to make his family suffer.'

I hissed in my breath, but the shank was at my gut before I could stumble away. I panted, *in and out*, so fast, the stairwell spectre-dimmed.

Only the tip of the blade pressed at my kidneys, worming at the khaki, as if nuzzling kisses.

'It's just business, baby girl.' Bisi's stiffie pressed into me, but it was the excitement of the knife, not the closeness to me, which had him hard. 'You know the score. Your man needs some way to pay me back, so we've come to an arrangement. I clear his debt, and he sells me Jade.'

My boyfriend was planning to sell my sister to the sadistic boss of the estate? Blokes settled their debts in pain and sex. Women and men nothing but slaves. But I'd rescued my sister once already from that life. No way was she going back to it.

I roared, nutting back my head.

I heard Bisi's surprised *oomph*, just before he jabbed the knife forward and twisted.

I gasped at the clear brightness of the pain, as he stabbed me. The blade was inside me, alien and wrong. My skin was sticky with my own blood. Yet all I could think was...

Toben had sold my little sister. I hadn't kept her safe.

Bisi's breathing hitched as he eased the blade in further.

A familiar light-headedness invaded me; I stared unseeingly at the arm snaking around my waist.

I could hardly think, but if I had to beg, there was only one person – J – real or not, who could help me.

J, I'll rescue the punk and I'll never ignore you again...please.

You only had to ask.

At once, the violet built, like ozone on the ocean air.

The power that terrified me because of the nightmares it whispered.

And those nightmares were me.

Bones and feathers, sugar and blood, all was crushed in the maelstrom of my howl. Whatever had been hidden inside, the fever had birthed it phoenix-like from the ashes.

And now I no longer knew if I was even human.

I snapped my elbow back into Bisi's guts, stamping on his foot and grinding down the heel of my boot. He hollered, letting go of the blade's handle.

I spun away, kicking his feet out from under him.

Then I reached behind my back, struggling in the slippery blood to get a tight grip, before yanking out the shank with a sickening jerk. When I staggered, Bisi snatched my ankle, tipping me on top of him.

His teeth glinted, as he rubbed himself against me in the struggle. 'I chose the wrong sister.'

I slapped him, my bloody hands marking his cheek, and then it was *me* pressing the knife to Bisi's chest. The handle of the Zombie Slayer glowed in the shadowy stairwell, as the tip of its blade broke the skin.

I was tripping on that drugged moment of elation and godlike power.

'Go on,' Bisi's gaze was feverish as he whispered, like we were performing a holy ritual, 'you need this. Take it.'

I pushed down harder.

My new power flowed through me in furious, hissing waves. It did need this: to control, consume, and kill.

But you don't, Feathers-pie, and it's time to put the tricks back into the box.

Ice-cold froze the fury; it cracked, and shattered, fragile as glass.

I quivered, throwing myself off Bisi.

His eyes were unfocused and confused. I wondered if he'd ever been the one under the knife before, his soul at another's mercy. Whether that would now become his new addiction.

'Where's my sister?' I demanded.

'I didn't touch her, I swear. I only made the deal with Toben. He said he'd step-up and deliver Jade this evening.'

I lurched backwards, the Zombie Slayer still clutched in my crimson hands. Then I stumbled up the stairs towards Jade.

College was finished; Jade knew to be back at this time.

I gripped the steel handrail, hauling myself up, but my feet were heavy and each step was torture. My back blazed. Blood dripped down to stain my jeans.

A *clatter* of footsteps, and a giggle of schoolgirls surrounded me, sucking on lollipops and filming me with their phones. I snarled at them, but they only tittered, waving their phones at me. I'd be plastered over social media at a press of their hyperactive thumbs.

Feathery-puss, welcome to Screwed City.

I slammed into the door of my apartment, hammering on the white wood — *bang, bang, bang* — leaving scarlet daubs, like a serial killer's finger painting. No way could I fumble for my own key.

When Toben opened the door, and I tumbled inside — knifed, ashen, and grasping a bloody blade — he almost looked concerned.

Toben reached out to me: a toxic mix of gentle giant meets predator in designer trainers. 'Hey, what's going on, sweet thing?'

'You turning slave trader, bastard.'

He shrugged. 'Sometimes you've got to take the licks, and it was Jade or us. That little bitch isn't even true fam.'

I bristled, barging past him through the narrow corridor and into Jade's room.

It was empty.

I wandered into the black-painted bedroom, running my hand over the purple velvet curtains and throws. I plumped the skull embroidered cushions, which were heaped on the bed. I gazed around at the wilting flowers, with which Jade had decorated the walls one weekend, and the sad blinking of the Christmas lights that hung from the ceiling.

Yeah, Jade's gang was emo.

I glared at Toben. 'Where is she?'

'How should I know? Now a man has food to sell and p's to make.'

Because life is all about p's — money — when you come from Utopia Estate.

Toben with his alpha prick and designer...*everything*...reckoned his drug money gave him the power. Except, there's always someone further up the ladder. There was Bisi: top boy. Boss of the Estate.

When Toben strolled into the sitting room, snatching up a wad of cash to count from the neat piles on the tacky carpet, I stalked after him. Tasers, guns, and shanks lay on our sunken brown leather sofa as casual as guests.

'I'm not going to stop asking.'

He continued to flip through the notes; I could see the numbers whirring through his mind. He was a bright bastard. It was why I fell for him.

I have a habit of falling for bastards. I've been trying to break it, but then they give me *that look*...

Yet in the light of day, I'd always kicked them out of bed in the morning. That was, before Toben, when I was trapped.

Because men were only good in fantasy.

When I hurled the Zombie Slayer onto the coffee table, it scattered the white and brown bags, scales and needles like a drug waterfall.

Toben's lips thinned. 'Stop playing, sweet thing.'

'You sell my sister to pay off a debt, and now she's missing? You can't *sweet thing* out of this.'

He dropped the cash onto the sofa, before pressing me gently down next to it. His hard chest pinned me against the leather.

I gasped. My wound throbbed dully at the pressure. My vision greyed.

When I pushed at his shoulders, my hands

trembled. After a moment, they fell back.

He stroked my cheek with his rough finger. 'You need to go to hospital, *sweet thing.*'

I shook my head. 'Jade—'

His lips stopped my words, as he tongued open my mouth.

You know what I said about Screwed City...?

And you know what you promised about only having to ask...?

It doesn't work like a switch, on and off when you showboat your ass and need saving from Satan. If you tempt the devil, then you better be ready to battle the flames.

Toben wrenched back my head by the hair, feather-kissing up my throat.

A tear chased down my cheek, but I rested my neck on the leather, closing my eyes. I couldn't feel my body.

Maybe this was death.

Maybe I didn't care.

Then drowsily, I opened my eyes again.

A flash of red and black.

I forced my heavy eyelids to open further, before shock widened them.

Rebel lounged in the doorway, his arms crossed and pierced eyebrow raised. His lip was split bloody, but he didn't need rescuing.

I did.

Yet ambling into a drug dealer's den looking like a punk rocker with a flame for hair, was either brave or dim.

I was going with dim.

Toben was too lost in licking down my throat to notice the new bloke on his turf. I jerked away from the wet slurping of his tongue with my last burst of strength.

He gripped my chin. 'You don't say *no* to me, bitch. Or do you want me to sell you too?'

A roar of rage-shadowed punk, and Toben was tossed across the sitting room; he slammed into the striped wallpaper with a *crack*.

Rebel's face was hard, cold, and suddenly ancient in a way so terrifying, I quailed.

How had I ever reckoned the bloke was *innocent*?

Toben hauled himself up, snatching a taser from the scattered weapons. 'You come to my yard and play the big man?' He wiped his hand across his nose, smearing the scarlet. 'You're going to get dashed.'

He charged the taser, and a blue flame leapt.

Rebel didn't move. Yet he burned with a power that paled my fury to child's play. Then he smiled: dark and terrible.

As if emerging from a black cocoon, he shed his leather jacket, and I gasped.

Violet wings unfolded in a glorious flutter of sparks. One swept upwards in a blazing arc, yet Rebel's left wing was bent like it'd been broken. The feathers glowed, each one more beautiful than any fantasy I'd designed.

They sang to me in words I didn't understand and of worlds I'd never imagined.

It was...awe-inspiring.

The Irish punk was a proper angel. I guess that made me a *unicorn*. And Toben no longer the alpha prick.

Toben dropped the taser, falling to his knees instead. He gibbered prayers like a rap song.

Rebel prowled closer. When he placed his hands on the sides of Toben's head, *hushing* him softly, Toben quietened.

Toben held his breath, his eyes wide and dazed.

Rebel's wings beat, just once. Their breath kissed my face.

Crack — Rebel twisted, breaking Toben's neck.

Hell, hell, hell...

I tried to struggle away but I couldn't move.

Rebel wiped his hands down his trousers and then hung his head for a moment, as if calming himself, before turning back to me. The glow in his wings faded. The same spark as I'd seen (and then doubted) in his eyes outside Spirit and Fire Gaming Company died. His wings folded close to his back like a bird's at rest. 'Bloody ape,' his smile was triumphant. 'Brilliant the way he fell on his knees like—'

'I thought angels were good,' I whispered.

Rebel frowned. 'Righteous. It's not the same thing.'

'You're a killer. That makes you the Big Bad, not the hero.'

He tilted his head. 'Who said I was the hero?'

This isn't the devil I've temped, J, this is an angel. What do I do?

You can't let him know about me. If he finds out, then he'll snap your neck, as quickly as he did your asshole boyfriend's.

Why?

Because I'm special, of course. And so are you.

Rebel sauntered closer, peering down at the burgundy pooling from my back onto the sofa. He grimaced. 'That's a brutal wound. You're dying.'

'Angel and social inadequate.'

A flash of hurt, before he smothered it.

Why the hell did that boot me in the gut?

'I'm taking you home,' Rebel crouched down, winding his arm around my waist.

'Heaven?'

This was it then. Game over. At least a demon wasn't hoisting me downstairs to the stink of sulfur.

Rebel's lips quirked. 'Kingston upon Thames.'

'No way, bro. I'm not swag to carry home all shiny.'

He sighed. 'You'll be my prisoner then.'

When he pressed into the base of my neck, I juddered with an electric jolt that shocked my shoulder blades. It overwhelmed me with an unexpected sense of violation.

See? All men are bastards. And angels are the worst.

I stared into Rebel's eyes, which were blurred to indigo skies through the blur of my tears, as I slipped into the dark.

3

Flying, fluttering, floating. Nothing to hold onto, only the threads of a vision: flaming wings and raging righteousness.

Angels were real. Rebel was a kidnapper. And I was lost in the black.

I flailed, battling to rise up to the light.

J, this is no time for the strong and silent act. I've been abducted and I can't wake up.

Silence.

Alone, I stomped hard on the sickening terror rising in my gut.

I need you. I'm asking.

My own thoughts echoed deafening, now that the voice in my head had been silenced.

Help me, help me, help me...

My eyes opened. And I awoke from the dark...into the dark.

I gasped, shivering. Then I sniffed: spicy cinnamon spelled the air. Whatever I was stretched on, hugged me softly like a...bed?

I tried to sit up but I couldn't. Something tight

but caressing encircled my wrists and ankles. When I tugged at my arms experimentally, a chain clanked.

Kinky bastard angel.

I'd been spread-eagled to a bed by the punk who'd slaughtered Toben.

And I'd reckoned losing my job had been a screw up?

I sighed, booting my foot and *clinking* the chains.

I'd never played the damsel before and no way in any kinky angel's dream was I playing it sacrificial now.

Yet it was there again: the *slam — slam — slam* of sweetness in line with my heartbeat. A rhythmic, tingling tide of sensation and taste. Sweet, coppery, and impossible to deny.

It was in me. For me. *Rebel's blood*, I knew now. Familiar, I rode it.

Hell, it was my new addiction. And it told me that Rebel must be near.

Creak — a white ray of light bled in through the opened door, along with a burst of anarchic punk music: Angelic Upstarts' "Teenage Warning".

Then came a throaty giggle — but it wasn't Rebel's. Some bitch was out there with him.

Punk rebellion, giggles, and chains? It wasn't as if I'd expected a freakshow like Rebel to kidnap regular style.

I blinked as the room awoke from the gloom in all its Tudor, oak panelled glory. When stone carvings of wolf heads snarled out of the ceiling's corners, I flinched. The four-poster bed I was shackled to by suede lined gold cuffs had twisted front posts, intricate roses carved into the bedrails and frilly burgundy curtains: a princess' wet dream.

Yet I was no captured princess; I was the beast.

I thumped my head back against a pile of scarlet rose embroidered pillows.

When the music died, Rebel slunk into my fancy prison cell. His studded leather once more hid his wings.

I screwed shut my eyes.

Rebel wanted a fairy tale? Then I'd play Sleeping Beauty, but he'd better hope he didn't awake what was hidden, slithering inside me since my twenty-first, with a kiss.

Except, I hated the relief. It flooded me when I'd glimpsed Rebel's familiar flame of hair and slouch around the door, his hands tucked into the pockets of his trousers.

I'd been caught in that shank-sharp line between craving my kidnapper, so I wouldn't be abandoned, and terror at being powerless.

I don't do powerless, not even for angels, the kinky sort who were stroking the backs of their fingers down my arm.

My bare arm.

I was naked, under the caress of a black wolf fur throw; the midnight strands tickled my tits. 'Call a bitch romantic,' I bit out, 'but I like to save the bondage for the second date.'

My eyes snapped open, only to be staring directly into Rebel's startled gaze.

A true angel with violet eyes.

So, what did that make me, with my one violet eye, and one black?

Rebel drew in his breath, stumbling backwards and landing on his arse. He gazed up at me with such meekness, the bloke could be mistaken for a cherub, not a killer angel.

Fool me once...

'You're awake then?' Rebel grinned, bottom shuffling to the four-poster, before kneeling next to me, as if he was the slave, and I wasn't bound to the bed. 'You gave me a fierce scare with the almost dying bollocks these two weeks gone.'

I gawped at him. 'Two weeks?'

'Some git stabbed you.' I jolted with the flash shot memory of Bisi twisting the Zombie Slayer into my kidney. But there was no pain remaining, not even a dull ache. I felt the strongest...fittest...most powerful...I ever had. 'We've been healing you.'

'You mean stripping me? Where are my clothes?'

He flushed. 'I didn't... I mean, I haven't...'

'The newbie desperate to see a human woman's—'

'Lay off, Lady Muck. Ma said—'

'Angels have mummies?'

'It was humans who helped you, like Ma. And she said you should be dead.' He smoothed his fingers through the wolf fur throw, soothing himself. 'I'm adopted.'

Who wouldn't want to adopt an angel? Just as no one had wanted to adopt a freak with mismatched eyes.

Rebel's scrutiny was suddenly too intense.

Hell, where were my sunglasses?

I bit my tongue to stop the scream. Clothes were nothing but cloth. But stealing my sunglasses was a violation that burrowed deep to the places where the nightmares gnawed.

I thrashed in the chains; my shoulder sockets pulled. I arched like a wild cat, until even the suede chaffed my ankles.

Someone lay over me, holding me down and still.

Safe.

I sobbed, resting my cheek against this someone's cheek, as their heartbeat throbbed against mine and our legs tangled.

I was cocooned in the sugar copper of their scent.

'My sunglasses,' I gulped out.

'I'm a muppet.' Rebel petted my hair, and — in that moment — I didn't want to break his fingers.

A gossamer press of lips to my forehead, before he eased off me. He opened a drawer in an oak chest of drawers beside the bed, snatching out my sunglasses. When he pushed them onto my nose, I cringed.

How had I allowed myself to sob in Rebel's arms exactly like that captured princess?

'If you ever touch my neck again, like you did when you kidnapped me?' At my snarl, Rebel slumped onto the bed, his own collared neck swan-like and exposed, as if in supplication. 'I'll snap yours.'

Rebel fidgeted with the frilly edges of my pillow, before nodding. 'I'm sorry,' I was shocked by the pained contrition in his eyes, 'I had no right. But you're alive—'

'I'm your prisoner. In a creepy arsed mansion. Strange, but I'm all out of happy juice.'

'Ma said you had to keep still for the herbs to work.'

'To hell with that, mummy's boy. Where are the other angels? Because if I believe in you, then there must be others, you get me?'

'They're not here.'

Rebel's gaze slid away from mine: definite shiftiness.

'Cheers, Mr Specific.' I banged my wrist cuffs together. 'Now I'm all fixed up, where's the key?'

He rubbed his thumb over the bruises, where I'd pulled against the cuffs. 'It's too soon. I have to protect you.'

'From what?'

His thumb traced circles on my inner wrist. 'Everything.'

'Too late, pretty boy,' I hissed, hating that I couldn't move or shank with more than words, 'epic fail. I've lost my job, apartment...*life*. Oh yeah, and you killed my boyfriend.'

This time there was no contrition. 'Git deserved to die. He was after selling you. And your sister.'

Jade.

Rebel could shank with a word.

'You reckon I'd cower here, whilst my sis is missing?'

He leaned closer as he whispered, 'Don't tell.'

Then his fingers pressed into my neck, and I shuddered at the invasion, as unexpectedly our bodies, minds, and souls became melded. His power surged through me, holding me motionless in its thrall.

In the bondage of my chains, Rebel also held me in the bondage of my mind, suspended above an abyss, whilst he flicked through my memories, so quickly they blurred like life seen from the back of a motorbike. Narrower and narrower, they focused on Jade: the flick of her pink-streaked black hair and shy beam, when she'd curled up with me to open her birthday present.

A crystal angel on delicate gold chain.

Suddenly, as if the memory was the launching pad he'd been searching for, Rebel was soaring. Then he was gone. And I was alone above an abyss.

I howled into the void, before a pull dragged me back to the wood-panelled room scented with cinnamon.

'I warned you, bro, I'd snap your neck.'

'Away with you, an empty threat,' Rebel shrugged, even as he peered at me anxiously. 'I'm

thinking you'll be after knowing about your sister?'
I didn't understand his glance at the open door or
the flash of guilt across his pale face, before he
murmured against my ear, 'All I know for sure is
she's no longer connected to you.'

My heart thudded. 'Listen, bastard, Jade will
always be—'

'Rebel, come here. You are in need of your
lesson.' A man's deep, aristocratic command from
the corridor outside.

Rebel jumped and grimaced.

I remembered his urgent *Don't tell.*

What the hell frightened an angel? Or made him
hang his head like a naughty school kid?

Rebel dawdled across the bedroom, *clomping*
his boots on the oak floor, before glancing over his
shoulder at me with a tight smile. He curled his
hand around the door, glancing back at me with a
rebellious grimace. 'I won't leave you in the dark.'

Except, without my sister, or J, and now
without Rebel, that's all I was.

Not *connected* to me? Screw that.

A long moment's silence and then...

Whish — crack.

I startled.

Whish — crack.

Then a stifled yelp. *Rebel's* yelp.

Whish — crack.

The beating washed over me in a whistling
wave, as Rebel's cries broke to weeping.

This was the *lesson* being taught by the owner

of that deep voice, which Rebel had jumped to obey?

Despite the cuffs at my wrists and the annihilation of my world on Utopia Estate, I remembered the glory of Rebel's wings and the awe that had pushed Toben to his knees. I whirlwind spun, a rage of bone and feathers, that a *human* would dare thrash an angel.

Whish — crack.

Rebel keened.

I hid my face against the pillow, clenching my fists. Then I let out a strangled choke.

A rattan cane bit into my throat like a garrote.

My eyes rolled back. I couldn't breathe. My skin bruised.

'When I first saw what the naughty boy had dragged home, I voted to feed you to the wolves.' That throaty giggle again. The brush of petalled silk, as the woman slithered onto me like a rose oil scented snake; I gagged. 'But no, I can't touch what's *special*. Are you, I wonder, worth the price?'

The cane eased at my throat. I retched, struggling to scrutinize the skank in crimson velvet sweater and billowing emerald skirt who was straddling me. Her wild black curls thwapped me in the face, as she swung the whippy cane like she was trying to hypnotise me.

One of Rebel's humans. And a definite Big Bad.

'Let me go and maybe you'll find out,' I growled.

The rose and thorn bitch smirked. 'I'm not naïve like Rebel. Try harder, or don't.' She shrugged. A sickly rose perfume clung to her clothes, hair, and eyelashes; it sweated from her skin. 'In Tudor times, this House of Rose, Wolf, and Fox was a schoolhouse. My uncle and aunt are, you could say, teachers of sorts. And I've grown up here,' she scowled, and I shrank back, 'in the shadow of one thing: the angel they loved as teenagers and lost.'

'Boo hoo, yeah? Poor little rich girl. Do you want to swap childhood survival stories? Because I'm not in the mood.'

Swish — the savage with curls raised the cane above her head to cut it down across my cheek.

I recoiled against the pillows.

'If you're vexed, Evie, then punish me.' Rebel caught the blow. It raised a livid red line down his palm, but he clung onto the thin cane.

Evie wrenched away the cane, flinging it to the other side of the room against the oak panelling.

Tear tracks stained Rebel's face, and he avoided meeting my gaze.

Why would my own abductor protect me? But then why had he saved me from Toben?

Evie made a point of sneering at me, before simpering at Rebel. She wound her arms around his neck. Then she snogged him like he was the sacrifice at a cannibal's feast.

'You didn't tell me your new toy was awake, my wicked love,' Evie pouted, her ruby lips thick and wet, when she finally drew back.

'Didn't get the chance,' Rebel shifted uncomfortably.

'Want me to kiss it all better?' When Evie dragged Rebel towards the door, I noticed he was limping.

He glanced back at me with an apologetic shrug.

'Why are you letting these humans own you?' I asked.

He stiffened, faltering in the doorway. 'They don't own me, but I'm their boy because they adopted me.'

Naïve? That'd be right. These humans had twisted the beauty of true adoption, but Rebel didn't have a clue.

I lay in the twilight, amongst the silk, fur, and chains, unable to escape the *squeak* of bedsprings, *banging* of the headboard, and the moaned ecstasy, whilst my enemies screwed.

As Evie shrieked her way to a climax, an older woman clopped into my bedroom in over the knee boots. 'As Rebel's Ma, I should introduce myself.'

I lay motionless, expecting another vicious attack, but unlike her niece, Ma was English country woman does mindfulness, in a vintage ruched black dress lined with fur and a sharp silver bob. A large wolf pendant glowered at me from around her neck.

Ma perched on the edge of the bed, before pressing a gold goblet of water to my lips.

Too parched to do careful, I gulped. 'Cheers.'

Ma didn't reply. Instead, she broke off a piece of dry toast from an oak platter, and I nibbled from her thin fingers like a baby.

It hurt to swallow.

Ma's gaze was shuttered, as if she wasn't handfeeding a naked prisoner to the soundtrack of shagging just next door.

How had my life become being the prisoner of an angel and his crazy adoptive family?

At least Ma was acting kind. When she brushed crumbs from my mouth, I smiled.

Until Ma murmured, soft as honey but sharp as a shank, 'Fool that you are, little girl, you imagine you've faced this world's nightmares or — dream on — that *you're* the nightmare. Whatever.' Her lip curled, like a surly teenager. 'The angel is ours. And if you ever think to steal him...'

A dry hand clamped over my mouth. Another

pinched shut my nose. I hollered against the gag. My lungs struggled and strained. Panic clawed.

Ma's eyes — crinkled at the edges but not with kindness, I realised with shock, rather with a dancing cruelty — chased me into the dark.

4

There are dark kisses that bruise your soul as well as your mouth. Kisses as soft as feathers. Light. Gentle. Kind. Whereas others blaze and burn to ash.

And then there are kisses that are a revelation.

As I drifted back towards the grey, once more out of the black, soft lips kissed mine.

The kiss didn't bruise or burn but it was firm and possessive.

Right.

Until it wasn't.

I bit hard. The bastard gasped, and the mouth pulled back. But not before a coppery sweet blood crescendo exploded; my tongue chased after heaven.

It'd been Rebel's kiss...and blood.

The new, fluttering forces deep within me awoke and roared at the taste, claiming Rebel. Wanting him, even if *I* didn't.

How had I lost control even of myself?

Then I blinked awake.

Rebel peered down at me, concerned. He stroked my arm, as he had when I'd first awoken; I reckon it soothed him more than me. He hadn't chained me this time, only snapped steel handcuffs around my wrists.

Maybe he was experimenting with bondage techniques.

When he leaned closer, I elbowed him — *oomph* — in the guts. 'Congratulations, you've just made my List of Asses to Kick.'

'You have a list?' He grinned uncertainly, like a kid discovering Father Christmas was real but had written him onto his Naughty List.

'Yeah, it helps when men molest you.'

Rebel snatched up his ripped t-shirt from the wolf throw and began sewing on leather patches around slashes in the back, even though his hand shook. I realised the gaps were for his wings and then, with a jolt, that he must've been sitting on the edge of my four-poster, under the burgundy frills and enshrouded in cinnamon and saffron — sewing — and watching me whilst I slept.

Or guarding me.

At last, Rebel's fingers hesitated. 'Angel kisses are fierce powerful. They heal. And you were...'

I jacked up, kicking off the fur throw and wriggling to the far side of the bed.

I steeled myself for the bump as I hit the floor, but a hand grasped my ankle and I was hauled back amongst the pillows like a winded catch of the day.

I bucked again, hissing.

'Take it easy, princess.' Rebel glanced at the open door, before whispering, his body taut with tension against mine, 'If you promise to stay here with me and my family, the Deadmans, then I'll promise to help find your sister. Deal?'

I became still. My freedom to find my sister?

Hell, no contest.

'Deal. But you're taking me back to Utopia Estate. I adopted Jade. And what you don't seem to understand is that doesn't mean I own her, yet she's still mine. She's my *estate sister*. And that's closer than blood.' Rebel's confusion was painful. My gaze softened. 'Angels kisses can't heal me, whilst my fam is missing.'

Clank — my handcuffed wrist jangled against Rebel's in the pocket of his leather jacket.

Handcuffed together, we stumbled through London Fields park, between taekwondo classes, bike trails, and shabby buggies in the clear winter sunlight like a lame-arsed comedy duo.

I tripped against Rebel, and we tangled in a crazy waltz. My nose pressed to his jacket; I took a snort of leather and metal.

But no copper sweetness.

Its loss was a boot to my gut, and I didn't know either why I cared, or why it'd faded. Yet the chance to escape the danger of Rebel's family was like being able to breath, after being crushed under heavy stones. I dreaded being dragged back there.

With a growl of frustration, I shoved away Rebel, and we both crashed into the scaly trunk of a London Plane tree.

He raised an unamused pierced eyebrow. 'Problem, princess?'

I snatched his fingers inside the pocket and squeezed.

He smothered a yelp, struggling underneath me to get away.

Just as I'd done in the bedroom.

Yet when Rebel discovered he was trapped, he

melted into me, trembling with pain.

It was...delicious.

Violet snaked between us, licking, tasting, and feasting.

Put the pretty boy down before you break him.

Where have you been, J? You left me chained in that Tudor mansion. Alone.

You're never alone. But sometimes, Feathery-puss, you can't hear me.

At last I let Rebel go, with a final warning stroke of my thumb. 'I'm still in handcuffs, even outside the house. You're a proper kinky bastard.'

He tilted his head, his wide eyes thoughtful, as he bit at his lip. 'Trust is a brilliant thing, to be sure. You can fly on trust. But you?' He flexed his swollen hand. 'I don't trust.'

And that was the true boot to the gut.

I scowled. 'Because I'm all down with trusting the killer angel. Look, kids took pictures of me with a knife in my hand. Then I disappeared from a murder scene. You don't reckon the pigs will be looking for me?'

Rebel shrugged, but he shuffled from foot to foot. When a football bounced against his ankle, his face lit up with a childish joy I hadn't seen before. He kicked it back to the lads in grey hoodies, who skulked by the benches, in a flawless arc that had the lads whistling and clapping. They gestured for Rebel — the bondage punk — to join the game.

In London Fields, Hackney.

Yeah, nothing was *regular* anymore.

I reckon if Rebel hadn't been handcuffed to me, he'd have bounded to join his new gang, with their designer saddlebags of cocaine, knives, and bottled acid stashed underneath the slanted benches, as if he was Peter Pan leading the Lost Boys.

I shivered, battling to drag my khaki jacket closer.

Hell, I'm wearing a stab victim's clothes, even if <u>I'm</u> the victim.

The punk cleaned and mended your clothes.

Want to tell me how the wallad magicked out bloodstains?

Magic...interesting word to choose.

Magic too?

I wasn't sure I was ready to believe that yet. In fact, all I wanted was to find my sister and get as far from Rebel and his freaky secret world as I could.

When I yanked Rebel, he strolled after me across the playing field towards the road looping Utopia Estate like we were any couple, huddled against the cold.

Waves of grease from the burger bar on the corner melded with spice from the kebab shop opposite.

'Why'd you bother rescuing my clothes?' I patted at my jacket.

'Duds are important,' Rebel glanced at me from underneath his eyelashes. 'Ma helped.'

I clenched my handcuffed fist, only for Rebel's bruised fingers to gently caress over it. Yet somehow his — kindness, calmness, submission — only made me madder. 'Your family, these Deadmans, are bastards. Why are you hiding with them?'

'I warned you I wasn't good, I was righteous. But I fibbed.' He gnawed at his sore lip again. 'I'm a bad angel. I ask for your trust and say you can fly on it. But you shouldn't trust me.' He stared at the ground, refusing to look up. 'I did a flit from Angel World and bolted here to yours. Now I'm the hunted.'

Finally, he sneaked a glance at me, as if expecting me to either clout him or recoil.

Instead, I clutched his hand in mine, stroking him as he had me. Because his shame called to my own.

For the first time, he released his tortured lip.

'Still, why stay with humans who beat—'

'They know magics that keep me safe.'

On the edge of the road, in the shadow of Tower Block A, I pulled him to a stop. I steeled myself, wishing I didn't have to ask. 'Are you telling me I'm the prisoner of spell lobbers?'

'You're a guest of my family. Who happen to be witches.'

An angel had been adopted by witches, and now I was their *guest* in handcuffs?

A flash of neon blue and the wail of siren, as a panda car — all blues and twos — flew through the estate.

Rebel spun me, as if to haul me into a snog, but I jerked backwards. 'We're not in a movie, hiding from the feds. Learn some swag, if you don't want to get licked.' His smacked puppy nose pout made me wish I'd snogged him, even more than the strange new buzzing murmur inside: *mine, take, devour...* And stoked my rage even higher. 'But you've already been licked. How's the arse?'

'I can sit down again, thank you.'

'See, kinky angel.'

'I'm Da's.' Rebel bristled, dragging me after him across the road between the beeping cars and vans. 'I left him. So, he punished me. How's that turn you on?'

I flushed, as he marched us up the stairs into Tower Block A. The guard was missing: Toben's soldiers weren't stretched out, like a lion pride on weed, along the concrete.

Everything had changed.

We slipped into the inky dark of the stairwell. The quiet suffocated me.

Suddenly the idea of someone else's hands touching Rebel — punishing, exciting, or comforting — made the hidden force that'd claimed him boil.

'You can kill a bloke with your hands,' *Toben kneeling, adoring, and then dead with a snap of his chicken neck*, 'but you'll let this slipper wearing, daddy issues perv turn you over his knee because you were late home?'

Rebel smiled brightly. 'Get on with you. Da would be mortified to wear slippers. And I wasn't just late. I disappeared for over forty years.'

When we clattered up the stairs, a schoolgirl paled as she passed us.

Before I could duck, the kid had snapped me with a *whoop* and a victory dance. She'd been there on the night I'd fought with Bisi too.

The bitch had pulled down the world on us, simply with her mobile.

Rebel and me glanced at each other once, and then we ran. When Rebel booted in the door to Apartment 333, we burst inside, diving for the death-quiet of Jade's room.

'She's not here. Maybe...she's just with mates.'

I didn't even dare say *back on the streets.*

I wandered through the stale room to the pine wardrobe that Jade had painted black and then decorated with glow-in-the-dark skulls, yanking open the door.

Rebel jittered. 'I told you, you're not—'

'Connected,' I muttered, running my hand over Jade's favourite pink-and-white striped tunic.

If Jade bolted to be with some boy, or...if she's alive...why didn't she take her clothes?

Your sis's alive, Violet-sweets. What scares you, is that you can choose the world you want now. You're free of Jade and this Estate.

For the first time, you can choose who you are.

I recoiled from J's truth. The devil's whisper and temptation.

Sirens wailed outside the block; the police's panda cars circled like hyenas.

'Time to scatter,' Rebel pulled me towards the door.

I caught a glimpse of gold on the bedside table.

I dug in my heels, leading Rebel to the necklace, before threading it between my fingers. When I heard his intake of breath, I knew he recognised it from my memories.

We shared Jade now and the promise to find her.

Jade would never have left without her necklace. It was my last birthday gift to her. The only present she'd been given that day because I alone loved her.

But she hadn't cared. Because we'd been *sisters*. *Someone must've taken her.*

Rebel's forehead against mine brought me down from the rush; he raised the necklace to my neck and with one hand each, we did up the catch. I longed to rip off the handcuffs and escape the claustrophobic closeness, at the same time as the other half of me relaxed into it.

Then I gave a nod, and we bolted.

Halfway down the open stairs that overlooked the playground and sweeping crescent of the Estate's main road, we peered over at the swarming pigs in blue amidst the snarling pandas.

Click — my stomach dropped, like I'd tumbled

over the ledge, when I heard the trigger cocked on a shooter.

Yet when I risked peeking over my shoulder, the gun was pressed to Rebel's head.

By Bisi.

Bisi met my glare, but he was trembling. I'd never seen him tremble. 'You stole my shank.' He rammed the snout of the gun harder into the base of Rebel's skull. 'So, I stepped-up. It's all about the straps.'

I'd wondered what becoming the victim would do to Bisi.

Now I knew. If you took a man's shank, he bought a shooter. No one could risk being invisible in London. And no one ignored a bloke with a gun.

Except Rebel.

'Friend of yours, Feathers?' Rebel leaned his arms on the ledge, as if he was sightseeing.

Bisi puffed up, rubbing one hand against his stiffie. 'Word on the street is this freak took out Toben. Are you muscling in on my turf? Monsters and murderers hungering to be the new top boys?'

I shrank against Rebel. 'Do your *righteous* thing.'

Rebel stretched his shoulders, flexing his wings underneath his jacket. 'It doesn't work like that.' He pushed back against the shooter, like he didn't realise Bisi wasn't bluffing. 'Lay off, muppet.'

At last, Bisi eased off the trigger, before grinning — a slash of gold in the concrete grey of the day — and turning the shooter on me. He pressed almost as close to me as the cold round snout of the gun.

I'd been knifed, beaten, dodged acid and meat cleavers but I'd never had a gun to my head.

Since Rebel had fallen from the ceiling, it'd been nothing but a world of firsts.

I hadn't expected the wash of terror, edged by impotent fury; I vibrated with it.

Then I yowled, as my wrist was wrenched up, and Rebel spun us, his expression transformed from studied boredom to tight grimness. He knocked the shooter up and away from my head, before clouting Bisi across the mouth.

'This is what a bro gets for going soft,' Bisi scrambled backwards. 'As soon as your man fell short, I should've shanked you and your sis.'

Violet hit like a tsunami.

I rode it to a plateau of feathers, where I was stronger, faster, more powerful and nothing mattered but...righteousness.

I ruled over the land of bones below, gnashing my teeth in vicious victory.

Someone was battling me, holding me back.

'Princess...mind yourself.'

But there was nothing beyond the feathers and bones.

I was lost, as something else took over, and *it wasn't human.*

A *scream. Bang. Howl.*

I couldn't stop. My hand was around Bisi's neck. He hung ragdoll limp over the ledge.

'Feathers, wise up! Let him go!' The voice came out in gulped gasps, as an angel tugged at my arm.

My angel...

The world blurred back to multicolour.

And I was balanced on the open stairs of Tower Block A, with my hand clutched around Bisi's throat, as he dangled over the sweep of flashing lights below.

I eased my hold, heart beating wildly. Yet when Bisi edged himself back over the ledge, he jerked me off balance, and then snapped at my thumb with his golden teeth, trying to bite and kiss me all at once.

I shoved Bisi back, and he fell, windmilling through the cold winter sky like a dark angel with broken wings.

Crash — Bisi slammed onto the windscreen of a panda car; the crack spider webbed scarlet.

The alarm screamed; pigs hollered and pointed up at me.

Bisi had been right: I was a monster and, like Rebel, I was a murderer too.

Maybe that's what being an angel meant.

Sometimes kisses are a revelation because it wasn't the soft lips that'd awoken me, but the *blood* when I'd bitten.

I'd known ever since Rebel had kissed me: I was part angel. His blood had sung to my own.

Sirens shrieked, whilst the heavy *stomp* of police boots echoed up the stairwell.

I clutched at Rebel, only to be dragged down, as he sank to the floor.

When he touched his shoulder, his hand came back sticky crimson from a gunshot wound. I pulled him up; he swayed, and I clasped him close to my chest.

Then we became the hunted.

5

Ever since Jerusalem Children's Home spat me out at sixteen, I'd expected to end up stumbling home with some bloke bleeding out from a gunshot wound.

What I'd never expected...?

Home to be a witches' house. The bloke to be an angel. And to have just discovered my own angelic heritage.

When Rebel shivered, I held him tight, yet I was frozen too. His feet dragged, tripping against mine.

The House of Rose, Wolf, and Fox rose out of the damp fog beside the silver snake of the Thames. Ancient woodland glowered behind the stone and blackened diagonal timbered mansion. Smoke snorted in furious bursts from the high spiralled chimneys.

I shuddered.

Did you know spell lobbers were real, J?

There isn't space on earth for what I know. But right now? You need to dump the

punk, turn your hoochie ass around, and use your brain, rather than the sweet tingles between your legs.

I jolted to a stop.

Rebel groaned, grasping the stone sundial that marked the centre of the sweeping drive. 'Princess?'

'We'll be at your yard any moment, bro.'

He shivered again. But this time, I didn't reckon it was with cold.

Was Rebel frightened because he'd defied the witches to help me? How big a risk had he taken?

Yet how dangerous was the world Rebel had fled, if a witches' house still meant safety?

I'm done with being afraid. So, no arse turning.

You're playing with fire. If you go inside, the witches will kill you for breaking their toy.

They can try.

And there's the Feathers-bitch I love.

I could hear J's smile. For once, it disturbed me, although I didn't know why.

I unfurled Rebel's hand, finger by finger from its death grip on the sundial, and then dragged him crunching over the gravel to the rounded arch of the pillared porch.

Rebel had sneaked me out of a side door in the early hours, when the house had still been veiled in black. Now I saw the red daubed symbols around the high oak door and wicker angel effigies swinging in the porch like they'd been hung.

Hell, the Blair Witch had nothing on Evie, Louisa, and Richard Deadman: witches, angel tamers, and my true captors.

Strange, since Rebel's kiss and his exchange of blood, this truth was clearer. I could read his feelings, spiderwebs at the corners of my mind, but only fleeting sensations.

Before I could knock, the door was wrenched open — *creak* — and a bearded bloke loomed over us. He held himself motionless, yet every giant inch of him radiated fury.

Rebel shrank back.

Da, in slim russet wool suit and waistcoat, his white shirt matching his perfect teeth, asked crisply, 'Where have you been, Zach?'

'Zach?' I mouthed at Rebel, but he didn't hear me; his gaze was fixed on Da.

'I'm sorry, but it's like this, see,' Rebel faltered, 'I made a deal—'

'Do you get to decide on what's best? To make *deals*, boy?'

When Rebel shook his head, I grasped his hand in my pocket. He winced, expecting me to hurt him like I had earlier, and that flushed me with unexpected shame. But I only held his hand lightly in mine.

'And why is that?'

'Because you're in charge, Da.'

I'd faced the disappointment of agency staff each time I'd swaggered back in the early hours to Jerusalem.

Curfews were for geeks and losers. The kids who took the beatings and ended up at the end of a shank.

So, if you didn't want to get dashed, you broke the rules.

This? Returning to face the music of a parent who actually gave a damn? If it hadn't been for the danger in Da's steel eyes and his headmaster sadist vibe, I'd have found reassuring.

Maybe *I* had daddy issues.

Da rubbed at his grey beard, which was as regimented as his hair.

'I believe we shall have to reinforce that lesson.' Stanbury had been the wannabe, but here was the true Christian Grey, only all grownup. But Rebel was such an innocent, I don't think he even understood what they were playing. 'Inside.'

Rebel flinched.

I'd only glimpsed a grand oak galley running above the wooden entryway and gold threaded tapestries, as we reluctantly stepped past Da, before Rebel dropped to his knees. I fell next to him. His eyes were screwed shut, and it was only me stopping him from collapsing.

'Up.' Da barked. 'You shan't think kneeling will reduce—'

'Back off, Sir Canesalot. Your boy here's been shot. *Bang, bang*?' I mimicked a shooter at Rebel's back.

Da's face drained to chalk.

After that? Everything blurred into a burst of frenetic commotion.

Da patted Rebel down for the key to the handcuffs, before releasing him.

I tried to pull away, but Da snapped the handcuffs back over both my wrists, before tenderly scooping Rebel up into his arms, as if he was a kid.

I tagged behind Da, the sudden outsider, as he marched into a vast kitchen of inky-black cabinets and exotic marbles. My eyes watered from the smoke that wafted out of the open inglenook fireplace, which was large enough to spit an angel.

Ma and Evie glanced up from sorting through a sea of washed underwear — lace bras, cotton boxers, and silk corsets — on the central counter.

The glow from the chandelier and the vibrant modern punk of Slaves' "Cheer up London" (no way that wasn't Rebel's iPod hooked up to the speakers), shocked me like a bullet to the head.

And in the one second before the everyday transformed to horror — when I glimpsed beneath the labels and the drama — I got it.

This was what Rebel loved. Why, after everything, he came back.

A home.

Rebel had known this family (when I'd only ever struggled to make my own), for decades. How could I compete with that? And why the hell did I crave to?

Then Evie exploded.

With a shriek, she swept the neat piles of bras flying across the kitchen. An ivory and rose underwire landed in the hearth with a bright flare and then sizzle.

Evie vaulted the kitchen counter, thrusting me aside to stroke Rebel's hair.

I lounged against the stone wall.

Ma merely pursed her lips, as Da laid Rebel on the long oak table. 'Be still, Evie.' When Ma turned to scrutinise me, I gagged, overwhelmed by the memory of her papery dry hand clamped over my nose and mouth. 'Why is our angel bleeding?'

I didn't mean to say it. I don't even know where it came from. But it still slipped out. 'He was trying to save me. He was being a hero.'

Evie snorted, but Da's shock melted to pride, before he smiled.

I smiled too, until Da shucked his jacket and undid his cufflinks. Then with an alpha display that made me even more definite he was never going anywhere near my arse with his large hands, he folded back his shirtsleeves to the elbow.

I launched myself between the witch headmaster and his whipping boy. No way was Da laying a hand on Rebel, when I'd just hauled him across London.

The new, possessive part of me stirred. But there was something else as well, even darker and deeper. It snarled just as loudly that Rebel — and his blood —was *mine*.

Da's thin lips twitched. 'Zach has a bullet lodged in his bad wing. He'll heal but only once the bullet's taken out. I don't imagine you know how to remove it, but please do enlighten me.'

I gestured *go ahead* with my handcuffed hands.

When Da massaged his thumb into Rebel's bent wing, Rebel's eyes shot open. He stared up at me like he was drowning. Then his eyelids fluttered, whilst Da massaged across his back, working into the feathers.

I examined the folded wings, as Da stretched out each one, working his fingers into the layers of soft feathers, skirting the gunshot wound.

Did all angels have bent wings, or only the bad ones?

When Rebel purred deep in this throat — a thrilling, growly purr that called to me — I grinned. Hell, I itched to wring that sound from him. To ease the pain in his wing and coax that purr out of his soul.

It was unsettling, this new closeness to Rebel. Yet just as I'd experience the urge to sooth his pain, I'd be blasted with the impulse to hurt him. Like the two powers inside me were warring.

The way Rebel relaxed under Da's touch, I realised he must've been in agony with his wing, even before he was shot.

Rebel was good at hiding pain.

And the truth.

I reached out to stroke the tip of Rebel's wing, as he'd stroked my bare arm; I was desperate suddenly to see if it was silky soft.

Evie batted me away. 'No touching, my lovely.

You're not invited to the party.'

Ma selected a bundle of dried herbs, which hung from an oak beam on the ceiling, but Da waved her away. 'Boys who disobey do not warrant spells of healing. I'll dig out the bullet the old-fashioned way.'

Evie sidled to Pa, winding a curl around her little finger. 'Uncle Richard, at least allow me to whip up a Rose Anti-Pain. When I broke my arm—'

'And if the other angels had located Zach? He didn't take an effigy. If we'd lost him again?' Da's hard gaze had found out Ma's.

Ma hurled the dried herbs onto the hearth next to the ivory and rose bra. The fire sprang up — *bang* — like a fountain of blood. 'That's it, for real. He's grounded.'

'You're grounding an *angel*?' I stared from one witch to the other, with Rebel stretched out on the oak table between them, bleeding from his wing.

The crazy bastards kept Rebel safe by stealing his freedom. Yet their fear of these other *angels* was real.

What the hell was an angelic top boy like?

When Ma pressed the blade into Da's hand, and he burrowed it into Rebel's wing, I winced on the angel's holler.

The shadow of his emotions tugged on me. *His pain...* It crawled across my own skin like claws screeching down slate.

Hell, if they wouldn't heal him, then I would.

I leant down and snogged Rebel.

The angel kiss wasn't a revelation. It was comfort.

I might only be half angel, but spell casters weren't the only ones with magic.

I nipped at Rebel's lip, swiping at the sweet copper in case that was the key, losing myself in the gentle intimacy. In the blood.

Until a long-nailed hand wound round my hair, wrenching back my head. My wet lips kissed the air.

'Gatecrashers,' Evie spat out each word, like I'd maimed her favourite Ken doll. 'Will. Be. Turned. Into. Gargoyles.'

'An angel kiss to heal him,' I panted.

'And where would you acquire such a silly,' Da twisted the knife, and Rebel whimpered, 'conceit?'

'Yeah, about that,' Rebel blushed, 'I lied.'

For something that wasn't a surprise, it still hurt.

Just like Evie's kick to the back of my knees and her vicious whisper, 'Even special ones have to drink. And when you do, it'll be the most scintillating surprise to discover what a changed woman you become.' Her chuckle was low, like water over crystals in an underground cavern.

Instantly, Rebel had risen off the oak table, his wings glowing and glorious, as they *beat — beat — beat* the wind against our faces. He was the ancient angel of my apartment, not Da's boy. There was not one submissive atom in him; the spiked collar around his neck was armour.

I quaked, as Rebel towered over me, but he only held out his hand, pulling me to my feet.

Slam.

Sugary copper zinged through me, lighting up my shoulder blades.

Rebel rocked, righteousness alone holding him on his feet. His wings wrapped around, hugging me to his body like I was a part of him.

I'd never felt closer to anyone.

And that terrified me.

I didn't know if I wanted to escape or surrender.

His tone was hard, 'No one harms Violet. If anyone tries, then I'll bolt. And this time, I'll never come back.'

Ma gasped. Then one-by-one Rebel's family crowded around us, stroking, soothing, and promising.

Who was in *charge* now?

Yet as Evie butterflied reverential kisses along Rebel's feathers, she cast me looks laced with venom.

The Deadmans' promises were as empty as the ones adults had thrown at me all my life. They were no more than gags to shut you up and shape you into their good little soldier.

J had been right: The witches would kill me, one way or another.

Because I'd stolen their angel.

Every bitch had to drink. And I couldn't forget the stone wolves, with their fangs bared in pain, trapped in the corners of my new bedroom.

Gargoyles.

How many toys had Rebel dragged home as guests to that room before me?

And how many had ever been allowed to leave?

The flickering light from the beeswax candles caught the snout of the stone wolf in the corner of my bedroom; shadows danced across its sneer.

Hell, the wolves were mocking me. I didn't blame them. I was a wallad for sitting my arse on the soft fur of its slain brother and forgetting *my* lesson.

Since I'd been old enough to toddle, I'd been taught the harsh lesson to look out for number one alone. Why? Because no one else would.

And certainly not some bloke.

Rebel held out the goblet to me again, 'Will you have a drink?' I turned away, pressing my chin to my raised knees as I hunched on the bed. He sighed. 'I made it myself.'

'Flashing wings and threats were all for show then? You don't trust your family either?'

Rebel slammed down the goblet onto the oak chest of drawers. When water spilt down the rim, pooling onto the wood, he smeared at it frantically with the sleeve of his leathers.

His fear of punishment itched at my mind.

I shuffled off the bed, swiping my arm to absorb the spill with my jacket.

He smiled shyly. 'I broke one of the rules. Da would call it a *loss of control*. Or sometimes just a *tantrum*.'

'How about this rule?' I shoved Rebel back against the drawers. 'You shouldn't have rules.'

He didn't try to escape but his expression was troubled. 'That's still a rule. And you're wrong.'

'And you're all healed up. So, does that mean angel kisses work? Or want to tell me about the miracle juice, Zach?'

'Don't be after calling me that.' He pushed me back, but his arms strained with the effort. So, not *all healed up* after all. 'It's not my name. Not now.'

'I hear you. But what's with the chores when you should be resting? And how do anarchists rock *grounded*?'

Rebel pulled a face. 'I took the risk for *you*.' My cheeks pinked. 'And I'm here to protect *you*.' Suddenly he grinned, grabbing my hand and pressing it to his back. I jumped at the feel of his left wing lifting and then settling. 'We angels heal fast.'

We angels? No one had said it out loud before. Somehow it made it too real.

He must've read the doubt on my face because he rocked on his heels. 'Before, you just hadn't grown into your powers yet. I know you haven't wings and...you're not the same as...anyone. But it'll be brilliant. You have no idea. The problem is both sides—'

'Allow it.'

A migraine throbbed behind my left eye; flashes of purple stars haloed Rebel.

The world faded, unreal and distant. Suddenly everything shrank Alice in Wonderland small.

If I hurled, I'd hit Rebel's red leather trousers.

Yeah, launder that, Evie.

'You look awful shattered,' he leaned closer.

'What I am, is pissed off,' I snarled. 'I've discovered I'm a supernatural creature dragged up by humans. And now I'm a prisoner of spell lobbers who've threatened to turn me to stone. What I want, is for you to set me free.'

Rebel gently brushed the hair back from my forehead, before feathering a kiss there again. 'I'm sorry.'

'I'm not.'

Crack — I nutted Rebel. His nose broke with a splatter of scarlet.

In a street fight you have a split second of surprise, so you fight vicious. Even if inside you're bawling.

So, I kneed him in the bollocks.

When he doubled up with a *squeal*, I shoved him to the floorboards, stamping on his hands with the heel of my boots.

Snap — snap —snap.

His fingers crunched like winter twigs.

My throat burned with vomit, but I booted the

left-hand side of Rebel's back before he could struggle up again, pummeling his bad wing.

He howled.

Then I legged it, out into the wide oak galley that overhung the hallway with its gilt framed portraits of generations of dark witches in ruffs and starched collars. As I hammered down the twisty staircase, my boots *clop clopping* an alarm to the Deadmans, the adrenaline rush had me soaring.

Utopia's Bitch was back in control. Nobody's toy. This was the tip of the shank sinking into flesh.

The moment of god-like power.

If I was part angel — and the fever, tingles, and rages were my growing pains — then I'd unleash my powers.

I wouldn't be tamed by witches.

When Evie blocked the front door, I was too high to hear her words, or even hesitate.

I elbowed her aside and reached for the doorknob...

Then I screamed.

Blinding electric crimson and gold sparks. Guy Fawkes Night in my head, and I was the Guy, writhing in agony on the bonfire.

I juddered, falling back, as the current coursed through me in punishing waves. The scent of my own singed hair curled up my nostrils.

Rebel caught me.

'I warned you,' Evie's sulky smirk, 'Rebel's grounded. The spell works to keep *all* angels out. And in.'

An invisible electric fence to trap us like animals...?

Or criminals.

Rebel had called himself *bad*. But why were these witches his gaolers? And what could a pretty boy like Rebel have done to need a witches' prison?

No way was I doing time because some punk had fallen onto my lap.

I twisted to escape the cool band of Rebel's arms. Instead he turned me, and I found myself staring into his sad gaze.

Anger, disappointment, hate...they were old friends. I could've coped with them. But not the wounded hurt in Rebel's gaze.

Slap — I wiped off that *look*.

I raised my hand again, but this time he snatched my wrist to stop the blow.

Now there was a glare I recognised: cold, serious, and determined.

'I'm telling Uncle Richard,' Evie pouted, 'that your precious here tried to escape—'

Rebel curled his arm tighter around me, 'I'll deal with her.'

I'd busted the bastard's nose, fingers, and balls...

Deal with? I'd heard that before. It always meant *screwed*.

'Angel mine, what will you do for me if I keep yet more of your secrets?' Evie flitted around Rebel like a scarlet butterfly, kissing his shoulders and the tip of his broken nose. As she lisped *secrets*, she licked at a dribble of Rebel's blood, and I struggled not to rip out her tongue for tasting what was mine.

Maybe Rebel's blood was addictive?

He dropped his gaze. 'Anything that pleases you, Evie. I'm yours.'

The world lurched, as I was tipped over Rebel's good shoulder in a fireman's lift.

My migraine shrieked to an inferno. I snatched at my glasses to stop them from falling as I dangled upside down. Each step up the staircase jolted me; I hung, staring at Rebel's tight arse.

He didn't say a word as he carried me into my

wolf stone bedroom. Nor as he dumped me amidst the rose pillows. Instead, he studiously undid my handcuffs, before dragging my hands above my head, rechaining me.

I figured protesting was taking the piss, especially as my slap had shadowed to a bruise along his cheekbone.

I fidgeted.

Guilt? It was for losers who looked back, rather than living in each danger-tainted moment. And if you did that, you missed the acid spraying at your face.

Yet why did an ice-cold ball chill my gut when Rebel drew the wolf fur throw one-handed over me because his right hand was swollen with shattered fingers?

There wasn't room for guilt; fear melted it.

I was chained, alone, with a killer angel.

When Rebel lay next to me on the bed, tucking the throw over himself with gentle strokes of the soft strands, as if the wolf was still alive, his studs nipping into my side like pinprick reminders of my stupidity, I shrank away.

Not this, hell, please, not this...

But this was what happened if you disrespected anyone on the Estate. Pain and sex. Despite everything, we were still enemies.

Yet all I heard in the dark was Rebel's quiet distress, 'We had a deal. I help with your sister, and you don't try to escape. I'm a muppet for trusting you.'

It shanked — his simple, honest words — sharper than any rant.

How had I become the untrustworthy one in this world of child-like angel crims and skank witch gaolers?

When Rebel didn't touch me but only turned

over, gasping with pain when his reinjured wing jostled, that ball of ice in my gut grew.

After everything, he was guarding me.

Rebel wasn't the man I'd expected.

Yet here was the screwed truth: I wasn't the woman I'd reckoned either.

I'd become the worst monster in this witches' house because I'd hurt an angel.

J had warned I'd die in the House of Rose, Wolf, and Fox. Now I feared that by trapping us together, the witches had condemned us all to die.

And I'd be the killer.

6

The Death by Chocolate mix dripped from the spoon, only for Rebel to catch it with his long tongue. His moan should've been rated Suitable for Adults, as his eyelids fluttered like he was taking a hit.

Evie trilled with laughter. She dabbed a rich splodge on his (perfect once again) nose, before licking it off.

A punk angel and dark witch baking and flirting in the kitchen?

If Rebel hadn't beamed with such relaxed happiness, like the simplicity of slipping the baking tin into the yellow Bertrazzoni Range fed a need — or calmed a demon — I'd have figured him under a spell.

Lucky bastard.

Except this twisted, homely morning after the storm, with me handcuffed on a charcoal swivel stool at the central island, Rebel doing his baker of the year impression, and Evie prancing around like it was Christmas day already and Rebel was her pressie, only reminded me of one thing: Jade was still missing.

My family was broken.

I clutched at my throat, stroking my sister's crystal necklace.

I promise you, Jade, I'll find you. And when I do, I'll hunt down any bastard who made you suffer.

I saw myself atop a mountain of feathers, above a sea of bones and for the first time, I didn't fear the vision I'd been hiding since I'd turned twenty-one, I opened my arms to it.

I embraced the new creature inside me, or maybe it was the true *me*, if only I hadn't been raised human. Maybe I'd fought, and shanked, and kicked against the world because I didn't belong. And if in turn I'd been rejected, abandoned, and shunned because the human world sensed it too.

But now I could open my mind and let out the darkness.

Revenge was purifying. Righteous. It would be my christening.

Evie chucked a wicker angel effigy at my head, and it bounced to the oak floor. 'Trance-girl, at least help me weave these. They're for your protection.'

I shook myself. 'You see *slave* tattooed on me, bitch?'

Evie rested her hand on her hip. Sunlight pierced the high arch window, flaming the edges of her hair to bronze. 'Behind those glasses, I do believe you're blind.' I shifted uncomfortably. 'I've lived in a shadow of grief all my life, but you, my lovely, *are* the shadow.'

Then she snatched Rebel's hand and twirled around, spilling the flour in a ghost cascade.

The kitchen was cocooned in the warm scent of baking. A deceptive safety that I ached to sink into.

Until I caught sight of the panel behind the Bertrazzoni.

A painting of a red rose entrapped a howling black wolf and snarling golden fox.

I bet those poor bastards had been deceived by the addictive offer of *family* by these spell casters too.

Rebel smiled, grasping my hands in his flour mitts to pull me up, but stopped when I sneered, 'Anyone would reckon your daddy had given you to Evie.'

Rebel blinked. 'He did.'

Why did that not surprise me?

Evie yanked Rebel towards her, pushing him into the ceramic mixing bowls with a *clink*. Swiping her forefinger through the chocolate, she fed the mix to Rebel, who sucked on each offering, as she teased him, *in and out*.

Disgusted (and I didn't know whether with them or myself), I turned away.

Evie's iPhone: sleek, scarlet, and *slipped out of her pocket* to the oak floor in the dance.

I struggled to keep my breathing even, whilst I peeked at the finger fellating couple.

Nope, still at it.

I edged the iPhone forwards with my foot and then ducked down to snatch it, hiding it in my jean's pocket. I could work wonders with a mobile. But I had to be alone.

I peered over at Rebel. 'Get a room, yeah?'

Evie wrapped her arm around his neck. 'What a perfectly splendid idea.'

I didn't miss Rebel's wince, his raised eyebrow at me, or that now familiar flash of hurt in his kohl-smudged eyes.

Scarlet, silk, and more gadgets than a teenage boy: Evie's bedroom, overflowing with glitter, selfies stuck to heart mirrors, and trophies.

A Queen Bee's bedroom.

I sank down into the embrace of a fluffy beanbag, as Evie thrust Rebel, with a lick of her lips, onto the satin sheets of her bed.

Naked.

The wallads were both naked, of course.

Hell, Rebel was beautiful.

I didn't mean to watch, but Evie had insisted they were *babysitting*, so here I was. The most irregular baby meets the most irregular babysitters.

Rebels wings were outstretched, hanging over the lip of the bed. They pulsed, as Evie straddled his lower back, gently running her fingers up and down from shoulder blade to tip, until he was arching off the bed and...

'Turning around now.' I bottom shuffled on the beanbag, facing away from the...couple.

My brain — heart — rebelled at the thought. At Evie's hands on Rebel's wings. At the sound of Rebel's purr and Evie's groans.

A hot possessiveness snaked around me in tight coils. It craved to whip Evie bloody.

Evie's laughter chased me. 'Suit yourself, prude.'

I bristled but then slumped.

Wet snogging *smacks*, flesh *slapping* on flesh, and grunting *squeals*. Rose oil hung thick and cloying.

I slipped the iPhone out of my pocket; the couple had forgotten all about their babysitting duties.

When I pressed on the iPhone, it sprang to life without a password locking it down; so much for protection.

Then again, who'd dare steal from a witch?

Looks like the Bitch of Utopia.

I swiped to send a message to Gizem because the girl had always had my back. All through our time together at Jerusalem Children's Home, and then afterwards when she'd studied hard, swinging the swanky job at Spirit and Fire Gaming Company and vouching for me.

But then I hesitated.

This wasn't school bullies beating me up because I didn't have designer trainers.

This was angels and witches.

And I was one of them.

Could I drag Gizem and her sis into this world?

A *slap* and *bad angels are punished* hissed from the bed behind me, jolted me to action.

I tapped Safari, searching for Toben's murder.

It was still a shock to see a photo from my college yearbook of my pallid face without glasses — one violet and one black eye staring out like the psycho villain in a Bond movie — up as the suspect.

'Do not approach,' screamed the text underneath.

The way I looked? *I* wouldn't have approached me.

Yet as I scanned the report, flicking from page to page, face after face of disappeared teenagers the same as Jade, stared back at me.

Boys and girls. All young, beautiful, and from Hackney.

I hugged the iPhone, as if I could hug those kids.

Why hadn't there been more press coverage of their disappearances before or was it only getting the media circus now because of the murder? After all, when a kid goes missing in middle class suburbia, it's headline news. But when a bunch of kids disappear from an estate in Hackney, it's shunted to the back pages.

Before, I'd have guessed a grooming ring. But now I knew the supernatural existed...?

I read through the info more slowly. Nothing but names and dates of birth. Yet for a hacker, that's a gift.

I lost myself in the Internet, crosschecking sites to tease out the truth of those missing kids.

And then I found it. The link.

My stomach lurched.

Jerusalem Children's Home.

Our children's home.

The disappeared kids were the cared for: orphans and the vulnerable. And they were being targeted.

Just like Jade.

'Fascinating, your precious new toy is a thief.'

Crack — I startled, dropping the iPhone to the floorboards. The screen smashed.

Evie snatched me by the arm, hauling me up. She and Rebel both wore matching red silk dressing gowns, with gold threaded initials *RWF* over the pockets like they were newly-weds.

Rebel's gaze was cool. 'She'll only be after avoiding our shenanigans.'

'You shan't blarney your way out of it. Not this time.' Evie gripped my elbow, dragging me out into the galley, before forcing me in front of a high oak door. 'We shall take a trip to Uncle Richard, and *you* shall confess her wicked behaviour.'

I craned to see Rebel, but he trailed behind, his hands stuck deep in his dressing gown pockets.

Bang — bang — bang.

Evie's sharp rap on the oak door echoed to the

timbered roof.

'Come in.'

Had I travelled back in time to a Victorian boarding school?

Evie smirked, before twisting the door knob. She gave a simpering wave as she pushed both Rebel and me inside. She didn't dare enter herself; she disappeared back into the gloom of the galley.

Bitch.

Da examined us from behind an oak desk that was carved with a wolf head at one end and a fox head at the other; its feet were paws. Then he carefully closed the leather-bound book he'd been reading, before making a mocking gesture for us to stand in front of the desk.

There was a spot marked by a luxuriously soft fox tip sheepskin rug

I'd never shrivelled inside with nerves like this before. I rubbed my boot backwards and forwards through the mottled red of the sheepskin.

Behind Da, an arched window looked out on a golden garden, which had been stripped bare by winter. I glimpsed a fountain and a maze, as well as the ragged line of woodland. It was easier to study the garden than Da's stern face.

Da leaned back in his chocolate leather chair, steepling his fingers. 'Do you wish to expand on the reasons for your unscheduled visit to my study?'

Rebel's bare toes squirmed into the rug. 'It's nothing, so it is.'

'Do I allow you to lie to me?' Sharp as a fox's bared fangs.

Just for a moment, I reckoned Rebel wouldn't grass. Then his toes curled deeper into the fleece. 'Violet stole Evie's phone.'

And my trust burst to flames.

Karma's a bitch.

When Da tapped on the head of a thick curved cane, which lay like a warning across the desk, Rebel flinched. 'Precision, if you please. To play games, or contact someone who risks us all?' Rebel fidgeted with the ties of his dressing gown. 'I asked you a question, boy.'

'I'm not invisible, beardface.' I took a step forward. 'If you want to know what I did with the mobile? Ask.'

A ghost of a smile, as Da slid his hand along the smooth cane. 'Very well then. Why did you purloin the phone?'

'To search for my sister. I didn't call anyone.' Rebel's gaze flickered to mine, his expression softening. 'I just want to find her.'

'And what did you discover?'

'Nothing.' I didn't trust Da. Any of the witches. I wasn't finding Jade, only for her to be taken prisoner too.

Da arched a manicured brow. 'You have permission, Zach, to utilize your Angelic Power to access this young lady's memories.'

I backed up against the book-lined wall, banging my head on a low beam. I held my hands up to ward off the violation of my mind.

But I'd forgotten how fast Rebel could move. He was on me, cradling me against his silk side, as he swept his fingers across the back of my neck.

Then he was in me: seeking, touching, and prying.

Yet this time was different. Rebel didn't want to be there, as much as I didn't want him.

When he pulled back, he studied me, before saying, 'She's no fibbing.'

Furious at his invasion, I shoved him.

Yet...he'd lied for me.

I'd stolen a phone, landed him in trouble, and

he'd covered.

Why the hell had Rebel kept my secret?

'I see. Well then, escort madam to her room. And Zach?' Rebel faltered in the doorway at the *swish* of the cane. 'Do be sure to present yourself back here before bed for a lesson in the correct manner of babysitting.'

'I will, Da.' Rebel's shoulders sagged as he led me to my bedroom.

When Rebel pulled shut the door, trapping us in the wolf dark, apart from a spear of light, I eyed him warily. Then I took a careful breath. 'Sorry about the—'

'We have to do something. Those poor lads and lasses.' When Rebel clasped my arms, his dressing gown fell open and I got an eyeful. 'I can help.'

'Cheers Intensity-1000. The kids, Jade included, disappeared from my estate. You say you want to help? The question is, how?'

Rebel's gaze burned feverishly. His fingers curled into my skin hard enough to bruise. 'I'm not the best at...anything. Words least of all. I've ballsed things up, princess. But if you have something of your sister's, then I can search for her.' He tapped his head. 'Here. It's brutal dangerous but—'

I broke away from his hold. 'Then why haven't you done it already?'

'Because it's forbidden.' We both jumped at the sharp rebuke, like naughty teenagers, swinging to the now opened doorway, where Da loomed statuesque.

I expected Rebel to slink away with his tail between his legs, but instead his shoulders straightened. 'I'm not a babby to be watched over. I need to do this.'

You could've carved your name in the silence.

Then Da smoothed down his waistcoat, flicking

off imaginary fluff. 'If you would be so kind as to step into my study, I believe we need to have a discussion.'

'I'm not a cub to be belted every time I have my own thought. The lass' sister is missing, please, let me—'

'It's not up for debate.'

Rebel stamped to Da, tipping up his chin defiantly to look him in the eye. 'I'm no sap, hiding behind my family.'

Da grabbed Rebel by the scruff of the neck, digging in his thumb.

When Rebel yowled, crumpling to his knees, I collapsed onto the bed, clasping the wolf throw and caressing it as I'd seen Rebel doing.

Rebel's suffering lapped at me in painful waves.

Da pulled the russet handkerchief out of his suit pocket, wiping his hands fastidiously. 'No, you're an addict searching for your next hit. One I have no intention of allowing you.' He twisted Rebel, his fingers wrapped tightly in his hair, holding him on his knees. 'You see here, little girl, a Human Addict. The weakest of angels. Our House is sworn to find and protect such Addicts, and have for generations. I was only a teenager myself when I first guided and trained Zach. I hoped to save the bad boy. I love him, we all do.' His hold gentled. 'Yet, after all, he'd betray me because once an addict, always an addict.' The pink in Rebel's cheeks spread down his neck as he swallowed; his spiked collar bobbed around the repressed sobs.

'But if he can find my sis—'

'You have no comprehension of what you're asking,' Da bit out. 'Don't you care who you hurt? If my boy were to reach through the minds of that many humans searching only for one...it would be overwhelming. Like a hit, after being clean.'

If feeding Rebel's addiction saved my sister, then Da was right: I didn't care if Rebel overdosed.

Or at least, I told myself that lie, silencing the protesting howls inside

Da read my expression, encircling Rebel's throat with his large hand. 'This is a direct order, Zach, do not use your Angelic Power to search for the missing children. If you disobey me...' Rebel winced. '...the consequences — to you both — will be severe.'

What would happen when we defied this sadist of a witch who held an angel by the throat?

Because despite the risk, we had to try.

Actions had consequences. And I was certain we'd discover the brutal cost of disobedience.

Right now, however, I had a sister to save, even if it meant unleashing an Addict.

7

Shocked out of the blackness of sleep, I booted at the intruder before swinging out of bed.

'Sweet Jesus, woman, would you take it easy?' Rebel popped up at the side of the four-poster, shuffling closer on his knees as he rubbed his bruised forehead.

I shivered in the cold draught seeping through the open door. A weak glow bled from the galley. Crossing my arms, I slouched against the bedpost.

I peered through the gloom at him. 'You're braving Da's *severe consequences*?'

Rebel pulled at his scarlet pyjama trousers as they slipped, before resting his elbows on the wolf throw. He wasn't wearing a top, and his wings beat slowly. 'I'm an Addict, it's true, but I'll help you because I saw your memories and...I'm not always a ball-bag.'

If it hadn't been for Rebel's melancholic thoughtfulness, I'd have spluttered with laughter. Instead, I patted his shoulder. 'Yeah, not always.'

This was it: I was freeing...something. Rebel had blazed to glory when he'd broken Toben's neck and saved me. Now I knew he was a Human Addict too. Piece by piece, he was fitting together.

Except, I didn't know if it was as the golden hero, or the Big Bad crawling from the pit.

And by using Rebel, I was hurting him.

My hand shook, as I unclasped Jade's crystal necklace, placing it into Rebel's palm — the snake tempting Eve — before pressing his fingers around it.

He smiled at me, relaxed and unguarded, innocent beneath his thick lashes, before he lay back on the oak floorboards.

I hovered over him, as his breathing slowed and he closed his eyes. I scrutinized the movements behind his eyelids and the twitching of his legs.

Could he see my sis? Had he found her?

Then he arched, thumping his back against the hard wood. His legs kicked.

I remembered Da's hand around Rebel's neck, forcing his collar to dig into his chaffed skin. *If you disobey me...*

I glanced at the door.

The witches would come swooping in, if they heard a racket.

Bang.

Rebel's head raised and then cracked down again.

Bang.

I hissed, cushioning Rebel's head with my hands, but now his feet drummed a jerky beat, and his arms spasmed.

His eyes rolled open and then back. His mouth gaped.

Hell, hell, hell...

I prised the necklace out of his claw fist, hanging it around my neck. 'Come back to the real world.'

I slapped him, before someone grabbed my shoulders.

'Stupid child,' Ma threw me to the side against the wood panelling.

I clutched my ribs, whilst three figures in silk dressing gowns crouched around the flailing angel, whispering and pressing their hands to his neck.

Da rose like a primitive god, the white-tipped brush of a fox swinging around his neck and a shank gripped in his hand.

I quailed, shrinking against the hard oak.

When Da stretched Rebel's bad wing, like a pheasant's ready for plucking, and set the tip of the blade to the base, I hurled myself on his back.

Da tutted, but still plunged in the shank.

Rebel shrieked awake.

I tumbled from Da's back to pet the feathers, trying to draw out the pain. Wherever Da had jolted Rebel from by force, he was bleeding back by degrees, staring wildly between us. His wings thrummed, as soft as I'd imagined under my fingertips.

Da pulled out the blade sharply, but Rebel didn't make a sound. At last, his gaze settled on mine, and then as one we looked up at his family, who were standing around us now in a silent circle.

'What happens when you intentionally disobey?' Da demanded.

To my surprise, Rebel's hand crept into mine, like a kid turning to the monster in the wardrobe for protection when he's threatened by the one living under the bed.

'It was *her*,' Evie lunged at me, but Ma caught her shoulders. Evie stamped her foot like a curly-haired toddler. 'She'll destroy...devour...him. Can't you see? Please don't punish my angel. After what's been done to him...'

'He defied me. He knew what discipline would follow. She may share the consequences since she's the temptress.'

Da yanked us both up, with a hand at the back of our necks.

Rebel still clutched my hand; his palm was sweating.

I struggled, spitting like a cat.

When we were hauled into the study, I couldn't help the anxious glance at the cane. The same panic as the last time I'd been brought to this room curdled in my stomach.

Ma unlocked a small door that was engraved with a rose, wolf, and fox. It matched the picture above the range. The door was hidden amongst the books and opened into a square, black space.

A box inlaid with gold. Not big enough for a man — or angel — to do more than kneel...

'Wings open, Zach.' Da rapped the door. Shuddering, Rebel obeyed. 'On your knees.'

Rebel dropped down with a beautiful grace, although there was a terrible bleakness in his eyes. He edged into the ornate gold box in the wall. It forced him to bow his head and curl around his wings. By the time he was contorted into the space, his muscles must already have been cramping.

I booted Da's shin; Da's mouth thinned.

Yet I couldn't allow Rebel to suffer alone, when I was the devil who'd whispered rebellion in his ear.

I didn't need Evie's smug tap on my shoulder to fall to my knees and shuffle in facing Rebel.

Without wings, I fitted.

I nestled against Rebel's chest, in the cradle of his wings, cocooned in his feathers and I was flooded by a sense of *coming home.*

Slam — the door was shut, and we were locked in the dark.

Rebel grabbed both my hands. His wings trembled. Fast, panted breaths filled the black. His chest rose and fell like a terrified horse's.

Now I knew why the sadists punished Rebel in this way. It was the same lesson I'd learned at J's knee: Find a bloke's weakness and shank sharp.

I stroked my thumbs in gentle circles over the backs of his knuckles. 'You're having a panic attack.' The same words I'd repeated to Jade, every time she'd cowered in corners. 'You're safe. Just breath.' I squeezed his hand in time with his slowing breaths, until at last he slumped, resting his forehead against mine. I shifted on my aching knees. 'So, you really are one of these Addicts, huh?'

In the long silence, I reckoned Rebel wouldn't answer. Then he replied, 'Ages ago, I looked beyond Angel World to the human one. And when I did, I was screwed...the call and thrill of it was too much. The gentle beauty of human family, love, music, food, drink, dancing, duds...and freedom.' He laughed. 'See? Bad. Look, but not touch. Ever. And I was after touching. So, Human Addict. The House of Rose, Wolf, and Fox saved me.'

I snorted. 'Transformed you into a torture doll.'

'Discipline, not torture. To remind me. Outside here, I'm hunted because I'm an Addict.'

'You're locked in a box. What's worse than this?'

'Forty years in one.' I bit my tongue. Just sometimes I wished I could hold back the bitch. 'I was captured,' he murmured, sad and soft. 'A birdcage prison in the dark.'

The bloke's voice was haunted; I didn't blame him.

Then realisation hit me. 'You couldn't open your left wing?'

'The gits strapped it down. They only allowed it to open a little, never to fly. You do that? It's the worst pain an angel can endure. They're after making sure you never forget how far you've fallen because you're an Addict.' His tone was tear-tinged. 'I hoped I'd have the strength to break it this time. But *once an addict, always an addict.*' I bumped my forehead hard against Rebel's. 'By all the saints...'

'Better an Addict than some tight-arsed angelic bastard. I'm sorry...I shouldn't have encouraged you to...overdose. But you helped me when you knew the risk and that makes you fam.'

His breath caught, before he whispered, 'I couldn't find your sister because she's no longer on earth.'

I didn't know I'd whimpered, until Rebel's lips were pressed to mine in apology. 'And she's not dead, you dope. She's in Angel World or...'

'You leave me hanging, I'll twist your balls.'

'She's no longer fully human. Just like the other lads and lasses, I reckon.'

It was my turn to gasp in the blackness of that box.

Slam — the sugar copper swallowed me, until I was bubbled in its — *slam* — tingling warmth — *slam* — soft feathers and — *slam* — sweetness.

Despite everything, the waves of sugar stroked me down from my panic.

Taken by the angels or not human? I didn't know which to hope for after the birdcage story.

'It doesn't matter. Fam is fam.'

'Then I made a mistake,' Rebel's tone hardened.

Here again was the warrior with the flaming wings and righteousness. 'Now we know who could've taken your sister, we can't hide like babbies. I'm more than an Addict; I'm a hunter. And you, princess? You don't know it yet, but you can fly higher than I can even dream.'

As I nested in Rebel's wings, I could pretend I'd found fam.

But that was the lie.

Hunted or hunter, Rebel's addiction would free me from the witches' house.

Find the weakness and shank it sharp.

You can be a prisoner in a cell or in your mind. A prisoner to society, your conscience, or whispered self-doubts. In a prison of family or love.

Yet you can choose whether you fly, even in chains, or remain forever shackled in the dark.

Evie led Rebel and me stumbling towards the gloom of the Great Hall; heavy gold velvet curtains suffocated the light. My legs cramped after being trapped all night in the box. Rebel wrapped his wings around me like a feather coat; they twitched with tiny spasms of pain.

Yet we'd survived, together. And now we had a plan.

When Evie spun with a mocking bow to usher us into the hall, which was hung with black wolf skins and russet, white-tipped fox brushes, I faltered.

A vast contoured map of London — Westminster, Buckingham Palace (her Maj's yard), and even my Hackney — pulsated in rose quartz across the entire hall like a heartbeat.

A crystal world, the human London, in the hands of the witches.

The Deadmans crouched over the map, whispering to the air, like they were commanding invisible legions.

I tripped, dragging Rebel down too in a tangle of *sweet Jesuses*.

Then Rebel hauled me up, the righteous fire sparking in his eyes again. He raised his boot and...*crunch*.

Big Ben stomped by an angel.

Take that, Godzilla.

The map glowed violently, as if convulsing from a bleeding wound.

Da and Ma merely straightened. Ma gave a casual shrug.

'Tantrum over?' Da unclasped the fox brush from around his neck.

'Take them off her,' Rebel raised my hands, jangling the handcuffs.

I wouldn't be a prisoner anymore. That's what we'd agreed in the long night. And Rebel would teach me what it meant to be an angel, so I could save my sister.

'I don't think so.' Da waved his hand dismissively.

Rebel raised his foot to stomp on Parliament, but I gripped his elbow. 'Before you get medieval on the politicians, why don't you just snap these cuffs with your super strength?'

Evie sniggered as she knelt by the map, stroking the crystal Big Ben; the quartz fused back into shape. 'They're angel proof, of course, else how could we chain *him*? Where do you imagine we magicked the bondage-wear from, special one?'

Rebel avoided my eye.

I flushed. I should've guessed I wasn't the first angel to be chained by these witches.

'I'm surprised last night taught you nothing,

Zach,' Da held the fox brush above the map, sweeping an outline through the air.

I expected Rebel to flinch, but instead he squared his shoulders. 'You're wrong, Da. When you locked us up, it taught me I'm more than an Addict. To face the worst. That this isn't about *me* anymore. It's about—'

'Princess, princess, princess,' Evie exploded, shoving Rebel back, but he caught her hands.

'And that's why you need to uncuff her,' Rebel insisted gently, winding Evie's curl around his finger, 'because we need to train. She has the right to be taught her powers.'

When Evie glanced between us, I was surprised by the wetness trickling down her cheeks. She nodded, but before she could reach my cuffs, she was stopped by Da.

'Train?' Da's lip curled, before he raised the brush even higher, stroking it from base to tip, *one — two — three —* times. Rebel paled. Da bit his lip savagely, trailing the white fur through the crimson, as if the fox had only just been torn bloody. 'Vulpes Vulpes.' The crystals hummed, a dangerous, furious whine. Da barked again, 'Vulpes Vulpes.'

The walls shook; the fox brushes hanging as trophies thumped a beat.

Rebel clasped my hand, dragging me back towards the door, without once looking away from his scarlet mouthed Da.

'I knew I hated spell lobbers,' I muttered, clinging to Rebel.

Then in the centre of the crystal London, a tail appeared.

A fox's brush. Bushy and black-fringed.

Then heavy flanks and a huge rusty-red body, larger than any regular fox. But then regular foxes didn't materialise body part by body part like a screwed-up version of the Cheshire Cat. Black paws, legs, and finally a narrow head with pointed black ears and...

Dangerous but intelligent amber eyes, studying me.

I froze. The fox's unblinking scrutiny called to the dark under my skin.

'Send them back,' Rebel pleaded. 'We don't need Spark and Blaze.'

That's when the second fox materialised at the large fox's shoulder.

Except, this fox appeared all in a rush, like it was late. Bright red, with a brilliant white throat, chest and white-tipped tail, it was as pretty as its brother. It ducked its head and whined, nuzzling the first fox.

Then it too turned its green gaze towards me.

'You wished to train,' Da nodded at the foxes. Their tails lifted. 'Now train.'

When the foxes stalked towards us, we backed away.

The witches had set new demons on us. Creatures they were using to hurt — *train* — us.

Just like I'd used and hurt Rebel.

The foxes prowled closer, baring their sharp thin teeth.

8

When Rebel reached for my hand, my first instinct was to pull back.

The foxes watched us with their sharp eyes as they prowled either side of the hissing map towards us.

The walls in the shadowy Great Hall trembled; the curtains swayed in a wild dance. I grabbed Rebel's fingers between mine, unnerved. The handcuffs clinked, cold against my skin.

What the hell did it matter if I'd used Rebel or he was an Addict? Fam was fam, these demons were free, and our arses were being hunted.

'Bolt!' Rebel hauled me after him through the hallway.

There was the *skitter* of claws on the oak floors behind us. A primal fear spiked my adrenaline.

Rebel booted open the rough side-door, and we scrambled through to the stone terrace.

Rusty-red on one side, bright red on the other.

The foxes circled hungrily.

We dodged through the stone pieces of the giant red and green chess set, as the foxes slunk close to the ground on either side, into the thickets of thorny rose bushes, stripped bare in winter, before weaving in and out between the stems.

I pricked myself on a thorn, and watched the blood bead; well, I'd wanted to be Sleeping Beauty.

I frowned. 'So, which of these bastards is Spark?'

'The one with green eyes and white tail,' Rebel spun round, his wings beating, as Spark danced towards him, before retreating. The little wallad was playing us. 'The big fellah with amber eyes and black paws? That's Blaze. They're brothers. *Christ...*'

Blaze had jumped from the bushes and sunk his canines into Rebel's ankle.

I swirled with fury that the fox had tasted my angel. Taken blood that should only be mine.

Yet Rebel's blood was his own; I'd never enslave him. I wasn't like Bisi.

Was I?

When Spark tried the same trick on me, I booted him in the head. He rolled onto his back and wriggled, whining.

'Lay off,' Rebel panted, trying to prise Blaze off his ankle, 'don't hurt the idiots.'

'You're joking?' I met Blaze's serious stare with a snarl, and he let go of Rebel's leg.

Blaze lashed his tail back and forth and bounded over to his brother. He nudged Spark with a nip that made Spark *yelp*, and together they skulked deeper into the gardens.

Rebel had snapped my boyfriend's neck like it was a game at a funfair but he drew the line at kicking a magic fox?

Rebel took one limping step towards the

mansion.

A furious guttural *chattering* howl. Dark shapes flittered fast across the path.

'They're after hounding us. It's a fox hunt in reverse.' Rebel's mouth became a tight line. 'Sometimes you can't face the worst. You have to hide.' He drew me towards a maze of high privet hedges; foxes were pruned into the topiary like plant gargoyles. I pulled back, but he shook his head. 'No other way, Feathers.'

'Not until you tell me why we're hiding from a pair of juiced foxes.'

'They're Blood Familiars.' Rebel fiddled with the skull on his bondage trousers. 'Da owns them. Please, they've been *ordered* to hurt us.'

Rebel knew because he'd suffered this *training* before.

That was all it took to kick my arse into dashing after him down the gravel paths of the maze. Every twist and turn was as familiar as the routine in the study for Rebel.

I trusted Rebel because otherwise I was lost.

Howls.

As we darted to the centre of the maze, they echoed around us. I remembered the slice of those teeth biting into Rebel's ankle, noticing the blood trail he left behind like breadcrumbs for the foxes.

The *howls* were closer. The familiars' hot panted breath on my boots. Flashes of red.

The centre of the maze arose up ahead like the holy land.

Rebel hobbled towards the fountain, which was a carved marble rose, blossoming open and as if being born from it, a fox and a wolf. The fountain wasn't running because it'd been frozen to ice.

I snorted. This was the big prize that would save us?

Rebel clambered over the lip of the fountain, before skidding across the thick ice to the statue of the fox.

I stared at him blankly. 'For real?'

He slipped, bumping to his arse. 'They don't cross ice. Muppets can swim though; I found that out the hard way.'

I slapped my hand against my thigh. 'Then step-up and work the bastards.'

Amber and green beamed out of the dark. The two brothers stalked into the centre of the maze.

Towards us.

'Spark and Blaze don't have a choice. They're under my family's power.' Rebel was clutching hard to the fountain; his breath came in dragon puffs. He looked troubled and distant as he murmured, 'And I refuse to hurt slaves.'

'Even if they're about to hurt me?'

The Blood Familiars slunk closer in ever decreasing circles. They held their brushes — one black and one white — proudly aloft, *chattering*. Never once did they look away from me.

'Princess,' Rebel hissed, flapping his wings in agonised indecision, 'please will you stir yourself?'

Blaze rested back on his haunches next to Spark, and I sensed it. The moment he'd signalled to his brother for the attack.

Yet as they leapt through the air towards me, I didn't hesitate. I wrenched off my sunglasses, and then held out my handcuffed hands.

The familiars didn't stop.

Then I was being knocked backwards, the air driven from my lungs. I hit my head on the gravel path.

Rebel's *cries*, shrieking *whines,* and soft heavy creatures trampling me.

I shoved at the handfuls of dense silky fur, until

I could sit up. The two foxes crouched, with their ears pressed to their skulls, *whining* and doing everything but batting their eyelashes at me in submission.

It'd been a risk, taken on nothing but the urging of the shadows under my skin. A certainty the familiars would recognise its power.

Spark nudged his head cautiously into my hand.

'What did you do?' Rebel murmured, 'I've never seen them like this.'

I grinned. 'I tamed them. Now I'm top boy.' I stroked Blaze's back. 'They're mine.'

When I slipped on my sunglasses, I was still high: I welcomed the surge of strength. This was flying, no longer prisoner to the dark but mistress of it.

Until Rebel's cautious hand on my shoulder. 'You're taking slaves?'

I surveyed the fox brothers cowering at my feet. Then ran my hand lightly over their heads, tickling behind Spark's ears. He glanced up at me, through laughing green eyes. 'No, bro, I'm freeing them.'

I marched back towards the house, with the foxes trotting at my heels.

When I burst into the Great Hall, with the Blood Familiars winding around me like my guard dogs, the Deadmans startled. Then they gawped at me, as if I was the one with the magic.

'Training's over,' I held out my handcuffed wrists, 'time to free me.'

Da glanced at Ma, for once uncertain. Then he abandoned the rose quartz crystals he'd been examining and prowled towards me, the grisly brush, stained with his own blood, still at his neck. He scowled at the familiars. 'I see you have mastered my children. Very clever.'

I tilted my head. 'You have daddy issues. And

your kids are going Hackney style.'

Da snatched my hands, roughly pulling them forward, before a snarl from the familiars stilled him.

'Zach, go and wait for me for me in the study.' Da's intent gaze never left mine, as he withdrew a key from his waistcoat pocket, and the handcuffs clattered to the floorboards. 'You seem to have forgotten important lessons.' I saw the struggle, but Rebel still nodded, before disappearing out into the hallway. 'You may dominate my children, but not my angel.'

The Blood Familiars' tails lashed.

'I freed your familiars. And I will free Rebel. Just like I'll get free. And when I do, you'll be the one in the dark.'

Da stepped back, as if I'd bitten him.

Yeah, I was flying.

The short coal-black sword flamed in the bleak underground cellar, like the eclipse of a violet sun.

Rebel trembled as he held the sword, his wings vibrating.

I lounged against the wall, next to a cobwebbed wire rack of pricey bottles of wine, Spark and Blaze smart at my heels. I smirked, when the Deadmans dropped to their knees in worship.

Was it possible to worship a prisoner?

When the witches had opened the iron trapdoor, shoving us down the stone steps into the musty pitch-black cellar, I'd been dreading the shooter to the head or wand action into gargoyle.

Instead?

Da had spun the lock on a fire-proof safe that hung on the wall, before reverentially drawing out a sword.

Rebel had stared at him in confusion. 'My Eclipse? But you said—'

'You've earned your sword back.' Da had lifted out a light leather harness that was threaded with gold and a scabbard, which he'd thrown to Rebel. 'You deserve to wear it again.'

'Thank you,' Rebel had murmured, shucking his leathers and buckling the harness and scabbard between his folded wings. 'Does this mean I'm not grounded?'

Da had glanced at me and then the Blood Familiars, who'd bared a flash of sharp canine. 'It means, boy, someone convinced me to free you. I do not believe you can be trusted. You ran once. Abandoning others is what you do, is it not? But we shall see. Do you prefer prisoner, or hunter?'

Something in me had thrilled at *hunter*. And between hunter or prisoner? I'd train any way Rebel wanted to become even a half-arsed angel without wings, if I'd also be a *huntress*.

A flash of hot thrumming excitement had shot through me.

I'd needed Rebel. And part of me...?

Wanted him.

Da had finally passed Rebel the sword, although he'd hesitated at the last moment, and his hands had met Rebel's. They'd both tugged on the hilt, before at last Da had let go.

'This is *your* choice,' Da had stared at me, swiping his forehead with his russet handkerchief. 'Are we safe now?'

Then Rebel had raised the sword, his thumb caressing the sparkling crescent moon hilt. He'd been lost in it; I'd recognised the surge of power, the same as mine, curling through him. He'd shuddered as he'd whispered, 'Eclipse'.

Then the sword had blazed to life, Rebel's wings

had burst wide, and the witches had prostrated themselves at his feet.

What had I just freed? And could I trust Rebel?

I shrank back against the damp wall, away from the zoned angel; the pretty punk was flying.

When the flame cooled, Rebel swung to me. His pupils were dilated and his skin feverish. 'See, princess, I'm more than an Addict. I'm Zachriel — the Rebel — and this is Eclipse,' he slashed the sword in an overexcited cross through the air. 'I've made a hash of things but I'm free now and—'

'Blitzed. You're broken, so how about you put the sword down?'

'If I were mad, I would! I'm a hunter. I'm on the hunt.'

'You're tripping.' I stepped towards him.

Rebel didn't even hesitate. He raised Eclipse to my throat.

9

Slash, stab, slice... A shank could carve your skin in a thousand ways. I was intimate with every single one but I'd never heard skin *sizzle* on the tip of a blade...smelt it *sear*...until it was my own.

And it was Rebel's sword pressed to my throat.

Bad angel. Rebel had warned me. Why hadn't I wanted to believe?

Shocked, I held my breath, resting my hands on the silky heads of the two foxes who'd leapt up in the shadows of the cellar. The Blood Familiars squirmed but didn't attack.

'Rebel,' I entreated softly.

Rebel's gaze was glazed, but there was a flash of recognition and pain. Then he twirled and drifted up the stone steps.

Lost, confused, and blitzed.

He was going to get himself hurt. Thrown in gaol. Or dead.

I curled to the concrete floor, wrapping my arms around the familiars.

Spark whined, nudging me. His green eyes, which were rimmed with thick black lashes, were thoughtful, as he rested his chin on my shoulder. His brother arched his back, on guard.

'Still believe you can trust him?' Da asked, shoving himself to his feet. He dusted off his suit with efficient flicks. 'Actions have consequences, little girl.'

Evie burst up, like a rose sprung to violent life. Ma grasped her waist, holding her back.

'Interlopers who hurt angels,' Evie spat, her fingers clawed around the petals at her throat, 'must face their own worst terrors. My wicked love has left you alone, who shall save you now?'

Ma smiled, deadly as a panther, loosening her hold on Evie.

I stiffened, pressing back against the wall.

Rebel had held me in the safety of his wings all night. We'd plotted how to both free and control my powers. But now he'd left me here with his family who wanted me dead.

Evie was right: Rebel had abandoned me. Like every other bastard man.

Da frowned, but his shoulders were stooped. 'Go to your room. Now.'

I jumped at his urgency, glimpsing the savage fire in Ma and Evie's eyes, as they prowled towards me.

I bolted.

There was no use pretending. I was still as much a prisoner as when I'd worn handcuffs.

Yet I was the wallad who'd freed Rebel. He wasn't tame at my heel like the foxes. He was wild and free.

And he'd left me because of a sword called Eclipse and the call of the hunt.

When I heard the *creak* on the stairs and hurried whispers in the galley outside my doorway that night, I slipped out from under the wolf throw and crept to my bedroom door.

Rebel's pained groan and stumbled step.

I hesitated with my fingers clutched around the doorknob, shaking with the effort not to throw it open and...

The question was whether I'd boot Rebel in the balls for burning and then abandoning me, or snog him for coming back, before chaining *him* to the bed, so he couldn't leave me again.

I rested my forehead against the cold oak door, before slipping down onto my knees.

I frowned at the shock of Rebel's emotions; his fear and shame spun a web around me, which I ripped down as fast it touched my skin.

Why the hell had Rebel kidnapped me and forced me to...*feel*?

I slipped out into the hallway, shuffling along in my bare feet to peer around the crack of Da and Ma's bedroom, as if I was spying on a boyfriend's parents.

Rebel was stretched bound across the bed. His wrists and ankles were strapped in hard leather cuffs, even if he lay on gold silk sheets. The air was thick with the scent of cinnamon, candles cast cavorting shadows, and the room was a sunburst of sensual velvets and damask.

Rebel had been stripped naked, except for his spiked collar, whilst Da and Ma in their dressing gowns crawled over him like he was a sacrifice.

When Rebel's eyes screwed shut in pain, I clenched my fists.

Slashes.

There were scarlet gashes across Rebel's chest,

as if he'd been repeatedly knifed.

The memory shot through me of a blade at my neck, and then slicing Gizem's cheek.

Who — what — had Rebel been hunting?

I'd been scorched by his sword. Yet someone — or something — had managed to knife him, like a bear's claws raking his guts.

Had the other angels done this? The ones he hid from?

Rebel moaned, as Ma swabbed at the blood tearing from the wounds with balled cotton wool. Then as she kissed him, hard and possessive.

I stiffened.

Da circled one of Rebel's nipples into a peak, before bending his head to the other and lapping. Rebel squirmed in his bonds but couldn't move away.

I realised the Deadmans had stopped Rebel escaping, exactly as I'd imagined doing. But now I saw it...?

I wished Rebel was wild and free again.

Ma lay on one side of Rebel, Da on the other side, predatory and dark.

This wasn't the same as when I'd seen Rebel shagging Evie.

It was a claiming. A possession. Ownership.

I shook to rip them from Rebel. Not only to save him, but to save him for myself. I'd never felt this...jealous...before. But then I hadn't been part angel until six weeks ago either. At least, this new side to myself hadn't awoken.

And I didn't like it.

Ma and Da kissed and licked down Rebel's chest and neck, worshipping him: their shackled god. Shocked, I realised I wished I could climb into those golden sheets with them.

I stumbled back, rushing into my bedroom. It

was too much. These new...feelings.

Slam — I crashed the door behind me, satisfied by the bang.

The Bitch of Utopia didn't do fear but I was trembling from the temptation to sink into the dark.

Instead, I climbed onto the bed — alone — unable to block out the image of Rebel stretched and bound naked, sweat glistening on his neck beneath his collar, before taking a swig of water from my goblet — alone — and burrowing back under the wolf skin — alone.

I hadn't abandoned Rebel, he'd abandoned me.

But why the hell couldn't I believe that?

Suddenly, everything blurred.

I retched.

Clutching my stomach, I blinked, and the world pixeled.

I hugged a rose pillow, as the bedroom merry-go-round spun. The wolves snarled, howling out of the ceiling.

I whimpered.

What was happening?

Then I glimpsed the goblet. It meant something. A terrible truth.

Gargoyles... Face your terrors... Actions have consequences...

I giggled. Then my eyes rolled back, and I collapsed onto the bed.

I stood on the top of a mountain of violet feathers, above a land of bones. I reigned, even though below me was nothing but death.

I was death. The End. Destroyer.

A wind whipped across the desolate valley; sizzling energy coursed across my crackling palms.

No, no, no... Time to wake up.

Calm down, J is with you...because you're inside yourself. Your own mind. That shady bitch poisoned you.

But it's real as...

Oh, it's real, Feathery-cakes. If you don't slay your demons in here, you'll be the one slayed. And I'm talking a fabulous new gargoyle for the witch floozy.

Where have you been?

They're witches. If they discover me, then you'll be in more danger than you're in right now.

Take me back. Away from me. I can't be trapped—

Only you can do that. Only you have ever been in control. And you can't escape yourself forever.

My feet sank into the ticklish wave of feathers, and then I fell.

Soft and suffocating, I tumbled down until...

Crack — my foot snapped delicate wing bones. I tiptoed between charred skulls and femurs.

My legacy.

I'm bad, just like Rebel. I kill and I hurt, and the things I imagine are even worse. Not only since my birthday: always.

So, you need your ass shut away in a tower? We're all demons. Perfection's the lie.

I rose up with a roar, bursting through the feathers and casting them like violet snow across the land. The bones glowed

My land.

I was birth. The Beginning. Saviour.

I burned with power, twining in two whirlwinds furious around me, both ancient and possessive.

102

And I smiled as I became the monster.

My eyes blinked open, fuzzy from the poison. Yet it was still there: the power from the drugged nightmare.

It hissed one taunting word, 'Rebel.'

I swayed, staggering out into the hallway and barging into Da's room. Then I caught my breath.

Rebel was alone. Tied to the golden bed naked as before, his eyes were shut like he was asleep. But the wallad was pretending because his fists clenched at the sound of my footsteps.

I was part angel, but I was also something *more*.

Why was Rebel keeping it secret from me?

If I wanted to claim Rebel too, then he was mine.

Lost still in the sensation of the dream, I struggled to catch at the sense of wrongness tugging at me, but it slipped away.

I sidled closer.

The slashes stood crimson against the pale white of Rebel's skin; they burnt livid, like the flame of his hair.

Fury surged that someone had dared hurt him. *Somebody but me.* I scored my fingers into a gash across his gut.

He gasped, his eyes shooting open. 'I know I'm on that List of Asses to Kick, especially after what I did, but could you not leave off until the morning?'

'You abandoned me,' I purred. And when did I *purr*? 'You allowed the bastard witches to touch what's mine.'

'Downed a few bevvies while I was hunting, Feathers?' He eyed me warily, like he'd seen the Queen drink one too many sherries and muddle up her Christmas speech.

'And what were you hunting? Who gave you these...?' I traced over each slash, as if taking ownership of them.

'I'm a hunter. I wasn't fibbing when I told you gits were after you.'

I froze. He'd been wounded protecting me?

'Who?'

When Rebel didn't reply, biting his lip hard, I climbed onto the bed, straddling him. That's what I'd craved to do earlier, when I'd seen the Deadmans crawling over him. Yet I didn't want to worship him, I wanted *his* worship.

The angel was helpless underneath me.

I ground down, Rebel's cock as trapped as the rest of him, and he groaned.

'Not like this,' he whispered.

I reached my hands around his neck, and he stiffened.

The collar's spikes pricked my palms, as I teased at the skin underneath. Then I began to unbuckle the collar. Someone else's mark of ownership, it incensed me. I'd mark Rebel with bruises, shank him myself, brand my own mark on him until everybody knew...

'Stop it,' Rebel's voice was hard and yet trembled with tears, 'it's not yours to touch.'

I stared down into shocked eyes, the eyelashes matted wet. 'If that's not mine to touch, how about this?'

I dropped my mouth to Rebel's, hard and relentless, as my hand found out his balls, squeezing just as hard.

Far back in my mind, I screamed and booted to be free. To stop my assault. But I wasn't in charge anymore. The growling, dominant bad bitch inside had been freed by Evie's toxin.

Rebel's body thrust and arched, but he was struggling, wrenching his head from side-to-side.

I pinned him, fire coursing through me, tingling with the taste of stolen sugar sweetness and electric wings.

I'd force Rebel to make me fly.

But then Rebel bit.

My mouth flooded with my own blood; I pulled back.

'No, stop, this isn't... Take it easy, what's the rush?' He panted.

I backhanded him, jerking his head by the hair to nibble at the base of his neck.

'I said *no*,' Rebel repeated, 'you're not yourself. Is this to get back at me for...? I'm sorry, so I am. Or maybe...' His expression gentled, even under the bruise — my mark — around his swollen eye. 'You're under a spell. Evie's rose potions are brutal—'

'Not offering marriage, wallad, shagging. Your lucky night in hell,' I grinned.

He bucked. 'Offer again when you love me.'

Shocked, I stared down at him.

The bastard was rejecting me?

I growled, gripping his wings by their delicate tips. I remembered the sensation of standing atop the mountain of feathers, above the land of bones, coursing with power.

Destroyer or saviour.

Crack — my foot snapping the light wing bones... I could bend Rebel's wing back and break...

Rebel whimpered.

I eased the pressure, shoving away from him. 'I can't love my kidnapper.'

Dizzy, the world lurched. I stumbled to my knees and then crawled to the door.

Large bare feet, hairy legs, and powerful

thighs...

I gazed up at the glowering giant of Da, who stood akimbo, like a devil in a kid's play.

I wobbled to my feet, edging out of the bedroom.

When I peered back, Da had stalked to Rebel, who lay motionless. Yet Rebel's eyes were wide and supplicating, as Da ran his hand along Rebel's collar.

It was no longer worship: Da's love was toxic.

Yet Rebel had abducted me. Why should I save him from the witches?

I closed the door behind me, trapping Rebel with his Da. But even through the blurred fog of the poison, I knew Rebel was a prisoner, just the same as me. An angel, ensnared by witches. And we'd need each other to escape.

Because his family had tried to murder me.

I screamed, battering at my own mind to return me to that room and help Rebel. But the poison's hold was too strong.

Tonight, we were both alone.

10

Monster, *freak* and *mutant*...with one black and one violet eye, I'd worn the labels from Jerusalem Children's Home to the schoolyard like Victoria Crosses. No one had seen my secret face beneath.

And we all have one.

Now I knew a true monster had lurked all that time behind the mask of my humanity. For all those years, I'd struggled to be human, when I'd never been one to start with.

Discovering I was part angel should've been an ugly duckling to swan fairy tale.

Except, the one angel I knew was bad.

The kitchen crouched in evening shadows; the open fire dragon smouldered.

Snip, snip, snip.

Ma cut a bundle of herbs on the marble counter,

her silver bob swaying with each sharp movement.

I hunkered on the swivel stool, elbows on the cool side, losing myself in the music on Jade's iPod...in Jade.

EELS' "Your Lucky Day in Hell" caught me in its demented dance, swinging from melancholia to bright choruses in twisted bass jumps.

Then I was spun and with a gasp, reached out to stop myself falling, before Rebel caught me.

Laughing, Rebel plucked the buds from my ears and into his own, as if he wasn't touching...violating...my memory of Jade.

He grinned. 'Maybe it'll be *our* lucky—'

I punched him in the nose.

He bounced backwards, tumbling onto his arse.

Shaking, I stuffed the iPod back into my pocket.

Rebel looked up with a mix of comical surprise and betrayal. He tilted his head, with that blinking innocence I craved to slap out of him.

The two clashing sides inside me, like static, prickled over my skin, until I scratched frantically at the backs of my hands.

I glanced away from Rebel's scrutiny. He had his secrets and I had mine.

He gnawed at his lip. 'If I've been a muppet, princess, just tell me.'

I stared down at him. 'List. Asses. Kick.'

He smirked. 'I reckon you made your point last night.'

I blushed.

This morning when I'd awoken with a thumping headache — and almost reached for the water again before I remembered just why I felt so rough — the details of my...molesting...Rebel were fuzzy.

But I'd remembered throwing myself at Rebel because of the poison. Worse...he'd rejected me. And worse even than that...? I'd abandoned him to

Da's abuse.

I'd hidden up in my bedroom for the rest of the day, until Rebel had coaxed me down with promises of chocolate cake.

Ma pressed the herbs into a velvet pouch, her emerald eyes watchful.

At last, I held out my hand and hauled up Rebel. 'I want to know who shanked you. I'm not going to hide behind you. Hide in this house. I want to...stop running away.' I looked up and our gazes met. 'Do you reckon I'm frightened of some Big Bad?'

'*What* shanked me,' Rebel amended.

'Angel?' I held my breath. I was surprised how much it excited me. The idea there were others like me. Even more thrilling, that'd I'd meet them, even in a fight.

He frowned. 'You're not ready.'

I shoved him back against the yellow Bertrazzoni, and he scrabbled against the range, as I boxed him in. 'Don't get all Jedi mentor on me because I was ready before some punk bitch fell in my lap.'

'Cop on! What you're ready for is about as useful as a lighthouse in a bog.'

Violet rage flushed my cheeks. 'Then tell me what can school an angel?'

He smiled. 'How about I show you?'

Heart pounding, I nodded.

This was it: Rebel's weakness. The moment I slipped in the shank sharp. I knew he was defying Da by taking me out, but this was the only way to push him into freeing us for real.

I hadn't expected the shudder of guilt but I hid it with a smile. I snatched Rebel's hand, dragging him across the kitchen.

Ma blocked the door. 'Do not think, little girl, you can win this game.' Her lip curled, petulant.

'You sneak like a snake, so who else will save my boy?' Rebel glanced between us, his brow furrowed. 'Here,' Ma slipped the pouch of herbs she'd been mixing over his head, tying it on a gold cord, 'if you must play at hunter and with your friend. And never forget your protection.' She snapped two tiny wicker angel effigies from a string by the door and held them out.

Rebel hung his on a chain of his bondage trousers. I didn't reach for the second one.

Ma's fingers shot out, clutching my wrist. 'You don't wish to hide? Stupid brat. Because without the effigies *you're* the hunted. They stop every sort of angel from tracking you. They also bind you to Rebel,' she smiled, suddenly I wondered if she could read minds, 'in case you think to escape.'

I swung to Rebel, but he shrugged. 'You say you can't love me? Well, I can't *trust* you.'

It turns out, it was Rebel shanking *me*.

Naïve?

The punk knew about hurt: taking and inflicting it.

Ma shoved the effigy into the pocket of my jeans, and I squirmed under Rebel's scrutiny.

Yet maybe Rebel was only so good at seeing through my mask because he had so many of his own secrets.

The stars sharp and silent, sparked from the black shroud of the sky.

Rebel's pale neck stretched long and exposed, as he tipped back his head, ambling up the slope of Kingston Hill, lost in the heavens.

'What's up, bro?'

Rebel startled. 'I'm hunting.'

'If you're going to work a lie, you need to stop

the Bambi's had his mummy shot impression.'

'Forty years,' he murmured, 'in a cage. Now at least I can look at the stars.'

When I stared out into the infinite dark, I shuddered. The spiralling loss of control sucked at me.

Richmond Royal Park beneath us was a shadowed blanket of woodland and greens, with peaks of brick and pitched roofs, and a snaking boundary wall.

Around us was a suburb for the wealthy stockbrokers and city bankers. Glimpses of Victorian manors and Georgian mansions peeked out between the plane trees and the oaks.

'Told you I was after hunting,' Rebel muttered, before unexpectedly tearing down the gated driveway of a modern designer house that was a box of pine and glass.

I retched, bent over.

Crimson — one spot, two, now three dropped shining onto the grass.

I touched my mouth; I was spitting blood.

Zachriel, Zachriel, Zachriel...

I slammed my hands over my ears, but the voice still echoed through my brain.

Ma's voice.

The angel effigy dug into my thigh through my jeans. Now I understood about it binding me to Rebel. I smeared my bloody mouth across the back of my hand and marched down the wide driveway after Rebel.

Bang — the red Range Rover that was parked in front of the millionaire's house trembled.

Bang — it rose up and then down, dancing.

Then Rebel, like a streak of fire, was hurled over

111

the roof.

Oomph — Rebel skidded, before landing in a tangled heap at my feet.

Yet he still sprang up, grinning. 'See? Hunting.'

A figure leapt panther-like onto the roof of the car. His coffee suede coat swept the metal as he stalked towards us. He was dressed in a brown suit as if for a bankers' meeting beneath his coat, but the silver snake bite lip piercings and his long black hair that swept to his waist would've made them stare up in Canary Wharf.

That and Mr Snake Bite's eyes were as black as his hair.

I raised my hand to my sunglasses; my own black eye throbbed.

What the hell was he? And why did he have eyes...like mine?

Snake Bite leapt over the back of the Range Rover, landing in a perfect feline crouch. Then he looked up at me and smiled.

Bastard fangs.

I stumbled backwards.

Snake Bite's lips curled in amusement around his canines and he stroked over his smooth ebony cheek.

'Vampire,' I hissed. 'But this is real life, not—'

'*Angels vs Vampires*?' Rebels' lips quirked, as two...dark creatures...united in their taunting of my tiny human world. Then Rebel threw off his leathers, and his wings burst free in flashing arcs.

Yet if this was a vampire, what did it make *me*? Half angel, half vampire? Was that even a *thing*?

Because I didn't have fangs, just as I didn't have wings. I also didn't have a thirst for blood, unless it was Rebel's...

Was there a reason I'd designed my computer game with supernatural creatures?

I shook.

Until the vampire laughed. 'A cripple?' His voice was rich and cultured. I don't know what I'd been expecting. I was still too dazed by the *vampire with black eyes* jumping off a Range Rover to expect much beyond a snarl. 'If you desired to be taken and played with, you should've asked.'

Rebel stiffened, his bent wing shrivelling closer to his body. I ached to stroke it back to its glory. 'Do I look like I'm playing, muppet?'

Rebel reached back between his wings, grasping for Eclipse. Only to pat his t-shirt, like the sword could've slipped under the cotton.

I rolled my eyes.

Snake Bite chuckled, tossing his locks like a wild cat before a kill. 'Why yes, and it's quite delicious.'

When the vampire's gaze slid to me, Rebel hurled himself at the bastard with a growl.

Snake Bite sidestepped, hooking his arm around Rebel's throat and slamming him against the boot of the Range Rover. Silver slashing shanks shot from his fingers like claws. 'You see, you may have forgotten your toy, but I always have both my weapons.' When Snake Bite grinned, his fangs grew longer.

I gasped.

A flash of silver, a tumble of black, and Rebel being pulled into a side alley by a bloke with tattooed birds exploding across his face...

Rebel had saved me from a *vampire* that first day.

Evie had a point: behind these glasses, I was blind. Because I'd abandoned Rebel, both on that first day and to Da in his bedroom. Just as now every screaming, straining nerve begged me to run.

But there was no way I was bailing on Rebel, even if I hadn't been bound to him by Ma's magic.

Not again.

Go visit some Feathery realness on that Fang!

You told you me to dump the angel before. If I'd played your game, he'd be the prisoner to the spell lobbers. And what would I be?

Free. But you're showboating, Violet-cakes, you want every man at your feet and every woman in your shadow. Secrets all revealed like candy.

This isn't my battle. I'm not a trained huntress yet.

The vampire sank his artificial steel fingernails into Rebel's shoulder, pinning him against the car.

The slashes across Rebel's chest? One mystery solved.

This is your move: fight or hide.

Snake Bite licked up Rebel's neck, nibbling his ear. Rebel shuddered.

For all I know the vampires are the heroes. Rebel's bad, yeah?

And I'm Jiminy Cricket, the voice of your conscience.

Rebel flapped his wings with a sudden, brutal *crack* across the vampire's suede jacketed back.

Snake Bite howled, his claw grip loosening, until Rebel wrenched away, diving beneath the vampire.

I was mesmerized by the savage beauty of the dance.

Rebel spun, his eyes burning as fiercely as his wings, and swept Snake Bite in a blur of suede and black to the drive. His wings that'd been soft and welcoming to me, were now as hard as the vampire's steel nails.

You have a choice. Are you on the side of the angels or the vampires?

How do I know, when I'm half of each? I've only been prisoner of one side, maybe I shouldn't choose either?

I stood stock-still, whilst they grappled at my feet.

Then claws slashed across Rebel's bad wing. A line of red fire. He hissed.

Blood had been drawn on Rebel's wing. It hit me harder than I'd reckoned possible. A volcano erupted inside me in a searing ash cloud.

To hell with who was the hero or the villain. To hell with games. And to hell with choices.

Rebel was mine, whether I'd chosen him, or the newly awoken powers within me had. And if he was a hunter, then so was I.

I stepped mechanically to the Range Rover, snapping off the steel antenna.

Swish — it whipped through the air like a cane.

I gripped it in my sweaty palm. The two bitches didn't even glance up.

Their mistake.

This was the god-like moment, when you held life in your hands. I was light-headed from the punch of potency curling the ash in black tinged clouds.

Then I skewered the vampire through the heart.

I didn't expect the chortle.

Snake Bite glanced back over his shoulder at me, the antenna sticking out of his back like a fashion accessory gone wrong. Rebel lay subdued under him, his wings beating feebly.

'I would say I'm surprised by how badly trained you are, monster,' Snake Bite gritted his teeth as he plucked the antenna out of his back and then tossed it into the bushes with a patronising smile, 'but then when I see who your Custodian is...'

Rebel frowned. 'We're not in your computer

game, princess. You can only kill these ball-bags by destroying their idiot heads.'

I dove into the bushes, wildly scrabbling for the antenna. Skin was grazed from my palms, and my knees smarted as I sank down onto the twigs. A branch thwacked against my cheek; I flinched at the sting.

At last, my questing hand closed around cold steel. It fitted, as well as any shank.

When I marched back to the vampire, he still had Rebel pinned to the ground. He licked his tongue over his lip piercings and jabbed a claw into Rebel's wing.

Rebel writhed, gritting his teeth not to holler. There were scarlet holes patterning his wings; Snake Bite had been using him as a pin cushion.

Then I swung.

The antenna sliced into the back of the vampire's head. He grunted and tried to stand, but I swung again.

Snake Bite grabbed hold of the gory end of the steel and yanked. I stumbled forward, but Rebel launched himself upwards, headbutting the vampire. Snake Bite groaned; his grip loosened.

I wrenched back the antenna, and then swung again, and again and... I was nothing but a blur of *swishing* steel.

The vampire fell on top of Rebel.

Beneath me was a mess of smashed skull, matted black hair, and crimson blood, sprawled over Rebel's wings.

My land of bones and feathers had scuttled into the real world.

I dropped to my knees, hurling down the sticky red antenna.

Then I chucked up.

Rebel struggled out from underneath the body,

slipping his leathers back over his wings. 'That'll do it,' he glanced down at the vampire. 'That was brilliant!'

I wiped the spittle from my chin.

The bondage punk bounced on his toes like we'd been to a rave not a murder.

'If you're my Custodian,' I gasped out, 'I want to be taught how to hunt. But also...how to control...myself.'

To my surprise, Rebel nodded. 'I was a dope. You're ready to become a hunter.'

He opened the velvet pouch that Ma had hung around his neck and scattered the herbs over Snake Bite's body. Like a ciggie held to a lighter, the edges caught to embers. The vampire's hair flamed, his coffee coat and soles of his boots curled to black, and his insides tumbled to ash. In a matter of moments, his corpse disintegrated to a stain on the ground.

I caught Rebel's arm. 'Hold it, punk boy, why didn't we spray this acid Hackney style at the bastard?'

'It doesn't work on the living. Only the dead.'

I scrunched up my nose. 'And vampires aren't dead?'

Rebel gave me a long look. 'I told you. This isn't your game. And vampires...aren't what you think.'

If I was truly half vampire, then I hoped that was true.

A powerful, ancient monster burnt to nothing.

I'd done that. *We'd* done that. Simply because he was a vampire.

I shifted uncomfortably.

Snake Bite had called me a *monster*. And he was right.

The cane swung like a hypnotist's watch — back and forth — from Da's hand, as he waited for Rebel and me to creep into the study. He perched on the edge of his desk, his leg swinging in time with the cane.

I squinted through the shadows. Star-shaped lamps shimmered around the corners: a sultan's tent.

Da's face was drawn, and for the first time I noticed tiny wrinkles radiating from the edges of his eyes.

No way had the bastard earned those through laughter.

'Close the door,' Da fixed Rebel with a hard stare, 'you took...*her*...away from our protection without my permission. Why?'

Rebel clicked shut the door with a sigh. 'We're not sprogs to be protected. You trained me to be a hunter, and Feathers had to see.'

'So, did she?'

'Yeah, bro,' *the vampire with black hair and eyes – like mine – leaping panther-like onto the back of the car, his fangs at Rebel's pale throat, and then burning into nothing but ash,* 'I saw.'

'I'm delighted. Then you can also witness Rebel's punishment,' Da gripped Rebel's arm, propelling him towards the desk.

Except this time, Rebel stuck his heels into the sheepskin rug: a lamb refusing to be dragged to slaughter.

Da tutted, swinging the cane arcing towards Rebel's arse, but Rebel reached his hand behind him and caught it with his palm. With an effortless flick of his wrist, he twisted the evil length of cane out of Da's grip.

Crack — Rebel snapped the thick wood over his leather encased knee. Then with a clatter, he sent it skittering over Da's wolf and fox oak desk.

It was easy to forget how strong he was and how much he fought to control that strength. I craved to have the same self-discipline when the rages roared.

In the silence, Da gawked at him.

'I don't need your lessons now,' Rebel never dropped his gaze from Da's. 'I'm after being a Custodian myself, with my own student.'

I smirked. 'Harsh.'

Da raised his hand, and my smile died.

That's all bastard men knew: how to dash, beat, and shank.

But Da only pulled Rebel close, stroking his wings with a whispered, 'I'm proud of you.'

It gutted me, those tender words, more than the clout I'd been expecting.

Maybe because I'd never heard them.

Maybe because I'd always dreamed I would from someone, whilst lying to myself I didn't care that I never had.

Maybe because I reckoned I never would.

When Rebel yelped, I found myself raising my fists, ready for a fight. Wanting one.

Needing one.

Da, however, only held up a dove-grey feather, which he'd plucked from the tip of Rebel's wing. 'Good god! I had no idea you were this close. You must go back to Angel World. I know the brutality of your life there but—'

'That's bloody blarney. You don't know.' Rebel's distress shocked me. His arms curled around Da's neck.

Da rubbed Rebel's back. 'But if you don't return—'

'I can't,' he shot me a look through tear-trembling eyes.

Rebel had fled persecution. A bird cage prison. I

knew that, but not why he looked to me as he said he couldn't go back to his home. Or why he wept from fear.

At the same time, I craved to rip him from Da and punish him for taking comfort in someone else's arms.

For keeping secrets again.

What unknown terror was held within that dove-grey feather?

11

To hunt is to hurt.

To hurt others and to be hurt by them is a line I've walked, unable to trust anyone but the voice in my head, since the day I was discovered — abandoned — in Hackney Cemetery.

Yet there's more to a hunt than the hurt. There's the very thing I'd been struggling for: control.

The steel sweep of feathers, *slam* of sugary copper, and anarchic blast of The Sex Pistols' "God Save the Queen" shuddered tingles from my shoulder blades to my fingertips.

I stumbled, driven back by Rebel's onslaught.

Tall oaks speared up to a grey sky, trapping me in the glade with Johnny Rotten's swag punk vocals, a propulsive beat, and a killer 3-chord guitar riff.

Rebel grinned, hopping from foot to foot. He hummed along to the subversive music spitting from the iPod speakers buried beneath the twigs on the edges of our training circle.

These sessions — calling out my powers, and then battling to leash them — had been the highlight of my imprisonment with the witches. Every day out in the woods, we'd danced like only two vicious bitches can.

I shivered, as the first snowflakes drifted between us like confetti.

Then I booted Rebel in the gut.

Rebel groaned but then grabbed my leg, spinning me round in the air and sprawling me onto my back.

I scrambled away, but he launched himself onto me. His wings beat, silhouetted bat-like above me; grey speckled the violet. Each session one more grey feather appeared amongst the violet.

He held my arms above my head. When I struggled, arching against him, his eyes fluttered closed.

Either there was a shooter in his trousers, or the wallad was pleased to see me.

'In a hunt, you must work out the weakness,' Rebel stroked his wing down my cheek. 'Vampires, like angels, can be hurt.' He drew the soft tip of his wing across my pinned wrists, and I shook. His lips were close to mine. Snowflakes settled on the dark curves of his eyelashes. 'Go for the hands. A bandjaxed vampire is still dangerous. Fire hurts them. But you're after wanting the quick kill. Their weakness? Neck and head.' A feathery touch swept across my throat: safety and danger all at once.

I choked, 'Get off me.'

'Make me.'

I gaped at him. 'Are you sure you want to play this game, pretty boy?'

He smirked. 'If you win, I'll take you out to fight a vampire by yourself.'

I licked my lips. That was what I'd been training towards in this woodland at the bottom of the House of Rose, Wolf, and Fox.

To be a *huntress*...

'And if I don't win?'

Rebel's gaze was suddenly serious. 'You could keep your promise not to escape.' Then he smiled shyly. 'And call me Custodian...?'

'In your dreams.'

I kneed him in the balls, wriggling away from him like a snake, as he doubled over.

I jumped up, rolling my shoulders. 'My advantage? A bitch fights dirty.'

Rebel's eyes blazed as he straightened, his wings beating, whilst the snow fell in a furious flurry around him.

'My advantage?' He unsheathed Eclipse; its flames coursed around its black core. 'I fight with a sword.'

'Wait...before you gank me into chunky salsa,' I backed up against the rough bark of an oak, snapping fallen branches on each step, 'are you compensating for the Fang and his *always having his weapon* disrespect? Because I don't have claws or—'

Violet fire shot from the end of Eclipse, burning through the snowing glade.

Crash.

A branch above my head splintered under the impact.

I ducked, shrieking. My heart thundered. 'Bastard! That could've been my head.'

He shrugged. 'Away with you, like I could miss those glasses if I was aiming for them. Now, shoot at me.'

I stared at him blankly. 'What with? My magical invisible mind blast?'

He snorted with laughter. '*Your* violet fire, of course. It's deadly special to you alone. Don't look so gobsmacked. You're half angel, you must've felt it.'

I shook my head, but it was there already because of Rebel's attack, trembling in my fingers.

'And what about the other half?'

He avoided my gaze.

We hadn't spoken about the vampire having black eyes like me. Was it shameful for an angel to be...part vampire? Was that why I was a *monster*?

Crack.

An explosion blasted just above my shoulder.

I hissed and patted at the sparks dancing across my jacket, but Rebel was wearing his innocent expression, even as he raised Eclipse again and arced the fiery streak across my feet.

I yelped, hopping away.

It burst out then. The wrath. A crackling inferno fizzed across my fingertips but it was ice-cold.

I'd unleashed a fire storm on Rebel, before I'd even remembered we were training and I should be aiming to miss.

But all I wanted to do was *hurt*.

Rebel screamed, as the flames caught his right hand. His sword clattered down; the violet clung to his skin.

I watched, fascinated, whilst his fingers seared

and blistered. He held his hand to his chest, gritting his teeth.

I threw another fireball past his head to make him jump towards me.

If I controlled the fire, I controlled Rebel. And that was even better than controlling myself.

Caught in his pain, Rebel didn't realise I'd trapped him, until I'd thrown him against the tree and wrenched both his hands above his head against the trunk, just as he'd held me on the ground.

When he did? It was too late.

I leant against him and couldn't tell if it was snow melting down his cheeks or tears. When he struggled, the fast *beat* of his heart through his thin t-shirt, fluttered against my chest.

'Hands and fire,' I circled my thumbs over his burnt, captured hand. 'Cheers for the pointer.'

I ghosted my mouth over Rebel's, and he stilled.

Angels, vampires, blokes. They were all the same.

'Who are my real parents?' I murmured.

He stiffened in surprise and then went lax.

I pressed my face close to his neck, licking and nibbling at its base. I tightened my hold on his wrists. He was still hiding the truth from me.

He gasped. 'Lay off. I don't know.'

'Yeah, you do.' I held him in place with one hand, stroking through his feathers and tracing the patterns of grey and violet, as he trembled. 'I get why the angels are hunting an Addict like you, but why are they hunting me? Is it because I'm too much of a *vampire* too?'

Rebel bucked, but I snogged him. Hard, deep, and demanding. At first, he fought it, frozen. The slam of copper was twice as sweet, however, when he thawed, lounging back into his imprisonment against the tree.

The bastard wasn't rejecting me now.

That's when I held Rebel's own sword to his throat, nicking a cut just deep enough to make him gasp. 'You're dead.' I lifted an eyebrow, pushing away from him and rejecting the kiss and unspoken offer the moment he'd melted against the oak. I grinned. 'I win.'

This time, Rebel didn't even attempt to hide his hurt. His wings curled around himself. 'You cheated, princess. Be proud when you win without tricks.'

I'd warned him I fought dirty.

And all that mattered? I'd won the chance to fight my first vampire as a huntress.

The pack of vampires jostled and joked their way across Kingston Bridge under the snow-wreathed moon. Except, only the tingling in my shoulder blades that Rebel had taught me to notice told me they weren't humans.

Kids.

They looked like a gang of college kids with a kiss of the Emo, with their arms slung around each other, snogging and balancing along the ledge above the frozen waters.

They reminded me of Jade.

Except, Rebel had sworn this gang had been ripping out the throats of humans at the local park. Vampires of the fangs, claws, and blood thirsty variety.

Not like me. At least, that's what I told myself.

I hunkered on the bank of the icy river in the shadows, fidgeting against the cold. Rebel lay sprawled on his back — a real snow angel — his wings wide either side.

Finally, our prey straggled past: the last in the gang.

The vampire was tiny. His hair was sprayed in a pink spike, his pretty bowed lips pierced, and his clothes black, ripped, and out punked Rebel. He flicked distracted through an app on his iPhone, as he fell further behind.

Separated from the herd.

It takes a fierce warrior to shake their thing at baby vamps.

He looks like a sweet cherub, but I'll go with demon child.

Rebel winked at me, before screwing shut his eyes.

Slam.

You could see the moment Tiny Fang tasted the sugary sweetness. His pupils dilated and he swallowed.

Slam.

Tiny Fang juddered.

Slam.

Gang forgotten, iPhone dropped, and Tiny Fang scrambled down the cold bank towards Rebel.

Trap set.

'Can you hear me, mate?' Tiny Fang crouched next to Rebel, and I tensed. 'What happened?' He gnawed at his beringed lip, caressing his hand over Rebel's bent wing. 'Sodding wankers always hurt—'

When Rebel surged up, Tiny Fang let out a shocked *eep*.

Rebel enveloped the vampire in his mottled

wings, like he was comforting Tiny Fang on his knee. Yet at the same time, Rebel slipped a leather ball gag around Tiny Fang's head, forcing it between his snapping fangs, before padlocking it on.

'I'm sorry, little one,' Rebel muttered, stroking over Tiny Fang's shaking shoulders.

Then Rebel shoved the vampire sacrificial off his knee towards me: the gladiator waiting for him.

And the vampire was the lion, although one with his jaw wired shut.

Tiny Fang's stare at me was confused terror, and back at Rebel sprawled in the snow, outraged betrayal.

I didn't blame him, but I had Rebel to impress. This was my first fight, and no false vampire solidarity would risk me showing Rebel what I'd learnt.

Then Tiny Fang snarled around the ball gag, and his steel nails descended.

The lion still had his claws.

Don't con yourself. This isn't a fight. It's an execution.

The pretty vampire was made for riding, not slaying. Let him go.

Sometimes, J, bastards are made for both riding and slaying. These beautiful kids are the enemy.

Humans need saving. I'm training to be strong enough to find my sister. And that means right now I'm a vampire hunter, yeah?

Executing is what I do.

Executing isn't something you do. It's what you are. Do you want to be the destroyer?

It's your choice. It always was.

I swallowed, circling Tiny Fang, slow and

predatory.

The vampire crouched, his dark eyes assessing. Then he sprang in a slashing whirlwind, faster than I'd even seen Rebel move.

I hollered, as his claws carved through my shoulder. I bent over, pressing my hand to the gashes that burned and throbbed like I'd been savaged by a big cat.

The pain ignited my rage. I couldn't hold it back.

I hooked Tiny Fang under the chin, and he staggered, breathing hard through his nose.

When Tiny Fang leapt at me again, a pink-and-black doll in the vast white, I twirled out of reach of his claws and booted him in the back. He sprawled into a snowbank, struggling onto his front through the icy chill — a snow vampire — just as I shot violet fire at his right hand.

Tiny Fang's scream was muffled by his gag into a gurgle. Searing flames skipped around his skin like evil fae in the winter night. His claws shrivelled back into his knuckles.

When I swaggered towards Tiny Fang, he shrank back into the snow, as if I was a wrathful god.

We stared at each other in silence.

Then I unleashed the fire on his left hand.

Tiny Fang howled, arching from side-to-side in agony. His blackened hands were thrown out on either side of him, stark against the white snow.

Hands and fire.

Tiny Fang was babbling something desperately through his gag.

Begging, pleading, praying?

It didn't matter.

Tiny Fang trembled, as I leant over him, balancing my hands on either side of his small head.

One twist and the bloke's neck would be... But I hesitated.

Fury still boiled inside, unsatisfied.

Too quick, it whispered, *too easy.*

I glanced back at Rebel, who watched from his seat on the bank.

The *Custodian* deserved a show.

I grinned, whispering into Tiny Fang's ear, 'Run, pretty vampire.'

Shocked, Tiny Fang stared at me, before struggling to push up from the crumbling snowbank with his blistered hands. Then he stumbled towards the frozen curl of the river.

I counted to ten, studying my nails, because even a bitch has to give the prey a chance. 'Coming, ready or not.'

The angelic righteousness swelled; I laughed. I hadn't expected the buzz and flood of adrenaline. I was high on it, and the chase had only just begun.

Tiny Fang skidded on the ice, thudding to his knees. I waited until he'd hauled himself to his feet. Then I threw a blast at the ice directly underneath him.

Tiny Fang disappeared into the hole in the ice.

I sauntered onto the slippery river, over to the jagged black hole. Looking down into the freezing river, a pink head surfaced, burnt hands scrabbling to hold onto the side and not be swept away.

When I crouched down and considered him, Tiny Fang's eyes were wide and pleading.

This your choice. Destroyer or saviour.

How is any of this my choice?

I smiled, stroking my hand through Tiny Fang's soaking hair. 'You're It, pretty vampire.'

Then I grasped Tiny Fang by his hair and hauled him out of the river.

Tiny Fang could've skewered me. *I* would've skewered me, despite the pain in my hands.

Yet he didn't. The wallad even looked grateful. He just lay on the ice, his skin tinged blue by the cold, shivering.

I shook my head.

Then he flung himself on his stomach and squirmed away, in the feeblest escape attempt I'd ever seen.

It was enough, however, to ignite the vampiric power underneath the angelic, entwining them. I dragged him back by his leg, flipping him onto his back.

It wouldn't have mattered at that moment if he'd been human. The vampire was nothing more than my enemy.

And I'd caught him.

Tiny Fang shook and sobbed, whilst I held out his arms crucifixion-style, pinning them with my knees. I trailed a flaming finger down his cheek, watching as it left a blistering trail, before I reached to rip open his t-shirt.

A sudden burst of wind blasted across my face, before a dark shadow swallowed me.

Broken out of my violent refuge, I looked up.

Rebel towered over us, his gaze coldly furious. 'Kill him.'

Tiny Fang cast Rebel the same look of gratitude, he'd earlier shown me.

I crushed Tiny Fang's throat, and he screamed.

Crackle — the blaze brightened and then...

Silence.

Triumphant, I bounced up. But all joy died, when I caught the disgust on Rebel's face.

'Had a deadly brilliant time tonight then, Feathers?' Rebel's tone was tight and hard. 'Playing your little games?'

Unsure, I shifted from foot to foot, whilst Rebel dropped to one knee and tenderly closed Tiny Fang's eyes. 'He's a fine red mist. Didn't you watch? I went for the hands and—'

'I watched all right,' Rebel gently scattered the herbs over Tiny Fang's body, like scattering ashes at a funeral, and the vampire burned down to a black stain on the river's ice. 'I watched you enjoy the kill. How it amused you. I watched two monsters in the snow.'

My breath came in short gasps. The cold suddenly chilled through me; I hugged myself.

No one had ever been proud of me before. The Bitch of Utopia demanded respect, not pride.

But somehow, making Rebel proud of me tonight had mattered.

And I'd failed.

'You wanted me to—'

'Go for the quick kill.' Rebel stood, wiping his hands down his trousers like he could wipe clean his role in Tiny Fang's *execution*. 'A hunter brings death to save others. We're not after getting off on it, or we'll become monsters too.'

The explosion burst from me, catching Rebel's shoulder in a shower of sparks and spinning him back along the ice.

'What am I?' I howled.

He panted, his expression softening. 'Different. Like me.' He straightened: an angel with a bent wing, still awe-inspiring in his punk bondage disguise. 'You wanted to know why the others were hunting us? It's because we're different. The gits would call it *imperfect* or *impure*. That's why we can't be the same as them. We have to be better.'

When I nodded, he smiled.

Yet in the hunt, there'd been both hurt and control, and I'd craved them both.

Destroyer or saviour. That was the true choice.
And now I'd had a taste of death, I knew how tempting the thrill was to become the destroyer.

12

Teachers had never picked me to be an angel in the school Christmas nativity plays. That honour had gone to the geek kids with shiny haloes and even shinier parents to make them out of tinsel.

Yet because no one had wanted me, I'd watched and built up my own fantasy, where angels hadn't been spoilt brats in dresses prancing through the heavens but powerful, terrifying, and dark.

And strong enough to save me.

Every night after my third Christmas in Jerusalem Children's Home, I'd prayed an angel would come for me.

That they'd want me as their own.

Every night no one had answered, apart from J,

who'd always lived in my head. Except for when I'd tried to question him about who *he* truly was, and then he'd pull the silent act on me.

Once, J had ignored me for a whole week as punishment.

I'd stumbled around in such a frantic panic that he'd abandoned me, my teachers had even called the children's home.

I'd learned my lesson.

At last, J had told me to stop calling to the angels, so I had. Yet deep down, I never let go of the hope that one would save me from my human life.

Then Rebel fell from the ceiling, and it was too late.

I was all grown up, I wasn't human, and I no longer believed angels would want me as their own.

Half an angel wouldn't be good enough, just as I'd never been picked for the nativity plays.

And now it was Christmas Eve again, I didn't want to hide any more.

It was time to face the real world.

As if enthralled, I tiptoed down the wooden stairs towards the Great Hall, drawn by Rob Dougan's gritty, bluesy vocals that itched into my soul.

Slam.

A surge of coppery sweetness hit me; Rebel was in the Great Hall.

Then Rebel laughed, followed by Evie's throaty giggle.

I gritted my teeth as I peered round at the vast crystal map of London. "Furious Angels" exploded in an anguished, epic burst of drums and orchestral violins.

Rebel (wings out, grey and violet dappled), hung mistletoe and holly from the beams and around the wolf throws and fox brushes. The cold air was rich with cinnamon.

Rebel was happy: his content clawed me through our bond.

Evie clasped her arms around Rebel's shoulders, swaying to the beat, as Ma and Da lounged on a pile of rose cushions like sultans, sipping egg nog from goblets.

Rebel's family.

I crossed my arms, hugging myself.

At Christmas in Jerusalem, we had a competition for the most screwed-up Christmas. Real life stories because none of us had to use make believe.

To the winner?

The honour of telling the spookiest story to freak out the newbies.

Jade had loved the tradition.

I missed Jade. I missed...

Humanity.

My chest tightened. I was breathing too fast but couldn't fight it.

Hell, was this what Rebel had experienced in the box or Jade in her panic attacks?

My heart thundered. Sweat dripped from my forehead. Terror shook me like a tiger had me cornered.

Evie grinned, snaking around Rebel. She snogged him, drawing him into the dance.

As the song climaxed in a soulful howl, Evie swung Rebel across rose quartz London like they'd conquered the human world.

'See, love is pain, angel mine.' Evie paused under the mistletoe.

I fell to my knees, struggling to breathe, as Evie

raked her nails through Rebel's wings, only for his wail to be swallowed in her kiss.

I'd allowed myself to relax, safe in the routine of my training. But the bitch who'd tried to murder me was snogging — hurting — Rebel. Because she only knew one destructive version of love.

How had I forgotten, even for a moment, that this was a witches' lair? I wasn't a guest to be trained, I was a prisoner.

Yet I'd craved to let out the forces, which had been trapped inside for twenty-one years. I'd been greedy for a taste of death.

Rebel had offered it, and I'd devoured it.

I cringed when I remembered Rebel's disgust at my display with the pink-haired punk. My hands trembled at the memory of how I'd executed Tiny Fang.

Yet that was the mirage to keep me from finding my sister.

My heart slowed. I could breathe again, now the fog had lifted.

I clutched Jade's necklace. Whether she was with the angels or not human...it didn't matter. I'd save her, just like the angels had never saved me.

For the past week, I'd watched at night, whilst Rebel had crept out through the side-door, and then flitted away through the woods.

Da had asked whether I trusted Rebel. Yet every morning, I wondered what I'd unleashed on the night.

I had one final glance at Rebel. He was sprawled in front of Ma and Da now, with his head cradled in Da's lap. Da's fingers carded his hair. Ma stroked circles through his feathers.

Rebel purred, his eyes closed.

My fists clenched: it didn't look like the bastard would miss me...

Then I pushed myself to my feet, slinking up the stairs. I snatched my khaki jacket from my bedroom, before slipping into Evie's.

The skank had hidden her iPhone after I'd stolen it, but you're not the Bitch of Utopia without having skills.

Where would Evie hide her stash?

I sneered round at the scarlet, silk, and glitter. Under the bed, bedside table, and wardrobe were all too obvious.

Then my lip curled. *The trophy cabinet.* I bet Evie reckoned it was *ironic.*

This was one trophy I was winning.

I slid open the glass, tipping the trophies onto the bed, until a sleek iPhone was revealed.

I grinned. 'Trophy Thief of Kingston Upon Thames.'

When I shoved the mobile into my pocket, my fingers brushed the prickly corners of the wicker angel effigy, which bound me to Rebel.

I plucked out the effigy, crushing it under my boot.

Freedom flared brighter than it had in weeks.

Evie's casement window opened outwards on a hinge; the frozen ground was a long way down.

Ivy flourished around the leaded window pane. I swung my foot out into the thick tendrils: I wasn't a princess waiting to be saved.

For the first time since I'd been dragged into this supernatural world, I set out on a quest.

Alone.

Two wide frightened green eyes stared up at me through a frizz of fringe.

Bang — the apartment's door caught on its chain.

'Go get your mum, Aylin.' I smiled.

'Mummy says not to talk to strangers.'

'Then what are you doing opening the door? Learn some basics, before your auntie Feathers goes Hulk that you disrespected her with the label *stranger*.'

A gasp. *Crash*, as the door slammed. Whispers.

I sighed, leaning against the rough graffiti tagged wall of floor eleven, Tower Block B. The corners were junked with used needles and dirty nappies. The concrete stairwell reeked of urine.

I was coming home for Christmas. Or the closest thing I had left: Gizem's home.

When the battered door swung open, I fought not to force myself into their *human* world.

Then I caught sight of Gizem.

She slouched in a stained white bathrobe, with a towel around her neck; her scar stood out livid down her ashen cheek. Her hair wound like black snake corpses down her shoulders, and her eyes were just as lifeless.

It was like the sun had died.

Aylin peeked around her mum, wearing pink pyjamas with fluffy winged angels. She clutched *The Night Before Christmas*. I snorted; when Gizem had tried to read that story to me as a kid, I'd chucked it at her head.

'Get into bed,' Gizem ran her hand down Aylin's hair, never taking her gaze from mine, 'I'll be in to read your book soon.'

'And Father Christmas? Will he... If I go to sleep, will he visit tonight?'

I raised an eyebrow, but Gizem didn't smile, she just pushed Aylin towards her room. 'Bed. Now.'

Then Gizem shoved me deeper into the urine stinking corridor, before closing the door behind her. 'What are you doing? Showing up at my yard?'

I blinked. 'Merry Christmas to you too. And *we* didn't believe in any of that Santa crap.'

Her scowl lightened. 'I know, that's why I'm making sure Aylin does.'

'I don't understand.'

Gizem sighed, brushing my shoulder in a gesture so familiar, it made me ache. 'I know. You never did.' She slid out a packet of ciggies from her pocket and lit one with a disposable.

'So, your little one didn't recognise me.'

'They grow fast. And you...seem different.' When Gizem took a deep drag, she exhaled with a sigh, and then relaxed back against the concrete wall.

I slouched next to her. 'Remember last Christmas she was obsessed with some pricey princess doll, until—'

'You took her to see a knight's dressing up outfit and told her the story of *Buffy the Vampire Slayer* who was just like King Arthur and ever since—'

'She's said she wants to be *Sir Buffy* when she grows up?'

We sniggered.

Just for a moment, I could pretend Rebel had never fallen into my life.

'You always had my back,' Gizem said softly.

'Because you always had mine.'

'I looked for you,' she tumbled ash from her ciggie between her feet. 'The feds interviewed us. You know what they're saying about you?'

I stiffened, before forcing myself to smile. 'That I'm a kickass bitch?'

'That you're a killer,' she licked at her dry lips, 'who took out Toben and then Bisi.'

'And Jade?'

Gizem shrugged, although the movement seemed to cost her. 'Casualty of turf war.'

'And what do *you* say?'

Gizem threw down her ciggie, grinding it with her bare heel. I flinched. 'You want to guess how much I wouldn't be out here if I reckoned you'd ganked Jade?' Then she hugged me fiercely, something she hadn't done since I was a kid, and I struggled not to lose any Hackney respect and bawl. 'I saw those pictures and I knew—'

'Hell, you saw...?' I'd forgotten, in the joy of the familiar, that my old life's annihilation had been caught on film.

'Someone's going to turn you in. It's all over social media.' Gizem edged back towards her apartment. I could see the light through the crack. A world of *The Night Before Christmas* and belief in a good magic that didn't come tainted with death. 'And the gang that took over the business,' she shuddered, her hand straying to rub at the towel around her neck, 'they're bastards who make Bisi look like a pussy. You can't let them catch you.'

'I won't let them mess with you either.' I couldn't help the growl. This was Gizem, and we were the Two Orphan Musketeers. Ever since we'd been kids, we'd looked out for each other because we'd had no one else. 'I'll protect you.'

Her smile was sad. 'Can you even protect yourself?'

I caught her arm before she could slam the door closed on me. 'You're saying there's no room at the inn?'

Gizem looked trapped in that agonizing choice between laughing and weeping. 'Maybe you're just trying to win the most screwed-up Christmas this year, Feathers?'

I couldn't help the wetness pricking my eyes. Gizem had never shut me out before. It hadn't mattered what I'd done, she'd always been there to put me back together again.

Suddenly desperate, I found myself babbling, 'I'm claiming that medal. I've earned it. So, do I tell the spooky story?'

Gizem's gaze hardened as she slammed the door, but I didn't miss her mutter, 'You're spooky enough already, girl.'

I stared at the closed door, blankly.

Then I allowed the tears to fall.

Blindly, I stumbled out of Tower Block B into a snow world, blurred to ice white by my tears. I grasped onto the frozen chain, dropping onto the swing.

I shivered as I swung.

Homeless, alone, abandoned.

Time for the spooky ass story, Violet-sweets. Make us fear and forget.

I bent my legs, lolling my head back, with my eyes screwed shut against a world I didn't want to remember. I swung higher and higher.

There was once a foundling. No one knew who'd left her in the human world. But she was powerful and swore one day, when she was all grown up, she'd take her rightful place in the magical world and her vengeance...

Lips on my neck. Arms around my waist, trapping me. Someone stopping the swing and stealing me back into the snow world *with a kiss.*

My eyes snapped open.

The bloke's hair was auburn and smoothed into a boy band chic I remembered. His skin was tanned, and his cheek bones were high and aristocratic. His long black wool coat and leather gloves marked him as Romantic Boyfriend material.

He was beautiful.

No wonder I'd risked everything that night to be

with him. The bastard did everything but sparkle.

Phoenix.

And he hadn't aged since the night he'd tried to kill me, shanked Gizem, and given me my first kiss.

Yet his pupils appeared charcoal-grey, rather than black. Was that why I hadn't clocked he wasn't human? And did vampires hide themselves that way?

Phoenix frowned, like he'd expected a bigger reaction. He leaned closer, as if to steal a kiss, but I wrenched his arm off my waist and scrambled away.

He sauntered after me. 'You smell divine. A Christmas gift just for me. But why are you so sad?' He smiled, with that dimple I'd found so cute before.

Now I wanted to curb stamp the pretty bitch's face into the snow.

I shrugged. 'Because a psycho reckons we're into sharing our feelings.'

Run, isn't that what you said to the Fang? Do it now, before this asshole twists your mind.

Why? I'm a huntress, remember?

But this was the first time I'd been alone without Rebel. Alone with a vampire.

And Phoenix wasn't a gagged baby vamp.

Phoenix ran a hand through his thick wave of hair. 'You're sad, I believe, because nobody wants you.' When I flinched, his smile broadened. 'Except, I want you. You want me too, if you'd only let go. You crave death, seeking it out with your foolishness. Yet I can give you something that will take you further than death. Just relax, and allow it to take you. Let me in.'

Phoenix's eyes were burning coals against the white of the snow. His move to me so fast, I felt his breath against my neck before I'd tensed for it. When he tongued my skin, I stiffened.

I didn't want this, but I was frozen because I did *crave death*.

Only not how he imagined it.

With a sigh, I elbowed Phoenix, and he staggered back with a startled *oomph*.

'Just bounce, yeah?' I booted the merry-go-round; it slowly spun.

Run, Pretty Feathers, run...

An outraged roar, then hands dragged me back by my hair.

I yelped, but my neck was twisted. Fingers dug in at the base.

Coming, ready or not...

Agony. Blinding and pure.

I screamed as my muscles and nerves melted in a wave of weakness. I submitted, falling to my knees in the wet snow.

I had the sudden memory of Rebel, risking this same pain at Da's hands.

I hadn't prayed to the angels for many years, but I prayed now for Rebel to save me.

I juddered with pain, like I'd been tasered, so weak I couldn't lift my arms. Then I stared up at Phoenix's face full of fangs.

That's a proper screwed-up Christmas for you.

Phoenix stroked down my cheek; the leather was soft and cold against my skin. He dragged my throat closer to his gleaming teeth. 'I've waited a long time to taste you.'

'Sweet Jesus, you're not using those idiot lines?' Rebel wrenched Phoenix away from me, smashing his head against the merry-go-round.

Phoenix snarled, trying to escape, but Rebel held him down with a boot on his throat.

I panted, gaping at Rebel in his swirl of black

leather, as — *bang* — he lifted up Phoenix's head and crushed it against the merry-go-round again.

Maybe a Christmas prayer could come true? I'd never been so relieved to see anyone as that psychotic angel pounding Phoenix's head.

I struggled to crawl closer to the bastard who'd scarred Gizem and stolen my trust in men. After Phoenix, blokes were disposable toys: shag and throw away. That way, you couldn't be hurt or shanked.

All because my first kiss was with a vampire.

I dragged myself through the snow towards Phoenix.

Phoenix flailed under Rebel's boot, but Rebel grimly held him down.

'You're right: I crave death. Let's see what happens when I let it in.' I kissed Phoenix lightly.

When Phoenix snapped at me with his fangs, Rebel ground his heel into his neck and he stilled.

I forced my tongue into Phoenix's resisting mouth. For the first time, violet death flowed through my lips and into my intimate tonguing.

Phoenix jerked. The silver knives, which had haunted so many of my nightmares, shot from his nails.

But now they were impotent.

Rebel swung Eclipse, slicing off the hands that'd dared to touch me, at the same time as a hissing, searing path of flames flared through Phoenix's head, until he burned like a candle.

When I settled back on my heels, the sparking fire ate through the vampire's convulsing body, until in a flash that speared up to the army of stars, Phoenix crumbled to ash.

I am death. The End. Destroyer.

You should've run. Remember I gave you the choice to run.

A huntress doesn't run.

I'll read you until the Christmas bells ring out: you're an addict, the same as Rebel.

Shocked, I sprawled backwards.

Rebel leapt over the pile of ash and threw himself onto me.

His body was hard. Supporting. Anchoring.

His face was as white as the snow, and his hands shook.

He touched every inch of me, patting down for injuries and turning my head from side-to-side to check my neck. He sighed, when he saw it was unmarked. Then he caressed his fingertips over my face, as if memorising it. When he slowly removed my glasses, I stiffened but allowed it.

He'd earned that...intimacy.

I blinked, as first Rebel touched one eyelid, and then the other. Carefully, he pushed my glasses back on. At last, he pressed a kiss to my forehead, before collapsing onto me. 'You're a muppet.'

I smiled. 'Yeah, and you're a wallad.'

Rebel touched his forehead to mine. 'I'm sorry. It's Christmas and your sister... You know I don't do—'

'Talking?'

'I say it all arseway but I understand. And before you eat my head off, I've lost family too. It doesn't make me seek death, but life. Look, princess,' he glanced down, his lashes curling onto his cheek, 'I'm a bad angel. I've fibbed to you about...everything. There are things I can't tell you. But if you come back with me — to my family — I'll tell you what I've been hiding...'

I clutched Rebel, my heart pounding.

This was it. The secret he hid behind his shuttered eyes. Where he went when he stole out of the witches' house at night.

Whether I'd been right to trust and free him.

And if I hadn't, I'd be forced to set him alight like a violet sparkler.

Then this Christmas Eve night, Rebel would be just another pretty death.

13

When the House of Rose, Wolf and Fox beckoned in a blaze of light in the freezing black — no way had my Christmas Eve vanishing gone unnoticed — I swung to Rebel.

My breath came in icy mists, puffing out like a fairy train down the driveway. My fingers swept the frosty stone of the sundial.

Crunch — I dug my heels into the gravel as I dragged Rebel to a stop.

Rebel glanced down at my fingers, which dug into his arm, with a nervous smile. 'Time to pay the piper then?'

Family is the angel in eyeliner's weakness. He's a loyal little punk. He'll tell

you his secret...out here.

But if you let that sweet ass of his inside, then his adoptive psychos will smother the darling until—

Got it, J, shank the weakness.

Shank the punk. Is it not sinking in yet? If they're not yours, then they're dead.

I shuddered, closing my eyes.

'Feathers, you're not looking so well.' Rebel stroked across the back of my elbow.

My eyes snapped open, and I wrenched away my arm. 'I'll look better, bro, when you trust me with the truth. Like where you go at night.'

He clutched at his collar, as if for protection. 'Do Ma and Da know...?'

'Focus.'

'What happened to *your* da?' He glanced carefully at me from underneath his eyelashes but he'd crossed his arms defiantly.

My stomach twisted. I'd never known my parents. But it'd been clear they hadn't wanted me.

Rebel knew that. *He was playing me.*

I shrank from his cruelty, even as I seethed that he'd use my dad to distract me.

Who's getting shanked here?

You don't need your dad; you have me.

'I reckon you know more about my dad than I do.' My hands shook as I gripped the edge of the sundial, but I tilted my head. 'You have one sentence to convince me not to burn you alive.'

Rebel's eyes widened. He paced in a tight circle around me and the sundial. My head spun. 'My real da's here on earth because I abandoned him.' Then he licked his lips. 'Oh, and please don't kill me.'

I snatched the cold sleeve of his leathers, holding him still. 'You have an angel dad?'

'It's...complicated. But I've been searching for

149

him. Even though the Deadmans would whip my arse for it, but that's why—'

I shoved Rebel across the gravelled driveway, slamming him against the timbered porch; the wicker effigies that swung by their necks trembled. The protection spells glowed, snaking crimson symbols in the shadows.

Rebel let out a startled yelp.

'I'm the mug who believed you were here to save *me*. My own angel at last. Where's my head been at, reckoning you were *family*? Because all along, you've been on earth to find your *true* family. I never reckoned I could feel sorry for the bastard witches.'

My vampiric and angelic sides crashed together in a dominating, enraged flood.

Mine, mine, mine...

I lowered my lips to Rebel's, as I had Phoenix's, whilst an ice-cold inferno spat and sparked from my toes to my mouth.

You can do this.

Remember the anger. The betrayal. I'm all you need.

Rebel struggled, his heels cracking against the oak door, but then he went limp. 'Hurt me,' he whispered, as if it was a prayer, 'kiss me, burn me...'

The sizzling flames leapt, from my lips to his, and he gasped.

What the hell was I doing?

I staggered back from him. The enraged wave broke, and the waters bled away. I vibrated with shock.

His gaze was dazed, before he swiped his knuckles across his seared lips.

'Don't lie to me again,' I shook, terrified at what I'd almost done — what I'd *craved* to do. And into what J had tempted me. 'If your dad is missing...then we can search for him, the same as Jade.' How little control I had still over the powers inside horrified me. 'You're not alone in that birdcage anymore. Fam is fam, remember?'

He nodded, although his smile was fragile. 'Brilliant! Although, could you call me Custodian once in a while? I'm already making a big enough balls of the job.'

'Safe, Custodian.'

'See? Now I'm all tingly.'

I smacked his arm, but he'd stilled, scanning the woods along the drive.

A flicker of movement like bats...

'Inside.' Rebel had paled. He dashed through the high door, fiddling with the effigy on his trousers.

I stalked after him into the halo light of the hallway that was glaring after the gloom of the porch, reaching for my own effigy...except it wasn't there.

I'd crushed it under my boot in Evie's room.

Hadn't Ma warned me that without the effigy I'd be the hunted?

Rebel scowled at me. He slammed the door, resting his forehead against it.

He'd guessed.

I banged my boot against the panelled wall. 'So, what have I done and how bad is it?' I asked, trying for casual.

Rebel's gaze was hard. 'You've brought down the vampires on us...on my family.'

'But I thought the effigies were to hide us from angels?'

'You want to discuss this now? Those creatures outside are here to kill us all.'

'Why?'

'Hunters? Witches? Angels? And you're....' He

caught himself, biting at his lip. 'We're they're enemies in a war that's been battled for centuries. There's no talking or dealing or... To them, *we're* the villains.'

In a flurry of silk dressing gowns, the Deadmans clattered down the staircase to paw Rebel, twirling him round to check for injuries and hissing over his burnt lips.

Da gave me a level look. 'Do you enjoy the chase? I have Blood Familiars who were once like you. After they were...tamed...they enjoyed it considerably less.'

'Sorry, bro, but your damaged psyche — freaky as it is — has to wait. There's a gang of Fangs outside.'

Evie's wild curls danced as she spun to me, but I was shocked to see the tears trapped in the corners of her eyes. 'I have powers, but no one listens to my warnings; I'm the Cassandra of London. And you, my lovely, are the destroyer. You bring death to this house.'

'Nobody will hurt you, I promise,' Rebel pulled his family around him. In silence, they held each other in a tight circle at the base of the staircase.

I ached, hugging my arms around myself. 'What can I do?' I asked quietly. 'Do we go out there, hunter style?'

'As if leading the enemy to our hidden door was not your intention,' Evie sneered, pulling away from the circle and breaking it. But Rebel held onto Ma's hand; her fingers clasped around his. 'Precious thing, how much will you cost us?'

Evie swayed in a trance, tracing invisible visions in the air with twitching fingers.

'You have two hunters now,' I shifted awkwardly, 'I have your back.'

Da nodded, but it was Rebel's brief smile that

straightened my shoulders.

Fight mode.

'Too many of the gits to go out sword waving,' Rebel jerked his head towards the door. 'This is different; they're fanatics.'

'Then we build up the house's protection.' Ma tugged Rebel after her towards Evie, before smoothing down Evie's cheek. Evie blinked, as if rising from sleep. 'You too,' she threw over her shoulder at me.

I jolted, surprised at the flush of warmth. Then I gave a crisp nod.

Together, we rushed into the kitchen, throwing down herbs from the low beams at Ma's orders, before dragging out a huge ceramic pestle and mortar from the ink-black cabinet.

Who knew it took a vampire siege to bring together a dysfunctional family of witches, angels and...whatever supernatural hybrid I was?

The golden chandelier warmed us against the night. The low flames in the inglenook fireplace sparked and stung my eyes with smoke.

Snip, snip, snip...

In the haze of the night-time kitchen, as Ma mixed the spell — and hell, I still struggled to accept magic was real — the world hazed.

Until Ma said, gazing intently at the herbs and never raising her head, 'The House of Rose, Wolf, and Fox has stood since humans burnt our kind on bonfires. It has life, the same as us. And it would die to protect us. Why are the nightmares pulling down our home?'

Ma sounded like a kid, asking why her new daddy crept into her room at night.

Rebel snatched the long carving knife so quickly

from the marble counter it was a nothing but a gleam of silver and then crimson as he slashed across his palm.

Drip, drip, drip...

Rebel's blood bled into the protection spell mix like it was just another herb: the red milk that bound it together.

When the scent hit me, sugary and intoxicating, I remembered the tangy sweetness on my own tongue. I hungered to sink in my blunt teeth again...

'Angel blood,' Rebel shook off the last drops, before licking the gash clean like a cat, 'fierce powerful.' Rebel dropped the knife, with a rueful smile. 'Not like angel kisses.'

Slash — a flash of silver, scream of red, and my palm sacrificial bled over the potion. I avoided Rebel's wide gaze: there was something too close to surprised pride there.

The one thing I'd pretended not to want was shining from Rebel just when we were about to die.

Because of me.

'Non-designer angel blood will still boost the spell, yeah?' I hunched my shoulders, shaking my hand and splattering scarlet across the oak floor.

'Bandage her wound,' Da said softly.

A kitchen towel was whipped off the range and tied carefully around my palm...by Evie.

I lifted an eyebrow, but she only smirked. Then she edged to the bowl of blood and herbs; she plucked a petal from her rose necklace and ground it into the mix.

Ma stroked Evie's hair, before untying her wolf pendant. She submerged it into the sticky paste, at the same time as Da ripped the cord around his neck and dashed in the already blood tipped fox brush. Then Ma stuck her hand into the oozing potion and smacked the rose, wolf, and fox picture behind the range, branding it with a bloody hand print.

Again, and again, Ma marked the painting, until it was covered with fingers and palms, like crimson birds with their insides exploded out, and nothing was left of the rose, wolf, or fox.

The house had been extinguished.

Exhausted, Ma fell back, and Rebel caught her.

At last, the family drew together, kissing each other gently on the lips.

Hell, what a time to shag... Except, then I realised it was a *goodbye*.

I swallowed. The family's display was too intimate. Personal. And why did it shank so deep that I had no one to kiss me?

Wiping the back of my hand across my eyes, I stumbled out of the kitchen, pushing into the first room on the wood-panelled hallway.

I reached to switch on the light, blinking as a small library with rows of faded books to the stone ceiling blossomed out of the dark. A calm corner of leather armchairs and chocolate sofa, hushed by swathes of gold curtains.

I could imagine Da, hands smartly behind his back, striding around his private retreat. A god in his own household.

I straightened my shoulders and set my jaw.

Why did it matter if I was alone, when I was going to die tonight?

I kicked closed the door. At the *bang*, two narrow heads peeked up over the back of the sofa.

I grinned. 'This is where you've been hiding?' Rebel had accused me of taking the Blood Familiars as *slaves*, but the foxes had wandered around the Estate as they'd like, since the day I'd freed them.

I'd seen barely more than a flash of red, except when they'd whined and begged for treats. 'Sitting on the furniture? Careful, you don't want to be chained in a kennel, bitches.' I sighed, throwing myself down between the Blood Familiars' furry bodies and allowing Blaze to lay his black paws possessively across my lap.

'Now hold on, you wouldn't put us in a kennel? And we're no bitches.' Spark scowled at me, aggrieved.

The fox's lips hadn't moved but a soft Scottish voice had lit up my mind, just like J's did.

Spark's expressive eyes were watching mine.

Auditory hallucinations...? But I wasn't in a migraine. *A spell?* But I hadn't drunk anything.

Then Spark yipped, as Blaze leapt across my knee in a heavy tangle of rusty-red flanks and whippy tail. Blaze pinned his smaller brother underneath him with his forelegs.

Spark grinned in submission, his white throat exposed.

'I told you not to speak to her, but you wouldn't listen. So, now she can hear us, you numptie, and my teeth are taking a trip to your backside.' Blaze: bolder, less geeky than his brother, and fuming...

I had the sudden instinct to teach one brother how to kick the bullies' arses, and the other how to read poetry.

Is that what it's like for parents?

I snatched Blaze by the neck before he could bite down. 'Not happening, bro. And if you don't like *bitches*, Spark, how about I call you *foxies* instead?'

'Nay, I don't think—'

'So, Blaze, how come I have fox radio playing in my head?'

Blaze settled back on his haunches with a snarl.

'Telepathy. You wouldn't be telling the witches? Because they'll—'

'Hurt us, hurt us, hurt us.' Spark nuzzled against my hand, and I stroked his ears, until he calmed.

'Our secret,' I murmured, wriggling down on the sofa.

'Told you,' Spark simpered at his brother, 'we can trust our new Keeper.'

I sat up, shoving away Spark's head. 'Rewind, foxies. Despite Rebel's bondage themed dates, I'm not into kinky slave and mistress—'

'You saved us from Da,' Blaze's amber eyes shone, 'and you can't know what that means. We didn't choose to be Blood Familiars, but you made a choice to be our Keeper when you claimed us. We'll always serve you. We're yours.'

Yours...

The thrill of Blaze's words wound deeper than the violet, to the river of black.

'Yeah, you're mine,' I dug my fingers into the familiars' thick fur.

I tightened my hold; Spark whimpered.

My nails were digging into the foxes' necks. I quickly let go, with a grimace. Then I stroked over their backs in apology. 'I always wanted a dog.'

I laughed at Blaze's snarl. But then I shivered.

I was being watched.

I pushed myself up, sidling to the high arched windows. Twitching the curtains wider apart, I peered out and then gasped.

An army of vampires lined the drive in dark ranks. Silent and watchful beneath the stripped trees. Their black eyes sparked, like fallen stars. Too far from the house to be caught in its light, they were nothing but shadows.

Except for their leader.

The fanatic's top boy smiled. He strolled closer towards the house, his hands in the pockets of his navy cargo trousers.

With a sweep of brunet hair and brooding mutton chops, the handsome bastard lounged in a dreamy, sky-blue velvet coat, as if he was a movie star. When his gaze locked with mine — searching and malicious — his plump lips pouted into a kiss.

Then he waved.

I jumped at a sudden scrambling, thudding sound, like mutant rats in the attic. The vampires must've sneaked around the back of the house and were now climbing up, onto the roof.

But what were they waiting for?

As soon as the sun rose on Christmas day, they were in for a splitting headache. Rebel had told me enough in my sessions: vampires could only suffer small doses of sunlight without the mother of all migraines. It explained *my* migraines in my feverish 'second puberty'. Maybe Rebel's blood was the reason my symptoms had eased.

So, what was the vampires' Big Plan? Had Ma's protection spell worked?

Then I smelled the sickly stink of gasoline.

'Rebel!' I backed away from the window, cracking my shoulder against the wall of books. I winced as hard leather spines dug into my shoulders.

The Blood Familiars leapt off the sofa, winding around me, their tails aloft.

Rebel skidded into the room, the Deadmans close behind him. Their faces were drawn and their hair tangled; I'd forgotten it was the middle of the night and they were up because of me.

About to be burnt alive...and hadn't I threatened to do that to Rebel?

I wanted to hurl. Instead, I nodded out of the

window at the tall figure of the perfectly styled fanatic.

Rebel stomped to peek out but then stared back helplessly at Da. 'It's Eden himself.'

'We always knew the risks.' Da pulled at his cuffs, yet I understood how much the simple gesture was hiding. 'Eden, the deluded and damned boy, is one such risk.'

Rebel sniffed, before stiffening. 'Can the spell hold off fire?'

'The house is wooden,' Ma's mouth twisted, like a teenager explaining something to her thick parents, 'it'll burn. No spell can change the nature of fire.'

'We're screwed.' When the others turned to gawk at me, I shrugged. 'Just keeping it real.'

'The iron cellar.' Evie snatched Rebel by the hand, dragging him to the door. 'Lucky boys and girls that we are, it already has extra protection inbuilt around the stone, for the fun toys stored inside. The fire may devour, but we'll be hidden cool enough beneath.'

'Monster, monster,' the singsong voice caught me, trapping me before I could follow Rebel to the door.

I shuddered.

'Eden.' Rebel stormed to the window, ripping back the curtain.

Two sparkling black eyes in an ashen face watched us from just outside the glass.

When I squealed, Eden laughed. He leant his forehead against the window; his breath steamed the glass. 'Come and play.' He considered Rebel, who tilted up his chin to meet his gaze. 'Oh, and the lost angel. Let me guide him to purity.'

'Let me guide my boot to your balls.' A wave of heat and orange flames was reflected in the glass from the other side of the mansion. The Great Hall, with its rose quartz London, was burning down. A city in flames... Still Eden didn't move back. 'Do one.'

Eden's smile widened; his canines curved to fangs. 'The angels so love their captors, they fight against their own freedom. Yet I'm fair, so let me extend an offer.' Then he sang, 'Angel and monster, come out to me, then I won't roast, the witches for tea.'

Eden tipped an imaginary hat to me, before disappearing in a blue velvet swirl back to his army.

Rebel was breathing hard. Then he dropped to his knees before Da. 'I'll go out to him. I'll give myself up—'

'Who's in charge, Zach?'

Rebel blinked. 'You are, Da.'

'So, who decides who protects whom? And whether your life is to be thrown away, after we've spent ours saving, waiting for, and loving you?'

When Rebel didn't reply, Da shook him.

'You do,' Rebel replied quietly. 'But I can't lose my family. Not again. Please—'

'I believe Evie suggested the cellar,' Ma announced like it was a ball invitation, but I didn't miss how her hand shook as she lifted Rebel back to his feet.

Eden had called to *me*. Rebel could spin it anyway he wanted, ancient war or not: Eden was hunting me.

I trailed after Rebel, with the fox brothers at my heels, following him and his family down the stone steps into the musty cellar.

Bang — Rebel slammed shut the iron cellar door.

Clang — the lock slid into place.

I hadn't felt claustrophobic before but I did

now; I quivered, swaying with dizziness.

Beads of sweat dripped off Rebel's forehead. It was heating up even here. The house above groaned and shook, whilst it burned.

The house was dying.

A screaming *crash*, shocking shudder, and shrieking *smash*.

We threw ourselves to the floor as stone dust from the trembling ceiling ghosted us.

I panted, pulling my arms over my head.

The lights went out, casting us — and the House of Rose, Wolf, and Fox — into the dark.

I lay, listening to the ragged breaths of Rebel and his family, whilst we waited to burn like their house. And the only thought spiralling through me was that I'd killed us all.

Just like Evie had prophesied. Just like I'd always known I would.

I was the cuckoo in the nest.

The monster.

Hurt me, kiss me, burn me...

14

Horrified, tearstained faces ghost flickered back into existence in the black, as Rebel flamed Eclipse like a candle between us.

Crouching on the concrete floor of the cellar, I swept my fingers in jerky arcs through the dust. Nauseous at the dry warmth, I scrubbed my hands down my jeans, gulping panicked breaths.

Then Rebel's shoulder knocked mine. I glanced at him, and he attempted a smile.

The Blood Familiars whined, nuzzling my knees. Their eyes were heavy-lidded and drowsy; Blaze curled around his brother. Their weight, each time they bumped me, was a reminder this was real.

Witches, an angel, Blood Familiars and me...huddled in the dank cellar, whilst vampires skittered and scampered above our heads across the iron ceiling.

I never reckoned I'd miss just a regular — human — screwed-up Christmas.

I wiped the sweat off my forehead with the back of my sleeve. 'If I'm going to be the roasted turkey, then someone's telling me who the bastards are that'll be munching on my—'

'Tiny breasts?' Evie pouted.

'Burnt wings,' I growled.

'The gits call themselves The Pure. Their boss is Eden. I've killed enough of them to know my balls would be sliced off, before my wings, and then...'

'But what's their beef with me?'

Rebel's breath hitched. He pulled his knees close and hugged them with his arms. 'Like me, you're not pure. They're extremists who see you as nothing but abnormal. And any creature not like them is destroyed or forced to convert.'

The violet fury, which had withered before the fire, frightened into submission, burst to life, dragging with it an oily slick of black dominance. The twin sensations carried me to my feet. I towered over Rebel, staring down at his startled face. 'Secrets. How many more are there?'

'A whole world — worlds — of them. I didn't mean to hide this.'

'Liar,' I was cold, even as I swayed with the heat. 'Why didn't you want me to know there were different types of vampires? And who did you have me killing?'

'That's indeed an excellent question,' Da undid the top button of his shirt and shucked his jacket; he was struggling to breathe.

Rebel glanced between us, biting his lip. 'The

Pure,' he whispered at last.

By the way the Deadmans exclaimed, I knew it was the wrong answer. But this time he was on his own.

'If we live tonight,' when I pointed at Rebel, he quailed; the light from Eclipse wavered, 'we're going to talk about respect, trust, and how angels don't fib to monsters.'

He gave a tight nod. 'If we live tonight.' He ducked his head, but I could still see his lips quirk. 'I told you I was bad.'

Rap, rap, rap.

The three sharp knocks on the cellar door echoed in the dark.

We all stilled.

Silence.

Then Eden's charming, teasing voice, 'Angel and monster, come out to me, then I won't roast, the witches for tea.' A shrill laugh. 'Whoops, I have burnt them, well, burnt down the witches' house.'

'I bet you were the kid no one played with at school. I'm right, yeah? So, you put your teddies in the corner, sang them freaky songs, and set alight the one with the fraying fur.'

'How rude,' Eden sounded genuinely disappointed in me. 'There's so much darkness in you, I can hardly see the light. Yet your angel loves his gaolers, so let me offer him the choice: in ten minutes, we'll dig out this cellar. Then I'll feast on the witches, whilst you watch.'

Rebel gasped, struggling to his feet. 'You won't—'

'That's right, I won't. If you and your monster walk up the cellar steps before the watch ticks and surrender yourself to me. There's always a choice.'

Rap, rap, rap.

'Ten minutes.'

I clenched my teeth so hard my jaw ached. Hell, I itched to smash Eden in the nose. To see the smug bastard struggle in ice-cold water, as Tiny Fang had, or kiss him to ash, like Phoenix.

I was a hunter. We'd trained to fight.

'What do I...?' Rebel spun on the spot with Eclipse, like a Catherine wheel. The violet spectre-trailed through the gloom.

'On your knees,' Da's curt command tumbled Rebel into position, his head hanging low. When Da stroked through Rebel's flame of hair, he leant into the touch. 'This belongs to your...true father.' Rebel's head shot up in shock. Da had taken out a glistening silver dagger from the safe. A star was carved into the hilt. A silver threaded scabbard dangled from Da's other hand. 'We acquired Star after... Did you think we were unaware of your search? That we'd allow you to leave the house without permission, if it was not our will?'

Rebel trembled, never looking away from the dagger. 'I'm sorry.'

'You didn't come back for us. Because you *wanted* us. We guessed as much. But that doesn't change that you're ours to guide. And love. Now you'll need your true father and brother again.'

Brother?

I cast Rebel a baleful glare — yeah, we were having a quiet little chat about *fibbing*, if Eden didn't cut off Rebel's balls first — and he ducked his head.

Da offered Star's hilt to Rebel, but he recoiled. 'I've no right.'

'You have every right.' Da glanced at Ma, and

she nodded. Da gripped Rebel's chin softly, raising his gaze. 'Please remember, Zach, finding your father may not be what you expect. It certainly will not set everything back to how it was. Don't fly on false hope.'

When Rebel sheathed Eclipse, we were plunged into the pitch-black.

Then Star burst alive in piercing bright violet. Shards of light shot out like the points of a star.

Rap, rap, rap.

'Five minutes until we play,' Eden crooned.

When Rebel leapt at me with the dagger, the fox brothers snarled, even though they were panting and battling to stand in the heat. Yet he only threw the scabbard at me. 'Put it on, around your waist.' I pulled on the scabbard, pulling my jacket down to hide it. It fitted, like it'd always meant to be there. Something stirred under my skin. A need...or a memory. I held my breath, trembling with the desire to touch Star. 'Ages it's been since I could give anyone a present.' His hands were steady as he raised Star. 'Sorry I couldn't wrap your Christmas gift.'

Mine, mine, mine...

It was a reclaiming. No longer fear held within a blade. Because the top boy shank was mine.

A knife that would burn and slice: I'd be god-like for real.

I backed against the cobwebbed wall. 'Don't tempt me, bro.'

'Every angel has an ancient weapon,' Rebel pressed. I didn't understand the anguish in his expression, as he whispered, 'You deserve it. Not me.'

I'd snatched the hilt from him, before I'd even

made the decision.

I gasped, and my eyes rolled back, flying on the power of the weapon. I was as baked as Rebel had been with Eclipse. I understood now: his joy.

The power.

After everything, it was Rebel who'd unleashed me.

With a jolt, the land of bones, beneath the mountain of feathers, flashed as if I was back there, cracking over wing bones. When I shook my head, the vision cleared.

But if that was tonight — *our* bones and *our* feathers in this cellar — then I needed to give Rebel a Christmas gift as well. Something just as special as Rebel's only link to his true father.

I scrabbled at Jade's necklace one-handed, undoing it and holding it out in the palm of my hand. 'Sorry I couldn't wrap it.'

He stared at me for a long moment. Then he lifted the necklace, placing it tenderly into the pouch around his neck, as if it was a wedding ring. 'Thank you.'

Awkward, I shrugged. 'Doesn't mean you've made it off my List of Asses to Kick.'

Rap, rap, rap.

'Four minutes, my lost ones,' Eden purred.

'You're after having to wait in line,' Rebel tried to smirk but he was tearing at his lower lip too hard with his teeth.

'We've loved since we were nothing but kids.' Ma tilted her head; her smile was soft. The Deadmans were hunkered at the back of the cellar in a circle, their hands entwined. 'We dreamed our lives away, lost in the shadow of you. You were all we needed.'

Da pulled his family even closer; his hand passed across their mouths. 'Now we die at your altar.'

'I don't.' Evie's gaze was razor-sharp; her eyes gleamed with unshed tears. 'But love is pain, remember?'

'Away with you, I won't...can't...' Rebel unsheathed Eclipse. And when he turned to me, I understood.

This was his family. And we were the hunters.

I knelt next to the Blood Familiars, stroking their heads. They pushed hard against my palms. I wished they dared talk to me, so I could say...something...to them.

Yet I had a feeling the familiars understood, even without me speaking, because they fought to their feet.

I shook my head. 'Your Keeper is ordering your arses to stay with the witches.' At their mournful whines, I held them close, whispering, 'And the first chance you get, I'm telling you to run, yeah?'

Then I held Star, like absolute power in my hands, and stalked after Rebel to the foot of the stone steps.

Rap, rap, rap.

'Three minutes. If you force me to come down there, I shall be quite put out with you,' Eden fretted. 'Purifying can be such a painful business, if I wish it.'

I rested my hand on Rebel's shoulder. Our gazes met. Whatever happened with Eden, we'd have each other's back.

I'd never had that with a bloke before.

We trudged up the cellar steps.

Rebel turned back to his family; his fingertips

rested on the hot iron trapdoor. 'I never meant to be a shadow or cause you pain. And I won't let you die on my altar. You wanted me, and I love you for that.'

I shrugged, 'I just hate you. But you're his family, so...'

Evie's eyes were closed. She murmured, her words slurring, 'I knew our angel would save us.'

Da dropped to his knees, before slumping on his front, but he forced out, 'Remember how proud I am.'

I stumbled mid-step, grabbing Rebel's sleeve. 'They've taken something. Poison? A spell?'

Rebel bolted down the stairs, leaping the final two and hurling away Eclipse, as he fell next to his family, who were sprawled, convulsing on the concrete floor.

'Help me,' Rebel pleaded, pressing shaking hands first to Ma, who was spasming, then to Da who was foaming at the mouth, and finally to Evie, whose legs jerked violently.

I froze, remembering the way Da had pressed his hand across each of their mouths.

Rebel's family had sacrificed themselves to save him. His family were his weakness. And they'd shanked that weakness before Eden could.

Hell, what did I know about that type of love?

When the witches suddenly lay still, Rebel let out a sob. He lifted Evie's lifeless body into his arms, rocking her and stroking her silken curls.

'Two minutes. Witches burning, witches burning, fetch the monster, fetch the monster, fire fire, fire fire!' Eden sang in a mocking lullaby.

I sprang down the steps, light-headed and shaking. I seized Rebel's shoulder. 'They're gone, but we're here and still set to burn. They died to stop you from being sliced by Sir Purity, so how do we escape?'

Rebel only groaned, nuzzling his face into Evie's hair. His eyes were glazed: the punk was lost in his own grief.

Yet we only had two minutes left to escape this crematorium, or just like Rebel's witch family, who'd sacrificed themselves for their angel son, we'd be corpses in the dust.

15

Grief is a devourer. It consumes, until you're hollow. A husk.

Unless you let in the darkness, and let out the demons.

Rebel clutched Evie, as if he was terrified someone would snatch her away from him. He hunched on the dusty concrete floor of the cellar, surrounded by the family who'd killed themselves to save him, stroking Evie's once ruby lips like he could caress them to life.

Despite the heat that was cooking us, trapped below ground as above the witches' house burned, I shivered.

'Bad angels are punished. Bad angels are punished...' Rebel intoned like a Victorian school kid. His gaze was distant and lost.

Rebel wasn't at home anymore; the Big Bad Boss on the other side of the cellar door had murdered him along with his family.

I shuddered at the agonising howl of Rebel's grief that clung to me through our bond.

I snarled, slashing Star through the bottles of wine on the wire rack.

Smash — the glass shattered, spraying red like a fizzing slit artery, across the cellar.

The Blood Familiars shrank back against the wall, away from the puddling burgundy and my terrified frustration.

At last, Rebel's head snapped up at the *crash*...and the gush of cold across his cheek.

'Welcome back to the living.' I wrenched his head by the hair, forcing his dazed gaze to meet mine. 'Now how do we escape being purified?'

Rap, rap, rap.

'One minute,' Eden called through the cellar door. 'I shall be having words with you both when—'

'Oh, stick it, bro,' I growled, 'you're playing at top boy, but you're only brave when you have soldiers at your back. I've no respect for blokes who don't have the balls to fight their own battles. How about you take me on?'

Rebel was up off the floor, shoving me against the wall, before I'd even seen him move. His heart beat wildly, but his gaze was hard.

Alive.

Who knew it took being pissed at me to bring him back to himself?

'Not a chance, princess,' he hissed.

I shook my head, 'Not your choice.'

'My my, trouble in...hell.' There was a pause, as if Eden was considering, and then he sounded almost regretful, 'It would be fascinating to fight you. But a leader mustn't indulge themselves. It's the vainglorious fools, with their outdated weapons and wars, who worship combat. I'm too pure.'

172

'You mean a coward,' I hollered.

Rebel pressed his hand across my mouth.

I struggled, snapping at his palm with my teeth. My breath came in panicked snorts through my nostrils.

Rebel just backed me carefully through the crunching glass of the shattered bottles, however, until we'd edged behind the wine rack. Then he pushed down a corner of stone, and a black hole gaped.

A *tunnel*.

I glared at Rebel.

We'd roasted in this cellar — his family's coffin — and all along there'd been a tunnel out of here...?

The Blood Familiars hauled themselves up, trotting to my side.

Eden sang out, 'Your protection spell is dying, like the house. Maybe I shan't feast on the witches, instead we'll burn them in the flames. Would you like to watch?'

Rebel shoved me into the tunnel, sealing us in a narrow dark, which was lit only by the twin points of our weapons. At last, he pulled his hand away from my mouth, flinching at the bruised imprints of my teeth.

I twirled around, wiping my sleeve across my lips. 'Why?' I whispered.

I knew he understood.

'This is why they died,' Rebel's gaze was cast down. The light reflected on his tear tracks; they gleamed like violet pearls. 'This priest hole. The witches have always been after helping the persecuted. They rescued Catholic Priests. Hid them here. But...' he stumbled, unable to name his family; his grief had swallowed them. 'They couldn't run fast enough. Nor fight like us. The vampires would have their scent; they're hunters, the same as us. Except, they hunt humans.'

'Your family sacrificed themselves because they knew you'd never leave them behind?'

'I don't deserve it,' he muttered.

'Bastards don't get what they deserve.' I grabbed his arm, hauling him after me down the stone tunnel.

When black mud tumbled from above, I was smothered in the earthy underground stench. I shook my head, frantically patting at my hair to dislodge the mud. Next to me, Rebel trembled.

Burnt or buried alive?

This wasn't a day for good choices.

The Blood Familiars dashed between my feet, tripping me. One glance at Spark's anxious green eyes, however, and I forced myself to smile.

Spark's ears perked, and he barked softly.

I listened, expecting to hear echoed footsteps behind us, but there was nothing but a smothering silence.

Then my nose smashed into solid stone.

Groaning, I stepped back, stretching out my fingers to test the uneven wall.

We'd reached the end of the tunnel.

Hell, there had to be some way out. *After everything, please...*

I scrabbled against the stone, ripping my fingernails. Then Rebel's hands were over mine, stilling them, before he shunted his shoulder against the tunnel's ceiling.

A hidden trapdoor. And it was stuck.

I giggled: high and hysterical. *Bastards don't get what they deserve...*

Snap your losing it *The Shining* style ass out it and help your weeping angel lift the trapdoor.

I need you, J. Please... I'm asking.

Why didn't you say?

I sighed, as the familiar violet power swirled. I rolled my neck, like I was psyching up to enter a boxing ring. Then I shoved upwards next to Rebel.

The trapdoor burst open in a shower of dirt and twigs.

Rebel pulled himself out first, before offering me his hand.

I stared up, through the square opening, at the sharp stars in the night-time sky and the speared tops of trees.

And Rebel's hand, held out to pull me to safety. I took it, allowing him to haul me into the glade. It was the same one in which we'd trained to the punk blast of the Sex Pistols: I recognised the oaks charred by our flames.

I took deep breaths of the crisp night air. Smoke stung my nostrils, as if someone was having a bonfire.

Then I remembered.

Rebel leant back into the tunnel, lifting out the squirming Blood Familiars, whilst I turned to look back at the House of Rose, Wolf, and Fox, through the thin winter trees.

At the bonfire of Rebel's life.

A dull, smouldering light, like the embers of a ciggie, glowed from the blackened, tumbled shell of the mansion.

Only one section, in the middle, didn't burn. The iron cellar, where the protection spell must still be holding out and creating a barrier around it.

Dark shapes swarmed over the middle section, infesting their fallen enemy.

Suddenly, I sensed Rebel at my shoulder. His gaze was blank, however, as he watched. Yet neither of us looked away.

Until two vampires prowled into the glade.

They wore pinstripe suits and fancy bow ties. They could've been bankers. Except for the claws and the fangs.

No one spoke a word.

The dance was brutal and short.

Blaze and Spark launched themselves at grey pinstripe with the pink bow tie, knocking him onto his back, and then savaging his wrists. The vampire tried to scream, but I stabbed Star through his vocal chords.

Bright light exploded from Star, an imploding sun, bursting out into points, until the vampire's head fried.

A quick kill.

See, bastards don't get what they deserve.

I lurched over to where Rebel had golfing cufflinks and polka dot bow tie pinned to the hard ground. Rebel stabbed Eclipse in and out of the vampire like he was a voodoo doll.

The vampire's eyes were closed; he groaned on each thrust.

Rebel shook: *in and out, in and out...*

I didn't know if Rebel would hear me, but I said quietly, 'Kill him.'

Rebel jerked, his gaze focusing. He stumbled back, swallowing convulsively. He gave a shaky nod. Then he slashed Eclipse across the bastard's throat, before he turned to me, horrified. 'I'm not the same as them. I'm not...'

'We're all monsters. Just call it by different names.'

He was dazed; grief had devoured him.

I hauled him up. 'It's time you follow me for a change.'

He nodded, blinking.

I realised then that it was Christmas morning.

On the air was smoke and blood, and like I'd

promised, I'd left behind nothing but death.

Yeah, we were all monsters.

I stuck out my tongue to catch the snow lizard-like.

The snowflake melted to nothing. I stole its life.

Soft sun, suffused through the snow cloud, stained the sky.

Rebel shielded his eyes against the light, moaning at the throbbing between his temples.

Christmas day was born, as we staggered into Hackney Cemetery.

We'd clambered up the locked Egyptian gates, which had been flanked by plinths carved with hieroglyphics, like we'd been seeking refuge in the Underworld.

The Blood Familiars had slunk between the wrought iron bars. Their ears had been pressed to their heads, and they'd nudged each other forlornly, limping. I'd only then realised their paws must've been burnt by the heat in the cellar.

I didn't know why I'd dragged us here.

Yeah, I did.

Abney Park Cemetery, Hackney, was where, clutching nothing but a violet feather, I'd been found as a baby.

Foundling. Orphan. *Outcast.*

I'd always hoped someone would come to claim me. But now I'd witnessed the *somethings* that carved their way bloody through the world…?

I was better off on my own.

Rebel groaned, sinking down behind a stone monument of a majestic lion, which roared like Aslan risen from the dead. Rebel rested his head in its shadow, away from the dawn light.

The punk had a migraine: I'd suffered their kiss enough to know. Yet I'd never seen him shudder with one before. He curled up on himself, amongst a bed of green wood spurge, as if he could disappear. His shoulders were shaking, although he didn't make a sound.

I reckoned he was sobbing.

The soft granite gravestones, eaten away by lichen, tumbled amongst the dense woodland, feasting itself on human death.

Here was Sleeping Beauty's kingdom.

I dodged around the trunk of a pale grey hornbeam, before the fox brothers settled at its base. Then I ran my fingers over the sparkling white marble of a memorial gravestone. It was carved with a powerful but sorrowful angel; I'd visited it every weekend when I was a kid.

The epitaph read:

Violet Lazarus
1896 — 1918
I don't die; I sleep

I snorted.

Except, when I'd traced her name — *Violet* — given to me too because I'd been found at the statue's feet, I'd spent years hoping she'd wake up and claim me as hers.

Yet she'd been dead for a hundred years.

And I wasn't even human.

When I smashed my fist against the marble, I gasped with the pain, as my knuckles split.

But I needed it.

To wake up.

This is no dream, Feathery-death, this is a slab of hot reality.

You have to work out why that sky-blue cutie pie of crazy, and his merry band The Pure, want you so bad or—

Get out of my head, J.

You asked, remember?

For the first time in a month, this is my choice.

Since when was I a lodger? I own this mind, hooker, I don't get my hoochie ass booted out.

Who am I?

Mine.

I shrieked, tugging at my hair. I couldn't breathe.

Rebel stroking Evie's corpse lips... The tumble of mud in the tunnel... The rise and fall of Rebel's sword thrusting into the vampire...

'Stop that.' Rebel shoved himself up, his back against the stone. He held his leathered arm across his red-rimmed eyes; this time his eyeliner had run. 'Don't go hurting yourself because of—'

'You?' When I turned my predator gaze on Rebel, he shrank back. 'A liar? Kidnapper? Killer? How about we have that quiet chat about respect, trust, and how angels don't fib to monsters?'

I was breathing too fast but I couldn't control it.

Rebel scrabbled for Eclipse, at the same time as I drew Star. Twin violet flames lit up the snow shrouded cemetery.

Rebels eyes widened as he realized — at the same time as the twisted awareness coursed through me — that I was no longer his prisoner.

And he was now alone: a grieving angel in the snow.

I shuddered. Star's power surged and swelled with mine, driving me higher and higher, until I shook to slash and burn the world.

I craved my freedom, rather than a Custodian: to carve out Rebel's secrets bloody. Now I was no longer a prisoner of the witches, I wouldn't be Rebel's.

The powers coiled inside me, whispering that this was the only way to survive, save my sister, and stop the Hackney disappearances.

It was time for a bitch to wake up.

Yet weak and broken as he was, Rebel also knew the stakes of the fight; his lips thinned. Then he slashed his sword in a sizzling arc straight for my head.

16

As a teenager, I'd hacked and customized avatars for the geeks of the gaming world.

Hell, I'd *been* that geek gamer.

Angels, vampires, knights, or beasts... whatever a bitch desired to be, I'd woven their dream. Then watched, as my customers had disappeared into their drug of choice, far away from the real world.

Later, I'd followed them down the rabbit hole. But only because I'd been able to control the avatar. An avatar I'd created.

Mine.

Real blokes? I hadn't been able to control or create. Their free will had disappointed me.

Until I'd met Rebel.

A stream of flames hissed towards my face.

I spun away, raising Star.

My panted breaths were loud in the silence of Hackney Cemetery. Snowflakes landed on my pale eyelashes, melting when I blinked. A blast of light and tremors shook through me, as the blade reflected Rebel's attack.

The bastard had been aiming directly at me.

I flinched, pinching my lips together to stop them quivering.

This was nothing like training. This was kill or be killed. No game.

I booted the olive wood spurge, flattening it against the snowy ground. When I stared at Rebel, shuddering with a raw hurt I didn't know I could feel, even though I'd been the one to start this dance, I gasped.

Rebel crouched by the lion monument, his eyes sparking with the same righteous fury as the day he'd snapped Toben's neck.

I backed against the hornbeam, snaking my arm around the icy trunk.

Rebel's lips curled into a sneer. 'What's wrong, Feathers? You're woeful bold taking on an angel, but then you reckon I'm *broken*. You never did understand. Or are you after getting off on kicking me, when I've just lost...'

I thrust away from the trunk, leaping over a granite gravestone. Rage buzzed through me, hungering to taste his pain, just as he'd hurt me. A flash blasted from my hands at him, but he dodged, springing onto the lion's head. The wood spurge burst alight beneath him.

The Blood Familiars howled, hopping back from the blaze.

I was shocked by the fox brothers' furious *gekkering* chatter as they turned, shooting me accusing glares over their shoulders. Then they skulked away, flashes of red weaving between the gravestones, into the oak woodland.

'Hey, get your arses back here, foxies.' The familiars ignored me, although their ears twitched.

I swished Star through the air like a wand. 'How about always serving me?'

'Everything's about you, so it is, *princess*,' Rebel rubbed his throbbing temple. He might not be broken, but he was weak. And that's when you shanked sharp. 'I protect and train you. Risk my life. But it's never enough for Lady Muck. I fell that day for you, but when have you ever fallen?'

The fox brothers had vanished into the gardens of Hackney Cemetery.

There was nothing left to control me now. No Custodian or Blood Familiars.

I'd even banished J.

I shuddered, stiffening. Rebel had taught me self-discipline in his sessions. But the chains had snapped.

Time to let out the dark.

'Are you still channelling Bambi, wallad?' I smirked, licking my lips. 'You're the kidnapper, and I'm the innocent prisoner. You shackled me that day, and when I win, I'll be free.'

I roundhouse kicked Rebel, knocking him back.

He let out a shocked yowl. His knees buckled, and he staggered off the monument into the fire.

Bubbled in violet and soaring on Star's power, I swaggered to Rebel, who was crawling out of the burning patch of undergrowth and beating frantically at his smouldering leathers. When he flung himself on his back, swinging Eclipse at me, I stamped on his wrist.

He howled, dropping the sword; I kicked away Eclipse.

'Is your victory worth this?' He panted

I straddled him, pinning his hands above his head. The first flash of true panic skittered across his face.

Unlike the time we'd trained together in the

glade behind the House of Rose, Wolf, and Fox, and I'd pinned Rebel like this, he didn't arch or buck beneath me. Instead, there was only a resigned stillness. And nothing hard in his red bondage trousers.

I grinned. 'I won, and this time without tricks. We can be equals now. Partners.'

'You do talk some shite.'

'Then let's not talk, pretty boy.'

A wicked rapture surged at my triumph. Rebel didn't want to be equals? Then I'd be top boy.

Hurt me, kiss me, burn me...

I pushed my lips against Rebel's, forcing my tongue inside his resisting mouth. I bit his lip, sucking at the sweet copper, trembling as the — *slam* — sweetness shivered through me.

His blood was mine. I needed it. And I'd take it.

Then I tasted the salt.

It soured the sweet, shaking me out of the ecstatic haze.

Rebel's eyes were closed, and he was weeping.

His family had killed themselves. His home had been burnt to the ground. And I'd just tried to...

I scrambled off him, backing up onto my heels.

Rebel didn't move. His face was turned away from me. His hands were clenched.

Slowly, I stood up. Everything ached. Now the angelic power had ebbed, it all felt more...real.

Is this what it was like for Rebel? When he soared on his righteousness?

I flushed as I held out my hand to him. When I didn't say anything, he carefully opened his eyes. Then he glanced at me, startled. He wetted his lips, before grasping my hand and allowing me to haul him to his feet.

'It turns out,' I scuffed my foot backwards and forwards against a mossed gravestone, 'I talk a lot of shite.'

He stared at me, before barking with laughter through his tears. 'Nobody's perfect. Not even a princess.'

When I raised Star, I hated that Rebel flinched. But then, I had just forced him to fight for his life. 'We'll search for your dad.'

Rebel touched the velvet pouch at his neck. 'And your sister. But...'

'No secrets. Honesty only from here on, or the angry monster comes out to play.'

'No secrets,' he wiped away his tears against the back of his sleeve, 'just a promise. I'll punish Eden and the bloody gits who killed my family.'

I nodded.

After what Eden had put me through? The bastard was top of my List of Asses to Kick too.

Yet I reckoned there was more to this than a feud between angels and vampires, or even Rebel and Eden.

I didn't know why, but I was also top of Eden's List.

I was free. I'd defeated Rebel. Yet I was still the hunted.

I'd passed from Dr Watt's Walk onto the boggy heath of Chapel lawns, striding briskly through the crisp snow, crunching my boots on each step, when I'd sensed, like an electric buzzing in my shoulder blades, that I was being watched.

A Big Bad lounged in the shadows of Abney Park Chapel: a fanged stalker.

I stopped, clutching my plastic shopping bag protectively to my chest. I'd broken into the back of a closed corner shop for essentials: water, baked beans, and painkillers for Rebel's migraine.

It'd been a risk though, taking the precious cargo.

I glanced at a silver birch, whose white trunk was slashed with diamond wounds, before stashing my shopping at its base. I straightened, eyeing the path back towards Rebel and edged out Star from my waist. Finally, I swaggered towards the sharp spired chapel. It rose up: bleak and Gothic.

As the shadow of the Victorian stone chapel swallowed me, for a moment I couldn't see.

Then I was spun, a hard body tight against mine. Tall and powerful. A mouth murmured hot against my cheek, 'What's with the dagger, babe? This is a Christmas day parlay.'

Parlay? The Geek Fang could've been one of my gamer mates.

I elbowed Geek Fang in the guts. When his grip loosened, I reversed our holds, slamming him back until he was pinned against the dilapidated chapel. Slates tumbled from the roof at the impact, shattering across our shoulders.

We both yelped in unison.

Geek Fang laughed, but I scowled.

I raised Star to his throat.

The army of vampires...skittering on the roof...trying to burn us alive...

Geek Fang's charcoal-grey eyes widened.

I stilled, the blade slicing into the delicate olive skin across his neck; crimson beaded and teared down, staining his black shirt.

The Fang looked like he'd stepped out of the eighteenth-century military, in long red army coat, but it hung open, over casual black jeans and leather boots.

But then Eden had been beautiful too.

I pressed the knife harder, not understanding why I was hesitating, even as Geek Fang's aromatic scent wrapped me in warmth, like a clove studded orange.

Rebel had trained me to know one thing: between hunter and vampire, one of us equalled dead.

So why wasn't I pushing in the shank?

And why wasn't the Fang struggling to stop me?

Why wasn't he fighting back?

'Call me babe again,' I hissed, 'and I'll decapitate you with a butter knife.'

Geek Fang sniggered. 'Creative. And painful. But do you always kill first, kiss later?'

I wrinkled my nose. 'That's not nice.'

Geek Fang pushed his hips against mine, with a smirk. 'Who said I was nice?'

To my surprise, instead of burning his head from his shoulders, I slapped Geek Fang, and then shoved away from him as quickly as possible, back into the patch of sunlight beyond the chapel's shadow.

We stood staring at each other, as I panted...

Why was this all suddenly...so confusing?

Geek Fang slouched back against the chapel wall like it was a bed. He crossed his arms behind his head, with a small, secret smile, as if he *knew* what I was thinking.

It made me want to slap him again.

'All right, parlay time.' He rolled his shoulders and widened his legs, like he was settling down to sleep. 'I'm Ash.'

'I don't put a name to Fangs. It'd be like naming the cow you're about to butcher and eat.'

Ash's eyes sparked: silver flashes. Dangerous as a panther.

I took one step back.

Then Ash blinked, and his eyes were normal again.

For a vampire.

Except...Ash was different.

The fiend surged under my skin, seeking to touch him and whispering he was something *new*.

Rebel had admitted that not all vampires were the same, but that didn't mean they were good.

Yet Rebel was a bad angel, and I hadn't killed him.

Yet.

I paced back to the silver birch, before steeling myself. 'Hold out your hands.'

'You know, that's never a sentence that ends well.'

I sighed. 'I'm not going chop or burn happy, bro.'

Ash pushed away from the wall, sauntering towards me, although he winced as he stepped into the light. He ran one hand through his sable wave of hair thoughtfully.

I couldn't help the swell of desire to tangle my own hand through his mane and smooth it. Not push him to his knees, like I would with Rebel, but simply stroke the wildness.

For once, I didn't crave to control. Ash wasn't an avatar.

He was the gamer.

'Even my nails are clean on this special day,' Ash held out his hands for my inspection.

I traced the strong palms, turning them over and caressing the long fingers.

No steel claws.

'Wolverine up,' I tapped his knuckle.

'I don't have that mod,' Ash pulled his hands out of mine and shook them.

My mouth twisted. 'You're not *pure* enough?'

Ash dragged his scarlet army coat closer around himself. His eyes were suddenly vulnerable and fragile, as he looked away. 'I'm not pure, Violet. I wish I could be for you.' It took a moment for me to register that he'd used my name. But then he brightened. 'I've got a shooter. You pull a sword... I go *bang*, *bang*.'

I lifted my eyebrow. 'Fight a lot of hunters then?'

He shrugged. 'I don't fight. Unless someone fights me.'

There it was again. That sense Ash wasn't the same as Eden and his army. And that I'd been fed only secrets and half-truths by Rebel.

How could I be this relaxed, leaning against a silver birch, with my shopping at my feet in the snow, chatting to a vampire, like he was some bloke from Utopia Estate?

Yet this was the most...*human*...conversation I'd had since the supernatural had fallen into my world.

I rubbed my hand against the rough bark. 'Your lot don't call me Violet. Get down with the *monster* insulting already.'

Ash flinched. Then he pushed against me, gently but insistently, holding me against the birch.

I could've thrown Ash off, but I didn't want to give up the *thud* of his heart, the heat of his cheek, and his heavy coat warming me against the winter breeze.

In the arms of a Geek Fang, I felt...safe.

He stroked a light touch to the base of my neck and I shuddered; explosions of buzzing nerve endings, for once nothing but pure pleasure, radiated down from my shoulder blades.

As I quivered, he murmured, 'You're no monster: you're one of ours. Sexy, smart, gorgeous—'

I laughed. 'Yeah, got the point.'

'Do you?' He licked up my neck, over my quick beating artery. My breath faltered. How had I forgotten the fangs? Maybe about the time he'd been calling me *sexy*? Or maybe Phoenix had been right and I craved death. 'And your blood? Just like you, it's powerful.'

Ash's fangs grazed my neck.

I should've been disgusted. Furious. Terrified.

Instead, I closed my eyes and flew on the thrill.

A *growl*, and the reassuring weight of Ash was lifted away from me.

Bellows and *snarls* echoed through the heath and up to the grey snow skies.

Bereft, I opened my eyes.

Rebel — in all his righteous wings out glory — towered next to a veined marble memorial.

He'd yanked Ash away from me, tossing him into a patch of dead bracken.

Rebel's glance at me was assessing. Then he unsheathed his sword.

Ash sprawled in the bracken and beamed. 'What's with the possessive boyfriend act, *angel*.'

It was like two gang leaders at school fighting over the same girl.

Romeo and Juliet Hackney style.

Ash's hand edged towards his waist.

His shooter.

Heart pounding, I strode towards Rebel. 'Put your dick away, punk boy, this isn't a pissing competition.'

Rebel blushed, but he slipped his sword back.

Ash rested his hand across his stomach, as if he'd never intended to go for his weapon.

'What's with the Don Juan act, *Brigadier*?' Rebel hauled Ash up by the collar of his coat, backhanding him and splitting his lip.

Ash hissed, before clouting Rebel in the guts.

I shook my head as I dived between them. 'So much for your *I don't fight* routine.'

I gripped Ash by the arm, but he shook me off.

'I didn't lie,' Ash was watching me closely like it mattered to him that I believed him. 'I said, *unless someone fights me*. Including crazy retro angels.'

Rebel roared, launching himself at Ash, but Ash laughed as he dodged.

Then Ash slipped off his army coat, and his wings burst out in dove grey majesty.

What. The. Hell?

Ash's wings were larger than Rebel's. And their tips glowed fiery violet.

Ash was a vampire. Yet he had the wings of an angel.

I hadn't realised I was staring, until I heard Rebel's muttered, 'Poser.'

I caught the way Rebel's own bent wing drooped; he turned away his head.

How would it feel to have such a damaged wing?

When Ash spun his magnificent wings, and Rebel simply stood next to the marble memorial, his own wings hanging limply, waiting to be hit, enough was enough.

'Allow it!' I booted the back of Ash's calf, startling him out of his spin.

Ash only nodded, folding back his wings and shrugging into his army coat. When he patted Rebel on the head, Rebel winced.

Ash grinned, sauntering back with what sounded like a gasp of relief to the chapel shadows.

Hell, I was desperate to follow him into the dark.

When Ash shot me a kiss over his shoulder as he strolled away, the base of my neck throbbed. 'Happy Christmas! See you soon, Violet.'

'She won't,' Rebel yelled after him, hopping from foot to foot, 'be seeing you, that is.' When Ash disappeared into the shadows, Rebel shot off a final ineffectual volley like his honour depended on it, 'So...don't be after coming back.'

I put my hands on my hips and raised my eyebrow.

Rebel deflated. 'I told you some vampires were different.'

The vampiric nature still wreathed me, as I slunk closer to Rebel; he shivered. 'What am I?'

'A hunter?' He smiled tentatively.

I grabbed him by the throat; he let me. He choked, as I threw him onto his back across the monument. His head banged against the thick iron bar embedded across it. 'What. Am. I?'

His gaze darted anywhere but mine. 'Daughter of an angel.'

'Cheers Obvious-1000. And?'

A shake. Gasp. Struggling this time.

'Daughter of the Fallen. Humans call them vampires,' he bit his lip so hard it drew blood, 'but once they were also angels. Ages ago they rebelled and now they're forced to live here on earth.'

Daughter of an angel... Daughter of the Fallen.

I backed away, shuddering.

Violet and black...both sides warring or joining in a tidal rush.

Rebel's veiled truths had forged me into a huntress of Fallen Angels.

I shook. 'Why would that Fallen army boy risk...?'

Rebel grimaced. 'The muppet was after seducing you.'

'That was...seduction?'

Ash's touch to my neck bursting pleasure from my shoulder blades... The thrill as his fangs grazed

192

my neck...and the way he'd made me laugh.

Yeah, seduction.

'What makes these — Fallen — any better than Eden?' I demanded. 'You only had us ganking the Pure.'

Rebel's gaze hardened. 'Don't believe I said better, only different. And the Brigadier would carve the wings from my back as foreplay, just so we're clear.' He flicked the chains on his bondage trousers, struggling to find the words. 'The Pure? They slaughter humans. The Fallen? They feed, but they don't kill.'

Feed.

At last it rose up: a coiling, inky-black.

I slammed Rebel back, trapping him against the marble, pushed even higher on the spiral by his shocked growl.

Then I kissed the base of Rebel's neck, as Ash had kissed mine.

I relished his moans and knowing, whilst he writhed — my prisoner — the pleasure surging through him, just as the power pulsed through me.

This was the moment before the shank sliced...

'Everybody kills,' I whispered.

Rebel stiffened under me, but it was too late.

I bit, right over the base of his neck, shooting sparks to the surface and searing the skin.

He howled, his legs kicking. His body bucked and fought against mine.

I held him down, worrying him like a dog.

I was the gamer, and Rebel was my avatar.

I'd won my freedom, but now I was reborn: daughter of angel and the Fallen.

I pressed my teeth in deeper; my lips burned Rebel.

Finally, he stopped moving.

When I staggered back, I stared at the body of

the silent angel, sorrowful in the snow.

I shook because I didn't know whether Rebel was alive or dead.

17

Rebel lay — dead as a statue — across the top of the veined marble monument. His violet and grey streaked wings hung limply outstretched. Rusty chains shackled his wrists to the iron bar sunk in the marble. Snowflakes softly landed, before melting on his closed eyelids.

Sacrificial slaughter Hackney style.

I leant over Rebel, stroking his cold cheek.

A single moment's loss of control had ghosted the land of bones and feathers echoing through my mind: the *crack* of wing-bones splintered beneath my feet.

Death crawled across my skin with burning kisses.

I didn't know how long I'd been standing in the freezing silence of the cemetery.

'Why are you crying, princess?' Rebel's agonised rasp startled me to life.

I tripped back, stumbling over my split bag of shopping, before falling on my arse.

Rebel's spluttered laughter hacked into a cough.

Cautiously, I dragged myself up, hanging onto the cool lip of the marble. 'I'm not...' I wiped at my cheeks. *Wet*. I pinned Rebel's chained wrists. 'If I am? It's because of what I have to do.'

His gaze darted to mine, before he weakly tugged on the chains, which I'd nicked from the padlocked doors of Abney Park Chapel. Then he banged his head back on the monument with a hiss. The skin on his neck was still blistered around the bite. 'What in the Jesus...? Am I after being your prisoner now?'

'You tell me.' I bit out, tightening my hold. 'You're still hiding a world from me. How can I trust you?' He cringed. 'What's with the playing *vampire* hunter when they're Fallen Angels?'

I snatched my water bottle and the box of painkillers from the ripped plastic bag, before hopping onto the monument next to Rebel. Then I balanced the pills next to his head teasingly, as I took a deep swallow of water.

He licked his dry lips. 'I reckoned it a fine thing to give you a choice.'

'Not following you, crypto.' I slammed my hand over his mouth and nose, as Ma had done to me.

His lips were cracked under my palm. I quaked with the desire to balance the water up to them. To be the one to save and protect him. Yet first, *he was mine to hurt*.

I recoiled from the thought...and the way Rebel struggled, before submitting.

He stared up at me with wide eyes.

At last, I drew away my hand.

'Ages the angels and the Fallen have been in an ancient war,' his chest heaved as he prattled out the words, frightened I'd steal his air again. 'You, Feathers, are the special one both sides want back. I fancied you needed some time, so you didn't simply pick out of responsibility or duty. I know what that's like.'

'Yeah, so special they dumped me in a kiddies' home.' I glanced away, staring at the chapel spire's long shadow...and the darkness between the oaks where Ash had disappeared. 'And call me *monster*.'

'The Pure are fanatic bastards. There's no use grousing about—'

I shook the bottle and droplets of water sprayed onto Rebel's cheek. He arched into the cool. 'Punk prisoners watch their mouths.'

'Punk prisoners have a throat on them. And a fierce headache too.'

I shook the painkillers rattling next to his ear. He winced. 'Sore, yeah?'

'Love is pain.'

I drew back, hurling the pill box against his temple. I grimaced myself at the *smack*, as it bounced off. 'Why don't the Pure have wings?'

'They cut them off.' Rebel shuddered; the tips of his own wings folded across his chest. 'It's a sign they're cut off from the angels. Purified. Look, I've made a balls of my life so far, please don't make a balls of yours because I'm a muppet.'

I gaped at him. 'That was inspiring. The light has entered my life and—'

'Dry up,' he pouted, 'I told you I was no good at talking. Angels, the Pure, Fallen Angels. They're all hunting us, and you don't have an effigy to hide you. That's what matters. End of story.' He glanced up at me from underneath his dark eyelashes. 'Now give me water and blessed pain relief, woman.'

I tipped the water to his lips. He closed his eyes, breathing hard. The first drops touched his tongue.

Then I drew back the bottle. 'Just one question first: how much do you hate me?'

His eyes snapped open. The flash of shock? No bastard could fake that.

'I-I don't—'

'Part vampire here. You're a vampire hunter. And my kind just murdered your family. Am I missing something?'

Rebel writhed, testing the chains, as he tried to scrabble backwards away from me.

I wrenched his head up by his flame of hair. 'Are we on the same side, or are you playing me?'

'Everyone's playing you, but I'm the only one who's also protecting you.'

I leant down and whispered, close to his ear, 'How'd I know if I should be a vampire, or an *angel* hunter? Or kill you all?'

Rebel blinked, opening his mouth like he wanted to say something, before snapping it shut and frantically fighting against his chains.

I smirked, resting back on my elbows.

Rebel twisted his wrists, tugging them bloody. When scarlet snaked down his arms, I rested my fingers on his chest, stilling him. Panting, he scowled at me, like a teenager caught sneaking out after curfew.

The sugary scent of his blood, melding with the static sting of his fear, was electrifying.

I raised the bottle of water to his lips again. This time he didn't drink, but with a resigned sigh, turned away his head.

Then I remembered how Rebel had held out the goblet to me when I'd been manacled to his bed without taunting or demands that I beg. I gripped Rebel's chin, turning him back, as I tipped up the bottle.

For a moment, he choked. Then he was swallowing, his throat bobbing underneath his spiked collar.

When I finally drew back the bottle, dropping it to the ground, he gave me a cautious smile. Then yipped when I plucked a dove-grey feather from his wing.

'Is this why you're so weak you can't even escape those chains?' I asked. 'And your migraine...?'

He flushed, hunching with the same shame as when Da had discovered the first grey feather in the study. 'I'm Falling, princess, and it's fierce frightening. If a Human Addict stays too long on Earth...we become the Fallen.'

I traced a finger down his cheek. I didn't even know I was trailing a burning path, as I had with Tiny Fang, until I smelt the seared flesh. 'Why would you risk...? It doesn't matter. Get your arse back to Angel HQ.'

'I can't.'

'Not asking.'

Rebel shook his head.

'The bird cage and the dark? It can't be worse than turning into...'

'You?'

'I'm not a vampire,' I growled.

'And that's why I don't hate you,' Rebel said softly.

I booted the marble. 'But if you stay here, you'll Fall.'

His wings quivered. 'Sometimes we're not free to make choices, even between bad ones.'

'Why?'

'I believe myself to be the guilty party.' I jumped at the cool, light voice behind me. I twirled round, shielding Rebel. Then blinked. An angel with the purest violet eyes, creamy skin, and golden curls, leant against the silver birch. He met my scrutiny with a considering look. 'No, that'd be you, wouldn't it, Zachriel?'

'Commander Drake,' Rebel had frozen statue-still, but breathed so fast, he teetered on the precipice of panic attack, 'this isn't... I wasn't...'

'Hush now,' Drake strolled towards us, his pale violet wings spreading out in violent glory.

An earthy scent, like ancient church incense — or frankincense — washed over me.

When Rebel trembled, I rested my hand on his shoulder.

I'd wished to see other angels.

Be careful what you wish for.

Drake was a kid in nothing but silk indigo trousers, which hung off his slim hips like he'd escaped from a harem. He was exactly the type of achingly beautiful bastard I'd have let into my bed.

Then Drake smiled: cruel and knowing. His predatory eyes were ice-cold fire.

I shrank back.

'I had to see you at Christmas,' Drake stroked his fingers through Rebel's snow dampened hair, 'and look, you're already gift-wrapped.' He tapped the chains approvingly.

Why had I allowed myself to forget that the other angels were Rebel's enemies? I'd crushed the effigy to let them in and bound Rebel sacrificial for the slaughter.

'Not your gift,' I unsheathed Star, toying with the blade. 'Better get your arse back to your Master of the Lamp, before you're whipped Arabian style.'

I was surprised when Drake's eyes clouded with

hot hurt. 'Wish to fight for him, princess?'

Princess? Wasn't that just Rebel's pet name for me?

The word startled me enough to miss Drake's step forward. He didn't even raise his hands but suddenly he'd invaded my mind.

I screamed as I was blasted backwards.

Violet strands sliced into my brain like a thousand shanks, carving it bloody.

18

Sometimes you can't face the worst. You have to hide.

I struggled onto my elbows, wincing from my wrenched muscles. Then I sank into the bed of moss, where Drake had blasted me. A statue of an angel, fallen and broken, peeked from the snow dappled green. My fingers brushed Rebel's studded leathers, scabbard, and harness, which I'd tossed onto the moss when I'd stripped him, ready for sacrifice.

Taking a steadying breath to control the agony in my head, I concentrated on the day Rebel and I had run from the Blood Familiars. I blocked out the icy snow numbing my fingers and soaking through the knees of my jeans.

Instead, I imagined the thick privet hedges of the maze at the House of Rose, Wolf, and Fox.

With a dizzying lurch, the maze shot up in my mind, blocking the questing violet. And Drake's attempt to read my memories and my secrets.

I risked raising my head to glance at Drake.

Drake was scrutinizing me, his pale eyebrows raised in shock.

Then the strands slicing through my brain, in bursts of rich frankincense, twisted.

I shrieked.

'The Commander won't truly harm you,' Rebel's words were soft and distant through my pain. 'It's all games, so it is. He only hurts lesser angels. You can battle him.'

Hedge, right turn, left, fox shaped topiary, left turn, right...frozen statue in the centre...

The strands quivered, like ribbons of skin, twitching their way through the maze.

Through my head.

Searching.

I curled around myself, slapping my palms against the sides of my head.

I'm sorry I booted you out, J, I was wrong. Please...

Save the whole song and dance, you must hide me. If harem pants discovers—

You're scaring me. I've never heard you sound so—

Like I just won the scaredy pants award? Trust me, Commander golden curls would destroy us both if he found me. You don't get it yet, but the world needs our hoochie mama asses. And only you can save us.

How?

He wants to find something at the centre

of the maze? Then let him.

The strands turned the final corner, towards the fountain carved out of marble. A rose blossomed open and as if being born from it, a fox and a wolf.

I closed my eyes, weaving my creation for Drake.

The ribbons hesitated at the edge of the fountain.

A female warrior angel, with gold wings and wielding a blazing sword, exploded up from the ice. The heroine from my computer game, glorious in her perfection, cut down the ribbons, as quickly as they wrapped around her.

Slow *clapping.*

I opened my eyes, one at a time.

Drake assessed me, his head tilted for one long moment, before in a rush that winded me, he withdrew from my mind. Then he shrugged. 'You shall have your secrets, princess. But I shall have your angel.'

'Allow that,' I shoved myself to my knees, reaching for Star.

With a bored flick of his wrist, Drake ordered, 'Stay.'

'I'm a bitch, but I'm no dog,' I snarled.

Except, I couldn't move.

Panting in sudden terror, I pulled on my knees, but they were stuck to the icy moss. My hand was glued to the hilt of Star.

It had to be a trick, but I couldn't break it, even when Drake sauntered to Rebel's chained body, and Rebel writhed, jerking on the chains to escape.

Only hurts lesser angels?

And I was a captive spectator.

'You told the princess to battle me.' The back of Drake's small hand touched Rebel's cheek. 'Lay still when I'm talking.' Rebel stopped struggling, but refused to meet his enemy's gaze. Drake's soft curls swept Rebel's lips as he leant over him. 'Why is that?'

'You know me, Commander,' Rebel smirked, 'bad angel.'

I flinched, waiting for the clout.

Instead, Drake stroked Rebel's temple, which was still creased in pain from his migraine.

To my surprise, Rebel relaxed under the touch. Until Drake whispered, 'You've forgotten who you are, Zachriel.' He grasped Rebel's hair and twisted his head to one side, exposing the base of his neck. 'Who you belong to. And the only way to make the pain stop.'

Drake pressed on Rebel's neck, and I shrank back at Rebel's howl.

Rebel reared up, every muscle straining against the impossible pain, as if he'd been electrocuted.

'Be silent,' Drake commanded coldly.

Rebel's screams cut off, yet his agony continued. He twitched against the chains, his mouth wide but his shrieks silenced.

I hadn't expected the scalding wave of possessiveness released by being forced to watch another angel inflict pain on Rebel. He might be a bastard but he was *my* bastard.

Hurt me, kiss me, burn me...

Rebel had submitted to me. Only me.

I wanted him back.

At last, Drake lifted his hand from Rebel's neck; he forced Rebel to meet his intense gaze. 'Nod if you understand now?'

Rebel raised his middle finger.

'Wallad,' I muttered.

Drake glanced at me with detached curiosity, before he noticed the offending digit. To my surprise, he almost smiled, before he stopped himself and scowled instead.

It was a glimpse of a bloke like Rebel, rather than the cold creature that burned you to your knees.

Why was the true Drake hiding?

'I've missed these sessions,' Drake trailed his hand down Rebel's chest. 'Why have you left me alone so long?' When he stroked his fingers through Rebel's feathers, Rebel quivered. 'I should pluck out each of these grey feathers one by one.'

'You know, at first I thought maybe you were the top boy angel on a power trip,' I called over. I was paralyzed but I could still shank with words. 'But now? I reckon you're just the harem boy messenger.'

Drake's shoulders hunched; his curls fell over his face. 'You know nothing of our lives.'

And the angel was shanked.

'I've met blokes like you before. The bullies at school because at home they're hiding under their beds from the monsters that hurt them.'

Drake's head snapped up. He eyed me suspiciously, as if he reckoned I'd read *his* mind. 'Monsters?' He sneered, but with a weary despair. 'We all serve monsters.'

'Yeah, but some of us get off on it more than others.'

'Shall we see which of us it is who *gets off on it*?'

Hell, I was the *wallad*.

When Drake caressed Rebel's wings, circling the feathers and massaging, Rebel squirmed and bucked. Drake's gentle kisses on the remaining violet feathers, like veneration, were familiar and intimate.

I quaked in outraged jealousy at the touch, yet also at Rebel's excited response.

How old was Rebel?

Drake looked like he was the same age as Jade, but he was a Commander. He could've been battling in these supernatural wars for *centuries*. And playing these games with Rebel for just as long.

I wanted to look away, my mouth so dry I could barely swallow, but I couldn't.

Drake watched me closely, whilst he stroked his hand over the hardness in Rebel's trousers, then worked his pulsing wings again, before backing down to soft kisses once more.

Rebel thrashed his head from side-to-side. At last I saw the tears, silent down his cheeks.

Drake was edging my pretty punk, and it was as much a torture, as the pain Drake had inflicted before.

Yet if Rebel was shaking, so was Drake. 'Have you no idea what you've done to me, Zachriel?' He wiped Rebel's tears away tenderly. Then he glared at me, and my breath was taken by his hate. 'Why are *you* always to be protected? Whilst we...' He twisted the tip of Rebel's bent wing, and Rebel howled silently, '...suffer?'

Drake dived to kiss Rebel on the lips, yet this time it was hard and impulsive, as if a forbidden touch.

Then he drew back, and once again was beautiful but cold slave plays at Commander.

I outstared the bastard.

Yet he shook his head. 'Why would you weep for a son of the Fallen?'

I looked up sharply. 'Why would *you*?'

Drake blinked. He raised his hand in confusion. Tears trembled in the corners of his eyes, spilling when he wiped his hand across them. The glare he cast me was deadly. When he spun to Rebel, he was nothing but cool detachment. 'Remember, Addict, return to me soon.' He swept his fingers down Rebel's chest. 'You didn't think I'd miss spending Christmas together?'

When Drake stalked towards me, his wings beating, I fought not to flinch.

'Bounce, pretty genie, your Master's rubbing your lamp,' I taunted.

Drake dragged the indigo silk trousers up his hips, where they'd slipped down, self-consciously. 'You know, I have also met people of your kind before. And they *are* the monsters from which I hid.' I winced. 'Inside you're keeping something.... extraordinary...from me. No one does that.' He leant closer. 'Not even you.'

Then I was falling forward on my face onto the springy moss, Rebel was howling, and Drake had vanished.

And that, my Feathery-sweetness, is why you should never have called out to the heavens for the angels to save you.

I stopped calling, J, and they still fell. And now one of them is mine.

I scrambled up, diving to Rebel.

Rebel pulled away, as far as he could in the bonds. His wings pulsed. His body quivered.

When I gently unchained his bruised wrists, he wouldn't meet my eye. He pushed himself staggering to his feet; I struggled not to grab him by his shoulders and support him.

I knew when a bitch didn't want to be touched.

Rebel slumped to his knees next to Eclipse.

'So, son of the Fallen, huh?' I said, quietly.

Rebel rested his head against the statue's stone wing, stretching out on the moss bed. He sighed, as if fibbing took more energy than Drake's *session* had left him. 'A Human Addict *and* a son of the Fallen makes me almost the worst angel. You after punishing me now for that too?'

'I reckon Genie of the Lamp already had that covered.' When I sprawled next to Rebel, he shuffled away. My lips thinned. 'Who was that bastard?'

'Commander Duma Drake...' Rebel hesitated, before he muttered, 'My gaoler for forty years.'

A birdcage prison in the dark.

I swallowed, before crawling over to the bottle of water I'd dropped and the box of painkillers, which had been knocked into the bracken. Then I knelt next to Rebel, raising two pills to his lips.

He didn't take them, as if it was a test.

'I'm not one-man band playing good cop, bad cop. Swallow the happy pills.' I massaged Rebel's temples with my other hand. He opened his lips, and his pink tongue flicked out for the painkillers. He raised his arm to take the bottle, but sank back down again with a sigh. 'Here,' I held the water up for him. He swallowed, although he watched me guardedly. 'I guess being a chocoholic wasn't causing my migraines then.'

When I sat back, he grasped for the hilt of his sword. But exhausted by the movement, he sank down. 'Balls...'

'I'm not going to fight you again. Let's agree you've a hell of a long Pinocchio nose, and I'll snap it off if you grow it any longer. But are you broken because of what Drake did to you or because you're Falling?'

Rebel's glance was sharp. 'I've been banjaxed for so long, but with you...? Sweet Christ, I was flying again.' His shoulders drooped. 'But now I'm in tatters. And you're a huntress who's rejected me as Custodian.'

'I rejected being a prisoner.'

He gave a bitter laugh. 'Any ape can see you

don't need me anymore.'

My heart beat, a deafening roar, sweeping me up, until I trapped Rebel beneath me, my hands pressed either side of his head.

A goodbye.

No way was the wallad making this a goodbye.

'I won't let Drake take you again.' Rebel could try and hide his fear but it was written in the tension of his wings. 'No need for the *I'll only slow you down* hero dramatics. You're not returning with Drake, no matter what he threatens. Look at me,' reluctantly he raised his gaze; the fragile hurt he usually hid was breath-taking up close, 'I've got your back. I won't let you Fall.'

'I'm bad, but I'll never allow myself to be one of the Fallen.' His fingers tightened around Eclipse.

Slap — I'd smacked his hand away from his sword, like a schoolmistress whacking the back of a naughty kid's knuckles, before I'd even realised I meant to.

Rebel cradled his scarlet hand, but his gaze was thoughtful.

Violet and black spun webs round us, furious and possessive, cocooning us together.

'Killing yourself doesn't make you the noble knight,' I pulled back, balling the snow between my fingers, 'but the bloke who gives up, rather than battles to the end. Or do you just want to copy your family?'

'Don't talk about my family—'

'We're fighting this. And your punk arse isn't leaving me when my sister is still missing. We made a deal. What if the Hackney kids were taken by angels? Our next move is to take this beef to Eden's turf, rather than letting him hunt us. I need you.'

'You need me?'

I froze, shocked by Rebel's hushed awe. He

stroked one shaking hand down my arm.

I did need Rebel. To find my sister and the other kids. To fight beside me against the Pure...

Because he was mine.

Yet unless he healed, we'd be targets for Eden when night fell. And I'd be alone to protect us both.

'Better get you fixed up.' I shoved Rebel against the fallen angel, snogging him hard in the wet snow.

When his hands weakly pushed at me, I pulled away.

'A fib,' Rebel bit at his full lower lip, 'remember? Angel kisses don't heal.'

I swooped on his lip, taking it between my teeth instead of his...and then I sank in my teeth.

Hell, if I was honest...? The vampiric power coiling and snapping inside had wanted to do this every time he'd torn his lip between his teeth.

Rebel stiffened, as I sucked.

Slam.

Sugary copper hit me in a sweet wave.

But it was even sweeter, when I drew back and bit *my* lip, before forcing my own blood into Rebel's mouth.

This time, when he struggled under me, I didn't allow him to escape.

Instead, I fed him the trickle of blood.

Slam.

I juddered, snow pattering behind my closed eyelids, as every atom danced alive on the sensation of our shared blood.

Slam.

Better than the moment a shank sliced...

Slam.

An explosion of life: I was flying.

'If Angel kisses don't heal, how about their blood?' I murmured. 'Word on the street is mine's powerful.'

Rebel turned away his head. It booted me in the gut to see the...*disgust*...and tears in his eyes.

Yet when I shuffled back, he snatched my arms. Then he was snogging me fiercely, sucking at my lip.

Gently, I pushed him back, before holding out my palm and pulling out Star.

He blinked, before baring the long line of his throat above his collar, as if he expected me to cut his head from his shoulders even now for his sins. Instead, I curled closed my palm, his trust tempting me to pay him back in kind.

And I'd never trusted a bloke before. Not after Phoenix.

Don't do this. The pretty boy is one step from fangs and claws.

I bared my neck, as Rebel had; Rebel watched me from underneath his eyelashes. Then I sliced a thin cut down my throat.

You're feeding an Addict. If you bind the eyeliner punk to you with blood, you'll have to kill him to free yourself, else he'll kill you.

We're the same, J, he understands.

And we both know your choices...feathers and bones...violet and black. Do you trust another monster?

Rebel snarled, before leaping onto me and knocking me back onto the moss. The small amount of blood from my lip had already strengthened him. He held me down by my shoulders, his hard body heavy against mine.

Had I saved Rebel or birthed a vampire?

I gasped, when black flecks sparked in Rebel's eyes, before he lowered his mouth towards my bleeding neck.

19

Death had suckled at my neck every day on the Utopia Estate, so the question of where I'd bleed out lullabied me each night.

Still, I'd never reckoned I'd die in Hackney Cemetery, where I'd been abandoned as a baby, whilst the snow wept, in the arms of a Falling angel.

When Rebel thrust me back harder onto the damp moss, I cried out.

My cheek rubbed in the frozen snow as I twisted away my head. I gulped; sticky blood dribbled down my neck.

Rebel clawed at my shoulders: a wolf holding down its prey. His tongue flicked out, tasting the air.

This wasn't how I'd imagined Rebel feeding from me, and yet if he'd offered me his neck, I might have taken his blood with the same brutality.

I was only half vampire and I already knew what happened when I lost control.

Did that mean I had no choice?

Rebel panted, his teeth bared; he lowered his mouth to my throat.

Hell, I'd bitten and burned Rebel and I hadn't asked all pretty first.

You've awoken a vampire. Look at him. The idea of feasting on you has him salivating.

I froze.

Rebel sniffed at my neck, before he licked the long line of crimson, which had snaked down to my collar.

Death isn't noble, remember?

When I writhed, Rebel growled, yet he didn't bite.

Instead, he licked down the cut again, slow and gentle, before sucking.

I gasped, my body arching.

The thrill. Joy. Calm. As if Rebel was inside me, on each intimate lick and suck: his emotions and mind.

The cold snow feathered my face in ice fairy kisses.

Slam — coppery sweetness spun me to a silent world, where there was nothing but blood...and Rebel.

No Hackney, supernatural world, or land of bones and feathers.

Instead, there was only us: two monsters trapped together.

Needing each other.

Bound.

Rebel kissed along the cut, savouring the last traces of blood in worship. When he pulled back, his loss was shank sharp.

He smothered a yawn with the back of his hand, rolling next to me onto his back with a sigh. 'Fair play to you, that was brilliant!' He muttered sleepily, his eyes already half-closed.

Then his head lolled back and he was gone.

Asleep.

Typical bastard bloke.

I pulled myself up against the angel statue, pressing my fingers to the cut; I gasped at the pain, but my fingers came back unstained, as if the gash had been sealed.

'Sleeping beauty, I'm excited it was good for you too but wake up.' I shook Rebel's shoulder, but his face was as still as the time I'd bitten his neck. What if my...impure...blood had killed him? When I backhanded him, his head rocked to the side. I stared at the red mark over his cheekbone. 'Don't just lie there, it's almost night. The Pure will rip off your wings and purify the hell out of me. We have to go.'

Rebel slept undisturbed. The snow settled on him, shroud-like.

I howled in frustration, cradling him in my arms.

It's your blood, Violet-juice. It's fabulously powerful.

You said he'd turn on me and tear out my throat.

He could've...and he still could. Don't kid yourself, you're playing with dangerous toys now.

Come on, lighten up. The little punk just needs some sleep.

And if nap time doesn't end before nightfall...?

Then you're on your own. Except for me.

I glanced at the angel sleeping in my arms.

An angel with a bruise, purple and swollen, blossoming on his cheek.

The sky above the wide branches of oaks and Abney Park Chapel's spiked spire was a steely grey, low with snow clouds.

I couldn't protect us both.

I shoved Rebel towards the marble statue, scraping the bracken over him and masking the red of his trousers, until only his face showed between the prickly brown and the green of the moss.

And his face could've been a statue's.

Rebel still had the effigy on the chain of his trousers. He hadn't crushed his.

I'd crushed mine.

Sharing my blood with Rebel had transformed...something. I'd already had a small taste of Rebel; I could feel the shadow of him inside me. But now he'd fed fully from my blood.

He was bound to me.

My responsibility. Both sides of my nature chorused it in unison. Rebel was mine to hurt.

And protect.

When Eden and his soldiers came for us, they'd discover only one monster to purify.

Cold.

Dripping cold dribbled onto my lips.

My tongue flicked out.

Water: fresh and *purifying*.

I jolted to my knees; they sank into a thick blue carpet. I blinked against the bright light of a chandelier and suffocating warmth.

My shoulders ached because my arms were wrenched behind me.

Steel handcuffs bit into my wrists.

I launched myself on top of the bastard who was hovering over me holding a crystal glass.

The vampire *eeped* and struggled, before stilling like a bird in a cat's claws, when I shoved my knee between his legs.

Two black eyes, in an elfin face too young to be in Jade's class at college, scowled at me. His jet curls trembled; his wings beat, their tips pulsing violet.

Wings...?

I sighed, pushing up from the kid. He warily shuffled onto his bottom, patting at the spilt water with his palm.

The vampire wasn't the Pure: he was the Fallen, like Ash.

A prisoner, the same as me.

I'd hidden in Hackney Cemetery all Christmas Day, alongside Rebel, but he hadn't awoken. When night had come, I'd climbed onto the tallest stone cross monument and waited for Eden to cut me into a fine red mist.

The Pures' eyes had sparked in the dark. A hundred fallen stars on earth, when at last they'd found me. No one had spoken. Eden hadn't even been there.

I'd called for J, but the violet rage hadn't been righteous, it'd barely tingled down my arms.

I'd drawn my dagger, the question of where I'd bleed out, finally answered.

Yet knowing I'd saved Rebel had steeled me.

Except, when the Pure had swarmed over me, as if I'd been no more real than an avatar, they hadn't slashed or burned, but had knocked me out by pressing my neck.

And now I was here: in Eden's lair. A grand Victorian wedding hall, with tables and chairs in ivory silks and high sculptured ceiling.

I glanced down at my scabbard: no Star.

I groaned. I hoped I'd dropped the dagger in the battle in the Cemetery. At least then Rebel would have his father's weapon.

I eyed the exit: grand oak doors behind a ballroom dance floor. At the other end, there was only a raised polished wood stage. Above us, a high painted ceiling swirled in a glorious mural of the blue and white heavens.

'When he brings me here, sometimes I can pretend I'm flying,' the vampire smiled timidly, before he shrugged, 'and sometimes not.'

'We're not talking buddies, Fang Face,' I pushed into a crouch, my trapped shoulders protesting. I peered around an ornate table, which was laid out with silver cutlery, at the ballroom. There were hundreds of identical tables and high backed chairs. The scent from the lilies in glass bowl centrepieces was overwhelming. 'You? Vampire. Me? Huntress.'

Smash — the vampire booted the crystal goblet, shattering it. 'Me? Anarchy. You? Bitch.'

I gaped at him. Then I grinned.

The wallad had balls.

Suddenly, Anarchy reminded me of Jade.

The longing for my kid sister...loneliness...fear for her...rose up, until I gasped from it, doubled over.

Anarchy?

In only a pair of tatty blue jeans, with a curl hanging over his nervous eyes and a body battered with purple bruises, looked more like the poster boy for slavery.

I hadn't expected the outrage storming inside to drain the bastard who'd ripped away the kid's strength, manhood, and identity.

It roared to give Anarchy back his name.

Vampire huntress? Who the hell was I kidding?

Choice. It's always been yours. But be careful because you're in the Pures' world now.

They don't believe in true choice.

I'll just have to convince them different then, won't I?

Eden's not like our Irish punk. He doesn't love the world; he wants to feast on it.

I pulled my hands against the steel handcuffs.

No luck.

'Kinky bastard vampires,' I muttered.

Anarchy laughed. 'I'd help you but...' He edged closer. 'Eden's punishments are inventive. And it's enough the ceremony's tonight.'

Ceremony, J, tonight.

That's top of the things you don't want to hear when you're trussed up.

***Inventive punishments* comes in a close second.**

I glanced at Anarchy. 'How long was I out?'

'Since last night.'

When I pushed up and paced towards Anarchy, crunching over heart-shaped confetti that was ground into the carpet, he backed against the striped white-and-blue wallpaper. 'The Big Bad here is Eden. I don't give a hell about anything else. He's my only enemy right now. So, how do we gank him?'

Anarchy blinked, before a shy smile curled his split lip. 'Burn the wanker,' he rubbed his hand over burns that patterned his chest, like a child had been playing with matches. 'He hurts with fire because it terrifies him.'

'And I just trust you, yeah?'

Anarchy shook his head, his dark gaze serious.

'Never.' When he reached towards me, I backed away, but he only stroked my hair with quivering fingers. 'I'm sorry. Eden brainwashes to purify. To make you one of *them*. I've fought but I can't even save myself. Forgive me for not saving you, princess?'

I jerked away. 'I save myself. And you're not one of them yet. My blokes don't give up.'

His lips parted, before he straightened his shoulders. 'Then I won't.'

Bang — the grand doors at the end of the Victorian ballroom swung open.

Anarchy cringed back at the *tap, tap, tap* of footsteps down the central wooden dancing strip of the ballroom.

Although my heart raced, I turned to Eden with a smirk. 'Why not let me free, so we can play?'

Eden faltered, his wide smile frozen. Then he tilted his head, his brunet sweep of hair falling over his brood of mutton chops. He stuck his hands in the pockets of his sky-blue velvet coat. 'Why, I'm delighted you're already feeling at home. Welcome to Perfection Hotel!' He sprang on a table, shattering a glass centrepiece in a spray of white lilies. 'All may enter, but only the pure may leave.' His smile widened, canines lengthening to fangs. 'Except the Pure don't leave because they're mine. Soldiers, soldiers, pure in a row, and one day soon, they're going to kill, you know.'

I tilted my head. 'What are you, the storyteller for Fang kiddies?'

Eden pouted, before calling, 'Stephanie, we have a lost soul to save tonight.'

When Anarchy let out a strangled cry, I stiffened.

A Pure vampire had prowled behind us, whilst Eden had been posturing.

In charcoal business suit, lilac shirt and smart blonde hair in a ponytail, you'd have reckoned Stephanie a mild receptionist...until the claws slashed from her knuckles and her gaze hardened with the look of a torturer offered their favourite treat.

Before Anarchy could dash to the other side of the ballroom, Stephanie had crushed her arm around his slim neck, dragging his wrist high up his back. 'Where are you going, sweetie?'

Pop — Anarchy's shoulder dislocated.

Eden leapt off the table, before glancing back at me. 'And where is *your* angel? Was it his decision or yours to allow the witches to burn in your place?' He twirled around, holding out his hand. Stephanie shoved me with her heel onto the wooden strip towards him. 'Dance with me.'

I shuddered. 'In your dreams, bastard.'

'Indeed, monster, every night for the last twenty-one years.' Eden gestured across the ballroom.

A willowy vampire in mauve evening dress stepped out of a hidden door onto the stage.

I rolled my eyes when she raised a violin.

A gentle, romantic waltz started up.

Eden was a dramatic bitch.

Eden slipped his arms, as if around the waist of an invisible partner, before waltzing across the gleaming floor towards me.

I grimaced, backing against the ivory table with a *clatter* of cutlery.

The calming coils of the violin drowned out Anarchy's cries, as Stephanie dragged him up onto the stage, before backhanding him. He fell in front of a long wooden block.

Anarchy's terrified gaze met mine over its top.

It was an executioner's block.

My breath caught.

'Such a sad boy and a rare failure.' I jumped: Eden's pale face was inches from mine. He scrutinized me, resting his hand lightly on my hip. I cringed as his fingers drew circles. 'Purity, I offered, but impure he wished to be,' his lips whispered onto mine, 'but tonight we try one last time to save the Fallen.'

'And me?'

Eden clutched me tighter around the waist, swinging me out onto the dance floor. When I fell over my own feet, he laughed, pulling me into the dance. All was lilies, sky-blue, and the sweet sickening glide of the violin. He sniffed my hair. 'You, my monster, have a choice.'

Do I play the game?

Whatever this dancing ass offers, it's not a true choice.

Trust no one.

Eden brushed my cheek. 'Time to take the first step to purity.'

Eden's canines slowly descended into glistening fangs; he grazed his teeth against my skin. Then he licked up the cut on my neck.

I stiffened.

My blood belonged to Rebel.

I snarled, kneeing Eden in the balls. He collapsed to the floor with a satisfying groan.

Stephanie roared, leaping down onto the dance floor. She twisted my hair, yanking me away from her leader. 'Who said you could play rough?'

She hauled me onto the stage.

I kicked and stamped at her matching lilac kitten heels, but with my hands cuffed, it was like being the fly bothering the lion.

She elbowed the violin player in the guts to stop her playing and then thrust me onto my knees next to Anarchy.

Anarchy shot me an apologetic smile around his tears.

I bumped his shoulder. 'A bitch doesn't give up.'

Anarchy nodded, tossing back his curls. He glared defiantly at Stephanie.

Surprised, Stephanie raised an eyebrow, her lips thinning; Anarchy's shoulders drooped.

Eden dragged an ivory silk chair scraping along the wood, until he sprawled across it in front of the stage: his throne.

When Stephanie drew a silver staff from her belt, Anarchy shook.

'Please, I'll try harder...' Anarchy's eyes were wide and desperate.

Why did it have to remind me of Tiny Fang? He'd been begging through his gag for me not to hurt and kill him.

Yet I still had.

And I'd got off on it, as much as Stephanie was now.

A black flame exploded from the staff on one side, turning it into a giant burning axe.

Stephanie booted my neck, bending me over the block.

When I twisted my head, two dark eyes sparked, looking straight back into mine. Anarchy was bent over right next to me.

Both our necks were for the chop.

I fought not to squirm.

'Your choice,' Eden's light voice made it sound like he was merely offering us raspberry or strawberry jam with our scone, 'is between who is saved and who dies. You've both forced upon me the unwelcome truth that not everyone is fit to live in my new world. But here's the game: shall the monster or the Fallen die?'

My gaze never left Anarchy's. Suddenly, his small fingers reached for mine behind my back.

A vampire hunter comforting a vampire?

Except, maybe it was a vampire comforting a vampire hunter. And wasn't that a bitch?

Eden's tone became shriller. 'Tick tock, goes the clock. In one minute, you shall each offer your choice and reason for it. If you refuse, then you both die.' I stroked my thumb over the back of Anarchy's quivering hand. 'I'll be playing your judge tonight, and Stephanie will be your executioner.'

The scorching heat from the axe seared my neck. Tendrils of smoke curled from Anarchy's skin.

What had J told me about *choice*?

I wet my dry lips. 'I don't need a minute. You want to know who to kill? Ask.'

Anarchy's eyes widened, his eyelashes matted wet, whilst he braced himself.

I gritted my teeth. The executioner's blistering axe pressed closer.

Eden was nothing but a puppet master playing with his toys.

I wasn't any bitch's puppet.

When Eden waved his hand, the oppressive heat lifted from my neck. 'Then I shall ask: who dies, monster or Fallen?'

Anarchy squeezed my hand, giving a resigned smile.

'Monster.' Anarchy goggled at my response. I smirked back. 'My reason? Do I look like a bitch who could be purified?'

Now it was my turn to squeeze Anarchy's hand. He swallowed.

'Rebellious Fallen?' Eden's smooth voice trembled with rage.

Anarchy's mouth quirked upwards, copying my

own smile. 'Fallen.' He poked his tongue out at me, and I stifled a laugh. 'Reasons? Do I look like a bitch who could be purified?'

A *bellow*. Followed by a *crash*. Then *tap, tap, tap...*

You're playing with fire and to save a Fang who's young enough to be Jade's kid brother.

He's cute, but you'd be a cradle snatcher if you rode that ass—

Not everything's about...not anymore.

You can't trust him. You don't know him.

Save it. I'm not shanking Anarchy in the back to save my own arse.

I won't play this wingless sadist's game.

Sometimes you're caught in a game, whether you want to be or not.

Eden hauled me up by the hair, hurling me across the stage.

I gasped, as my arms twisted, trapped beneath me by the handcuffs.

Anarchy tried to stand, but Eden shoved him with a *crack* back to his knees.

'I judge between the pure and impure.' Eden stretched out Anarchy's ash-grey left wing, caressing the tip, until Anarchy shuddered. 'Only the perfect may come to tea.' He mock bowed towards me, as if we were courtiers in a dance. 'Monster and Fallen choose death at a ball, my oh my, what shall become of them all?'

'We shank ourselves because of your bad poetry?'

Eden's eyes blazed. 'Monsters with no heads can't hear poetry.'

I'd known it from the moment I'd woken up in the white-and-blue heaven swirled ballroom. In fact, from when I'd been carried into the blackness by the waves of the Pure on Hackney Cemetery.

I'd been a dead woman walking. My true choice had been how I died.

20

Choice is a crown only worn by the free and the powerful.

Trapped on the Utopia Estate, a shank had earned respect but not choice.

Imprisoned in Jerusalem Children's Home, rules had guided my every breath, until breaking them hadn't been a choice but survival.

Eden loved to offer choice because the trick was for the poor bastard to condemn themselves.

'Please...kill me, not my princess,' Anarchy struggled up, and again Eden pushed him back over the wooden block.

I twisted on the cold floor of the stage; the citrus polish caught in my nostrils reminding me of sitting cross-legged at the back of the stage in school assemblies. But I hadn't been handcuffed then.

Or about to die.

'The death of a monster should be a grand affair. I shall hold a special party here for the Pure.' Eden clapped his hands, giddy as a kid before his birthday. 'But first, we have a disobedient Fallen to save. And then we all have dinner reservations.'

Eden wrenched Anarchy's wing along the wooden block. He stretched it out, twisting Anarchy's back, until his shoulder blade pressed against the block.

I thumped my forehead on the stage, growling in my throat.

I warned you, Violet-kitty: the game still plays, even if you storm away from the board. You have to be playing to win.

When Stephanie tested her flaming axe to the base of Anarchy's wing, he whimpered.

'You're breaking your own rules.' I squirmed onto my knees, panting. The Victorian ballroom lay before us, dressed for a wedding, whilst Eden threatened death. It swept in a grand slice of blue-and-white heaven; and we were trapped in hell. 'You said monster or Fallen. Not both.'

Eden's grin was wide. 'Your choice was between who was saved and who died. You shall die, and the Fallen here will be saved through purification. When we carve his wings from his back, he will be clean. How sad you believed yourself the hero. Rejoice, rejoice, for today Anarchy will be pure!'

I wrenched my arms against the handcuffs, until my wrists bruised. 'And I'll burn your sky-blue world to violet, if you touch his wings—'

The violin struck up a soaring joyful ode.

Black flames blazed. The axe fell.

And Anarchy screamed.

Anarchy quivered, kneeling on the angel mosaic floor at Stephanie's feet. His wings were bloody cauterised stumps. When he glanced up, he caught me looking and flushed.

Eden lounged at the head of the mahogany table, with Stephanie and me at either side of him. Plush, blue velvet drapes swung at the windows of the restaurant, and a wing shaped mirror hung above a marble fireplace.

Eden had chosen the table furthest from the spitting roar of the open fire; I wondered if Anarchy was right about fire being Eden's weakness.

What type of bloke took his own fear and spent his life shanking others with it?

The restaurant inside Perfection Hotel — Eden's Lounge — was crammed with the Pure. They could've passed for human, except for the blackness of their eyes, when they scrutinized me.

And that tingle between my shoulder blades.

I shifted on my padded leather, sinking further into it. The rich meaty aromas of roasts — gravy, potatoes, and lamb — made my stomach growl.

All I'd had for Christmas dinner had been cold baked beans out of a can.

Where was the condemned woman's last meal?

Anarchy whined, wrapping his arms around himself, as his body spasmed with pain.

Stephanie, however, gripped Anarchy's curls and jerked him back into position on his knees.

'Feed our newest soldier,' Eden speared a large slice of beef wellington into his own mouth, 'it's hard on them in the first days. Transformation into purity. He's a lucky boy, he has Stephanie here to teach him his lessons.'

'Are you hungry, darling?' Stephanie tore a thin

shred of lettuce from her Caesar salad and held it out on her palm, like Anarchy was her pet rabbit.

I'd have sneered...something...but Eden had rammed a leather gag in my mouth, before he'd led me into his joint.

I guess the bloke was touchy about his poetry.

I bit the leather, hating the way it tasted; I sucked down my saliva.

How screwed was my Boxing Day, when I was sitting gagged and handcuffed in the fanciest restaurant I'd ever been in, surrounded by psycho vampire fanatics?

Anarchy nibbled at the lettuce, wincing when Stephanie tapped his head.

Stephanie's gaze was flat and hard as she simpered, 'Good job, sweetie.'

'I imagine you've been told lies about us,' Eden touched his chest with his long pale hand, as if it hurt, 'that's why you've *murdered* so many of my friends.' I flinched, remembering searing my touch down Tiny Fang's cheek. Eden brushed his cheeks, wiping away imaginary tears. 'No more to play with me, dead are they, can't come to tea.'

'She's a hunter,' Stephanie scoffed, 'their hearts are stone.'

I shrank back.

Hell, they were right: I'd revelled in the kills because what was one dead vampire?

One dead Fallen Angel. One dead the Pure. One dead *friend.*

'Lies like we're the vampires who kill?' When I straightened in my chair, Eden nodded smugly, banging his fork *clinking* against his plate for emphasis now he had my full attention. 'Angels kill. The Fallen too. There's only righteousness and perfection, not good or evil in this dance. Besides, now I've learnt a new trick to feed without killing. A delicious Utopia dessert of my own.'

Utopia? Eden was talking about feeding on *my Utopia Estate?*

Anarchy moaned, juddering as a new wave of pain swept through him. Stephanie pushed his jet curls, which had fallen in front of his eyes, gently behind his ears. Then her hand slipped lower, between his shoulder blades, and then to the base of his back. She played her fingers around the waistband of his jeans.

Anarchy tensed, suddenly motionless. His breathing became raspy and uneven. His feverish gaze darted to mine.

'With wings we fall, without wings we rise,' Eden forked a broccoli tree, crunching hard. 'I wonder though, my monster, whether an abomination such as you could ever be pure?'

I bristled. If I got free, Eden was going down Hackney style.

Eden carefully crossed his silver cutlery on his plate, before leaning closer. 'Do you even know who you are? *What* you are?'

I choked on my own spittle.

You have to be playing to win?

I tilted my head, as if interested.

Eden wiped at the corners of his mouth with an ivory napkin. 'Eyes are the windows to your soul, you know...'

He reached forward to pull down my sunglasses.

I jerked backwards, tumbling out of my chair and cracking the back of my head against the mosaic floor. I was breathing so hard through my nose, white stars danced.

Then Anarchy was cradling me, and through the haze, I heard his calm voice, 'Trick is to breathe slowly in these wankering gags. I've got you.'

Slowly, the globe lamps of the restaurant fuzzed back above my head, along with Anarchy's anxious face. Despite his agony, he held me close.

Until Stephanie booted him in the stump of his right wing, and he howled.

'You're the Pure now, darling, so don't go dirtying yourself by touching monsters, or I'll have to cleanse you, well, more than I will anyway.' Stephanie ground her kitten heel into Anarchy's shoulder blade. 'Little soldiers need training.'

I arose, vibrating with a fury at the abuse to the Fallen who'd cared for me. I kicked, sweeping Stephanie's legs out from under her. She flailed, before stumbling onto her arse. Her business suit ripped along its expensive hem, as she let out a startled *squawk*.

The other diners suddenly hushed, before sniggering and snorting behind their hands.

I might be handcuffed and gagged, but I could still fight dirty.

Stephanie twisted to me, her ponytail spilling onto her shoulders and her lilac shirt half hanging out of her trousers. She raised her fist.

Anarchy dove in front of her. 'Cleanse me, bitch.'

Eden chuckled, so close to my ear, I jumped. 'Two rebels in Perfection Hotel, what shall I do?'

'Let us go?'

Eden kissed my hair, wrapping his fingers around the ash blonde strands. I tried to pull away, but he held me still. 'Here comes a candle to light you to bed, and here comes a chopper to chop off your head.'

I blanched, forcing myself not to cringe from his touch, as Eden spun me in a wild dance, before yanking me close against his velvet coat. Trapped in his lily scent, I battled to breathe through my nose, against the rising panic.

...Here comes a chopper to chop off your head...

It was easier to tip back my head and lose myself in the sparking stars in the night sky, than to stare ahead at the ranks of the Pure on Perfection Hotel's roof terrace, and see the stars fallen to earth in their glowing eyes.

As I knelt in the ice-freeze, cheeks whipped raw by the snow breeze, it was dying like a war criminal — a monster — that caught the sob at the back of my throat.

Dying alone.

You're not alone, never forget that.

I'm sorry, J, I let you down.

Hold on, the diva awards are mine. How's your choice going?

Too busy dying to talk now. Unless you violet me up...?

Righteousness isn't a trick to pull out of your slutty hat, or do you want to transform into the wingless wonder in blue? A tyrant, mad on his own power?

I glanced at Eden, who was sauntering in front of his followers, sweeping his coat back and forth like he was posing for photographs.

I rolled my shoulders, rubbing at my wrists. Stephanie had taken off my handcuffs and gag once the army had assembled.

A *squeal*. *Guffaws*. And the *blast* of Stephanie's axe.

I pushed myself up onto shaky legs.

Decorative wrought iron tables and chairs dotted the terrace beneath the melting snow and Eden's army, slouching or gossiping between them, looked so...ordinary. Suits and wool coats, mixed with dresses and scarfs. If it hadn't been for their eyes, they'd have passed for human. But then their fangs and claws were hidden. And they'd hacked off their wings.

Anarchy was trapped between a jeering circle. Every time he stumbled to escape, he was shoved back into the centre with Stephanie: his tormentor.

His trainer.

Rebel had been my Custodian. Yet when we'd trained in the glade, it'd been a thrilling dance: blade and fire, Sex Pistols and kisses, control and...love.

I glanced away, as Stephanie blistered a searing line along Anarchy's gut with her axe, before he could twist away.

Anarchy howled. When he spun, stumbling to the edge of the circle, Stephanie yanked him back by his curls, painting his back crimson.

'Roll up, roll up, death of a monster, lifetime special,' I hollered over Anarchy's weeping, spreading my arms like wings.

The army of the Pure fell silent.

Eden turned to me, his full lips curling up. 'My, you are eager to sacrifice yourself. Yet would you be, if you knew the truth?' His gaze clouded. 'Lazarus rises, and we shall say, all our goodbyes.'

'Hold the crazy line. Lazarus, what...?'

Eden only whirled to his disciples, pointing at the heavens. 'Exult, my soldiers, for tonight we purify the destroyer.'

Destroyer?

I stumbled backwards to the edge of the terrace. Eight floors below? The pavement, in front of the grand porch entrance. I clasped onto the crumbling stone ledge, before clambering up.

I'm sorry Jade...that I didn't find you...save you...

Eden held out his hand with a *click* of his fingers.

Stephanie glanced down at her axe, but then hesitated. 'I could slay the dragon, Eden darling, if the fire—'

With a growl, Eden snatched the weapon from her, although his shoulders stiffened and his fingers trembled.

'Don't worry, Eden,' I said, my voice as soft as silk, even though my mouth twisted, 'nobody's perfect. Not even a fanatic.'

Anarchy's gaze met mine, intense and steadying; tears streamed down his cheeks, but he still forced a smile.

Not every bastard Pure on that terrace hated me.

I wasn't alone.

Eden lunged, flames fizzing from the axe.

I took a deep breath. Then I closed my eyes and waited for Eden to execute a monster.

21

Feathers.

They cocooned me in the soft scent of safety and home.

Slam.

Coppery sweetness spun me to heaven.
I quivered, caught in the scent of angel blood.
Rebel's blood.
Hell, if this was dying, it kicked living's arse.
My eyes snapped open.
Rebel was holding me on the stone ledge of the roof terrace, before the furious glares of an army of the Pure.

His mottled wings, which he'd wrapped around me, were as hard as steel, but his smile was fragile.

'Hold on,' Rebel yanked my arms around his waist, as his wings stretched out. Then he dove upwards into the cold night sky.

'Guests may not leave the party early!' Eden shrieked, bouncing on his toes.

I sniggered. But then caught Rebel's flinch. 'You're... This is... You're saving me?' I blinked, gripping so hard to Rebel's hips, I must've been leaving bruises.

He nodded. 'I'm not the one who abandons people.'

Hollers, the *whoosh* of flames beneath my boots, and *bang* of gunshots.

Rebel swooped, dodging.

I gasped at the glorious buzz of soaring through the dark in the arms of an angel.

My heart thundered: I'd stood at the cliff edge of death — jumped — and flown.

'Lazarus rises, bitches,' I yelled down at Eden and his soldiers. Their eyes gleamed like hyenas' in the night. 'I bet you wish you weren't wingless now?'

Whizz — a bullet grazed my ear.

Best not to read the fanatic jackasses until you've actually escaped. After all, your ride could break down. The punk's wing is wrecked.

But he still risked saving me.

Why? Oh, that's right, girl, because you bound yourself by blood. Say hello to your baby vampire.

I shifted in Rebel's wings. The speckled violet feathers pulsed amongst a sea of grey.

Rebel clutched me closer.

The moon caught on the spear tips of the

Thames, which curled far beneath us, criss-crossed with bridges. Cars and black cabs sped between blocks of skyscrapers and curving terraces. Cathedral spires and cupolas rose like illuminated spectres.

A human world, spread like a kid's playset.

Violet and black seethed at the thought: to mould the world and make it mine.

When I shuddered, Rebel stroked my arm. Then suddenly, his bent wing spasmed.

I screamed, as we tumbled, spinning through the black.

Rebel beat his wings frantically, plunging us further towards Hackney.

We were about to get up and personal with London Fields.

I braced myself, as we crashed into the frozen green. We cracked over a bench, before barrelling into a wonky goal post.

My ankle twisted.

I scrubbed my face in the slushy snow, struggling to bring down the coursing adrenaline spike. My whole body shook, even my toes drummed on the grass.

I touched my throbbing ankle and yelped; I slammed my fist into the ground with a growl. 'I won't be flying Rebel Airlines again. You're lucky the army didn't shoot us down.'

Rebel's eyes flashed with hurt, before he smothered it with a smirk. 'You after going back? That's the first time I've flown since the gits hurt my wing.'

I started to shake my head, but then stopped.

Anarchy.

The kid Fallen who'd tried to save me was still trapped with Eden.

How the hell could I abandon him?

'Yeah, we're going back.'

Rebel gaped at me. Then he briskly snatched his leathers, which had been stashed behind the goal post.

Then it was my turn to gape. 'You *chose* to crash here?'

Rebel avoided my gaze, slipping on his studded jacket. 'Made a balls of the landing. But I've an important meeting.'

'Whilst I had fire at my neck, you were plotting *meetings*?'

Rebel swallowed under his spiked collar. 'Don't get narky. I arranged it before the Pure killed my family.'

His grief flayed him raw, but I couldn't allow it to reduce my fury. 'When you snuck out at night? Another secret?'

He stalked towards me, dragging me up onto my swollen ankle. 'What about *your* secrets, princess? Why are you after going back to terror hotel?'

Did I say baby vampire? Make that a fully-grown vampire bitch.

I bit back a groan. 'No secret, you're just not the only bloke in my screwed-up life.'

The Bitch of Utopia shanks again.

Rebel blanched. He steadied me against the goal post, before stepping back. His hands fluttered as if he didn't know what to do with them. 'Dry up, I never said...I didn't think... Who is this bleeding muppet?'

'Anarchy.'

Rebel snorted. 'Even has a muppet name.'

'You could create a punk duo.'

He tilted his head. 'I don't know any angels—'

I crossed my arms. 'Because he's a Fallen...*was* a Fallen Angel, until that bastard Eden chopped off

240

his wings. Now the kid's one of the Pure.'

Rebel slammed me against the goal post — *bang* — the goal trembled. 'Mind yourself, princess. The Pure play with minds, until you'll fly into the sun on Eden's word.'

'Anarchy helped me,' I rested my forehead against Rebel's. 'He lost his wings for me.' Rebel raised his pierced eyebrow. 'I won't leave the kid behind.'

Rebel's grip loosened as his turned away. 'Like you abandoned me?'

I blinked, confused.

Then I remembered how I'd left him hidden under the bracken.

What the hell had he thought waking up alone?

I touched his cheek, remembering as well the bruise I'd marked him with. There was nothing left to show for it now, only pale perfection.

Unwilling, his gaze rose to meet mine.

I smiled. 'I saved you, wallad.'

Surprise, followed by understanding and guilt, chased across Rebel's face, before he grinned. 'Fair play to you. I knew you wouldn't leave me...not after...' He reached round to the back of his jean's waistband, slipping out Star. He held it out to me on his palms like an offering. 'I found it in the cemetery. I hoped you hadn't rejected my gift.'

I reached for Star with trembling hands, sheathing it. 'Cheers. And I'd never do that. A gift's too special, bro.'

He scuffed his foot backwards and forwards through the snow. 'The meeting today? You might eat my head off.'

'I'll rein in the bitch, as long as we go back for Anarchy after.'

'Here's the thing of it with Anarchy, if they've taken his wings, he's already lost.'

I blinked away furious tears. Then I slipped my hand under Rebel's leathers, tracing his bent wing. 'And what does that make you? Broken? Grey feathers?'

He flinched. 'Don't touch me.'

I froze, before carefully pulling away my hand.

Rebel's gaze was flinty. 'We can rescue your toy boy Pure, but not until it's safe.'

'It's never going to be safe, don't you get it yet?' I snarled, stalking away across the field towards the line of London Plane trees. The cold bit my cheeks, and my fingers shook. 'We can't hide. The only way to survive is to be the scariest monster. If they burn down our house? We burn down theirs.'

Rebel drifted after me, his hands stuck in the pockets of his trousers. 'A ball-bag like me never should've been your Custodian. Bad angels have no place...' He hung his head. 'In the name of Jesus, what made you think you could trust a Fallen?'

'Fair question, Zachriel. Why do *you* trust us?' A hard, sneering Irish voice called out, startling me. A tall vampire, in faded black denim jacket and emerald shirt, sauntered from the shadows of the trees. He had thick black eyebrows and eyelashes, with the shark-eyed hardness of a soldier. His short buzz of hair blazed as red as Rebel's.

'Briathos!' Rebel breathed, stilling. Then before I could stop him, he bolted across the green towards the vampire, beaming with a joy that made him look younger than Anarchy. 'I've fierce missed—'

The vampire clouted Rebel in the nose.

I growled.

Crimson spurted down Rebel's chin.

'My name's Wings now,' Wings brushed his hand through his auburn bristles.

'And I'm Rebel,' Rebel pinched his nose,

although the wallad was still smiling.

'You see, there's the problem, git angel,' Wings shoved Rebel's shoulders, and Rebel stumbled backwards, 'you can play at being one of the Fallen but you chose not to Fall.'

This was Rebel's *meeting*?

Rebel wiped the blood away with the back of his sleeve. The hesitant way he still smiled, his kohl darkened eyes warily hopeful, made my stomach flip. 'I'm sorry—'

Oomph — Wings booted Rebel in the balls.

Rebel folded to the frozen earth, groaning.

Wings shrugged. 'Git angel.'

Wings turned, but before he could stroll back into the shadows, I sprang towards him. I snatched his denim sleeve and smashed him against a London Plane.

'Bastard Fang.' The knee to Wings' balls to punctuate each word sated the anger bleeding the park purple because he'd attacked Rebel.

My angel.

When Wings tried to curl around the pain, I pinned him to the tree by the throat.

A feathered tattoo, which reminded me of the one on the face of the vampire who'd attacked me on the day Rebel had first fallen into my lap, wove round Wings' neck like barbed wire.

Mesmerised, I stroked over the feathers.

The way Wings raised his pierced eyebrow, however, caught me off guard. How uncomfortably familiar it was. 'I'd heard you were a ball buster, princess, but you know just how to touch a bloke.'

Rebel struggled to his knees. 'You keep your hands to yourself, Briathos.'

'I'm not the one *caressing her neck*,' Wings purred. When I backed away quickly, he laughed. 'I don't blame you for wanting to pull a real fella, not if you've been stuck with this banjaxed idiot. He already has you fighting his battles.' He glanced at Rebel, assessing where to stick the shank next. 'Can Zachriel even get it up with a broken wing?'

Rebel surged to his feet. But I'd already spun Wings round and unsheathed Star.

Power surged through me, spiralling me higher, after a night of powerlessness trapped in Perfection Hotel.

I ached to slice and slash, until I'd reclaimed every shred of dignity stolen from me by Eden. Repaid terror with terror, starting with Wings...who was staring at Star with horrified shock.

'You're no warrior,' when Rebel hugged his arms tightly around himself, I knew Wings' taunt was meant for him. 'Star's not yours. How could you give it to...?'

'She has more right than me,' Rebel whispered.

'A swill munching sow has more right—'

I swung Star in a bright arc, and Wings danced backwards, steel claws springing from his nails. 'I'm not one for quipping during fights to the death.'

Wings smiled: brilliant and dangerous. 'You should try it.'

'Know something else I should try?' I hacked the dagger as if towards Wings' right hand, before shooting flames towards his left.

In a blur of black and red, Rebel dived in front of the blast, howling as it hit his back.

I threw myself over Rebel, rolling him across the ground, until the smouldering fire died. I pinned him down by his wrists, our bodies pressed together. I didn't want to stop touching him because if I did, I was certain I'd have burnt him to ash.

'Not with Star,' Rebel pleaded, his body quivering with pain, 'don't hurt him with my father's dagger.'

'Why?'

Wings' shadow caught us both in its dark; his gaze was guarded. 'I'm this git angel's brother.'

My hands tightened around Rebel's wrists. He hissed.

I warned you about trusting the killer angel.

The Fall divided families, friends, and lovers: a wall between worlds.

The question is whether your pretty boy, who tastes like heaven, is leading your sweet ass to hell.

I crawled off Rebel, backing away.

Rebel twisted his head to the side, unable to meet my eye. 'You knew my true da was one of the Fallen.'

'Your bro too? And how many others? What is this meeting? Your attempt to wheedle your way back with them? Am I the slave to pay off your debt?'

Rebel pushed himself onto his elbows. 'How can you...?'

I crouched and spun, catching Wings in a spinning heel kick.

He bellowed, as I swept him onto his back next to Rebel.

But when I slashed Star towards his throat, Rebel lunged forward.

The tip of Eclipse pressed against my neck.

'Don't make me choose,' Rebel's whisper shook with despair, 'fam is fam.'

Slam.

Rebel's sweet scent washed over me. Yet this time there was no safety.

It was an illusion.

Rebel had saved me, only to betray me to the vampires.

22

In the safety of my gamer world, I'd designed flawless angels soaring to the heavens, whilst vampires crawled deformed from the pit.

Yet beauty was the true monster because it hid the twisted truth beneath.

I'd been a blind bitch, just like Evie had prophesied.

Cold rain teared from the ragged night sky above London Fields; my hair plastered to my head in snakes. I blinked it out of my eyes, shivering.

Eclipse's blade sizzled at my throat; I swallowed, but held my dagger quivering at Wings' neck.

'*You* trained me as a vampire huntress,' I hissed

at Rebel. 'But instead of having my back, you're fighting against me on the side of a bastard Fang?'

'And what's Anarchy? A wingless fairy?' Rebel shoved the sword harder against my skin.

I winced at the searing burn and stink of my own flesh roasting.

Reluctantly, I sheathed Star.

Wings slinked to his feet with a shudder of distaste, straightening his faded denim coat.

The blade dropped from my neck. I grabbed the collar of Rebel's leather jacket and pulled him up.

'Princess, listen...'

I lobbed Rebel towards his brother. 'You made your choice.'

'Wouldn't you?' Rebel's gaze was defiant, although his shoulders had slumped. 'If this was Jade?'

When Rebel touched the pouch at his neck that held Jade's necklace, I stiffened.

Would I choose Jade over...everything?

'Is this where you go all Bond villain and hand me over to your Fang family?' I lounged against the tree, as if I wasn't set to bolt.

Rebel blinked. 'You think everything's to do with you. This is between—'

'A lost babby and his da.' When Wings gently hugged Rebel, I took a step towards them, but it was too late to stop Wings' shanking words, 'A traitor angel isn't family. My little brother is dead to me. The next time I see you, it'll be as my prisoner.'

Wings kissed Rebel's forehead, just as Rebel had kissed mine, before stalking away into the darkness between the London Planes.

Rebel stood motionless; his hands balled into fists and his long eyelashes curved onto his cheeks, as he gazed downwards at the icy undergrowth.

His despair was so bitter I choked on it.

I patted his shoulder, but he recoiled. 'I told you not to bleeding touch me.' His voice was low and hard. When he turned his steely glare on me, it was my turn to flinch. 'You were after murdering my brother. I hate the idiot, but he's still blood. After everything I've... You still don't trust me.' When I hesitated, he nodded. 'See? And what about if...I Fall? Would you get your kicks torturing and killing me then?'

Rebel knocked past me, striding away across the field.

Everything was happening too fast.

I spun, shouting after Rebel, 'Where the hell are you diva storming?'

'What do you care, Feathers?' He hollered, without looking back. 'I thought you had other *blokes in your screwed-up life?*'

Numb, I watched Rebel disappear into the black, leaving me stranded under the wizened trees.

Alone.

Loitering at the back of the burger bar on the Hackney Estate — alone — to the beat of grime music, stench of frying fat, and scowls of the wired kids in hoodies was like screaming *shank me now.*

But I was the Bitch of Utopia.

The swagger of the neon-haired girls and the boys with baseball hats should've been like coming home.

Except, this wasn't my world anymore. I didn't belong: I wasn't a human.

If I'd felt it before, I knew it now, huddled in this narrow alley in the dead freeze of night as the last flurries of rain spat down.

But what the hell did it matter, when I was summoning an angel?

I leant against the cold brick, remembering the sensation of violation when Commander Drake had attacked me. How the violet strands had invaded my mind.

Drake was the only other angel I knew; the only one who could help me. And I'd sensed it: the connection was still there.

I closed my eyes and sank deeper.

Have I told you how much this idea is going to bring down the house...on your cute ass?

Have I told you that you have a freaky obsession with my arse?

Your buns are for the gods. Why shouldn't I want a bite—

Banned word, J, biting.

Angels, aren't they banned?

You must hide me from Commander Goldilocks.

I snapped onto the thread of violet in my mind. It thrashed, panicked, but I yanked, dragging it back through the maze I'd built.

I wiped my hand through my soaked hair, focusing my brain in a startling way that flew me higher, flashing with a brilliant white that tasted of candy floss, and spun me in its softness.

Heady on the thrill, I hauled harder, until the strand trembled, tumbling out at my feet.

Commander Drake stared up at me.

He rubbed his eyes, as if he'd been asleep, before they widened in shock.

His golden curls were tousled; it made him look even younger than before.

When he stalked to his bare feet, they sank into a puddle. And they weren't the only part of him that was bare...

It seemed Drake slept naked.

I leant back against the wall and sniggered.

And the moment Drake realised why...

Hot rage flushed his cheeks, before his gaze froze ice-cold.

Drake curled his wings around his body, covering himself in frankincense scented feathers. 'I knew you were extraordinary. Yet I'd also hoped you were different.' He shuddered, casting an anxious glance up and down the alley. 'You summoned me, Mistress, your wish is my command.'

I stared at him blankly.

The smile was bitter, but it almost touched Drake's lips, before he killed it. 'Genie? Lamp? You may also wish to get in now insults about harem and whipping boys.'

He lifted one pale eyebrow, daring me to utter a word, as he turned.

Lashes — crimson and purple — marred his slim back. Interlaced welts wove bloody across his quivering body.

I bit my lip not to make a sound.

When he twisted to face me, his expression was cold again. 'I told you, we all serve monsters.'

Drake no longer appeared to be putting on a show.

But I was.

I stroked my fingers through Drake's wings, in the same way he had Rebel's, when Rebel had been chained to the monument.

Drake panted, struggling to back away. 'Enough. I can't be here...like this.'

'Stay.' Drake's eyes flashed dangerously. 'And be silent too, bro.' He shook but he stood still, submitting to my caress. 'Who's getting off now, Commander?'

Find the weakness and shank sharp.

A gentle touch hurt harem angel worse than any torture.

'My sister's missing and other Hackney kids. They could be in your world. I need an angel to take me there.' When I ran my fingers to the tips of his wings, pulling them away from his body and exposing him, Drake shuddered. 'You're the only other angel I know.' He arched away from me; his dick pulsed pretty and hard. He refused to look at me, as if I was an enemy interrogator, glowering over my shoulder instead. 'I tried to fit in here. But I don't know who to trust. All I know is my sister's gone.' He glanced at me in surprise. 'You have permission to speak.'

'Has Zachriel abandoned you? He excels at that.'

I dug my nails into the tips of Drake's wings, and he howled.

A gang of lads circled on bikes at the entrance to the alley, like sharks scenting blood. I shoved Drake down behind the stinking black bins, my arm across his slender throat.

Drake lay in the shallow puddle, shivering: he wouldn't hurt me, even when I hurt him. When I stared into his cool gaze, I remembered this was Rebel's gaoler for forty years.

The angel hunting him.

I stroked Drake's damp curls out of his face with an exaggerated tenderness that made him flinch. 'So, were you thrashed because you went psycho on Rebel or because you didn't bring him back to Angel World?'

'Does there need to be a reason?' He shrugged his slight shoulders. 'If you desire...' He took a deep breath, steadying himself, '...I am yours.' I reared back, studying him. He only continued with an uncomfortable earnestness, 'You don't belong amongst these humans. There's a whole world waiting for you.'

'You're mine?'

His gaze was understanding; it shook me. 'You may have me, if you return now to Angel World. Isn't that what you called me for? You allowed me back into your mind, and I glimpsed... I'll search for your sister, if you aid me in the Addict hunt.'

I pushed back from Drake. 'That's where you lost me. I'll burn your pretty head from your shoulders before—'

His mouth twisted. 'Be calm. Would you prefer Zachriel Falls? Because unless we save him, he will.'

I growled, wrenching his head to the side by the curls.

Why did the violet curling through me, entwine to Drake's?

I was electrified by his promise of a new world of angels.

Somewhere I belonged.

'You need to accept who you are,' Drake murmured. 'You're important. Special. Powerful. As much as I may hate it...'

I kissed his fluttering neck. Then I licked the raindrops, as they fled quivering down his chest. 'You hate it, bitch, but you're mine.'

When I bit his nipple, he tasted of frankincense.

He groaned, even though his body vibrated with repressed fury.

The control ignited by his words... *Important. Special. Powerful...* flooded me in violet hallelujahs, chorusing me to the heavens.

I was high on the dominance, after weeks of fear and helplessness.

Rebel had rejected me, when I'd pinned him down like this. Rebel had said *no*: not until I loved him.

Yet Drake was straining to lie still, as I stroked the back of his neck in teasing circles.

When I forced his mouth open, stabbing my tongue inside, his eyes shuttered to a studied blankness.

I knew that look: I'd used it myself to escape the abuser who worked at Jerusalem Children's Home.

Jade had worn it for years.

Yet Drake didn't stop me or say a word.

Why the hell was it so important I agreed to go with him that he'd sell himself?

Like ice water, Drake's blank look cooled the high. I pushed back from him, before crouching next to him.

Slowly, Drake pushed himself up, hugging his arms around his knees. He avoided my gaze. 'I can try harder,' he said softly, 'to make you want me.'

'Not the problem, bro,' I touched his pale knee gently, until he glanced up. 'The thing is, *you* don't want *me*.'

Confused, he shook his head. 'Irrelevant.'

'Not if you're a harem boy, but yeah, if you're my partner.'

'Maybe you *are* different,' he ran his hand through his curls. 'But if we're to return—'

'Deals off. You don't bring out the best side of me. And offering to be my slave clued me in that you don't come from the land of unicorns. Trust is a bitch, and your Angel World has lost mine.'

Drake surged up, prey to predator in a heartbeat, his wings outstretched in pulsating glory.

Hell, why had I ever reckoned I could control the Commander?

I stumbled to my feet, fumbling for Star with fingers made clumsy by the cold.

'I believe *you* to be the bitch,' Drake backed me against the brick wall, boxing me in. 'And payback to be one as well.'

'Hey, sexy,' Ash strolled from the shadows of the alley's entrance in his red military coat.

The scape of his fangs... Light touches to my neck... Pleasure buzzing through me...

'Don't call me sexy.' But when our gazes met, I couldn't help the grin.

Ash smirked, looking Drake up and down. 'Wasn't talking to you, Violet. Although for the record? You are sexy.'

Drake staggered back, blushing and shielding himself with his wings. 'Impure creatures, such as you, Seducer—'

'From what I just saw,' Ash toyed with the silver buttons down his coat, 'you're an easy lay yourself.' Then he sauntered past Drake, who shrank back, and placed his hands either side of my head on the wall. His shadow covered me, along with the tang of citrus cloves: I'd forgotten how tall Ash was. 'Told you I'd be seeing you again soon.' He snogged me, hard and fast, before drawing back. His charcoal-grey eyes sought mine. 'Don't choose the Ice Commander, just because you reckon he's the only one who can help you.' He rubbed his cheek against mine like a lion; his mane of hair tangled against my skin. 'You can crash with me, if you're over the whole *vampires are the Big Bads*. Although, I *am* bad, babe.'

I spluttered with laughter. 'You're such a geek. And decapitation with a butter knife, remember?'

'If only I had the time.' Drake sank his thumb into the base of Ash's neck.

Ash stiffened with agony, before falling to his knees.

His fingers curled into my thighs as he buried his face against my stomach, fighting not to make a sound.

'Allow it,' I snarled, sizzling violet fire at Drake and searing the creamy skin of his chest crimson.

Drake stumbled back, shaking.

He wrapped his wings even tighter around himself. 'You'd choose that...Fallen thing...over me?'

I hauled Ash up next to me, linking our arms like we were lovers. 'What can I say? At least the Fang knows how to kiss.'

Drake's blank look shattered.

He shattered.

For the moment before Drake vanished, I regretted the hurt in his eyes, which glittered with unshed tears.

Until I remembered Rebel's silent screams and his fear as he'd trembled in the dark box in the House of Rose, Wolf, and Fox.

I'd shanked the Commander's weakness sharp, but he knew it.

And yeah, I had a feeling payback *would* be a bitch.

'Home? Cup of tea? Bed?' Ash grinned.

'You're one weird arsed Fang,' I pinched Ash's side, and he squirmed.

I'd chosen a vampire Brigadier over an angel Commander.

Yet without Rebel in this supernatural world, I needed a guide.

I was no longer blind, however, to the dangers that had once been hidden but now were coming out to play.

Drake and Ash were both beautiful. But neither angel nor vampire were good.

We were all monsters.

And now a huntress, I was walking alone into the home of a Fallen.

No matter how delicious the death wish thrill of

his fangs at my neck, for all I knew, Ash planned to feed on me tonight.

23

Vampires' lairs were meant to be Gothic, dark, and freaky. Not geek heaven apartments with gamer pods looped with consoles, virtual reality headsets, computer monitors, pewter Princess Leia figurines, half-empty pizza boxes, and a Lara Croft poster stuck on the steel grey bedroom wall.

I snuggled down under the soft scarlet blankets of Ash's bed. If Ash meant to bite me, at least he'd made me comfy first. And with...everything...from the moment the Pure had swarmed around the witches' house crashing down on me, I was too knackered to care if he did.

Maybe I wanted Ash to, or maybe I just wanted what he was offering to be real. The first slice of...normal...since Rebel had fallen from the ceiling.

I'd shucked off my jacket before climbing into bed. But I wasn't stripping off; there was comfy and there was offering up your arse.

Ash pottered into the bedroom with a steaming mug of Earl Grey. Flushing, he kicked a dirty sock under the bed as he handed over my tea.

I arched my brow at Lara Croft. 'I said you were a geek.'

Ash grinned, sliding out of his military jacket and lobbing it at an oak chair by the wall.

It missed.

With a shrug, Ash stretched his wide wings, before sprawling next to me on the pillows. 'I need somewhere to relax from all the...' His fangs shot from his teeth and he growled.

Despite myself, I jumped, spilling my tea. 'Bastard.'

Ash laughed, before his fangs sank back into his gums. 'No worries, I'm not the bite and fight type.'

When I studied him, brushing his tumble of jet hair away from his long olive neck, I wondered whether I could allow myself to believe that was true.

At the same time, I quivered with the coiling urge to bite...*taste*...him.

I slurped the hot Earl Grey: black and strong. It warmed me, when I'd been frozen for days. 'And where are your little Fang friends?' I asked carefully.

His smile faded. He twisted away, pulling off his boots. 'Not here. After all, you're a hunter. It'd be like bringing Buffy to Spike...but then they ended up screwing each other...'

I snorted.

Ash shrugged. 'What? I can't do ironic human pop culture?'

I struggled to hide my smile. 'Tell me this then, do all you Fangs live in wealthy arsed apartments?'

'Only if we work.'

When he took my empty mug and tucked the blankets around me, I tensed. Once, I'd been sick with the flu, and Gizem had tucked the covers around me in just the same way. But only when she'd reckoned I was sleeping because she had a reputation to keep.

Why did that one small gesture matter?

Ash drew back. 'Bed? That's yours. Couch? That's for the sexy Fallen Angel, who'll be whinging about a bad back in the morning.'

'A bed without chains is a luxury.'

He shook his head. 'I always knew it about the crazy retro bastard. Angels are kinky underneath.'

I sniggered but then clutched the blankets tighter. My mouth was dry at the memory of waking to thick blue carpet underneath my knees, the light of a chandelier and suffocating warmth. 'The Pure didn't even have a bed. They just got with the chopping. The only one who had my back was Anarchy.'

'Anarchy?' Ash towered above me, his wings like a stormy sky. 'Where is he?'

'One of your soldiers, *Brigadier*?'

Ash winced. 'He's my mate, Violet. Like a kid brother.'

Now it was my turn to wince. 'You know I said *got with the chopping...*?'

Ash fell to his knees, his wings folded around himself like he was returning to a feathery womb. He keened.

I was a bitch. 'Not his head, wallad, his wings.'

Ash glanced up at me through wet eyelashes. 'They took his wings?'

'Eden said he was a rebel,' I smiled sadly. 'Sorry,

bro, that he's—'

Ash bounced up, with a grin. 'Purified? He's *Anarchy*. The little bastard'll fight them until they gank him. Except, we'll break him out tomorrow night.'

I pushed up from the pillows. 'We will?'

'Sleep. Great escape to plan when you wake.'

Somehow, I'd switched gangs. Rebel wouldn't save my new mate, but his enemy would. I forced myself not to think of the way Rebel's wings had drooped in the cemetery when he'd stopped even defending himself against Ash.

I grabbed Ash's hand, before he could saunter out. 'You can't plan with a bad back,' I muttered.

'Napoleon lost the whole Russian campaign because of a dodgy back.' Ash slunk over me, climbing under the covers without undressing.

When I turned on my side, Ash's velvety feathers curled around me, like a second bed. He sighed, his breathing soft and safe, against my neck.

I tensed, but then relaxed. Neither halves of my nature roared *danger* at the closeness of his fangs. Instead, they hummed in tired contentment. Slowly, his hands settled around my waist.

'Russian campaign? I thought you knew nothing about fighting, Brigadier?'

For a moment, Ash's breathing hitched, before it steadied. 'I used to,' he murmured, 'but not anymore. There are different ways a bloke can win a war than with a sword.'

So, this is your choice? Black, not violet? Bones, rather than feathers?

I'm not making a choice, just resting.

You better hope it's not eternal rest. At least you could try out the whore's dick. You don't want to waste a Seducer—

I'm not that kind of bitch now. Not since—

A couple of hours ago with the ice angel Commander?

You saw how I hurt Drake. I'm not doing that again.

You keep telling yourself that.

And what's so special about a Seducer?

You'll see.

I buried into the warmth of Ash's aromatic wings, as the dark rose and covered us, and I closed my eyes.

When I opened them, kisses were feathering along my shoulder blades, until they tingled.

I shivered. Still half-asleep, I licked my lips.

A small hand stroked my thigh through my jeans in hesitant circles. Then violet wings...

Violet?

Flames crackled in an instinctive rush of outraged fear, as I elbowed the violator.

Drake tumbled in a hissing, burned tangle onto the floor.

Suddenly wide awake, I scooted up on the bed, pulling the blankets over me.

Where the hell had I dropped Star last night?

When Drake pulled himself to his feet, holding up his indigo trousers carefully, I shot out of the bed. 'Is this your *pay back*?'

Drake eyed me coldly. 'Calm yourself. You're still sleeping with your vampire whore.'

I whirled round.

The bed was empty.

If this was real, what had Drake done to Ash? And if it wasn't...and Drake was messing with my mind...?

I took a step towards Drake. 'Next time you come playing in my head, you don't touch without permission. And you don't turn up without an invite.'

He rolled his eyes. 'As you wish. But I'm here because I've found your sister.'

My legs buckled; I slumped onto the bed. 'Where?'

Drake smiled with sudden childish innocence. He held out his hand to me. His fingers were mangled, as if they'd been broken one at a time. *I hadn't done that.* 'If you come with me now to Angel World, I'll take you to her.'

I let out a shaky breath. '*Please...*'

It'd been so many weeks since Jade had disappeared. Every day I'd imagined finding her, and the way she'd flick her pink-and-black fringe as she beamed. I battled not to think about what was happening to her. Only that one moment when she saw me...saving her.

I reached out to take Drake's hand.

But then I noticed his broken hand was shaking.

I drew back. 'I'll pass on the poisoned apple, cheers.'

Drake stared at me, before tossing his golden curls. 'I assure you, what happens next...? I didn't choose it. Watch.'

Suddenly, Ash was sprawled across the bed.

But his wings...

I gasped.

Blood dripped onto the blankets. Scarlet from the sodden outstretched wings stained the floor. Mutilated, the feathers had been plucked or carved out.

I clutched Ash's maimed shoulders, but my fingers clawed through air.

I blinked at the bed that was unexpectedly empty again.

Drake shrugged one lash streaked shoulder. 'I'm only *playing*, am I not? I apologise for the lack of invitation.'

Rebel, his fiery head bowed, prostrated himself before me.

And his wings were nothing but burnt stumps.

I twirled to Drake. 'Stop your little show of horrors. This bitch doesn't do threats.'

'This isn't a threat,' Drake waved his broken hand, and Rebel vanished. 'This is a possible future path if you don't come with me now.'

'I'm not buying what you sell.'

'Your choice,' Drake draped himself over the bed, like a cherub sacrificial on a vampire's altar. 'But you only have two nights. After that?' His violet eyes were ice cold. I remembered the cruel way I'd shattered him. Shanking an angel Commander was a dangerous move. 'I kill your sister.'

I froze.

The image of Jade appeared: her pale face on the pillow, with her pink streaked hair framing it in an Emo riot. Her eyes were closed, as if she was sleeping. She wore one of my baggy black t-shirts and a pair of shorts that matched her hair.

Drake kissed her.

I slammed forward, wringing the blanket like it was Drake's neck.

Not real, not real, not real...

Drake wound his hand into Jade's hair, watching me over her head, waiting for the fireworks. 'Your sister believes I can kiss,' he said quietly.

'You didn't even wake her, Prince Charming. And if you ever touch her for real...? I'll rip off your bollocks.'

'Yet you chose not to save her.' He shoved Jade out of the bed at my feet.

Not real...not real...just playing with my mind...

I couldn't stop myself. I crouched over Jade.

Scarlet.

It burst from Jade's guts.

Trembling, I pressed my hands over the knife wound.

When I pulled back my bloody hands, I sobbed.

Jade's murder stained me, and it was my fault

Death swallowed me. Blood, bones, and feathers.

My sister was the sacrifice.

'Two nights,' Drake skulked at my shoulder, whispering his poison into my ear. 'Call me and I am yours. We can't all choose our path, but you are fortunate. Is a human sister not worth more to you than a Fallen or an Addict?'

Then I startled awake. To a silent room, sheltered in the arms of a sleeping vampire.

A vampire Spike doll — complete with black coat and bleached blond hair — guarded the computer monitor opposite a pewter princess Leia.

Ash had a sense of irony about his vampiric heritage.

He didn't have a Buffy doll, but then I couldn't blame Ash for not welcoming a vampire slayer into his home.

Yet I was here — a huntress — spinning on Ash's leather computer chair.

I adjusted my earpiece and then snatched the Spike doll, stroking it like a stress toy as I peered at the monitor.

A marble lobby, with a silver and blue mural of the heavens on both floor and ceiling, leapt up and down in jerky movements at each step Ash took.

The camera and sound worked.

Now time for Ash to put on a bitch of a performance.

I grinned, bouncing in my seat.

'You're gorgeous, Violet, but can I just say, one more time, you're an evil bitch,' Ash murmured into the earpiece.

'You don't like the escape plan?' I smirked. 'Get in to Perfection hotel. Place the bugs, so we know what Eden is planning. Then rescue your mate. What's the problem, Brigadier? Too hard for you?'

Ash snorted. 'You're hot when you're all commanding. If I escape with my wings, let's play dress ups.'

My grin died. 'Just escape with your wings.'

The feathers carved out of Ash's wings... Rebel's bloody stumps... Scarlet seeping from Jade...

Blood on my hands.

Crack — Spike's head hung backwards from his body.

I'd decapitated him.

I always wondered what it'd be like when you met a guy who was as big a geek as you.

I didn't meet a guy: I'm working with a Fang.

Keep telling yourself that Miss Vampire Lover.

Yet seduction works in rainbow pretty ways. And you could end up seducing him.

Not listening...

But he's no slave like Rebel. If you try to tame him, you'll destroy him.

I shoved the broken doll behind the computer desk.

The camera, which we'd hidden in the button of Ash's military coat, projected the curve of the marble counter in the hotel's lobby.

Ash's strong fingers drummed on the counter top.

'I'd like to see Eden, please.' Ash sounded shy

and awe-struck (we'd worked on that). 'I...I don't know if I'm in the right place but...this is so hard... The others...the way they treat me...I feel—'

'Dirty?' I jumped at the sound of Eden's voice. Ash spun. Eden swanned towards Ash. His gaze was calculating. 'Seducer, you were once a soldier up on a hill, but then down you came tumbling onto your knees.' When Eden kissed Ash's lips softly, I growled. 'Whore, whore, three in a bed, bad little boy, will soon be dead.'

Ash's arms clasped around Eden's neck. 'Help me?'

Silence.

My nails sliced into my palm.

This was the hard part.

Whether Eden would believe Ash a willing convert.

Sitting there — remote and helpless — was more difficult than I'd ever imagined.

Eden delicately pushed Ash away, before stroking down his cheek. 'You want to be clean?'

'Yes.' Ash's voice was tight with tears.

Hell, even I could believe he meant it.

'You *need* to be purified?'

'Yes, sir.'

Eden twirled around the lobby, his arms out in an elegant waltz, before gripping Ash around the neck, as he whispered, 'I will train, save, and then free you of your wings.' I shuddered. 'You will be my solider, whore, and toy.'

I pressed my nose to the monitor, as if that could transport me closer to Ash.

Eden hauled Ash by the arm through the lobby and into a plush bronze lift.

When the doors shut, with Eden's sky-blue chest pushed against the camera, I snarled.

My plan...this was my plan...

Ash was wrong: I wasn't a bitch, I was a monster.

A *ping* of the lift, lush blue carpeted hallway, and then mahogany door.

'The entrance to your new life. Walk the path of the pure,' Eden turned a key and thrust Ash into the gloomy room, before locking him in.

I squinted at the outline of the blue-and-white striped bedroom: wood-carved silver bed, Victorian desk and...

Anarchy kneeling in the corner.

Anarchy's head was bowed to the carpet, in the same way Rebel's had been in my vision from Drake, his back blistered between the cauterised stumps of his wings.

He didn't even look up.

'Are you seeing this?' Ash muttered furiously. He sank down next to his friend, running his hand through Anarchy's curls. 'Hey, menace, I should kick your arse for dragging me into trouble again.' Anarchy flinched but didn't look up. 'But not until we're safe in my place, with a tub of chocolate fudge ice-cream and...don't tell me that only works on girls.'

For a moment, Anarchy's gaze flickered to Ash's, as his mouth curled into a smile, but then he quickly looked down again.

'Tell him my blokes never give up,' I insisted into the earpiece.

'Violet, demanding so-and-so that she is, says her blokes never give up.'

Anarchy's head shot up. 'You bloody wanker. The princess escaped. If you—'

When Ash hauled Anarchy to his feet by his neck, crushing him against the wall, Anarchy yelped. 'You get yourself captured, and I risk...everything...to rescue your ungrateful arse, so don't...'

They collapsed to the floor together, Anarchy clutching around Ash. 'I'm sorry... I lost... I couldn't stop them...'

'How adorable, my two darlings know each other.' Stephanie stood framed in the door, holding her short silver staff. 'Training will be much more fun. Eden called and told me about your conversion, Seducer. He doesn't believe you need restraining. But boys who don't behave are chained. So, be good.'

Violet snaked sickly in my stomach, as Stephanie prowled towards the two vampires on the screen.

I growled, 'Don't touch my fam, bitch.'

'The Fallen are your fam now, princess? So, it was just *my* brother who wasn't good enough?' Rebel leant against the steel back wall of the bedroom.

His eyes, however, sparked pure fire.

I startled, tumbling off the computer chair onto my arse.

Only now I wasn't transfixed by the danger on screen, I was flooded by the scent of sugary copper; I buzzed with the sweet high, which thrummed through me, until I was lost in a dangerous haze. I shook my head to force it to clear.

Then I ripped out my earpiece, edging backwards. 'How did you...?'

'Hunter.' Rebel shrugged, although he was shaking. 'Tracked you. Found you. Booted in the door. I may have made an arse of being your Custodian, but I won't let these gits seduce you. Even if it hurts both of us.'

Rebel's wings spread like a threat as he straightened.

He was awe-inspiring in his righteousness, and

I was the Big Bad.

Then Rebel stalked towards me, drawing Eclipse's flaming blade.

24

A tweed blazer: that's what I always remember. The way it'd wrapped me safe in the scent of oranges, as two strong arms had carried me away from Jerusalem Children's Home.

My first and only foster dad.

Six months later, I'd been carried back in the thin arms of his new wife.

Her cold brown eyes had avoided mine, as she'd dumped me back in Jerusalem's.

All I'd known was my foster dad hadn't wanted me enough.

Fought for me.

Loved me.

Because bastard blokes always abandon you.

Rebel circled me in Ash's bedroom, his sword at my head. His arm shook.

The backs of my knees hit the bed, and I caught my hand in the blankets to stop myself falling.

I caught a glimpse of Star on the ebony bedside table. Then I booted an empty pizza box scuffing across the carpet at Rebel.

He dodged back.

Stephanie had both Anarchy and Ash. I'd sent Ash into Perfection Hotel. It was *my* plan. And instead of having their back, I was battling with their enemy.

I glanced sideways at the monitor.

Ash had been forced to strip off his coat with the hidden camera, but he'd draped it over the desk, as if I didn't want to miss the floorshow.

When both vampires knelt at Stephanie's feet, I shuddered.

Rebel noticed my distraction and roared as he swung.

I ducked under Eclipse's glowing arc.

If we'd been in our training sessions, I'd have been certain Rebel had been aiming to miss.

Rip — the sword slashed through the Lara Croft poster, embedding in the wall's plaster.

As Rebel yanked, I booted him in the gut. He flailed away from the blade, before toppling over. Then he bottom shuffled across the carpet, clawing himself up when his back hit the wall.

Violet me up anytime now, J. I'm being hunted by the punk.

You're in the bedroom of his enemy, Feathery-Judas. Where's the righteousness if you burn him down?

And if he burns me?

Everybody burns. It's just a matter of when and how.

I twirled, slamming my fist into the wall next to Rebel's cheek. 'You want to hurt me, wallad?'

Rebel flinched but didn't pull away. 'I just want *you*, princess. To protect you.' He bit his lip, resting his head against the wall and exposing his neck around his dark collar, as if tempting me to bite. 'I know I'm bad. But you said you *needed* me.'

'And you abandoned me.'

We stared at each other, united in our hurt and confusion.

Then Rebel grinned, bouncing up on his toes. 'Let's put it down to six of one and half a dozen of the other. I came back, so I did.'

I looked away. 'Right now, Ash is risking his wings for Anarchy. Because you wouldn't.'

Rebel flushed, hugging his leathers closer around himself. He gave a curt nod and marched to Eclipse. He braced his foot against the wall, heaving the blade free in a sludge flurry of plaster. 'I made a balls of teaching you to be a vampire hunter,' he muttered, wiping clean his sword, before sheathing it, 'you're the vampire saviour.'

When I followed Rebel, turning him gently by the shoulders, he steeled himself, as if expecting to be clouted. *Love is pain...* What else had I ever given him? 'I sent the Brigadier into that Psycho Hotel, like a soldier into battle. If he's ganked, it's on me.'

Rebel's smile was soft. He rubbed my shoulder. 'Let's rescue these dopes then.' He strode to the computer, before flopping into the chair. 'Is this all part of the plan, Feathers?'

I pushed my earpiece back in and turned to the screen.

Three naked vampires in a tangle on the silver

bed, curves and hardness writhing in the silk, moans, wet kisses, and *slaps*.

Stephanie stretched along the bed like a goddess being worshipped, as Anarchy sprawled on his side, directed by her hand at the back of his neck to snog her lips and neck. At each hiss of *harder, soldier,* Ash screwed her, his wings beating up and down in time with his thrusts.

'Not part of the plan...?' Rebel ventured.

'Not *my* plan.' I snatched the Spike doll, twisting its head fully off, before hurling it across the bedroom.

Rebel lifted his eyebrow. 'Toy murder aside, the muppets may not have had a choice.'

I was going to hurl.

Suddenly, Stephanie convulsed, clutching the silk sheets. Ash held her down, curling his wings around her, whilst she shrieked. Then her eyes rolled back, and she collapsed.

'Hell, he's screwed her to death,' I breathed, staring at the screen.

'Not dead, just blacked out,' I jumped at Ash's whisper, 'and either I heard the angels because being used as a dildo flew me to heaven — note the sarcasm — or your possessive boyfriend reached the end of his leash and came back.' When Rebel growled, Ash laughed. 'That's the sound of your kinky angel.'

Rebel tilted his head at me, but I shrugged helplessly. 'No matter how much of a legend you are in bed, Ash, that skank shouldn't be comatose.'

Ash hurled Anarchy's tattered blue jeans at him, before scrambling into his own clothes. 'It's a Seducer thing. A secret superpower. She wanted it.'

I bit my tongue, not expecting the scorching surge of jealousy. 'Superpowers save people. How does...?'

'It's how the Brigadier feeds,' Rebel glanced at me. 'Take them to heaven and then...hell.'

Ash's shoulder's slumped as he buttoned up his shirt. 'Not hell. Just a quick nap in heaven, and I... They don't die, and we don't feed from the unwilling.'

'*We* don't,' Anarchy slipped his arms around Ash's neck just for a moment. 'The Pure are the wankers who take by force.'

Rebel snorted. 'See now why I didn't... Why I can't Fall?'

Ash grabbed his coat, and the camera jerked, whilst he pulled it on. Then he slunk around the room, sliding the bugs safely out of sight.

I licked my dry lips. 'Just get your arses back here.'

'I can't, princess,' Anarchy's small hands clasped the front of Ash's army coat, as if he could hold my hand. 'I'm sorry you wasted your time trying to rescue me. But I'm one of theirs now. They'd burn the world to find me.'

'*I'd* burn the world to keep you.' I didn't know if I was talking about Anarchy or Jade, but I knew I couldn't lose them both. My fingers trembled, as I caressed the edges of the monitor. 'If Ash escapes and you don't, then they'll punish—'

'It just gives them another excuse.' Anarchy peered at the camera. His face was pinched. 'I'm Stephanie's wankering pet; no one can change that. But I hear everything. How there's some big project in Hackney. How the Pure are divided between Eden and Stephanie. I'll be your secret agent. Behind enemy lines.'

Ash stroked Anarchy's curls. 'This isn't a game, mate.'

'I know, but look what the wankers did to me.' Anarchy fell to his knees, bowing his wingless back.

When he looked back at Ash, his cheeks were streaked with tears. 'I can't return to the Fallen. You know what they'd do to me.'

'I'd hide you,' Ash pleaded, grasping Anarchy's shoulders.

Anarchy shook his head. 'You reckon I'd risk that? Give them a reason to hurt you, even worse than they already do?'

How did the Fallen *hurt* Ash? He was a Brigadier with a wealthy arsed apartment.

Except, maybe there was a reason he didn't live with the other vampires.

Maybe he was an outcast too.

Rebel was watching the exchange thoughtfully. To my surprise, he hooked our pinkies together.

'Please,' Ash ran his hands down from Anarchy's shoulders to his arms, 'don't do this. We'll figure something out.'

The silver sheets stirred, as Stephanie roused from her orgasm blood high. I wished Ash had torn out her throat. 'Darlings, that was...acceptable,' she purred, 'but who gave you permission to dress? A cleansing session will remind you to be good little soldiers.'

Stephanie slid round on the bed.

'Out,' I hollered into the earpiece, 'now.'

Ash slipped off his coat, before hugging Anarchy. 'See you, mate.'

Smash — Ash booted the high window in a shatter of glass.

Stephanie screeched.

Then Ash dived out into the black.

Abandoning Anarchy to the Pure.

Ash crouched in the stone courtyard behind the apartment, his coat a scarlet pool spilling around him in the snow.

There was no breeze, only the cutting freeze of the night air. A broken shed leaned against the corner of the courtyard; white shrouded it ghost-like.

Ash stared up at the starless sky, which was blindfolded by cloud, as if he could fly back to Anarchy.

Save him.

If anyone understood what Ash had lost, it was me.

Yet Drake had offered me a Judas choice. And I had one more night to make it.

I could still save my sister: her blood didn't have to stain my hands bloody.

Sacrifice Rebel and Ash. Forget the danger to the Utopia Estate from the Pure. Go over to the side of the angels...and I wouldn't have to suffer this torment in the snow as well.

Did it make me a monster that if Drake appeared, I'd choose my sister?

I leaned in the frame of the back door, rubbing my arms against the cold, as I asked, 'Would you trust Commander Drake?'

Ash slipped on the slushy snow, his coat a tail around him. Finally, he looked away from the stars. He scrubbed his hand across his face. 'As much as I'd trust Darth Vader.'

'So, the real question is, who's the Emperor?'

Ash's lips thinned, before he turned his head. 'Why the need to know about Sexy Snake Drake?'

I crossed my arms. 'Is the bastard true to his word?'

'Not the same as *trust*,' Ash wiped the tears in his eyes away with his sleeve, like I hadn't already seen them. After a moment, he nodded. 'One soldier to another, in matters of war, he's true to it.'

What wars, J?

These angels and vampires have been fighting for centuries. It's gang warfare.

Worse than you can imagine.

Bones and feathers, carnage and genocide...

'But outside the battlefield...?' Ash twisted his hands together. 'It depends how badly Drake wants something. Or the Emperor does.' He sprang to his feet, his shoulders straightening. 'None of us are free, Violet, light or dark.'

'And just how dark is Drake? Is he a human killer?'

Ash laughed. 'I'm glad you're over the vampires being the Big Bads here, but save some of that for the angel boys. Humans are like heroin to angels. They're addicted, or else they're the preachers punishing the Addicts and flushing the heroin down the loo. One dead human is just one less Addict to Drake.'

I paled: Jade and the missing Hackney kids were nothing but *heroin* to the angels. Humans reduced to a drug.

Even if I went with Drake to Angel World, how could I trust him not to kill the kids anyway? To him, they were the cause of an addiction.

When I'd tortured Tiny Fang in the freezing water of the Thames, before blistering fire down his cheek, Rebel had towered over me, insisting we had a duty to kill only to *save* others.

Drake? He didn't sound like that.

He wasn't righteous: he was a zealot.

Rebel had been trained to believe himself a *bad angel*. But if Rebel was bad, then so was I, Anarchy, and Ash too.

We were all rebels.

I didn't belong in Drake's screwed-up world. Yet

if I didn't choose him, my sister died.

Ash was at my side, his hard arms around me, before I even knew I'd let out the sniffle.

Two flashes of red leapt from the stone wall.

My Blood Familiars.

Blaze and Spark wound around my ankles, their bellies close to the ground, whining.

Spark fluttered his long eyelashes at me, grinning with his green eyes.

I grabbed Spark by his whippy tail, swiping Blaze across his upturned muzzle.

The familiars yipped but didn't struggle.

I tilted my chin, struggling to keep my voice low. I remembered the terrifying loss when the familiars had abandoned me in Hackney Cemetery. 'Reckoned I was your Keeper, foxies? Maybe I should chain you in that kennel, yeah?'

'Nay, please...' Spark whimpered, his tail quivering in my hand, 'we're sorry, sorry, sorry—'

'Told you I wasn't into the kinky mistress vibe.' I let go of Spark's tail, stroking his head, until he nudged into my hand. 'But you're the ones who left me.'

When I glanced at Ash, he'd lounged back against the doorframe, with his hands behind his head.

Had he heard fox radio...?

'Urban foxes are a menace,' Ash grinned. 'I feed the little mischiefs whenever they show up. We all need a home.' He hunkered down beside Blaze, running his hand through his thick fur. 'Especially Blood Familiars. Earl Grey and a biscuit for us. And an apple for you, gorgeous?'

Blaze snapped at Ash's nose; Ash fell back with a laugh.

'Leave go, you dunderhead,' Blaze snarled, 'we belong to our Keeper now.'

I guess the familiars did also use telepathy on Ash.

So, they trusted him then?

But I was the one who'd slept in his arms...

Ash's expression darkened. 'You don't belong to any one.'

'We'll all belong to the Pure, so we will, if Eden's Utopia Project works,' Rebel shoved between us out of the apartment.

He hopped from one foot to the other, clutching the earpiece that still buzzed with feed from the bugs Ash had planted in Stephanie's hotel room.

I straightened.

If humans were only heroin to angels, were they only blood to the Pure?

Rebel ignored Ash, cast a curious glance at the Blood Familiars, and passed me the earpiece.

'...a mistake, darling,' Stephanie's steel wrapped in silk drawl from the earpiece, 'the soldiers think you're weak. They want to feast—'

'To purify the world, we must look to a new age,' Eden, and sharper than I'd heard before, 'and copy the humans' tricks, until we nest cuckooing amongst them. We'll drink from my Utopia fountain and purify the Fallen. Then I will be King. After that—'

'The angels.' Stephanie laughed.

'Poor lost Zachriel,' Eden sighed dreamily, 'and my monster.'

I ripped out the earpiece, shaking.

Think before you jump into the middle of a war.

Eden's on my turf: Utopia.

Gizem and her sis...the wingless bastards fed from her.

It's why she wore a towel around her neck: to hide the marks.

Are you forgetting you've been a blood donor to a baby vamp too?

Yeah, like I could forget the thrill of saving Rebel with my blood.

The bondage punk is mine because we both wanted it.

But the Pure are taking, not asking.

How'd you like to be nothing but a burger in a bar?

Maybe it's all any of us are: food to a predator.

'Violet?' Ash asked gently, 'are you OK?'

'I'm the Bitch of Utopia.' Violet surged through me, violent and righteous. 'No Pure king will take that title.'

'Holy Mary preserve us, we misfits are after saving the world then,' Rebel quirked his soft lips. 'Because Utopia is only the test run. London's the ancient seat, but we angels — and vampires — are like rats.'

'We're everywhere,' Ash nodded. 'If we don't stop Eden nesting in Utopia, we'll all end up like Anarchy. And humans around the world will be tasty fast-food snacks.'

I glanced around at the punk, Seducer, and brother foxes, hovering between the snow of the courtyard and the dark of the apartment.

My army.

'Then get ready bitches because we're going to war.' I hid my trembling hands in the pockets of my jacket.

If I saved the world, I condemned my sister to die.

My army against the legions of the Pure consisted of two ancient enemies, who hated each other, and a pair of Blood Familiars who'd abandoned me.

Standing there, our gazes met: we'd battle together.

But we also knew that we'd all die.

25

Sometimes kisses are a revelation.

But sometimes, in the wartime heat of *goodbyes* before the fiery fury of battle, they're also a mistake.

Especially if they taste of sugar and blood.

Rebel had overheard Eden on the earpiece ordering a limo to drive him out to Tower Block B on the Utopia Estate.

Gizem's block.

Stephanie and Anarchy were to stay behind in charge of business at the hotel.

We'd known then where to take the fight to Eden. How to save Utopia.

Yet tonight was also the deadline for Drake's ultimatum: Return to Angel World or Drake would kill Jade.

I hunkered with Rebel in the dank graffiti sprayed stairwell in my old tower block, across from the one now controlled by the Pure; Eden's new gang made Bisi's look like kids playing at gangster.

Toben's soldiers had once done their deals in this concrete stairwell, when it'd been splice, rather than blood, which was the *food* on the Estate.

I banged the heel of my boot against the wall, glowering at the floor. The tang of urine mingling with the spicy bursts of old dinners was reassuringly familiar.

And human.

Blaze and Spark were red shadows patrolling the block, whilst Ash took command of the tech side with his gadgets.

Yet I had to wrap my arms around my middle, not to yank Commander Drake through my mind and onto the floor at my feet.

Not to betray the world for my sister.

Betray Rebel.

Lips, gentle on my forehead.

I glanced up, as Rebel kissed me.

Then Rebel rested his cheek against mine. 'I promised to protect you. And I will.'

'Did you miss the part where I'm now top boy?' I gripped his chin. 'I'm the bitch with the flames.'

'Don't,' he whispered. His gaze was searching, and I squirmed. 'I'll kneel for you, but only if I fight by your side. Or do you want to rule like Eden?'

My cheeks pinked. I shook my head.

'Have you forgotten what I've lost? What the git

did to my family?'

I wished I could forget. But his family's true love — sacrifice — I got that now.

'Ash's lost someone too.' I traced my finger across Rebel's lower lip to silence his protest. 'I had to watch — twice — whilst Anarchy was sacrificed to those fanatics. Angels hate vampires: cheers for the newsflash. But now we have to unite against the Big Bad. And that's Eden.'

'Inspired for battle, so I am,' Rebel smirked. 'This could be Agincourt.'

I laughed, smacking his nose. Then, without realising I meant to, I snogged him.

His lips tasted of sugar and blood. His tongue twined gently with mine, until I thrust deeper.

When he pulled back, his cheeks flushed, he opened and closed his mouth, unable to know what to say, before he tilted his head and asked, 'Does this mean you've taken me off your List of Asses to Kick?'

'Could be.' I licked along his lips, until they parted.

Then I clutched him by the shoulders and snogged him again.

'007 at your service...' Ash slunk into the stairwell, balancing an Apple laptop and bundle of tech on the ledge, before noticing the kiss.

Then Ash roared, marching towards us into battle. He hauled Rebel up and away from me by his collar.

My lips kissed air.

Mistake, mashing your sweet lips with pretty in punk when you're trying to hold together a peace accord with his love rival.

I didn't blow the bastard; I only kissed him.

A kiss is life. Powerful. Love. I'm sorry you don't understand that yet...

Ash smashed Rebel back against the opposite wall. I winced at the *crunch*. 'I was giving you the benefit, mate, but now you'll tell her.'

I pushed myself up. 'Tell me what?' I asked flatly.

'Dry up, vampire,' Rebel spat, struggling, 'and get your *filthy* hands off me.'

Ash stiffened, weakness shanked. He lowered his head. Then he yanked off Rebel's leathers, so fast Rebel yelped. He pulled out Rebel's bent wing. 'This is the last night before he Falls,' his voice was clipped, 'we *vampires* can sense each other when we're close.'

'Lay off, git, I'd die before I turned into a *dirty thing*, like you.'

Snap — Ash cracked Rebel's bent wing at the violet tip.

Rebel wailed, clawing at Ash.

Ash plucked handfuls of grey feathers, tearing them from Rebel's broken wing.

At last, I shook myself awake from the shock, diving to Ash. I hooked my arm around his throat, pulling him back. He choked but didn't struggle. I chucked him to the opposite side of the stairwell.

The two blokes stood panting, scowling at each other across the shadowy concrete space.

I'd screwed up our truce.

For the first time, I truly realised the ancient war I'd stumbled into.

'These,' Ash held up the handfuls of Rebel's blood tipped grey feathers, 'are medals of honour, not shame. A traitor like you doesn't deserve to wear them.'

When Ash tossed them to the floor like dirty snow, Rebel shrank back.

'How's that *not fighting* working out for you?' I growled at Ash.

'Not great since I met you, Violet.'

Sharp *barks*: Blaze and Spark's signal for the arrival of Eden's midnight-blue limo.

I shot Ash a last warning glare, before rushing to the ledge. I peered down over the playground towards Tower Block B.

The building blazed with light, as if every Pure had woken alongside their humans to welcome the celebrity.

Rebel hugged his broken wing to his stomach. 'I don't mean to give out here about our chances, but I can't fly at all now, since some great idiot wounded their own side.'

I dropped to kneel in front of the laptop, *tapping* wildly as I hacked the fire alarm system.

A shrill alien *beeping* echoed out through the night. 'Anarchy told me fire is Eden's weakness.' At Anarchy's name, Ash's expression finally softened. 'And I promised to burn down their house, just like they burnt down yours, wallad.'

Rebel glanced up at Ash. The two men studied each other warily, before nodding.

'And we're nuking them into orbit from here...?' Ash asked hopefully.

I stood upright: lightning and thunder streaked inside me. A storm that exploded the violet fire hissing down my arms and across my palms.

This time, it was both vampire and angel shrinking back.

The shifting powers inside howled *warrior*.

I grinned. 'Bitch of Utopia is home.'

'Bitch of Utopia is fierce frightening,' Rebel whispered.

'And hot,' Ash muttered.

I fired flames at the ground between their feet, and they danced back. Then they shot each other a smile, before remembering they hated each other and scowling.

The storm died down. But static still fizzed along my skin. Supercharged, the savage sides to me had never felt so close to the surface before.

'We have to show up the Utopia Project.' I studied the bleak concrete and purple Tower Block B. 'If it fails it won't be copied around the world.'

The fox brothers' eyes gleamed in the dark, their claws skittering on the concrete as they prowled to stand sentry at my side.

When I peered down at the playground below, residents were milling around in dressing gowns, wrapped in thick duvets or wool coats over bare legs. Kids swung on the swings or spun on the merry-go-round.

In silence.

Why were they outside in the middle of the night?

'It's like *The Walking Dead.*' When Rebel blinked and cocked his head, Ash struggled to hide his smile. 'Catch up on the box set classics at least, angel.'

'The Pure are guarding them,' Rebel pointed down, into the shadows.

Faces with star sharp eyes were caught by the moon's pale rays.

The Pure patrolled amongst their humans — *food supply* — alert and...anxious?

They glanced over their shoulders, casting long looks out into the shadows between the tower blocks.

This is it then, the final curtain.

And what's your choice? Fill me in. Because from my fabulous throne, I can see you about to take on an army of the Pure.

For humans.

The same humans who abused,

abandoned, and treated you as a freak.

Now tell me this is a punchline to a lame ass joke.

Gizem saved me. She's trying to save her sister. And she's in that tower block.

Anyway, what could be better than going down in a blaze of glory?

I scanned the vampires. 'That can't be all of them.'

Ash shook his head. 'I can sense they're out of the rooms, but some are blocking the stairs, guarding the way in and out. Except for one floor. And that's Pure HQ.'

I knew the number, before Ash said it: eleven.

Gizem's floor.

I whirled on Ash. 'How do we get in there?'

Rebel backed away, fiddling with the skull chained to his bondage trousers. 'That won't be a problem, princess.'

My heart pounded. Inky spots danced in front of my eyes. I couldn't breathe.

I launched myself at Rebel, grabbing his t-shirt between my fists harder than I'd intended. Then I slammed him against the wall.

Rebel gasped as his injured wing cracked. He pushed back, but stilled when Blaze snarled warningly.

'You always said I didn't trust you.' I spat. 'Except now I do, and you've turned Judas?'

Rebel quivered, his hands fluttering, as if desperate to touch me, but not daring. When he finally answered, he collapsed back against the wall in submission, 'The Brigadier was right. I can sense the Fallen now. And that means—'

'They can sense you.'

Rebel's betrayal booted me in the gut. The bastard had known and he'd hidden it.

When my hand heated around his throat, branding as I choked him, he didn't struggle.

Instead, his gaze was...disappointed.

But he didn't struggle.

Hurt me, kiss me, burn me...

My vision cleared, and I pulled in raspy breaths. I pressed my lips to Rebel's, as my fingers scorched.

'Save your fire,' Ash wrapped his arms around my waist, gently pulling me back from my stranglehold. Rebel bent over, clasping his seared neck. 'The angel is a muppet,' Ash's gaze was hard. Yet I realised with a jolt that he was pissed with *me*. 'But I hoped you were better than that, Violet. And by the way?'

There was a thunder of running footsteps either side of the walkway.

Three female members of the Pure — fangs and claws out — in snarling attack mode and matching silver sequin evening dresses like they were on the red carpet, bowled us against the ledge.

I blasted a skank with neon pink lipstick shrieking in a blistered heap.

Ash ducked another's claws and mouthed over his shoulder, 'Told you so.'

Rebel drew Eclipse, struggling to swing, as a harpy with platinum curls and high heels stomped on his boot, and then sank her fangs into his broken wing.

Blaze and Spark circled, snapping at the vampire's thin ankles.

I jerked her head back by the bleached roots, dragging her teeth out of Rebel's brutalized wing.

But when something pronged jabbed into my neck, I lost my grip.

Electricity thrummed through the stun gun.

I gasped as my body cramped. A juddering current tore the muscles down my back and neck. I overbalanced onto my tiptoes, hunching my arms closer around myself against the pain.

Bang...bang...bang...

The pressure dropped away, along with the stun gun.

I juddered; the tremors slowed.

Breathing heavily, I stared around at the Pure, who were like dolls in their party dresses, with bullets through their brains.

Ash was tucking away his shooter, with a shrug. 'I go *bang, bang.*'

Still trembling, I managed a shaky smirk.

Until the *hollers* from below.

I'd wanted an entrance but not like this.

Ash flushed. 'I forgot about the stealthy, what with the electrocution. How do you want to play this?'

The vampires below were crowding towards Tower Block A...and our stairwell.

It was a suicide mission to get across that playground — through that many Pure — now they knew we were here.

And it was my decision to make alone...?

When I hesitated, Ash dropped to his knee. 'You're my princess, Violet,' he said softly with a smile.

I glanced at Rebel, and he simply nodded. Then he also dropped to his knee, next to Ash.

I flushed, looking away from them. 'Cheers for the pressure, wallads.'

Rebel spluttered with laughter, bouncing to his feet. He held out his hand to Ash. Grudgingly, Ash took it, allowing himself to be pulled up.

'Screw it, we came to burn down Eden's house. And I want a burning.' I allowed the violet and black to spark through me, until I was flying. I nodded, and we stalked towards the stairs. 'No hurting the humans.' It was strange that I didn't even stop to consider myself one of those anymore. 'Now let's take this bitch down.'

When we sprang down the final steps, and I drew Star in a blinding arc, I grinned.

A troop of the Pure in dinner jackets and bow ties (we'd crashed one hell of a party), marched towards us across the playground, between the terrified humans shivering in the cold night air.

At least if we were going to die, we'd have an audience.

The flash of fangs, gleam of shank claws, and *gekkering* howls.

Blaze and Spark leapt from the steps over my head, steering with their bristling tails, before thudding into a blue dinner jacket bastard and ripping out his throat.

An outraged roar, and we were swept under the well-dressed wave.

The fox brothers were nothing but flashes of red, rattling *yelps*, and *howls*.

I pressed my hand, as if in blessing, to one burly bloke's forehead, and he fell squealing in flames.

When I was dragged backwards by my jacket, I struck with a spinning kick, slicing Star through the pretty blond vampire's hand.

Hands and fire. I'd never forgotten Rebel's lessons.

The hand dropped at the feet of a human kid like an offering. Crimson sprayed my cheek.

I was a god.

Yet when the bloke — a kid buried in puffer jacket and swag — stared at me, it wasn't with awe. He looked at me in the same way I had Rebel, after he'd snapped Toben's neck. I stumbled away, but the Pure struggling with Rebel caught my elbow, shoving me towards the kid.

I hissed at a sudden sharp pain. Confused, I pressed my fingers to my shoulder. When I drew back my hand, it was sticky with blood.

The human kid in the puffer jacket had his chin tilted defiantly, but his hands that clutched the gory blade shook.

And these are the jackasses you're sacrificing Jade and your own hoochie ass for?

They're like me, J, can't you see that? That kid's just protecting his own.

I snapped the human kid's wrist — *crack* — and he squealed. 'Not your fight, soldier.' I glanced over at Ash, who was slamming a vampire with a peak of chestnut hair and classic dinner jacket repeatedly into the metal pole of the swings. 'Playtime's over,' I called, waving Star towards Tower Block B.

Ash nodded, before wrapping the swing's chain around the fanatic's neck and pulling.

Ash was no James Bond. He was the hot villain who strangled him.

The Blood Familiars snapped at ankles and calves, biting through our enemies.

When Rebel heard my call, he fell back, away from a snarling gang of the Pure. Limping and clutching his broken wing, he swung his glowing sword in front of him, as if its light could ward them off.

Then Rebel blew on the flames and they ignited, whooshing heat across the playground.

Red-hot screeches, as the Pure flared violet to the night sky. *Vampire fireworks*. Rebel burnt them Hackney style.

We edged closer to Tower Block B, which rose above us monstrous. The mirror of my old home.

And Eden's dream project that would cast the world to hell.

The bald bastard with the wing tattoos, as if birds had exploded from his mind, thrust through the ranks of the Pure towards us. In gleaming white tux and black bow tie, he hunkered with his claws primed at his knuckles: the claws I'd mistaken for a shank, and the reason I'd abandoned Rebel and run on the first day I'd met him.

I stiffened.

Maybe I abandoned Rebel as much as others had abandoned me.

Maybe I did it to punish Rebel *because* they'd abandoned me.

Rebel's hand squeezed mine.

Then a circle of humans stumbled around us, breathless and trembling. We shoved them away, but they pressed closer.

The vampires watched, smirking.

Stun guns... I noticed them casual in the fanatics' hands.

The Pure were stinging the humans' arses with shots of electricity to drive them towards us.

I growled, pushing a stout middle-aged bloke back, before catching Ash's arm to stop him clouting a woman who was burrowed in her faded duvet. When someone tripped into my back, I spun, pinning them with my sword.

A girl.

She shivered in her unicorn nightie, sobbing in the snow. Then she collapsed to the ground, curling into a ball and dragging her thin arms over her head.

As if she could hide from the monster.

I'd almost knifed her.

I still hungered to kill her.

'Stop,' I whispered and then hollered, 'bastard

stop.' When Rebel and Ash glanced at me, I tried not to let my voice waver, 'I won't do this by bringing bones and feathers to the world. I'm a hunter but I don't gank humans. So, fly away now, Brigadier, this mission is over.'

Ash shrugged. 'I've nowhere else to be. Anyway, would Han abandon Princess Leia?'

'What about you, pretty boy punk? If your wings weren't—'

'Nothing to do with my wings.' Rebel stroked the back of my hand. 'I'm yours.'

I smiled, before bending down to Blaze and Spark. When they whined, I stroked their ears. 'Run and be free. Ash was right, you don't belong to anyone.' Then I stood on tiptoe to wave at Bird Tattoo. 'Wing face, white flag's being waved over here, yeah?'

Bird Tattoo grimaced, shoving through the cowering humans. When he spun me, I braced myself.

I jumped at the spark and buzz of electrified cuffs, which bound my hands behind my back.

Bird Tattoo sneered, before shackling Ash and then Rebel. When he gobbed in Rebel's face and punched him in the gut, it was Ash who snarled. Then Bird Tattoo smoothed down his tux and grabbed my arm, parading me through the fanatics' ranks.

The Pure clapped and whooped.

I flushed, ducking my head to hide behind my hair, even as I glanced between the ash blonde strands at the looming tower block.

Floor Eleven — Eden and Gizem.

The battle with the Pure, on the night my sister was set to die.

Yet I was handcuffed, knifed in the shoulder, and my allies were defeated.

Bird Tattoo's hold on me tightened as he dragged me into the shadow of Block B, for a date with the bloke who craved to kill me and feast on the world.

26

Born and raised in the shadow of Hackney, my bloody death had haunted me ever since I'd clasped my first shank.

Bitches like me died on the streets.

Yet the chance to go out battling for something *righteous* had spiralled me to violet glory. Now I shook, however, that I'd bleed out shackled. Worse? My Brigadier and punk Rebel would suffer the same.

Tower Block B, floor eleven. Gizem's fiery orange apartment.

Violins, in an imperious waltz, soared from the sound system on the glass coffee table. The table was a riot of white lilies. The intense sweet scent was sickening.

I shifted from foot to foot, glancing down at Rebel and Ash's boots on either side of mine because it was easier than looking up at Eden. We were lined in front of him: peasants before a king.

Eden sprawled on a flame red armchair; his coat hung artfully open. His eyes glittered as he examined his captives, like we were tasty treats at a tea party.

Bird Tattoo prowled behind us in guard mode.

A soft kid's sobbing was coming from behind the closed door of Aylin's bedroom.

Gizem's bedroom door was closed. She wasn't sobbing. Hell, I wished she was because her silence hurt worse.

Carefully, I tested the cuffs, hissing as my skin blistered: these must be custom-made for angels and vampires. I scanned the apartment, from the fawn divan underneath the window, piled with fluffy cushions, to the corridor with the cracked radiator, through to the kitchen.

All ordinary. Except for the leader of the Pure and his prisoners.

'Kneel to your king.' Eden waved at the laminated flooring. When I hesitated, he nodded to Bird Tattoo. 'A pawn must learn when the game is lost.'

Bird Tattoo shoved me in the back, and I gasped from the sudden jolt to my knife wound.

I stumbled forward a step. But I didn't kneel.

Bird Tattoo stomped to Aylin's bedroom. When he wrenched open the door, and Aylin's wail rose in crescendo with the violin, I dropped to my knees.

Aylin believed in bastard Father Christmas. Gizem was trying to give her a life — *hope* — that we'd never had.

In a single moment, Bird Tattoo could've torn it

from her.

What if he had already?

To my surprise, Rebel and Ash sank to their knees next to me. Both their shoulders brushed mine — one on either side — warm and solid.

It gave me strength.

Eden clapped his hands. 'How delightful: three wicked rebels on their knees, soon to be punished by the Pure armies.'

'Crack on with it then, bro,' I tilted my chin, 'or are you killing us with your rhymes?'

Eden leant forward on his blazing throne. 'If you wish to burn my house, I shall burn yours. The birthing pains of all ancient blood feuds.' When Ash stiffened, Eden chuckled. 'Whore, your bugs were such a short game of hide-and-seek. Although,' he kicked his bare feet up onto the glass table, 'you shall still make a pretty soldier on your hands and knees.'

I snarled, struggling to stand, but Ash shook his head.

Eden pouted. 'Do you now wish to know why my purified are dressed for the ball?'

I lifted my eyebrow. 'They're waiting for you to turn into a pumpkin?'

Eden pointed his long foot at me. 'This is the night I catch a monster by the toe, and if it squeals, gut it in the snow.'

I recoiled.

He knew all along, J, about tonight. He set us up.

Eden plays with the mind. He's a vampire Drake.

With the power inside, you could bleed the world dry, but you're the only one who can choose it.

'How.... Who grassed?' I didn't look either side

at Rebel or Ash; I didn't want to catch the flash of guilt before I knew the truth.

But I could still sense they'd both stiffened.

Eden glanced around at the tiny apartment. 'You own an enemy, by owning those they love.' He sprang across the coffee table, booting the sound system to stuttering silence. He bent me backwards, sweeping me into his arms. 'Monster and vampire, sitting in a tree, K-I-S-S-I-N-G.' Then he kissed me tenderly on the lips as he murmured, 'I could've chosen anywhere in the City, but I nest with the girl who loved you enough to save you from a vampire's embrace. I told you, I have been dreaming of this from the moment of your birth.'

I struggled then, snapping at Eden's full lips, until he backed away.

No one had grassed; Eden had planned this.

Eden's played me — all of us.

Our mistake was not guessing just how long Eden has been in this game.

Eden gave a high laugh and strolled to the armchair, before throwing himself down.

Hell, everything here on the Estate — the cuckooing in Tower Block B and Gizem and her sis held as hostages — was happening because of *me*.

When I'd thought to blaze in the hero, I'd already painted the target on their backs.

I wasn't birth. The Beginning. Saviour. I was death. The End. Destroyer.

When I panted, sinking onto my arse, Rebel stooped over me. Suddenly, he gave me a hidden grin and whispered, 'I told you we'd get in. Now we hunt.'

I stared at Rebel like he'd snapped.

That had been his plan all along?

There'd been no betrayal because Rebel had *known* he'd be sensed, we'd be captured, and then dragged in here...where he reckoned I'd take out Eden?

More secrets.

Yet the problem with Rebel's plan was that Eden was right. He owned the people I loved, so he owned me. The vampires had herded the humans back into the tower block. If the choice was to save myself, my sister, Rebel and Brigadier by burning down this human world, then maybe I wasn't like Eden.

Because I wouldn't take it.

Yet Rebel was smiling at me with such faith, it made my heart ache. No one had ever looked at me like that.

Why the hell did Rebel have to look at me like that now?

'My sweet lost angel,' Eden crooned, casting a hooded glance between Rebel and me. The bastard had noticed Rebel's smile too. 'By the time the long night ends, you'll be the Fallen.'

You own an enemy, my owning those they love...

I drew in my breath, jerking away from Rebel.

Just getting it now?

But I don't love Rebel...I just...don't hate him.

That <u>he</u> loves <u>you</u>, hooker. The bondage angel loves you.

Eden nodded at Bird Tattoo again; Bird Tattoo hauled up Rebel under his arm like he was a kid and dropped him onto Eden's lap.

When Rebel squirmed, Eden encircled his throat with his hands, just brushing over the base of his neck in warning.

Rebel stilled, breathing heavily, yet his look at me was still hopeful, like he expected me to spring up and save him.

Save the world.

A tear escaped down my cheek, and I couldn't hide it.

I stared at the picture on the wall above Eden's head.

It was the first design I'd ever made for *Angels vs Vampires*: a warrior angel, victorious and rising to perfection.

Why had I ever reckoned I could be her?

Eden stroked down the front of Rebel's trousers, smacking the outside of Rebel's hip when he shrank back. 'Tomorrow, when you Fall, you'll make a pretty pet.'

'Don't touch him.' *Mine* — my blood sang — to touch, kiss, hurt...

Eden pushed Rebel's leather jacket off his trembling shoulders, twisting it over his handcuffs. When Rebel tried to keep his wings folded back, Eden pinched his sensitive shoulder blades, until his wings drooped limply at either side in their mangled ruin. Eden's face flushed with outrage. 'Who has so defiled my lost one? Such sacrilege! The wings must be whole, a perfect offering, when they're purified.' His gaze flickered to Ash. 'Crawl to lie at my feet.'

Ash raised his eyebrow at me, as if awaiting my command, but jumped when Rebel yowled.

Eden's steel claws were buried in Rebel's thigh, like a lion pinning down its prey. 'Crawl, whore.'

I nodded, and Ash crawled around the coffee table, before lying tensely on his face in front of Eden.

Bird Tattoo dragged down Ash's army coat, pulling out his soft grey wings.

Then he stalked to me and wrenched back my hair. The cold nick of a flick-knife pressed against my throat.

A *click* and Rebel was tumbled to the floor, with

the handcuff removed from his right wrist.

'Pretty matching pets with bloody wings.' Eden tossed a shank to Rebel. Then he drew his fingers through his hair with a dramatic sigh. 'A choice: carve the feathers from the Fallen, or allow us to slice the monster.'

As if an army order had already been given, Ash spread out his wings for the blade.

I shook.

Rebel bent over Ash, the shank tracing the violet tip feather.

When he looked round at me, the knife raised, I expected to see victory on his face — his revenge on the vampire, enemy, *rival* who'd broken and ripped the feathers from his own wing — not agonised despair.

He sank in the blade at the tip, and Ash screamed.

Then the shank was falling from Rebel's fingers. 'Do it to *me*.' His freed hand rubbed backwards and forwards pleadingly on Eden's bare feet. 'Don't be after making me—'

Ash surged up to his knees. 'That wasn't an option. Hack now, angst later.'

Eden stroked both their heads. 'Did the war end? Are you not hunter and hunted? But if you refuse, I'll pluck the whore myself and bleed a monster.'

Rebel snatched up the shank and drove it into Ash's wing.

When Ash hollered, I shuddered, sinking into my mind and searching for it: the violet righteousness, twined with seething black that could...if not save us...then *stop this*.

The one Rebel believed in.

Yet as Ash writhed in scarlet agony, and Rebel's quick glances at me became at first cautious, then doubting, and finally blank — the same as Drake's, Jade's, mine — nothing flared but my own powerlessness.

The sense that this truly was my night to die.

Crimson. Blood dripping from outstretched wings. Mutilated, the feathers carved out...

Here was the Ash of my dreams, lying in his own feathers and blood.

If I'd chosen to return to Angel World with Drake, I could've saved the Brigadier.

Future paths, memories, visions...

You can't trust them, believe me.

But what about Rebel wingless on his knees and Jade dying with a shank to the guts?

What if they...?

And what if you're so focused on them not coming true, you make them happen?

How could Angel World be any worse?

I made the wrong choice. Drake's pill was safety, and I chose suffering.

When Eden pulled Rebel back onto his lap, he slipped the shank from Rebel's scarlet hand, before flicking off the feathers and sucking the bloody fingers.

Ash lay motionless, struggling to breathe.

Eden caressed Rebel's slumped shoulders. 'There, let's have some refreshments with our entertainment.'

Gizem had never been silent.

I'd seen her beaten, dumped back from foster homes, fired from jobs, and on the day that she'd discovered she was pregnant.

She'd always had something to say.

Yet when Bird Tattoo led her out of Aylin's bedroom wrapped in a threadbare bathrobe, she shuffled with her head down, without saying a word.

Ash had been spot on: *Walking Dead.*

Gizem startled when she saw me on my knees, a vampire with his wings shanked bloody, and an angel like a little boy on his daddy's lap.

But barely.

Eden *clucked* at her, like she was a skittish chicken, before winding his hand through her lank hair and pulling her close enough to sink his fangs into her neck.

Gizem had saved me from Phoenix, taking the slash to the face, which should've been my throat.

But I had to watch as a vampire drank from her.

Yeah, Rebel had made *a balls* of teaching me to be a vampire hunter.

'Drink from my cup,' Eden pressed Gizem's scarlet neck against Rebel's resisting lips.

Rebel twisted away. When his tongue licked out, across the blood dribbling down his chin, he shuddered. 'I'm an Addict, a bad angel, and a ball-bag. But I'm not the Fallen. Not like you.'

'Yes, so like me, by dawn. Drink.'

He shook his head.

Then he screeched, as Eden sank his claw into the base of his neck.

'Allow it,' I leapt up, booting the coffee table, until — *shatter* — it cracked, cascading lilies across the floor. 'He'll drink.'

This time the glare Gizem shot me was venomous.

Hell, I deserved it.

'I can't, Feathers,' Rebel's voice was husky; his eyes red-rimmed. 'Your blood was like soaring to the heavens, but I'll be cursed to hell if I—'

'I trust you.' Rebel gave a shocked gasp. He'd trusted me to save the world, yet it'd taken me to this moment to realise it was true. And it was too late. 'You asked, if you Fell, what I'd do. I know

now. I'd be proud to have you at my side, the same as Ash, because it doesn't make any difference what's done to you or who you become...you're still *you*. My Irish punk bondage wallad.'

Rebel blinked, before he whispered, 'Thank you, princess.'

His teeth descended to Gizem's neck.

He worried at the skin, sucking at the blood.

Mine...bound by blood.

Only mine.

I hadn't realised I was growling, until Eden elbowed Gizem onto the fawn divan and stroked Rebel's shoulders, calming him from the blood high.

I shook my head, cutting off the growl.

'Now I own everyone you love, monster. I own *you*. Wait, not everyone.' Eden clutched Rebel by one hand, whirling into Aylin's bedroom and drawing out a weeping bundle in pink pyjamas in the other. 'One little pink bird sitting in the sun, she took a nap...and then there were none.'

'No...' This time, I didn't even think.

I sprang over the coffee table, low roundhouse kicking Eden.

Eden stumbled onto the glass, shrieking as his bare soles sliced.

Ash struggled up, sweeping out Eden's knees with his bleeding wings; Eden crashed over the armchair.

Rebel dived after Eden, hooking him across the chin with his freed fist.

Gizem snatched her sister's hand, pulling her down onto the divan's cushions.

Slam — Bird Tattoo headbutted me.

I stumbled, tasting my own blood down the back of my throat.

Dizzy, I tripped. The orange apartment blurred,

as my head throbbed.

Then the *snick* of a flick-knife at my throat, and just as the world was saved, it was lost.

27

The power of a shank isn't in the sharpness of its blade, but in the brutality of the bastard wielding it.

Bird Tattoo pressed his knife closer into my neck, before wrenching me onto tiptoe by my hair

I grunted. Pain shot down the backs of my calves, as I struggled to balance, aching from my wounded shoulder. I bared my teeth at Eden.

Gizem curled on the divan, trembling in shock.

Rebel and Ash knelt beside the armchair, their heads bowed, but darting glances between the blade and Eden.

Eden glowered in the centre of the apartment; his slashed soles dripped blood onto the laminate.

And Aylin dangled from Eden's hand, her legs kicking in the air.

At last my true angelic power awakened because of a child who was loved, rather than abandoned. With a home, big sister, and *a chance*.

Rage surged: waves crashing on rocks, each one bigger and more violent than the last, until they exploded across the land, carrying everything away.

Can you feel it? It's coming now. All you need to do is ask.

I'm asking.

Then you're ready.

I jolted, and Bird Tattoo's flick-knife nicked my neck.

'You're a Human Lover. No better than an Addict.' Eden scraped his fangs along Aylin's quivering throat. 'It's why you'll always be weak.'

I stared at the picture of the warrior angel; the cloying scent of the crushed lilies wound around me.

'I'm all monster,' my voice hissed with the fire winding through my lungs and heart, 'and loving the world's what makes me powerful enough to burn down your house, bitch.'

I was lost in a sea of violet.

Righteous anger bubbled hotter than ever before, taking me over. When I pulled my hands apart, this time the handcuffs snapped.

Bird Tattoo pulled the knife away from my neck, and I dropped back onto my aching feet.

Voices dimmed.

I'd retreated to the back of my mind, and the grim glory reigned.

When I held up my hands, frozen flames flowed across my skin, engulfing my whole body.

Eden stared at me in terror. Bird Tattoo fell back, cowering against the radiator.

I met Rebel's steady stare. His smile was soft and hopeful. My heart leapt.

Then an arcing bolt of electric violet exploded from my chest. I bowed backwards, hung on the beam that'd consumed me.

The electric bolt hit Bird Tattoo. He howled. The beam burnt a charred core through his chest, before flowing over him, until he was shrouded in flickering violet.

Eden leapt for the door, struggling with the handle. But then the ray arced away...and hit him. He squealed, as the bolt shanked him. It dragged *him* up onto tiptoe. Then violet wept over his skin.

We were all connected by the beam. I heard their terrified thoughts. Their fear was mine. Their pain worshipped at my feet.

Rebel threw himself over Ash, his wings wrapping around his taller frame.

When the electric beam shot towards the huddled vampire and angel, I battled from the prison of my mind to deflect the bolt. But I wasn't in charge; the violet ruled me.

And it was alive, ancient, and deadly.

It singed Rebel's wings, hovering over his back. His t-shirt burnt; his back blistered. The beam, however, didn't suspend them in its web.

I closed my eyes.

The arc's captives shuddered.

Then the angelic power burst in a tidal wave so intense I rose in the air. My arms were flung out wide, as if I'd been crucified.

The current flowed in one wave through the entire tower block, from vampire to vampire, skewering them through the chest and flaming them violet.

A legion of minds caught within mine.

I was the destroyer. The land of bones and

feathers had been birthed on earth.

The world echoed with the screams of the Pure.

The beam burned fiery hot in a sudden blaze.

And there was nothing but silence.

The rage ebbed inside; I opened my eyes, in control again, as I sank to my knees.

Nothing.

Eden and Bird Tattoo — every one of the Pure in Tower Block B — had been burned to ash.

I pushed up, my shoulder blades buzzing.

Tendrils of glory snaked through me: a power even greater than the moment a shank sinks through skin.

I shook with tremors, but I laughed.

Tune down the glory.

It's time to work your extravaganza amongst the mortals again.

But I'm not mortal. The human mask has been burnt away and now...

What the hell am I? Where do I fit?

This weapon...

A taste of power makes you thirst to discover the well.

Yet once you do...? Addiction creeps in.

But how do I give up this feeling? The strength? It can save us.

Or it can rule you.

I still pulsed with the power that had healed me.

I flexed my shoulder, laughing again when there was nothing but the slight tug of freshly knitted skin. I raised my arms, revelling in the sparks crackling along them, even though a dark edge pulled at my mind to...*destroy and control*...rather than *save*, as Rebel had taught me.

A *whimper*.

Blackened wings and blistered back. Rebel curled with his arms around his head

The Brigadier, who'd dragged himself out from underneath the angel, was now sprawled on the floor clasping Rebel's hand, whispering soothingly to him.

When I booted the broken coffee table smashing against the far wall and marched towards them across the sea of white lilies, they both cringed back.

A flash of fury slashed at their fear: I was the hero.

They'd both knelt to me.

They were mine.

Yet they were pulling away from me in the moment of my victory...?

The commanding darkness itched to punish them.

It must've shown on my face because Ash forced himself up onto his knees in front of Rebel to defend them both.

From me.

I paled and stumbled. Then I reached down, twirling Ash and breaking his handcuffs. He shook away the hissing metal and shrugged off his coat with a gasp.

When I reached for Rebel, Ash tried to push me back, but I shoved him to the floor in a sizzle of flames.

Then I snatched Rebel.

'Please, princess...' Rebel's shoulders trembled under my fingers.

Fear feathered me through our bond, agonising and accusing.

Snap — I pulled apart Rebel's handcuffs.

Ash gripped Rebel around his waist, helping him to stand, his own bloody wings limp. Rebel's leathers slipped from his wrist, along with the sparking handcuffs.

Hurt them...punish them...burn them...

I backed away, panting.

Hell, they were right to fear.

Help me, J, please.

I'm about to unleash friendly fire on my own side.

You're right, it's ruling me. I don't want this power if it—

Corrupts?

You're the only one who can decide what you want to become.

What's inside you isn't good or bad. It's all in how you use it.

I stumbled to the corner of the room, pressing my back against the wall.

Jade... Rebel stroking down the back of my arm... Ash cocooning me safe in his aromatic feathers...

Slowly, the furious buzz faded to a hum and then a tingle.

The crash from the high, when it came, doubled me over. I clutched my stomach, whilst I sobbed.

It was like soaring the heavens, only to fall to earth.

Now I understood a shadow of what the Fallen had lost.

At once, Rebel and Ash were crouched over me, their burnt and mutilated wings veils.

I stroked both their wings in comfort.

The tears dried on my cheeks, but I couldn't help the way my breath hitched, 'They'll mend, yeah?'

Ash swallowed. He looked away. 'With blood. It's a small sacrifice for you and the world.'

At Rebel's moan, I cradled him to the ground. His head rested on my shoulder; his hands clasped the corners of my jacket, soothing himself against the pain. 'I told you, remember?' His eyelashes fluttered. 'I knew you'd fly higher than I could even dream.'

I brushed Rebel's sweaty hair back from his forehead. 'I had a good Custodian.' *Hurt them...punish them...burn them...* I took a shaky breath. 'Who...what am I? Who are my parents?'

At last, he lifted his gaze to mine. 'Who do you think we've been protecting you from, princess?'

I jerked back. 'What...?'

'*Monster*,' Gizem stalked towards us across her shattered apartment. She was glaring at Rebel, but I knew the word was meant for all three of us.

Gizem held up Bird Tattoo's flick-knife like a promise. But she'd already shanked me.

We were no longer the two Orphan Musketeers: I was a stranger.

I tried to warn you. You'll only ever truly have me.

I know you, down to the bones.

'I promised to protect you,' I glanced at Aylin's fuzzy head, as she burrowed further into the pile of cushions on the divan to hide, 'and kick this new gang out of our yard. I saved you.'

'It's not your yard anymore.' Gizem prowled closer, dragging her stained bathrobe around herself. When she waved the knife at Rebel, I held him closer. 'You let that...*thing*...bite and violate me. I'd never let anyone touch you. Don't you remember all the times *I* saved *you*?' She rubbed at the scar down her cheek. 'But now I reckon what everyone is saying is true. You're a killer.'

Ash straightened; he loomed over Gizem. 'She's Princess Leia, saving the universe, you ungrateful—'

'Yeah, she's not into our brand of geekery. So, you're not making much of a point.'

Ash shrugged. 'Hero. World. Saved.'

Gizem backed towards the divan, spinning the shank between her fingers. 'I don't care about the world,' she said blankly, 'I just know my mate Feathers is dead. Whoever you are, bitch? You're not her.'

'I sacrificed...everything...for you,' I couldn't look at Gizem, not through the blur of tears. I didn't dare raise my head. 'I'm changed, but I'm still me. Jade will die tonight because I chose to save you.'

Rebel startled.

His fingers caressed the pouch with Jade's necklace, as his other hand ghosted over mine.

'Then I know you're not *my* Feathers,' Gizem looked me up and down, 'because she'd never let her sister die.'

Ash's strong fingers clawed into my shoulder, pulling me to my feet. I yelped in shock, before Ash whispered urgently, 'We have to go. I can sense the Fallen Army. They're not far from here. And it's rare for them to get medieval like this, unless there's an epic battle about to wage. Something must've happened that they've been waiting for because it takes planning and mind control to mask it from humans.'

'I'm not saving these humans from Eden, just to—'

Ash snatched up his coat, shrugging it on with a grimace. 'They're not after the humans.'

Rebel bounced up, wincing as he slid on his leathers. 'Bang on! They're after you, princess. Your power was a beacon to summon them. The Supreme Commander will have stirred himself after such a fine show.'

I froze; everything slowed.

Rebel spun me in a circle, before kissing my forehead.

It was gentle and tender.

As if it wasn't a Judas kiss.

As if Rebel hadn't been playing me all along and now had delivered me up to the Fallen Army.

Fat rain tears blurred the barren sludge of London Fields, masking the wetness streaming down my own cheeks, as I forged across the icy park.

Red tinged the clouds, like blood clouding water.

Dawn struggled to be born on a day in which my sister would die.

And Rebel would Fall.

I staggered to a stop in the downpour, shivering. My top stuck to my soaked skin.

Two bedraggled foxes wound between the London Planes.

My Blood Familiars had been following us since we'd left the tower block but they hadn't ventured any closer.

Maybe they were frightened of me too.

Yet now I was the prey.

I tried to sink back into that place where the violet flamed, alive and savage, but there was nothing but smouldering embers.

Bring it back, J.

When the Fallen find us—

It's too late. They've already found you because the punk played traitor.

Where's the righteousness in saving your own ass?

You need to learn to survive on your own.

I swung my arms, scuffing my boot through the muddy slush.

'No stopping,' Ash grabbed my hand, 'they're almost here. The military call this a strategic retreat. Basically? It's time to run away.'

I shook his hand off and backed up. 'I'm not running. I've been hiding...on the run...for months.' Rebel's shoulders slumped; the rain plastered his hair into his eyes. His gaze met mine for a moment, before he looked away. 'The bastards'll catch us, sooner or late. But I hunt bastards. So, this is as good a place as any to fight the Fallen.'

Ash glanced around at the wide park, before giving a brisk nod. 'Old-fashioned battlefield. We can work with that. If we'd had some time we could've gone guerrilla *Rambo* style...'

'And you'll fight against your own army...?'

Ash crossed his arms, staring fixedly away at the line of London Plane Trees. 'What about him?' He raised an eyebrow at Rebel, who shrank back

When I stalked towards Rebel, I hadn't expected the defiant scowl or tilt of the chin. 'In about an hour the sun comes up, and you Fall. Are we the bribes to buy yourself in with your new gang? Did you always plan to hand me over to the Fallen Army? Has everything been an act? Were you plotting to Fall all along?'

Rebel shook his head. 'You know me better than that, woman.'

I dragged him forward by his collar, not loosening my grip, even though he gagged. 'Trust, loyalty, fam.' He winced at each shanking word. 'You're like a kid, lost in the dark.'

'I *was* in the dark,' he choked out, 'for long black decades. Centuries before, I waited. Alone. I need you. But I also *needed* you to help me.'

I shook him so hard, he scrabbled at my hands. But he didn't fight back. 'Why?'

'Family,' he gasped. 'Redemption.'

I backhanded him; his lip split. 'You used me.'

Why the hell was my voice trembling?

Rebel's laugh was bitter. 'Just like you were after using me? To free yourself, find your sister, and fight the Pure? Tell me, when weren't you using me?'

I shoved him away, my hands shaking.

The denial died on my lips.

And he hadn't even said *when you snogged me...tried to screw me...hurt me...burnt me...*

Because they'd have been true too.

Why hadn't Rebel said...those other things?

I blushed, glancing away.

I knew why. Despite everything, the wallad loved me.

When Ash drew his shooter and held it to Rebel's temple, Rebel didn't even flinch. 'Permission to execute the traitor.'

Rebel's gaze met mine unwavering.

His mascara had run in the rain, like black tears. He didn't battle or beg, he simply waited on my judgement.

Like I was Eden on his throne.

My mouth was too dry to speak, as Ash's finger tightened on the trigger.

Rebel smiled sadly, but he didn't move.

Sugary copper warred with citrus cloves.

I knocked Ash's arm away from Rebel's head. 'Fam is fam,' I muttered.

Rebel sagged, pressing his palms to his eyes.

Then the red-tinged sky darkened, as if the newly birthed sun had been blocked out.

A wind blasted us, hurricane-style, from the direction of the City with the warrior flapping of hundreds of wings.

We drew together: monster, vampire, and angel.

Three against the legion of the Fallen Army, who flew like an ancient plague through the London skies to wage war.

Yet I didn't know if the truth was I stood alone, with two Fallen at my side ready to betray me.

28

I never expected I'd face down an army of vampires, who hadn't crawled deformed from a pit, but beautiful winged from the red-teared skies. War-moths, they soundlessly landed on the greens of London Fields, like black stars fallen.

War had come to Hackney.

And I was Violet of Troy: the bitch they battled to possess and carry home.

But I'd no longer be anybody's girl but my own.

The winged ranks marched towards us. The blood dawn haloed the Fallen Army.

Cold rain ran down the back of my collar; I

shivered. When Ash's arm snaked around my waist, I was wrapped — just for a moment — in the aromatic scent of safety.

Until an albino Fallen, with pure white hair swinging to his waist and hooped piercings through his nose and ears, like a goth elf in floor-length black leather coat, paced forward. He snapped his fingers at Ash, as if he was a dog. 'Here, Seducer.'

Ash coloured. Then he dragged his hand through his hair and took a step towards the Albino Fallen. Almost as quickly, he jerked backwards, shaking his head.

I snatched Ash's wrist. 'You told me you weren't nice,' I couldn't hide the edge of tears, even if I could stop them falling, 'but no way in hell did I take *you* to be a traitor.'

Ash spun, whispering, 'I'd never betray you. But you crave to own, and the thing about *being* owned...? It sucks.'

I dropped Ash's wrist, and he pulled away from me. He didn't look back, trudging towards the Albino Fallen, with his head down and his hands buried in the pockets of his coat.

The Albino Fallen seized Ash, tangling his hand in Ash's thick hair and slapping him, hard enough to make Ash stagger.

Sniggers ran along the line.

When the Albino Fallen clasped Ash to his chest, running his hand possessively down his chest, Rebel's snarl answered mine.

Owned.

Ash understood the powers inside me: the violet and black curling underneath my skin crooned that he *belonged to me.* Yet the danger of listening to the siren song was being played out in the way the Albino Fallen clamped his hand around Ash's neck, whilst he stroked down his jeans.

Ash closed his eyes, turning away his head.

The geek Seducer was never yours. Now the game must go on.

But there's only Rebel and the foxies...

There's only you, sweet cakes. There's always been only you. Didn't I raise you to remember that?

A sodden dash of rusty red — like blood streaking through the rain — and the familiars broke from the cover of the trees.

I smiled. I needed the little furry bastards winding around my ankles. Their *howl*, *shriek* and *snap*.

But instead, they wove away from me, towards Ash.

'Blaze! Spark!' I hollered.

The foxes turned their heads to gaze at me, sinking onto their haunches at Ash's feet. They nuzzled his calves to comfort him, as the Albino Fallen's hand gripped Ash's neck harder.

And then there were two...

Tower Block B? Lit up, like fairy lights, with rainbow arcs of the Pure strung together? There was only one then.

And what about you?

I'm part of you, hooker, whether you love or hate me.

'My brother...I have to try...' Rebel bounced on the balls of his feet, his pinkie linking with mine, before he dove towards Wings.

Wings stood at the front of the Fallen ranks, his arms crossed over his denim jacket. The red lit his auburn bristles like a halo. He held up his arm to stop the other Fallen attacking at Rebel's excited dash.

Rebel launched himself at his brother, clinging to him. 'Please, there's no need to fight. Give me a chance, Briathos. I know I've made a balls of things, but we're family.'

And then there was one...

Bondage boy was always bad, Featherylove. The question is why you ever wanted him to be good?

Wings rested his hand between his brother's shoulder blades.

I should've hoped Wings shanked the punk who'd betrayed me. Yet all my heart ached was...*don't hurt him...not again.*

Wings' other hand stroked across the barbed wire line of feathers, which were tattooed across his throat, before he spun Rebel and shoved him skidding face down in the slushy mud.

In front of his enemies.

His family.

The sniggers became *guffaws.*

Rebel slammed his fist — in a squelching spray — into the puddle. Then he raised his head and our gazes met. He couldn't mask the desperate pain fast enough: humiliated, rejected, and abandoned in front of his own.

Hell, if I ever discovered my fam, after years of searching, only to be kicked in the mud...?

I'd rent the world to ribbons.

Rebel struggled to stand, his cheeks streaked with dirt and rain. Wings took a run at him, booting him in the arse and sprawling him deeper into the mire.

A cheer erupted from the ranks; Wings lifted his arm in mocking salute.

I winced.

Rebel reddened, pushing himself to his knees again. This time, he turned half warily and half hopefully to the warrior next to Wings.

The Fallen warrior watched Rebel in stony

silence. He towered over everyone, in a sea green suede jacket. He was older, although with the same flame red bristles, and a beard like a Celtic Chieftain.

'Da...?' Rebel tilted his head, his neck exposed and vulnerable.

This...*hulk*...was Rebel's true da...?

I tensed, lurching a single pace forward, before stopping myself.

'You're dead to the Supreme Commander, git angel,' Wings raised one pieced eyebrow. 'Did you forget that if I saw you again, it'd be as my prisoner?'

Rebel ignored Wings. He repeated, more forcefully, 'Da?'

The Supreme Commander of the Fallen strode forward. His eyes blazed severe and pitiless.

I slipped my hand to Star's hilt.

Rebel breathed hard, his chest rapidly rising and falling, but like a lamb on the altar, he didn't reach for his sword. Instead, he knelt before his dad, with that terrible hope burning in his gaze.

Please...please don't...

The Supreme Commander stopped, close enough to have reached out and cupped his youngest son's trembling cheek. He examined him: from his rain drenched hair, to the collar tight at his neck.

Yet all without saying a word.

Rebel shook far more than could've been caused by the rain, as if in the grip of a fever. 'Da, please...'

Long, black steel claws unsheathed from the Supreme Commander's nails, a second before they slashed across Rebel's face.

As if at a signal, all along the line, the vampires' claws shot out.

I unsheathed Star, holding the dagger high in

front of me.

Rebel knelt in the muck at his dad's feet. Scarlet lines scored his cheek; the rain wept away the blood. And still he didn't reach for Eclipse.

This isn't your fight. The Irish boy delivered you up to the Fangs. He deserves this.

Nobody deserves this. Anyway, fam is fam. And I protect my own.

'Come to us, princess,' the Supreme Commander held out his large hand to me.

'Stick it, bro.' I lunged across London Fields, dragging Rebel back by the arm.

Rebel struggled. 'Why...? Da... Briathos...'

Slap — Rebel shook his head against my blow but then focused on me.

'They don't want you, and if you don't land back in reality, they'll claw your pretty head from your shoulders.' I shook Rebel and then caught a sob at the back of my throat, holding my sodden sleeve to my mouth to stop the broken screams. 'You're a monster. Bad, damaged goods, broken. A freak. That's why you've no family. Rejected. Abandoned. *Nobody could ever want you.*'

I choked, fighting for breath, as if my insides had already been shredded.

When I looked up, Rebel's pinkie brushed mine again.

Rebel's smile was shaky, but his look was one of such gentle understanding, I gasped. 'You're right, princess. But *we're* not alone.' He drew Eclipse. The light caught the metal studs on his leathers: punk armour. 'Who do you want to fight first, Feathers?' He smirked. 'Take your pick.'

'How about the bastard Fang who booted my Custodian in the arse?'

His smile wavered, before it broadened into a

grin. 'Your Custodian? If only for this battle, let's see if we can't boot his muppet arse.'

We rushed at Wings, lifting him by the waist and dividing him from the ranks. He yelped, but couldn't squirm away. We hurled him into the same slushy puddle into which he'd kicked Rebel.

Wings arose, shaking his head and dripping muddy water, to the chuckles and clapping of his own troops.

Fickle bastards the Fallen.

Surging towards us, Wings hooked Rebel under the chin, before sweeping his feet out from under him. Then he pounded Rebel in the guts; Rebel groaned.

I threw myself on Wings, gripping the back of his denim jacket and heaving him away from Rebel.

But I dropped Star away from Wings. I remembered the distress tearing through Rebel when I'd threatened his brother with the dagger out here before.

I wasn't the same bitch now.

Rebel sprang up and launched himself at his brother. He tackled Wings down to the ground, dropping Eclipse.

The two brothers grappled in the sludge, before Rebel pinned Wings beneath him.

I glanced at the Supreme Commander and the Fallen Army. Not a single vampire stirred, instead watching the gladiatorial combat with glee.

Rebel bit his lip so hard it bled; his shoulders quivered. He clouted his brother across the face, first one way and then the other. At each word he laid into Wings, 'Why...won't...you...forgive...me?'

Two swollen eyes scowled up at him. 'Because that's not redemption.'

Rebel scrambled back, like his brother had spewed fire.

I blinked, squinting up into the sky.

On the opposite side of Hackney to the red dawn crawling behind the Fallen, indigo bled into the sky.

A violet horizon...flew towards us.

Wings slunk to his feet. 'Still a traitor then? You brought your friends to the party?'

'The angels aren't my mates.' Rebel had become still; his face ashen. 'They're my gaolers.'

When Wings limped back towards his ranks, Rebel snatched up Eclipse.

'This is war then? Both sides are going to battle over me?' I clasped Star in sweaty hands. 'Why am I so special?'

Rebel grinned, but his eyes were achingly sad. 'You're so much more than I'll ever be. I wish... I'm sorry—'

'Save it. If we're not sliced into a fine red mist by either side, then I'll expect the best on your knees apology, with begging and chocolate. But first? We fight.'

He nodded.

Butterfly light, the angels landed: an army of pulsing violet winged beauty. I fought not to prostrate myself before them in adoration.

Yet every one of those angels hadn't saved me when I'd called out to them.

Drake marched forward: David to the Supreme Commander's Goliath. He ignored me, as if the monster in the midst of the two armies was nothing but a pawn.

Commander Drake was in for a shock.

'The princess belongs to us,' Drake faced down the Celtic giant, even as his bare feet sank into the mud, and his sheer trousers stuck to his arse in the rain.

'She's ours, and we intend to take her,' the

Supreme Commander of the Fallens' gruff response — the counter in a fierce business negotiation — shot flames coiling through my guts.

The bastard spoke about wanting me, but he wouldn't even talk to his own son...?

'Hey,' I yelled, 'better tell your soldiers to go home. Because nobody *owns* the Bitch of Utopia.'

Rebel grinned. We both spun, until we were back-to-back. Then we raised our weapons.

'Is she always like this?' The Supreme Commander grimaced.

Drake's lips curled up, before he coughed, hiding his smile with the back of his hand. 'Unfortunately, yes.'

'Commander Drake,' Rebel's dad asked, with the reluctant respect of one old war leader to another, 'in your judgement, is she insane enough to fight, regardless of our own battle?'

Drake lifted an eyebrow at me, before nodding, 'Supreme Commander Flynn, that would be another yes.'

Then both Commanders raised their arms in signal.

Listen to me, you make a choice: black or violet. Bones or feathers. This war is—

Crazy. A couple of months ago, I thought I was just a regular woman. Before my twenty-first birthday and the fever that changed me, I was only a gamer with a kid sister. But now there's angels, vampires, and wars between them <u>over me</u>. You want me to choose? I choose humans, J.

You didn't choose Jade. In an hour, she'll be dead. And the angel at your back? He'll have Fallen.

I grasped Star so hard the hilt bit into my palm.

Rebel glanced over his shoulder at me, before gripping my other hand.

Slam.

This time the sugary copper spiralled me high, until I was bouncing on my toes, like Rebel. Until we were both grinning like wallads, as Drake sighed...and brought down his arm.

The steel sweep of beating violet wings, mixed with a wall of grey feathers. Flashes of flame. *Shrieks, screams, screeches.* Tearing of flesh from tendon and bone: *hands and fire.*

Johnny Rotten's swag punk vocals and the killer guitar riff of "God Save the Queen" looped around my mind, whilst I shanked, barbequed, and booted in the balls.

Our brutal dance was beautiful.

Why had I ever let Rebel think he was a bad Custodian?

He'd freed me, as I'd freed him.

A hiss of pain, and I twisted to look over my shoulder.

The Albino Fallen's claws were sunk into Rebel's chest. Rebel struggled, pinned and panting. But the Albino Fallen raked his claws, like Legolas' evil twin, down Rebel's chest to his guts.

Rebel howled, swinging Eclipse, but the Albino Fallen crushed his wrist.

I didn't notice Ash in the melee, until he'd hooked his arm around the Albino Fallen's throat. Then he'd dragged the other vampire away from Rebel, into the sea of wings.

I thrust Star through the nearest wing; the feathers steamed. I yanked back my blade, booting the howling angel.

Suddenly Ash, his forehead streaked with scarlet, was at my back as well. I shuddered with the solid warmth of his touch.

And then there were three...
But for how long?
Don't you get it? That doesn't matter.

They have my back now when it counts. I won't forget it.

'I couldn't be in debt to you for saving me from frying,' Ash shot at Rebel, clouting an angel in the nose, 'or miss this *Game of Thrones* battle.'

'This is a game?' Rebel blinked.

'Box set marathon. Pizza. My place,' Ash twirled to kick the next vampire, but the vampire caught his foot, twisting his leg out of its socket. Then he hurled him back into the ranks of the Fallen.

Away from us.

Wings.

He was the bastard who'd dragged Ash back to the side of the Fallen.

I turned to help, only for Rebel to snatch my arm. 'He's after using the Brigadier as bait.'

'What?'

Wings jumped on Ash's arm.

Crack.

I flinched as Ash's arm broke, and then as Wings stomped on it again.

Ash's bellow rose above the clash of the battle.

I quivered, burying my shank in a vampire's guts; his squeal equaled Ash's.

Crack.

I cringed.

I couldn't lose myself in the beauty of the fight and the *beat* of the Sex Pistols anymore, only the *crunch* of bones, blast of fire, and gash of the shank.

Crack.

I turned my head towards Ash, almost missing the flash of movement behind me.

Rebel.

I whirled, but an angel with shiny jet braids to her waist and glowing ebony skin, had already pinned Rebel's arms at his side, wrapping her wings around him like a Venus flytrap.

One hard yank and Rebel had been swallowed into the pulsing angelic mouth.

I howled, searing a blistering path across grey and violet wings alike.

But Ash and Rebel were lost.

I was alone.

Crack.

I swung Star, shuddering at Ash's pain.

Then I sprang over crumpled bodies for a glimpse of Rebel.

He'd been pushed to his knees; Drake's fingers pressed at the base of his neck.

I'd sworn Rebel would never be touched by Drake again.

That he'd never go back into the dark.

Star fell limp in my hand as I collapsed to the muddy grass.

Tears joined the rain streaming down my face; their salt was tangy on my lips.

I'd saved the world but I'd sacrificed...everything.

I'd known I would. But that didn't make it easier.

Get that hoochie ass up. Since when did you give up?

It's not giving up to save my blokes.

They've earned that.

Someone dragged me backwards by my feet, banging my head against the ground.

Bump, bump, bump.

I sprawled in a dirt splattered heap.

Past the sound of my own quick breathing, the fast *thump* of my heart, and the heavy *drum* of rain against my face, I could hear how silent London Fields had fallen.

They'd stopped torturing Ash and hadn't violated Rebel then.

A bitch could get used to this positive thinking.

I stared up at the bearded Supreme Commander, who scrutinised me back. The soft corner of his coat swung against my face like seaweed. Then he tangled his meaty hand in my hair and wrenched me up onto my knees.

I hissed, stumbling to crawl after him, as he dragged me forward through the parting ranks across the battlefield. When he stopped, I looked up through panicked eyes — straight into Rebel's.

Drake held Rebel on his knees by a hand at his neck, inches from where the Supreme Commander gripped me.

This time, Rebel didn't even try to smile. Terror vibrated from him in shuddering waves.

'We both have something the other wants,' Drake shook Rebel, like he was a sewer rat. 'So, I propose an exchange: the princess, for your son.'

The Supreme Commander's hold tightened in my hair. 'Tactical error, Commander. Maybe because you were raised... broken? You never did understand emotion, Duma. You see, I already have my true son.'

The Supreme Commander glanced at Wings,

who stole to stand at his dad's shoulder, leaving Ash curled in a ball with his left arm shattered.

Wings' face was a swollen bruise, but he didn't look as satisfied to see his brother a prisoner as I'd expected. Instead, he glowered at me.

Rebel snarled, wrestling to break free from Drake. 'Da, please, I'll prove—'

'The *traitor* chose *you* when the battle lines were drawn.' The Supreme Commander's hand wound even tighter in my hair. 'Keep him. We only have room for true rebels.'

Whoops and *catcalls*.

Wings didn't join in.

Rebel slumped to the mud, and Drake didn't stop him.

'You know what will happen to me if I leave without the princess,' Drake's voice was low and careful.

The Supreme Commander nodded but his grin was feral. 'Now to win *her*, boy, you'll have to fight.'

The leader of the Fallen Armies launched me to the side, at the same time as Drake flung Rebel. Our foreheads banged in a star blinding *crack*.

Then Rebel's arms flung around me, pulling me against his chest, as if he could still save us. But it was too late. Because we were the winner's trophies.

The angel and vampire armies circled.

Wings passed the Supreme Commander a giant two headed black axe.

The Supreme Commander swung it from side-to-side. It hissed through the air, as he tested its weight.

Drake paced forward in nothing but silk harem trousers, which slipped down his hips. Then he stretched out his glorious wings, their beat loud in the hush, and rose into the sky.

The Supreme Commander rushed Drake like a bull, lifting up at the last moment.

They clashed mid-air, battling across the dawn-tinged heavens; the axe sliced and gashed, whilst Drake's speed was mesmerising. Drake slipped under the swing of the axe, booting the Supreme Commander bloody.

I gasped when I realised these supernatural creatures had only been playing with us before, like a cat does with a mouse it's already caught.

The ancient forces inside me rose up, greedy and thrilled, thirsting for this *power*. If this was what I could learn in Angel World, then I wouldn't be the one helpless on my knees.

Yeah, power, it's an addiction.

When Drake's wing slashed down across the Supreme Commander's back, crashing him to the ground like Zeus' thunderous fall to earth, I grinned.

Gank him... Do it... Do it now...

Then I heard Rebel's sob.

Rebel's dad was a bastard, but Rebel was about to witness...

The skank with the braids lobbed a huge sword with a hilt built out of violet feathers to Drake. He laid the blade, fizzing with fire, over the Supreme Commander's neck.

Then sliced it down.

'Christ, no...' Rebel hurled himself to his dad.

At the same time, Wings staggered to his knees next to Rebel.

Both their flame red heads bowed over the fallen vampire. Their backs shook with silent, united grief.

How could I've wished for that?

The shadow of Rebel's grief shrouded me through the bond.

In the veil of the rain swept park, less than an hour before dawn woke over London Fields, two armies stood in shock over the death of a leader.

Drake threw down his sword, before prowling towards me.

Both sides quailed before him.

'I've won you,' Drake held out his hand: it was shaking. 'You're my prize. Zachriel too.'

It was the shaking that did it.

So, Drake was dangerous? A killer of vampires?

How many had *I* killed in Tower Block B? Wasn't I a huntress? And now Drake was scared of *me*?

I clutched Drake's hand, surging up and crushing his fingers. 'You haven't won me, Commander.' He tried to pull away, but I squeezed harder; scarlet tears bled between where our hands joined. 'You're mine.'

He jerked. 'Don't—'

'You bastard angels lost me twenty-one years ago.' Dark pleasure snaked at the alarm dancing in his eyes. 'Now I'm coming home.'

He tossed his curls to control the pain. 'As you like. Angel World, however, may not be quite as you hope. Remember I warned you.'

The dark pleasure curdled to fear.

I dropped Drake's hand — his blood sticky on my palm — at the anguish that'd flashed across his face, before he'd buried it.

But I'd been brought up in Jerusalem Children's Home.

I'd savoured every flavour of trauma from the kids who'd passed through.

Drake wasn't kidding: Angel World was no heaven.

I drew back, but Drake cradled his small hand around my neck, his thumb pressing into the base.

'Allow me to escort you *home*, princess.'
    Dawn over London Fields exploded into violet.

29

Vampires? Angels? All I know is they're both bastards.

And I hunt bastards.

The problem is: I'm both vampire *and* angel.

So, what does that make me?

Monster? Princess?

When the violet fractured — jagged edges of a mirror reflecting my own dazed face back in an endless tunnel — I collapsed onto the cave floor. And into a crushing dark.

I shivered. My breath puffed in painful frozen wheezes. My knees bruised on the icy rock. A dank foulness caught at the back of my throat; I gagged.

I staggered up, feeling along the cavern's wall.

Hell, I thought it was vampires who didn't like the light?

Rebel had hated...

Rebel...

Weak violet pulsed from someone huddled in the corner.

If it was Rebel, then he hadn't Fallen. His wings were restored again.

I grinned, shuffling towards the light, but yelped when my foot hit something hard. I groped around testing the rock.

Bars speared from floor to ceiling.

Rebel's cell: *a birdcage prison.*

I dropped to my knees next to Rebel. He looked small. Toy-like. Broken.

I paled, and unsure what to do, gripped the cold bars.

Rebel didn't even look at me. He was bent over, his hands clutching his head as he whimpered, 'Bad angels are punished. Bad angels are punished. Bad angels...'

He was naked.

His punk clothes had been stripped away. Even his collar had been taken, and I flinched at that, remembering his distress when I'd touched it.

My sister's necklace in the pouch around his neck — my gift to him — stood out stark.

And Rebel's wings...

Yeah, they were violet. But his broken, bent left wing had been bound down with stiff leather straps against his back.

...The gits strapped it down...You do that? It's the worst pain an angel can endure...

I'd have fought battles right then to see Rebel's wings outstretched and whole.

For his freedom to fly.

Yet Rebel had betrayed me for his family.

I shouldn't care. Vengeful joy should've been spiralling through me to see the bloke who'd played me, kneeling back in his cell.

Then why was it despair howling through me instead?

The pretty boy fell into your lap for a reason. And you chose to bind him to you by blood.

So, what? Next step wedding dress shopping?

You shouldn't be alone, girl, not in Angel World.

Some of these angelic assholes can worm into your mind like Drake. If they find me? We both die.

But I am alone.

Are you listening? The punk bitch needs an ass whipping for what he did. But his daddy died today. And he's the only one, despite everything, that you can trust now.

I thought I was home.

Who said anything about home being safe?

I hesitated, before reaching my hand through the bars to stroke Rebel's soft hair.

'Bad angels are punished. Bad angels are punished...' Rebel hunched over.

I tilted his chin, trying to focus his gaze on me. His face was scored with scarlet slashes, where his dad had struck him.

'Bad angels are punished. Bad...' He faltered, like he was only just noticing me. Then he flushed with bright shame. 'I'm sorry. I didn't protect you.'

I couldn't stop the tears slipping down my cheeks.

His head tilted as he watched the tears, before raising his trembling hand to touch them.

I knocked him away harder than I'd intended;

he cried out, his wrist hitting the rock bar.

I scrubbed my eyes harshly with the back of my sleeve. 'We're not ganked, which means I'm waiting on your best apology with begging. If not, you're number one on my List of Asses to Kick.'

I wished I hadn't made the weak joke, the moment Rebel uncurled with agonising difficulty and pulled himself onto his knees.

Crimson gashes bloodied his chest and a band of bruises swelled over broken ribs. 'I'm kneeling, Feathers, and if it's begging you want: please forgive me. I'm not good. I never was. And I never fibbed about that but I tried, for you. To pretend I could be a Custodian...and give you the choices I never had. Even if you don't understand yet. But I don't expect you to forgive me.' Rebel's hands clenched into fists, and I remembered the way they'd pounded into his brother's face when Wings had refused to forgive...*what*? What terrible sin had Rebel been trying to make up for by sacrificing me? He hung his head. 'I don't deserve it.'

'And what do you deserve?'

'This,' Rebel whispered. It was so haunted, I shook. 'Alone. In the black. Never escaping...'

His breath came in short panicked gasps.

I thumped back on my heels. 'Harem boy doesn't plan to leave me...?'

The shadows...cold...clawed at me.

Rebel's laugh was short and bitter. 'Away with you, you're the guest of honour, not an Addict. You'll be showered in light, not shut in the dark.'

The thought of Rebel here in the silent black shanked me.

'But we'll both be alone.' I slipped Jade's iPod out of my pocket. My last connection to my sister if she'd died...

Rebel and I had been connected in her search. It

bound us as much as the blood. The hunt for all the missing kids of Hackney.

I gripped Rebel's hand, slipping him Jade's iPod. 'Your punk arse needs educating. Something more modern than the Buzzcocks.'

His look, as the iPod rested on his open palm, was one of shock, awe... and love.

I shook my head, my cheeks hot.

The wallad must be playing me again.

I reached to snatch back the iPod, but Rebel clutched it to his bare chest with quivering hands, like it was his salvation. Then he bottom shuffled to the corner of the cell and hid the iPod in the shadows.

I licked my dry lips, forcing myself to smile.

He relaxed, cautiously crawling back to the bars.

Frankincense burst in a rich woody cloud. Violet light flared through the cavern with the beating of wings.

I surged up, backing against the dripping wall and resting my hand on Star's hilt.

The purple glow lit up Rebel's petrified face, before he scrambled as far back in the cell as possible. He clutched the pouch at his neck, rocking and muttering to himself.

'Be still and silent, Addict,' Drake's voice was predator sharp and harder than even the time he'd played with our minds in Hackney Cemetery, when I'd chained Rebel up for him like a Christmas gift. 'Good. Now, come here.'

When Drake crouched beside the bars, his creamy back curved in unmarred beauty: no welts. Except, when he tipped his head forward to hold his arm through the bars to Rebel, his golden curls tumbled forward, revealing bruised bites down his neck.

Kinky bastard angels.

When Drake clicked his fingers, Rebel shuffled towards him, avoiding his gaze.

'Genie boy,' I booted at Drake, 'you didn't drag me to my new home, just to watch you break one of your toys.'

Drake's glare was cold. 'Zachriel isn't a toy. He's my prize.'

'Psycho definitions are a bitch. Whoever it is who rubs your lamp? Take me to them.'

Drake smudged the sooty kohl underneath Rebel's eyes, before mock tenderly wiping the blood from his injured cheek. 'It's time for a reminder of who owns you, son of the Fallen.' His fingers circled lower, down Rebel's throat. 'You left me here. Alone. To suffer.'

Rebel raised his gaze then. 'And you murdered...'

Drake froze. 'It was an honourable battle. And I was following orders. Your father was once a great man, before he Fell. But don't you see, Addict, Supreme Commander Flynn died because of *you.*' Drakes fingers swept lightly over the base of Rebel's neck as he whispered, 'Tell me you had a reason? Explain now, so I can save you.'

When Rebel caressed Drake's wrist, Drake gasped.

Then Rebel raised his shaky middle finger.

'Wallad,' I muttered.

Drake hissed, pressing into the base of Rebel's neck. Yet the moment Drake touched Rebel, a howling fury surged up inside me.

I launched myself at Drake, catching him around his slight waist and hurling him against the cavern wall.

Drake let out a startled *oomph*. Yet he didn't struggle, as I pinned him with my arm across his neck to the rock.

I brought my elbow back and ground it into his Adam's apple. Drake retched. 'You're mine. *My* toy.'

The words weren't my own. I fought against them.

But here in Angel World, my angelic power whispered louder, flickering across my skin. It snaked in brutal rapture at the fear in Drake's gaze and the tremble running through him.

I slammed him against the wall again. 'Where's my sister?'

'*Dead.*' Yet the waver in Drake's voice and the pearl tremble of tears matting the corner of his eyelashes, told me he was lying.

I backhanded him across the cheek, smashing his head — *bang* — against the wall.

I didn't miss his darted glance over my shoulder at Rebel.

'Try again, bro.'

He spat blood on the floor. 'It was never my intention to kill her.'

I raised my fist.

The *beat* — *beat* — *beat* of my heart entwined with Drake's own panicked breaths.

Drake glanced down, his eyelashes curved pale on his cheek, like Rebel's always had, resigned to my...

Abuse.

I lowered my fist, falling over my own feet onto my arse, as I stumbled away from him.

Why was Drake letting me treat him like this? And why did I crave to?

If he only hurt *lesser angels*, what did that make me?

Drake watched me guardedly; I breathed hard, pushing down the snaking rapture. When he held out his hand to help me up, I stared at it. His knuckles were still tacky with blood, where I'd crushed them.

The pull of Drake's smile was softly dangerous. 'This is the deepest level of Angel World, for only the worst sinner. You need never come here again.' When he helped me up, I flinched, as his hand tightened over mine, but then his thumb only traced tingling circles over the back of my hand. I quivered. 'I understand your fear. Why would you trust us? After the deceit of the Addict—'

'No, please, Commander Drake...' Rebel dragged himself onto his knees, clinging to the bars. He shot anxious glances between us, like we were two boxers sparring. 'Belt me, burn me, use me...' His cheeks flushed; he bit his trembling lip. 'I'll be good, but please don't tell her.'

'Pretending to care for you and whoring himself, I expect. My Zachriel is talented.' Drake's smile broke — just for a moment — and then it was back, more dangerous than before. 'Lying, however, he excels over us all. What was his story? Guardian Angel? Escaping my evil clutches?'

'What...? That's not... I don't...' I pulled my hand away from Drake's confusing caress, clutching Star's hilt like a comfort blanket.

'We all follow orders,' Drake's voice was cool, amused, and deadly. 'As an Addict, Zachriel knew your world better than most. He didn't escape: I *allowed* him out. His job was to watch over you and bring you back safely to Angel World. But the boy was too weak. You're his addiction. He couldn't give you up.'

I twisted away.

I wanted to hurl, weep, and gank Drake just so I wouldn't have to hear his poison.

Rebel's betrayal.

I'd been wrong: Drake could fight back. He

shanked with words.

Rebel slapped his hands against the bars. 'Sweet Jesus, woman, will you listen? I changed, and you saved me. When we—'

'No more lies.' Righteousness at Rebel's betrayal, from the moment I'd met him, kindled spitting sparks across my skin. 'Keep your bitch mouth shut.'

I'd trusted the wrong bastard bloke.

Yet Rebel *had* protected and trained me, had my back, and believed in me, until I'd burst into my new powers.

Had it all been a play because of *orders* or his *addiction*?

When I stalked to the cell, violet flames ghosting me, Rebel cowered like I was his executioner. But then he edged forwards. His face was turned up to mine, his gaze intent and searching.

He licked his lips, with painful hope.

Today he'd lost his dad, chance of redemption, freedom...

And me.

I leant over Rebel.

My sparking fingers stroked down his cheek, shocking him in bursts.

He jumped but didn't pull away.

His eyes were large in the luminous light; his long neck was bare without the collar. But the pouch still hung there: my gift to the bloke who'd lied to me for weeks.

I reached through into the cell, wrenching Rebel's head against the bars. I held him still by his hair.

Then I Judas kissed his forehead, as he'd kissed mine.

The angelic powers, freed and overwhelming,

roared.

Flames seared Rebel's skin.

He didn't flinch. Instead, he pressed closer into my cruel lips.

...hurt me, kiss me, burn me...

The inferno built, screaming for release. To burn Rebel, and the secrets and lies, to ash.

To purge the pain, weeping now down my face.

Slam.

The sugary copper scent blasted through me. But this time it tasted bitter because I knew it was nothing but a trap.

Yet it didn't stop my craving for Rebel's blood. Our bond. For *him.*

Hell, I was addicted too.

I battled the roar, dampening the flames to embers.

Shaking, I pulled back. Then I released Rebel's hair, shoving him away.

He snatched the bars to stop himself tumbling. Blisters branded his forehead, but he peered out at me, with a tentative smile. 'Princess...?'

'You were right,' I said, forcing myself not to choke on the quiet words. Rebel tilted his head. 'You *are* bad.'

Rebel's eyes widened, before he crumpled like I'd clouted him.

I clenched my jaw, before ripping the velvet pouch with my sister's necklace inside — the only thing shielding Rebel from complete nakedness — from around his neck.

'Please...it's all I have...and your gift...' Rebel scrabbled through the bars.

I stuffed the pouch into my jean's pocket with shaky fingers. 'You don't deserve my gift.'

I turned to Drake, as Rebel curled back on his side, keening.

I cringed, clenching my fists and refusing to watch Rebel's expression as I walked away from him.

If I had, I'd have forgiven his betrayal.

Despite everything, he was still fam. But he wasn't the only one who needed saving.

'I want to see my sister,' I demanded.

When Drake smiled, just as he had before he'd shanked me over Rebel, I stiffened. He beckoned me to follow him through the narrow cavern. 'Patience.'

I strode after him, as he marched faster along the freezing tunnel.

Through thin spears of rock, I glimpsed violet flashes.

More cells.

More prisoners like Rebel.

'Where's Jade?'

Drake bowed his head. 'First, you must meet your mother.'

I stumbled, hanging onto the wall.

My mother...?

I was trapped in the treacherous Angel World, where J had warned I could trust no one but the one ally, who was now locked in a birdcage prison.

Yet now I was being taken to meet the woman who'd abandoned me to the humans at birth.

And it terrified me worse than any fight.

Why had my mum abandoned me? And why had Rebel and Ash worked so hard to protect me from her?

I pushed my sunglasses more firmly onto my nose.

If my angelic mum expected an angel for a daughter, she was in for a bitch of a surprise.

I was all monster.
After all, nobody's perfect.

The End

Ready for the next instalment in the Rebel Angels series?

Check out **VAMPIRE PRINCESS**!

https://rosemaryajohns.com

Did you enjoy **Vampire Huntress: Rebel Angels Vol. One**?

Let me know by leaving a review!

Love Reading Gripping Fantasy?

If so, sign up to Rosemary A Johns' *VIP* Newsletter List to be notified of new promotions and never miss out on hot new releases.

Indulge yourself, grab a coffee, and then dive into a Fantasy Rebel book – they're fantasy for rebels.

Plus you'll also receive Rosemary's FREE and exclusive novella "All the Tin Soldiers".

It's our gift to you.

Visit Rosemary's website to subscribe and become a Rebel: rosemaryajohns.com

Hooked on *Rebel Angels*?

Read More from Rosemary A Johns

Website: https://rosemaryajohns.com
Bookbub:
https://www.bookbub.com/authors/rosemary-a-johns
Facebook:
https://www.facebook.com/RosemaryAnnJohns
Twitter: @RosemaryAJohns
Secret Rosemary's Rebels Fan Group:
https://www.facebook.com/groups/698811356958470/permalink/867211580118446

ABOUT THE AUTHOR

ROSEMARY A JOHNS is an award-winning, #1 Amazon bestselling fantasy author, music fanatic, and paranormal anti-hero addict. She writes sexy angels, savage vampires, and epic battles.

Winner of the Silver Award in the National Wishing Shelf Book Awards. Finalist in the IAN Book of the Year Awards. Honorable Mention in the Readers' Favorite Book Awards.
Shortlisted in the International Rubery Book awards.

Rosemary is also a traditionally published short story writer. She studied at Oxford University and ran her own theatre company. She's always been a rebel...

Want to read more and stay up to date on Rosemary's newest releases? Sign up for her *VIP* Rebel Newsletter and get a FREE novella!

Member of a Book Club?

Why not share *Vampire Huntress* with your group?

Series by Rosemary A Johns

Rebel Vampires
Rebel Angels

75534998R00210

Made in the USA
Middletown, DE
06 June 2018